LAST
FIRST
SNOW

Max Gladstone

TOR

A TOM DOHERTY ASSOCIATES BOOK

NEW YORK

LAST FIRST SNOW

Copyright © 2015 by Max Gladstone

A Tor Book
Published by Tom Doherty Associates, LLC
175 Fifth Avenue
New York, NY 10010

www.tor-forge.com

Tor® is a registered trademark of Tom Doherty Associates, LLC.

The Library of Congress has cataloged the hardcover edition as follows:

Gladstone, Max.
    Last first snow / Max Gladstone.—First edition.
        p. cm.—(Craft sequence ; 4)
    "A Tom Doherty Associates book."
    ISBN 978-0-7653-7940-5 (hardcover)
    ISBN 978-1-4668-6840-3 (e-book)
    1. Magic—Fiction.   2. Conspiracies—Fiction.   I. Title.
    PS3607.L343 L37 2015
    813'.6—dc23

                                                    2015015038

ISBN 978-0-7653-7941-2 (trade paperback)

Our books may be purchased in bulk for promotional, educational, or business use. Please contact your local bookseller or the Macmillan Corporate and Premium Sales Department at 1-800-221-7945, extension 5442, or by e-mail at MacmillanSpecialMarkets@macmillan.com.

First Edition: July 2015
First Trade Paperback Edition: April 2016

LAST
FIRST
SNOW

1

For false gods, they cast long shadows.

Elayne Kevarian, the King in Red, and Tan Batac towered over Dresediel Lex. The vast once-holy city spread at Elayne's feet, miles of adobe and steel and obsidian and chrome, concrete and asphalt, wood and glass and rock. Its arms enveloped the bay south to Stonewood and north to Worldsedge. Roads wound up the Drakspine slopes and down again, cascading east into Fisherman's Vale. Container ships the size of fallen leaves docked at the toy wharfs and piers of Longsands near the Skittersill.

The King in Red, a mile-tall skeleton in flowing robes, stood in the ocean. Waves broke around his anklebones and the tip of his staff. Tan Batac had found a comfortable saddle-ridge in the Drakspine upon which to sit and watch. But they were not Elayne's audience.

She looked up.

Judge Cafal's eyes blazed in the sky, twin suns watching Elayne for her first mistake.

"We've waited too long," Elayne said as she paced over a warren of close-curled alleys. Each tap of her black heels would have leveled a city block in the waking world, but when she passed on, buildings and termite-sized human beings remained intact. "Forty years since Liberation. Four decades since we won the God Wars in Dresediel Lex, and still this city languishes under the wards and edicts of deities long dead. Gods we killed." With a wave of her hand and a twist of chill Craft she peeled back the city's skin to reveal the wards she meant: lines of sick green light beneath the maze. "The old Gods and priests reserved the Skittersill district for their underclass. Slaves lived and died on these streets. Temple guards sought sacrifices here. The Skittersill has changed since Liberation, but the old wards endure."

Neither the King in Red nor Tan Batac interrupted. They had hired her months back to mediate their negotiations about the Skittersill, and they had come today, the skeleton and the small round man with the sharp eyes, to see their triumph. She suspected—hoped—each still thought he was getting the best of the deal.

"These wards mark the Skittersill as a divine protectorate. As a result, property there can't be bought or sold—which makes it difficult to insure or renovate, and depresses rent, inviting crime and decay. The old wards were meant to keep the Skittersill poor, its residents controlled. They have no place in a free city. As Dresediel Lex grows, they become a weakness. Modern Craftwork drains their strength. In the short term, they merely restrain growth, but in the long term they will fail."

She raised one hand like a conductor signaling crescendo.

The sky flashed black. Fire clawed at the green beneath her feet. The wards crumbled without gods to back them, and the city burned. Gouts of smoke spread north from the Skittersill to richer districts. Panic welded a million tiny screams into one unbroken cry.

When the city lay in ash Elayne returned the ruin to its former life, and destroyed it again. Plague, this time, the virus's spread tracked in a purple wash that soon leapt west to the Shining Empire across the rolling Pax. After plague, famine. Riots. Drought, leading to riots and famine and plague once more. Zombie revolution. Blackout. Terrorism. Crime. Demonic possession. Every snap of her fingers an apocalypse.

Each citizen of Dresediel Lex died a hundred deaths, screaming.

"The Skittersill is vulnerable. Undefended. These dooms will come to pass if the wards remain unchanged."

The judge watched from the sky, impassive as any real system of paired stars. Did she buy it? Or was she just playing along, giving Elayne more rope to hang herself?

Best continue. "Let me show you a better future."

She called upon her power, upon deals and contracts Crafted for this moment. Around her, beneath her, a crystal palace grew. Slums failed before towers of glass, warehouse warrens became courtyards where fountains ran clean. (The fountains were Tan Batac's touch, impractical in dry Dresediel Lex but clever for that very reason: a future of impossible luxury beckoned if the judge approved their deal.) The cracked lizard-skin of Dresediel Lex transformed to a jeweled oasis.

Meaningless of course. The reborn city could look any way they cared: floating spires, towering ziggurats, more pyramids even. The seeming was not the point. Under this translucent splendor, Craftwork replaced the green wards laid by the old dead gods. Machine-tooled spiderweb glyphs glittered, circles revolved within larger circles scribed in tongues forgotten and not yet made. Lines radiated out and in to clothe the Skittersill in Craft.

Elayne Kevarian permitted herself the slightest sliver of pride.

Five months' work to reach this moment. Five months of patient mediation between the King in Red, dread lord who'd ripped Dresediel Lex from its Gods' hands, and Tan Batac, landholder of the Skittersill. Five months to Craft new wards that were, in her own frank estimation, the equal of any she had seen.

Some artists settle for mirroring the world.

Elayne had built a new one altogether.

She subjected her wards to the same tests as the Gods'. Fires died, plagues flared out, revolts contained themselves, demonic hordes bounced back into the outer hells. The city stood.

"Our proposal will free the Skittersill from bad theology and worse urban planning. We will make this city better."

She stared up into the twin suns suspended in a sky the deep blue of paintings on porcelain. She waited for the verdict.

Time wound down, wound slow. The crystal towers of her triumph shone.

"No," the judge said.

The world broke open, and they fell.

"Why not?" Elayne asked later, in the judge's office, pacing.

For all its size, for all its brass and leather opulence, the office still felt small. Anything would, after standing astride the city in the Court's projection. Elayne's spirit had not yet settled back into her skin. Always took the mind awhile to re-accustom itself to fleshy constraint. Colors in the world of meat were less vivid. Time ticked by with slow rigidity. Even the sun outside the office's slit windows seemed dim.

Judge Cafal kept silent at her desk behind paper ramparts of case files and motions, immobile and squat as a Shining Empire idol. Her blue eyes, no longer suns, peered through thick-rimmed glasses—an unnatural gaze here in Dresediel Lex, where eyes were black and hair dark.

Elayne continued: "Do you see some problem with my work? The compromise is sound."

"It may be sound, but it is not a compromise." In person, Cafal sounded almost human. Her voice was old, withered, and strong, with a harsh buzz to its upper register that suggested recent throat surgery. "You've not accounted for all factors."

"Between the King in Red, and Tan Batac's merchant collective, we control property use rights in the Skittersill. Who else is there?"

Amateur mistake, she realized as she said the words: never ask a question when you're not certain of its answer.

Cafal's short fingers crawled down one rampart's edge, and withdrew a thick folder. The documents within flew out to hover between them at Elayne's eye level. "Here's a sample of the letters—I can't call them briefs—I received about the ward revisions. Contents range from well-reasoned arguments by educated laymen to bloody-minded rants calling for us all to be sacrificed to the old gods come the next eclipse. Add to that reports of unrest in the Skittersill—protesters and the like. It paints a picture."

Reports of which Elayne knew nothing, but she would never admit that to the judge. She scanned the papers in silence, and when she spoke it took effort to control her voice. "If these people wished to contribute to the process, they should have issued representatives."

"Were they invited to do that?" Cafal's too-wide mouth turned up at the corners.

"This is obstructionism, not policy."

"You may be right," Cafal said, "but my hands are tied. After the Alt Selene outbreak, the judiciary's decided to treat citizen complaints with heightened scrutiny. We don't cover a few isolated free cities anymore; our apparatus has to shelter half the globe. We're spread too thin to keep rolling over public opposition."

"We need these changes. Do you think a plague will stay confined to the Skittersill just because it starts there?"

"I know. If I thought your proposal frivolous, trust me, we'd be having a different conversation. And if we could ignore these letters, I would do so with joy in my iron heart." Elayne doubted she was joking about the heart. "But I need something to bring back to the judiciary. Show me an accord with these people, or prove their incoherence, and I can help. Otherwise, it's my will against the Higher Court, and you know how that goes."

"Thank you, Your Honor."

"Good luck, Elayne. You'll need it."

"When, exactly," said Elayne as she marched with the King in Red and Tan Batac down the Court's marble halls, "did you gentlemen plan to tell me about the Skittersill protests?"

"Elayne," said the King in Red. He reached for her arm, but she pulled away and wheeled on him. The skeleton skidded to a stop on marble, foot bones and copper-shod staff clattering. Imposing as Kopil could be in his current form, Elayne found him easier to handle than he had been back when he had skin and muscle and the normal range of human organs. For one thing, the skeletal King was shorter: the few inches the man lost in his transformation from creature of flesh to creature of Craft had reduced him to a manageable six feet, only an inch and a half taller than Elayne herself. Before, he had been a giant.

Still was a giant. Just easier to look in the eye—provided one knew the trick for making eye contact with a skull. Elayne did.

"Kopil." It was easy to keep her voice cold. "If you want to play games, don't do it in a way that makes me look stupid before a judge."

The skeleton shook his head. "What was her problem with our proposal?"

"Protesters? Letter-writing campaigns? Does any of that sound familiar?"

"Outrageous."

Not the King in Red's voice. Batac's. Elayne briefly considered gutting the man, and decided against it. In her experience spraying a Court hallway with blood and other humors was rarely a good idea. That one time in Iskar had been a special case. "These letters have no place here." Batac's face and voice flushed with anger. If Elayne did not know better she'd have sworn some petty god built the man for committee meetings and neighborhood politics. "The mob that sent them doesn't have any position, any goal beyond clogging the streets to keep decent folk away from work."

"So you both knew about this."

Kopil held up his hands. "It's a protest, Elayne. Since when have those been a problem? We ripped out divine wards every day in the God Wars. These people have no Craftsmen or Craftswomen. They're a job for law enforcement."

"Does the judge want us to invite every kid with a bad haircut off the Skittersill streets into Court?" Tan Batac fumed. "This is a vendetta. She wants to humiliate me in front of my partners."

Batac wasn't done, but Elayne did not wait for him to finish.

"Follow me." The Court of Craft was too public for this conversation. A few Craftsmen seated under the front hall's murals seemed suspiciously engrossed by their newspapers. A skeleton in a pencil skirt appeared to be arguing with a green-skinned woman—but neither had spoken in the last minute, and both had adjusted position so they could see the King in Red. Ears everywhere. Even when the ears were merely metaphorical, as in the skeletons' case.

She led Batac and Kopil through smoked-glass revolving doors, out of the Court's elemental chill into the heat of Dresediel Lex. Industry and the fumes of fourteen million people hazed the city's dry blue skies. Pyramids jutted from the earth, man-made mountains mocking the crystal knives of skyspires suspended upside down in air above, and the modern land-bound towers of glass and steel below. An airbus passed overhead, and the city's faceless Wardens flew by on their Couatl mounts. More Wardens stood guard outside the Court, humans with heads and faces covered by silver cauls. They bore ceremonial pikes to signify danger to those who didn't know the Wardens themselves were weapons.

Elayne hailed a cab. She did not spare a glance for the Wardens or the city. The city she knew, and she would never permit the Wardens to see that they unnerved her. Their masks predated her work in Alt Coulumb, predated the Blacksuits and Alexander Denovo's more misguided hobbies, but still she preferred to see the faces and know the names of potential obstacles.

A Craftswoman could do a great deal once she knew her enemy's name.

Batac and Kopil joined her in the cab's green velvet stomach. She told the horse to bring them to RKC's offices, closed the door and windows, and nodded, satisfied, as the carriage lurched to motion. They sat across from her, the businessman and the skeleton who once was mortal.

She closed her eyes, found her center, and opened her eyes again. "Cafal has to justify her actions to the judiciary, and a few months back the judiciary decided to be more careful with civil protest. They're spread thin. Last winter there was an outbreak in Alt Selene, and they won't risk the same here."

The skeleton nodded. The crimson sparks of his eyes dimmed in thought.

"I don't understand," Batac said. "The protesters have no Craftsmen. What threat do they pose?"

The King in Red answered for her: "They can break the world."

"Oh," Batac said. "If it's a little thing like that."

The carriage jolted over a bump in the cobblestones. Batac was a merchant, not a magus; Elayne spent a juddering minute considering how to frame the issue in layman's terms. "Belief shapes the world. Dreams have mass."

"Of course."

"We want to rewrite the Skittersill—to replace the gods' laws with our own."

"That's the idea."

"But these protesters resist us. Their vision wrestles with ours, and the struggle warps and weakens reality. Things from beyond push through. The Court thinks these people are determined enough that trying to overrule their objections would tear a hole in space, and let demons in."

"Five months of mediation. A year before that recruiting my partners. And now we go back to the conference table until we satisfy a gang of zealots?"

"Not exactly," Elayne said. "We don't need to satisfy them if there's no 'them' to satisfy. If these people are inconsistent— if we face not one movement but a thousand nuisances— then the Court's power can overwhelm them all, bit by bit. Of course, if we do that, we might trade magical conflict for physical. Either way, I need to know more. I should have known more from the beginning. From here on out, no secrets." That last she addressed to the King in Red. "Agreed?"

The horse veered around a traffic accident. Through the green velvet curtains, Elayne could not tell who was hurt and who at fault. She saw a black shadow of wreckage and heard screams, and men weeping.

As they passed the wreck, Batac lifted the curtain with one finger and peered out, blinking against the pure light or what he saw. He released the curtain, and falling velvet blocked light and tragedy alike.

"Agreed," Kopil said.

Tan Batac nodded. "Fine."

Not a ringing endorsement, but it would serve. "Send me what you know about these people," Elayne said. "Tomorrow, I'll go."

2

The next day before dawn Elayne hailed a driverless carriage and rode south to the Skittersill, to Chakal Square.

Glass towers and hulking repurposed pyramids gave way to squat strip malls, palm trees, and tiny bungalows. Optera buzzed and airbuses floated through a bluing sky. Road signs advertised sandwich shops, carriage mechanics, pawnbrokers, and lawn care. A few tall art deco posters of the King in Red, pasted in storefront windows, urged citizens to beware of fires.

Near the Skittersill the buildings changed again—adobe and plaster gave way to clapboard row houses painted in pastel green and pink. Streets narrowed and sidewalks widened; uneven cobblestones pitched the carriage from side to side. At last she dismounted, paid the fare from her expense account, and continued on foot.

Two blocks away she heard the protest. Not shouts, not chants, not so early—just movement. How many bodies? Hundreds if not thousands, breathing, rolling in sleep or grumbling to new unsteady wakefulness. Mumbled conversation melded to a rush of surf. Mixed together, all tongues sounded the same. She smelled bread frying, and eggs, and mostly she smelled people.

Then Bloodletter's Street crossed Crow, and Chakal Square opened to the south and east.

Chakal Square was not a square per se: a deep rectangle rather, five hundred feet long and three hundred wide, with a fountain in the center dedicated to Chakal himself—a Quechal deity killed early in the God Wars, a casualty in the southern Oxulhat skirmishes. Defaced, the statue, and dead, the god, but the name endured, attached to a stone expanse between wooden buildings, an open-air market most days, a space for festivals and concerts. Red King Consolidated's local office brooded to the east.

People thronged Chakal Square. Camp stove smoke curled above circled tents. Flags and protest signs in Kathic and Low Quechal studded the crowd near the fountain where a ramshackle stage stood. No one had taken the stage yet. Speeches would come later.

A loose line of mostly men sat or stood around the crowd's edge, facing out. They bore no weapons Elayne could see, and many dozed, but they maintained a ragged sentry air.

Elayne looked both ways down empty Crow, and crossed the road. The guard in front of her was sleeping, but a handful of others shook themselves alert and ran to intercept her, assembling into a loose arc. A thick young man with a broken, crooked-set nose spoke first. "You don't belong here."

"I do not," she said. "I am a messenger."

"You look like a Craftswoman."

She remembered that tone of voice—an echo of the time before the Wars, before her Wars anyway, when she'd still been weak, when at age twelve she fled from men with torches and pitchforks and hid from them in a muddy pond, breathing through a reed while leeches gorged on her blood. Memories only, the past long past yet present. Since that night of torches and pitchforks and teeth, she'd learned the ways of power. She had nothing to fear from this broken-nosed child or from the crowd at his back. "My name is Elayne Kevarian. The King in Red has sent me to speak with your leaders."

"To arrest them."

"To talk."

"Crafty talk has chains in it."

"Not this time. I've come to hear your demands."

"Demands," Broken-Nose said, and from his tone Elayne thought this might be a short meeting after all. "Here's a demand. Go back and tell your boss—"

"Tay!" A woman's voice. Broken-Nose turned. The one who'd spoken ran over from farther down the sentry line. The guards shifted stance as she approached. Embarrassed, maybe. "What's going on here?"

Broken-Nose—Tay?—pointed to Elayne. "She says the King in Red sent her."

Elayne examined the new arrival—short hair, loose sweater, broad stance. Promising. "I am Elayne Kevarian." She produced a business card. "From Kelethras, Albrecht, and Ao. I've been retained by the King in Red and Tan Batac in the matter of the Skittersill warding project. I'm here to meet with your leaders."

The woman's deep brown eyes weighed her. "How do we know you won't cause trouble? Last few days, folks have come into the camp just to start fights."

"I have no interest in starting fights. I hope to prevent them."

"We won't bow to you," Tay said, but the woman held out one hand, palm down, and he closed his mouth. Didn't relax, though. Held his muscles tense for battle or a blow. "Chel, we don't have to listen—"

"She look like one of Batac's axe-bearers to you?"

"She looks dangerous."

"She is dangerous. But she might be for real." Chel turned back to Elayne. "Are you?"

And this was the Craft that could not be learned: to answer plainly and honestly, to seem as if you spoke the truth, especially when you did. "Yes."

"No weapons?"

She opened her briefcase to show them the documents inside, and the few pens clipped into leather loops. Charms and tools, instruments of high Craft, were absent. She'd removed them this morning against just such an eventuality. No sense frightening the locals.

"Who do you want to see?"

"Anyone," Elayne said, "with the authority and will to talk."

Chel looked from her, to Tay, to the others gathered. At last, she nodded. "Come with me."

"Thank you," Elayne said when they had left the guards behind but had not yet reached the main body of the camp.

"For what? Tay wouldn't have started anything. Just acts tough when he's excited."

"If he would not have started anything, why did you run over to stop him?"

"It's been a long few days," Chel said, which was and was not an answer.

"Aren't sentries a bit exclusive for a populist movement?"

"We've had trouble. Burned food stores, fights. Folks that started the fights, nobody knew them—Batac's thugs."

"A serious accusation."

"Bosses did the same during the dockworker's strike. Got a lot of my friends arrested. Those of us who lived through that, we thought maybe we could calm things down, or scrap if scrapping's needed." She sounded proud. "So we stand guard."

"You're a dockhand?"

"Born and raised. About half the Skittersill works the Longsands port, or has family there."

"And your employers gave you leave to come protest?"

A heavy silence followed her question, which was all the answer Elayne needed. "I guess you're not from around here," Chel said.

"I lived in DL briefly awhile back. I'm a guest now."

"Maybe you didn't hear about the strike, then. This was last winter. We faced pay cuts, unsafe working conditions, long hours. People died. We took to the picket line. Turns out strikes against you people don't work out so well."

Elayne recognized that tone of voice—heavy and matter-of-fact as a rock chained around an ankle. She'd spoken that way, once, when she was younger than this woman. Come to think, she'd had the same walk: hands in pockets, bent forward as if against heavy wind.

"We didn't take leave," Chel continued. "Things have been hard since the strike. We read the broadsheets, same as everyone. If this deal goes through and our rent goes up, we won't be able to live here anymore. Moving costs. Traveling to work costs. Worse if you have a family. This was the best bad choice. You know how that goes, maybe."

"I do," Elayne said, though she hadn't planned to say anything. "What do you mean, broadsheets?"

Chel plucked a piece of newsprint from the ground. The headline ran: "Cabal Plans District's Death," over caricatures of the King in Red and Tan Batac. Elayne read the first few lines of the article, folded the sheet, and passed it back to Chel. Now that she knew what to look for, she saw more copies pasted to the sides of tents. No bylines anywhere she could see, nor any printer's mark.

The camp woke around them. Eyes emerged from sleeping bags, peered out of tents, glanced up from bowls of breakfast porridge. Some of those gazes confronted Elayne, some assessed, some merely noted her passage and dismissed her. She heard whispers, most in Low Quechal, which she did not know well enough to suss out, but some in common Kathic.

"Foreigner," they said, which didn't bother her, and "Iskari," which was wrong.

"Craftswoman," she heard as well, over and over, from women stretching, from men crouched to warm themselves at fires, from children (there were children here, a few) who stopped their game of ullamal to follow her. Others followed, too. They gathered in her wake, a sluggish V of rebel geese: a gnarled man covered with scars who might have fought in the Wars himself, on the wrong side. A pregnant woman, leading her husband by the hand. A trio of muscular bare-chested men, triplets maybe; she could tell them apart only by the different bruises.

As they neared the fountain, she felt a new power rising. These people had made themselves one. The air tinted green beneath their unity's weight.

Angry masses. Torches, pitchforks, and blood.

No. Approach the situation fresh, she told herself—these aren't the mobs of your childhood, just scared people gathered for protection. And if what Chel said was true, about fights and arson and strikebreakers, they had reason to fear.

Chel led Elayne past tents where volunteer cooks gave food to those who asked, past signs scrawled with crude cartoons of the King in Red as thief and monster, past the stage and around the fountain and its faceless god. Behind the fountain lay a stretch of square covered by dried grass mats upon which men and women sat cross-legged and rapt.

Elayne's heart clenched and she stopped breathing.

An altar rose before the grass mats, and on that altar a man lay bound. A priest, white-clad from waist down and bare and massive from waist up, stood with his back to the congregation. Intentional and intricate scars webbed the priest's torso. A long time ago, someone had sliced Quechal glyphwork into his skin.

The priest raised a knife. The captive did not scream. He stared into the dawning sky.

The knife swept down.

And stopped.

There had been no time for questions or context. Elayne caught the blade with Craft, and wrapped the priest in invisible bonds. Glyphs glowed blue on her fingers and wrists, beneath her collar and beside her temples.

The crowd gasped.

The sacrifice howled in terror and frustration.

The priest turned.

He should not have been able to move, and barely to breathe, but still he turned. Green light bloomed from his scars and glistened off the upturned blade of his knife, off his eyes.

His eyes, which widened in shock, though not so sharply as her own.

"Hello, Elayne," Temoc said.

3

In a respectful universe, crowd, parishioners, sacrifice, and guards would have all kept still, but of course they didn't. The faithful cried out. Temoc stepped toward her, but he was a less immediate concern than Chel, who tackled Elayne to the ground.

Elayne hit hard, taking the fall with shoulders and arm, but she kept her Craft locked around Temoc. Chel pinned her arms and grabbed her throat. Chel's teeth flashed white, and in the trembling of her whole body Elayne read shock and shame and anger. Mostly anger.

"Chel," Elayne croaked. "Stop."

A circle of faces formed above and around them, staring down. Breath came slow and thin.

"Let her go," Temoc said from somewhere far away. The circle broke into a U, though Elayne could not see the man himself.

Chel looked up, confused.

"I am not in danger. Elayne is an old friend. She does not understand our work."

He entered her field of view. Dawn broke through the mist and scissored his silhouette from the sky: a chthonic figure, a cave painting strong enough to burst free of the wall. Temoc Almotil, last of the Eagle Knights, priest of the old gods, looked better than she remembered. Green light from his scars cast the faces of his gathered faithful a weird pale jade. Chel released Elayne, sat back on her thighs, and stood. "Sir." That word held devotion, awe, curiosity, a little reproach.

Elayne examined Temoc's face.

Planes and angles composed him, like always, like she remembered when they'd first met under flag of truce when she was seventeen and he was twenty—and not long after, when he'd almost bled out in a Sansilva backstreet, impaled by a spear of ice, as a war raged overhead. Eyes of the deepest, roundest black, and a mouth an Ebon Sea sculptor might have immortalized in marble as the one honest detail in an otherwise flattering portrait: too broad, too sharp, like the rest of him. Muscular didn't begin to cover it. A man built on a different scale from other men.

Built, then scarred. He moved slowly, laboring against her bonds. He hadn't tried to break them; then again, she hadn't tried to break him, either.

He offered her the hand that didn't hold the knife. Mindful of the crowd and of her mission, she accepted, and used him as an anchor with which to pull herself upright. His arm did not twitch when he took her weight.

The sacrifice sat upon the altar, loose ropes trailing from his wrists, perplexed. Most of the faithful remained in their rows. The watching U retreated from Temoc, from them both.

"A long time," he repeated.

She nodded to the knife. "I thought you didn't kill these days."

"You don't understand."

"You have a knife, and there's a man on that altar. What do I not understand?"

"We've changed the sacrament." He gestured toward the altar with his blade. "The ceremony must be done at sunrise. Will you join me?"

"I won't let you kill him," she said.

"I pledge that this man will be alive, as you recognize it, at the rite's end. My blade will not pierce his flesh."

"Your specificity does not inspire confidence."

"Trust me." That smile had not changed. Neither had his teeth. "See how we remake ourselves." His voice brimmed with clerical assurance, a priest speaking for the groundlings. Not so different from the voice Elayne herself adopted at court. A priest was a man who made his face a mask.

Her presence by his side would confer legitimacy, which he knew as well as she did. But she'd come to parlay, at least ostensibly, and by his side she would be in a better position to stop him if he needed stopping.

She shot her cuffs, and swept the dust from her suit with a quick web of Craft. A small tear in her jacket rewove itself. Wasteful parlor tricks, dry cleaners and tailors being more efficient on the whole than sorcery. But there was value in impressing the locals. "I'm glad," she said, "you stepped in when you did."

"Chel wouldn't have hurt you." Temoc walked between his faithful toward the altar, under the pressure of their gathered gazes. His scars glowed, and shadows slicked his skin. His people did not see this side of him often, she expected.

She kept pace. "I was not concerned for my own safety." This, too, pitched to be overheard.

What Temoc said next, wasn't. "Would you mind letting me go? Your heathen magics sting."

"But you look so impressive lit up like a solstice tree." She smirked, and canceled her bonds upon him. The light dimmed first, the shadows after.

The erstwhile sacrifice spread-eagled again on the altar, which was not stone at all but a squat, sturdy table propped with four stone panels. Makeshift, make-believe.

Temoc raised his knife. Its black glass blade caught the sunlight. The audience sat in a rustle of grass mats. Chel watched from beyond the mats, and others watched with her, their numbers swelled by the commotion.

Worshippers fell silent. Gathered faith crystallized the air, arrested light in its passage, riveted this moment to a million others stretching back through eternity, that were not a million separate moments at all but a million reflections of the same moment in time, or its facets, revolving.

She was the only person here, she wagered, who understood

the Craftwork that underpinned the scene: the faithful giving pieces of their soul to the performance, to the priest, to the sacrifice transfixed in the ecstasy of his role, eyes open as he saw the faces of god. She was the only one here who could describe, in six pages perhaps with three figures and a few mathematical sidebars, the mechanics of Temoc's worship.

And she was the only one outside it all. So she watched.

Sun glinted off a raised blade. She tensed, remembering torchlight reflected in hunters' eyes. The knife fell.

Its pommel struck the sacrifice's chest with a rich echo like a knuckle's knock against the sound box of a guitar. The man twitched once. A small sigh escaped him.

Elayne closed her eyes to watch the sacrifice as a Craftswoman. Small distortions stitched through the lightning-lit spider world beyond her eyelids, like darting fish in seaweed: tiny gods. With eyes opened, she saw green ghosts rise from the altar to lick the sacrifice's skin. The spirits lingered where the wound in the man's chest would have been, if this was a sacrifice in truth as well as name. Spectral tongues lingered at the hole Temoc would have carved to draw his heart.

As the godlings drank their fill, their joy pulsed through the web of faith Temoc wove, to quicken his congregation's hearts and touch them with eternity—a sliver of bygone days and glories, a lingering aftertaste of ancient bloody history. The blood sacrifice was no more. The old gods were dead.

All as it should be.

But still, the crowd rejoiced.

The moment passed and the godlings faded back into ether. Temoc lowered his knife and spoke in High Quechal to the sacrifice, who nodded, unable to answer through his tears. Temoc addressed the faithful in High Quechal first, then Low. Said, at last, in Kathic, "the Miracle is Accomplished," so that Elayne heard the capitals.

And they repeated it to him, the hundreds here, words rippling through the gathered crowd and those beyond still waking.

Temoc slipped the ropes from the sacrifice's wrists and an-kles. The man stumbled into his embrace and wept.

I am an outsider, Elayne repeated to herself.

She did not know why she felt the need.

A winged shape crossed the sky, heavy subsonic bass to complement the cheers: a Warden come on Couatl-back to watch the outlaws below.

To watch, like her. And wonder.

4

"To what do I owe the honor?" Temoc asked after the ceremony. The sacrifice's friends helped him, staggering, sobbing, off to breakfast. The congregation bled out into the crowd. Elayne listened to their chatter: the word "Craftswoman" featured often.

"Can't you guess?" Elayne said.

"You might have heard about my work here. Come to see what I've done with my life, or even to join us. Wishful thinking, I suppose."

"Yes," she said. And: "How did you convince your gods to accept a mock sacrifice?"

"With difficulty. Most refuse. The great Lords and Ladies are dead, and the hungriest of those who survive, sleep. A few lesser corn gods and household spirits join us, though to them the bloodless rite feels like drinking from a dirty sponge. But it's this or nothing, for all of us."

"Must be hard."

He knelt behind the altar, and from the empty space beneath removed a towel with which he wiped himself down, and a white shirt he buttoned across his chest. "Our ways will not survive unchanged. The old sacrifice bound my people together. The celebrant whose heart we drew participated in godhood. Here, the celebrant acts out the sacrifice, and through that enters the community of gods. But he cannot stay—he must return bearing knowledge of what it is to die. Deeds once done are done forever. I've taught this to men and gods for twenty years. Someday they'll listen." The small buttons slipped under his thick fingers, and his muscles strained against the fabric. His hands did not shake. They never had, not down all the years she'd known him. Clean living, he'd said decades before, when she asked his secret. They had both been younger then.

He still looked young. And foolish, in that white shirt. Someone had tried to tailor it to his figure, and succeeded only in demonstrating the impossibility of their enterprise.

Chel remained, watching them across the grass mats. Temoc beckoned, and she approached. "Thank you," Temoc said, "for escorting my friend."

"She attacked you."

"She thought I was about to kill that man. In her position, would you have done differently?"

Chel's jaw tightened, and so did her eyes. Elayne sympathized: Chel had exposed herself to bring Elayne through the barricade, realized she had made a mistake, and was now being told her mistake was no mistake at all. She felt she'd failed on all counts. "No," she said at last. "She says she's from the King in Red."

"And you brought her to me."

"Would you rather I have brought her to the Major?"

Temoc laughed, a deep, echoing sound. "Come," he said. "The ceremony gives me a little power, and I must use it. Walk with me."

"So what brings you to this mob?" Elayne asked as they walked.

They moved among tents and throngs of protesters, some sleeping, some eating breakfast, some singing. A group of mostly men performed a martial exercise. Fathers cradled children. The place should have stunk but didn't, thanks to neon-colored alchemical toilets and—Elayne was shocked to note—to her own nostalgia. Odors of charcoal and desperation, sweat and hope, dirt and canvas and fear, evoked her youth, and the Wars, and not all those memories were bad. The camps were fun, for the most part. Pranks and drugs and sex and music and black magic relieved the tension of the battlefield.

"They're not a mob. They live here. They're trying to protect their homes."

"Against me."

"I hope not," he said. "You have to understand—Tan Batac and his partners live uptown. They want change for their own sakes. The people in this camp are fighting for their lives."

"And for the return of the old order, with you in charge?"

"I'm a priest, not a king."

"This city's never seen much difference between the two."

"But the Wars are over," he said. "Especially in the Skittersill."

"You're still here, and so am I."

"Your side won, in case you didn't notice." A woman waved to him and he waved back. "My king fell, and my gods are dead. I would have died with them, if not for you."

"I'm sorry I interrupted your . . . show," she said. There were other words for what she'd seen, but she could not use them. Especially not now the sun had risen and its clear morning light replaced the half-formed world in which she'd seen a man sacrificed who did not die.

"No trouble. Have you ever noticed that the followers of Glebland mystics rarely write about their teachers' normal days? They prefer to speak of interruption. For each surviving sermon there are ten tales of blind men who thrust themselves into private conferences, leprous mothers who tackle sages in the street, cripples whose friends lower them through the skylights of houses where masters sleep. You can trace the death of a faith by its decreasing tolerance of such interruption."

"So you're a prophet now?"

He laughed. "I am trying to be a good man. Or at least better than I was before."

As they walked she overheard snatches of fierce argument:

"—not as individuals, but as members of a class—"

"—a seed isn't insignificant—"

"—Any more wine?"

"Systems are like magicians, when they claim to be honest with you's when you need to watch them—"

"How's Food Com? Any word on stock after the fire, that's all, need to know if I should run out and get my own—"

"Where'd you find that coffee?"

"—Sleight of hand, that's all, sleight of—"

"—More to a city than just lying to people—"

But as they approached, the speakers saw Temoc and fell silent. The tremors of the priest's footfalls shook them from one record groove to the next. As a Craftswoman, as a partner in a large firm, Elayne was used to spreading fear. This was different. Fear was only a piece of it.

Wherever he went, Temoc bore a piece of his sunrise sacrament.

A young couple approached Temoc, cautious, escorting their five-year-old son. The boy's chest rattled when he breathed; when he saw Temoc he curled into a ball and began to cry and cough. The cough started last night, his mother said.

Temoc touched the child over his heart. The scars on his arm glowed green. A piece of the power he'd gathered at sunrise, the strength the godlings gave him, flowed into the boy and made him whole.

Simple trick. Medical Craft could accomplish as much with as little trouble. But there was no doctor here, and Elayne doubted a doctor would have received such tearful thanks.

"Chel mentioned a Major," she said when they left the couple and their laughing boy behind. "A rival leader?"

"I am not a leader, and so I have no rivals. But not everyone in this camp thinks peaceful protest is the best road. Some feel this crowd should be the core of a new army. Most of those have never fought a war, you understand."

"What about you? Do you want peace?"

"I want to help people," he said.

"So do I."

But before he could respond, a group of camo-clad men and women had a question about the distribution of supplies. After came a young man with a broken arm. Temoc ran his hand over the wound, smoothing the bone whole. Elayne watched. What the others made of her presence, she could guess: outsider who did not comprehend their ways, servant of the dark powers arrayed against them.

Fair.

Temoc slowed. He gave more thought to the decisions put before him, and grew more careful with the healing he offered. The power of the morning ceremony ebbed. Mock sacrifices, it seemed, did not impart as much glory to Temoc's gods as the blood-gushing kind.

A cluster of youths dressed in dust and ripped denim bore a stretcher to Temoc, and upon the stretcher lay a girl. Fallen in a dance, they said. She breathed, her heart beat, but she could not speak, or even move save when convulsions wracked her.

They set her at Temoc's feet, and Temoc looked down. Elayne recognized his fear only because she'd seen it before, in battle. He doubted he could heal this girl, and he did not want to try and fail. Beneath that doubt she saw anger, too: at his own hesitation, at her friends for not bringing her earlier, at the girl for falling, at Elayne for standing witness.

So it may have been sympathy that made her say, "I'll do it."

Elayne approached, but the dancers clustered around their fallen friend like dogs at bay. They said nothing, but she saw *witch* in the set of that young woman's jaw, and that boy's white-knuckled grip on the fallen girl's arm. Of course she seemed an enemy, briefcase-bearing, pinstripe-clad, shod in patent leather: portrait of a monster in her early fifties.

The girl trembled.

"Please," Elayne said. "I can help."

The dancers did not move.

"Let her," Temoc said.

They drew back, a knotted muscle unclenching.

Elayne knelt by the stretcher. Lines of time clung to her as spiderwebs—the moment thick with hagiography, each observer trapping Elayne and Temoc and the girl in a tale. Forget history, though. Forget politics, and focus on the patient.

Elayne closed her eyes.

A good doctor could describe the girl's ailment with a glance at the tangle of her being. A good doctor could fix her problem permanently, or recommend preventative drugs and exercises.

All Elayne could do was reach inside the girl's head with fingers finer than the edge of broken glass, grasp the snarled threads within, and restore them to their proper course.

Which looked impressive enough.

She opened her eyes. The sun had gained the high ground against the earth. The girl breathed deep. Her pupils dilated. She squinted against the light, and spoke. "I see." She did not say what she saw. Her friends embraced her.

Elayne shook with the cold her Craft left behind. Temoc offered her a hand up. For the second time that day she accepted, and for the first she did not begrudge the offer.

"Thank you," he said when they found a private space in the crowd. "For her."

She didn't reply at first. She'd come here to find evidence of inconsistence, weaknesses to exploit. She remembered the dancers' fear, and the sacrifice weeping, and sour breath through a reed and the tarry stink of hunters' torch-smoke. She wasn't sure how to say, *you're welcome.*

A cry interrupted her search for the proper words. "Temoc!" Chel's voice: the woman came running. "There's trouble."

5

They heard the argument from halfway across the Square.

"Rotten meat!" a man cried. Temoc forced through the crowd, and for once Elayne followed: if the priest gig didn't pan out some navy could hire the big man for an icebreaker. They approached what she judged, from the smoke and the smell of singed pork, to be a cook tent. The shouting continued: "My daughter and my son are puking up their guts from rotten meat you served!"

"There's nothing wrong with our food," a woman answered, firm, angry.

"You're a fraud, Kemal, you and your husband both, frauds and poisoners." When they pushed to the front of the crowd Elayne surveyed the tableau: the woman, evidently Ms. Kemal, with cleaver and blood-spattered apron, blocked the cook tent's entrance. A pale-skinned sous chef stood by her side. The shouting man before them had a voice meant for the stage, and a smolder that would have impressed the hells out of a jury. Classic case of missed calling. Bright eyes bulged from a lean hungry face, and his teeth were yellow. "You take our souls and poison us in return."

A drum beat in Elayne's chest, and she looked up: Wardens circled on Couatl-back overhead. A fight would draw them down.

And that fight wasn't far off. The corners of Kemal's mouth declined, and her grip tightened on the cleaver. "Shut your face. Bill and I pass the hat, and every godsdamned thaum goes for food and fuel. It's hard work to feed a camp and you're wasting our time. Nobody's taken sick from our food before, and nobody has now."

"You call me a liar?"

"We cooked yesterday for a thousand people. If our food hurt your kids, why's no one else sick?"

"I'm going in that tent. I'll show the world your rotten meat." Nods from the crowd. Shouts of support. Not many, but enough to cause trouble.

"There's nothing in that tent but a lot of work for us to do. It's a kitchen, for the gods' sake. If your kids really are sick, what they have might be catching. I won't let you dirty up our space."

"Dirty?"

Temoc stepped into the clearing and addressed the cooks: "Kapania," to the woman, and "Bill" to her helper. His voice carried, and people looked to him. "This man's worried about his children. It's a reasonable request. What's your name, sir?"

"Sim."

"Surely it won't be trouble to let Sim into the tent."

"Temoc." Kemal's jaw jutted forward, and she bared her lower teeth. "The whole camp eats our food. I can't trust anyone in here I don't know. We caught this man trying to sneak in."

Sim flushed. "Why post guards if you have nothing to hide?"

Grumbles of assent from the crowd. Temoc glanced back, and the grumblers fell silent. "What if I look myself, Sim? I give you my word I will tell you if I see anything unsavory."

"These are my kids. I trust no eyes but my own."

Kemal rolled hers. "Waste of time, Temoc. Sim, I'm sorry your kids are sick, but it's no fault of ours. We have work to do."

She must have thought the matter settled—she turned her back on Sim and lifted the tent flap.

Sim rushed her. Bill tried to block his path, but he wasn't a fighter. The angry man threw him to the ground and tried to shove past Kemal. Kemal shoved him back, turned with cleaver raised—not out of anger, Elayne thought, she just happened to have it in her hand, one of those thousand unhappy coincidences of which tragedies are made. Sim seized her wrist, twisted—the cleaver swept down toward their legs—Elayne woke a glyph in her arm, in case—

But suddenly Temoc stood between them.

Sim lay on the ground, staring up wide-eyed. Bill had caught Ms. Kemal before she fell. Temoc held the cleaver.

The crowd pressed close and angry. "Kapania," Temoc said. "People are upset. Let Sim look."

"No."

The new voice clamped like a fist around the murmurs of the crowd, and crushed them to silence. Elayne turned, Chel turned, the whole crowd turned, even Sim lying prone. When he saw the new arrival, he blanched.

A man of steel emerged from the crowd.

Golem, Elayne thought at first, but no, the movements were too fluid, the voice too wet—the figure was human, armored from helmet to boots in scrap metal plate, all sharp lines and jagged edges and dark leather. A lead pipe hung in a sheath by the figure's side, and a red enamel circle glinted on his left arm.

"Long time, Sim."

There was no trace of Craftwork about the armored man, but the crowd hushed all the same.

Save for Chel, who whispered to Elayne: "The Major."

As if Chel's voice broke some binding spell, Sim spasmed to his feet, shocked upright by terror. He hadn't quite gained his balance before he tried to run.

The Major's hand flicked out, and Sim crumpled. Craftwork, Elayne thought before she saw the blood on Sim's temple, and the small iron sphere that rolled from the man's fallen body. A good throw, that was all.

Sim tried to stand, but before he could the Major reached him, lifted him, struck him across the face with a mailed fist. Sim spun, gained balance, tried to tackle the Major—but that junk-metal armor didn't seem to slow the man. Sim slipped on the iron ball and fell face-first. The Major pressed his knee between Sim's shoulder blades and twisted the man's left arm up behind him. Armored fingers probed Sim's sleeve.

Temoc advanced. "What are you doing?"

"Temoc." Again the dark, heavy voice. "I'm saving you trouble."

"I don't understand."

"Bring me meat," the Major told Kapania Kemal.

"Excuse me?"

"Meat!"

And she moved.

"Sim and I," the Major said, "have a history, don't we, Sim? If that's your name." Sim cursed, then screamed when the Major jerked his arm. The Major found what he sought in the sleeve: a small phial that shimmered before Elayne's closed eyes. "Dockworker's strike last year, at the solstice, when the bosses were about to cave, this man visited our food tent. Half the camp took sick two days after. We turned on each other, and the Wardens came. Hard to put a protest back together after that, isn't it, Sim?" The fallen man groaned. "Didn't think you'd be dumb enough to try the same trick twice. Where's that meat?"

Bill brought it from the tent: a handful of raw ground beef. The Major uncorked the phial and poured its shimmering contents onto the meat. Elayne watched the transformation with clinical interest: the accelerated putrescence, the maggots that took writhing shape within the flesh. Basic decay agent—not over-the-shelf, but hardly traceable. Some in the audience retched. Chel staggered, and Elayne steadied her.

"That," the Major said, "is what happens when I pour so much onto so little. Spread through an entire stew this would sour the taste slowly—and tonight there'd be sickness all through camp. Just like last time." The Major drew his weighted pipe from its makeshift scabbard. Sim whimpered. "Not again." The Major raised the pipe.

"Stop," Temoc said.

The Major did. "Why?"

Temoc pointed up. The dark eyes behind the mask glittered as they peered into the blue, where Wardens circled.

"If sneaks try to break us, shouldn't we break them back?"

"We can't beat Wardens in a fight," Temoc said. "We are strong in peace."

"I've seen the strength of peace fail."

"If you want to give them an excuse to come for us," Temoc said, "you're no better than the man beneath you. And I will stop you."

The moment wobbled like a spinning top, and Elayne could not tell which way it would fall.

The Major let Sim go, and stood. Sim gasped and flopped on the stone like a landed fish. He rose slowly onto his hands and knees. Temoc and the Major stared at one another.

"Go," the Major said. "Before I change my mind."

Sim ran. The crowd parted for him, and followed him with their eyes as he hobbled to the edge of the Square. Elayne ignored Sim; she and Temoc watched the Major retreat toward the fountain.

Temoc almost followed, but walked away instead.

"Not a rival," Elayne said when she caught up. "I see."

"What do you want from me, Elayne?"

"The same thing you want. Peace. These people need someone to bring them to the table."

"Come home with me," he said.

She looked at him with mild disbelief: they were not what they once were, but time had refined them both. Still, there were some lines one did not cross.

"Temoc," she replied, and pondered her next words.

He almost succeeded at covering his laugh. "Not what I meant. We need to talk in private. Besides." And then something she had not expected to see: the rock face broke, and he smiled almost like a normal person would. "I want you to meet my family."

6

Chel guided them to the camp's edge. "Thank you," Elayne said.

The woman bowed. "Good luck." She set her hand to her heart when Temoc passed; they all did, the watchers on the border.

The crowds outside the camp were less respectful.

Wardens at attention paralleled the dockworkers' perimeter; Elayne and Temoc walked through their line, ignoring the poured-silver faces' reflective stares. Behind the Wardens gathered a second crowd, better dressed and angrier than the people of Chakal Square. Suited men waved signs shop-printed with the logo of the Skittersill Chamber of Commerce. Press passes sprouted from reporters' hatbands.

A sign-bearer spat at Temoc's feet. Temoc's stride hitched and he turned toward the spitter, slow as an executioner raising his axe. The man bore Temoc's gaze for a heartbeat, though it must have felt longer to him. His fingers twitched on his sign-haft, which was no larger around than Temoc's thumb.

Elayne saw Temoc fight a war with himself, and win.

When he turned away the little man with the sign began to shout again, louder than his fellows.

The pause had given reporters time to push through the crowd, pencils sharp, notebooks out. Elayne raised a hand to hail a cab. "Temoc?" A young woman with deep circles under her eyes shoved to the front of the journalist pack. "Gabby Jones, DL *Times*. A moment, please."

"We have none to spare."

"Who's your friend?"

"Another person who is leaving with me."

"Any comment on rumors the King in Red is reaching out to the Chakal Square camp?"

Temoc shook his head.

"Are you denying he's reached out, or—"

A cab tried to gallop past them. Elayne locked its wheels with a tine of Craft, and it skidded to a halt by the sidewalk. The horse shot her a reproachful glare, which she ignored. "He means, no comment."

"And you are?"

"A concerned citizen. If you'll excuse me." She ushered Temoc into the carriage, followed, and slammed the door on the reporter. She released the cab's wheels, and the horse surged down Bloodletter's Street.

"I need to learn the trick of that," Temoc said. "Handling the press."

"You did well, I thought. It's not as hard as the other thing you did. Or didn't do."

"When have I ever concerned myself with the ridicule of fools?"

But he did not speak again as they galloped south into the Skittersill.

Elayne opened the curtain to watch the city pass. She had worked on the Skittersill project from afar, and while she could plot their course on her mental map of the district, she did not recognize these shops and parks, the young claw-branched acacias or the hopscotch patterns children chalked on sidewalks.

They stopped by a stone gate in a windowless plaster wall. She paid for the cab, waving off Temoc's protest. Along the street only a few doors interrupted the smooth plaster. Old Quechal architecture presented a blank face to the world.

Temoc opened the gate and led her down a brief dark tunnel into light, and paradise.

Accustomed to a Dresediel Lex of arid brown—save for the manicured lawn of her hotel—Elayne stopped short, stunned by luxuriant green. The courtyard overflowed with flowering cactus and climbing vines. A table stood among the plants, set with a half-finished chess game. A three-stringed fiddle leaned in the shade near the front door. A boy sat cross-legged opposite the gate, playing solitaire.

"Welcome," Temoc said. The boy looked up from his game, and smiled a broad and shining smile. Elayne would have recognized that expression even had the child not left the game and run toward them across the courtyard, shouting, "Dad!"

Temoc grabbed the boy, lifted him in a hug, swung him around so the force of their revolution made his feet describe a circle. The priestly mask was gone. Grinning, he set the boy down, and presented him to Elayne. "This is Caleb, my son. Caleb, meet Elayne Kevarian."

Elayne accepted the boy's hand. His grip was strong.

She was still reeling when the screen door opened and a woman emerged: tall, tan, short-haired, with the elegant self-possession of minor royalty and tenured academics. She smiled, too, but there was tension in that smile. "I'm glad you're back," she said to Temoc.

Temoc moved to her, river-swift and inevitable, held her, kissed her. Her hands seemed sculpted to his shoulders, and their parting was the parting of tectonic plates. Elayne felt guilty for having seen it, for being the pretext on which Temoc drew back and turned and introduced her to, "My wife, Mina."

Lunch was leftovers—heavily spiced and roasted pork in a sauce touched with chocolate, and oranges for dessert. They ate outside, the dining room table being occupied at the moment by Mina's research, which topic gave Elayne, drowning in domesticity, a spar to clutch. "What do you study?"

"Migratory desert cultures. Mythography and foundational theology for the most part."

"Exciting field?"

"These days. We're just coming out from under the shadow of Abervas and Klemt, last century—the family-tree model of religious structure." She ate with her fork, sawing meat to pieces with its side, then spearing, and she leaned against the table when she spoke. "Very Gerhardtian—this sense that cultures grow more complex over time, and by studying modern 'primitive' cultures we can approximate the beliefs of previous generations."

"That isn't true?"

"No more than it's true monkeys evolve into men—in fact both came from something else. Cultural development and transformation happens everywhere, all the time—it's a disservice to modern nomads to see them as throwbacks who never made the jump to settled life. Klemt's students missed, well, basically everything pertinent about the subject. Turns out many of the cultures Klemt identified as 'primitive pretextual' were recovering from post-Contact plague; we got off easy, our gods were strong enough to keep us going until our immune systems caught up with Old World bugs, but Contact wasn't so easy for everyone. Klemt was such a dominant force in the field that people spent a solid century ignoring what their own eyes told them in favor of his theories. Nomadic peoples aren't any more timeless than urbanites—their history just works differently. I spend most of my time in the field, trying to trace it. That's how I met Temoc."

"We visited the same tribe at the same time," Temoc said, "while I was wandering. We did not have much in common."

"I thought he was a self-righteous prig. But adversity makes the heart grow fonder."

"We stopped a renegade Scorpionkind clutch from infesting the desert with unbound demons."

"That was the start, anyway." Mina grabbed Temoc's wrist, and squeezed.

"How did *you* meet Dad?" the boy asked Elayne. He had obviously heard these stories before, and run out of patience for them.

Temoc coughed into his hand.

"We didn't like each other at first, either," Elayne said. "Your father seems to have that effect on people."

"You did save my life," Temoc demurred.

"We met during Liberation. He worked with the old gods, and I was an attaché to the Liberating Forces."

"You fought for the King in Red?"

She nodded. "When I was not much older than you. I joined at thirteen."

"That young," Mina said.

"It was a different time. The good people of my hometown tried to kill me when they learned I'd taught myself the basics of Craft; I didn't even know that what I did had a name. Lots of Craftworkers my age have similar stories, women especially. I ran away to the Hidden Schools—but they were under threat so often back then, I'd just as well have joined an artillery battalion. Soon I entered the fight in earnest. When I met your father I was fresh from the Semioticists' Rebellion in Southern Kath. Bad business. They sent me here for an easy assignment: help Kopil broker peace with your gods. It wasn't so easy as we thought. Talks broke down. Peace failed." And snow fell on Dresediel Lex for the first and last time. Lightning crackled in the sky above, eternally, a tree of thorns on which Craftsmen impaled the gods they caught and killed. Engines of war rent the skies asunder. The King in Red blazed with hellfire in the heavens. She'd found Temoc in Sansilva snow, speared through the stomach with a thorn of ice. She had healed him. She wasn't sure even the King in Red knew that. "I run into your father once in a while—rarely when I expect, and always when he's up to something strange."

"You visited the camp this morning, then," Mina said, with evident distaste on the word "camp."

"For business, yes."

But at the mention of "business," Temoc stood to clear their empty plates, and when he returned he bore a deck of cards.

They played a few hands of bridge, Temoc and Mina against Elayne and the boy. Elayne and Caleb lost the first two hands, but by the third they worked out the conflict between their bidding conventions, and they made that contract, and the fourth.

The boy played the final hand, and though he ran two risky transports of which no teacher would approve, he made both good. In that garden courtyard, surrounded by cactus flowers, sun bright in the dry blue sky, sipping weak pale beer and playing cards, Elayne almost forgot Chakal Square.

Almost.

After the game, Caleb reclaimed the cards, and Mina retreated into the house and her work. Which left Elayne and Temoc alone under the sun, surrounded by cactus.

She finished her beer, and looked down into the bubbles that clung to the empty glass. "Why go to the camp at all, if you're worried about your family?"

He stood and began to pace, arms crossed, head down. In the silence, Elayne understood the role of the courtyards, of the inward-facing windows and the cactus and the vines. Green walled them round, warded them against the city outside.

"I have a church," Temoc said. "Not far from here. A small place I built ten years ago. My congregation brought me word of the King in Red's plan. The broadsheets warned them, and called them to act. If enough gathered to oppose him, he could not continue. We might save ourselves by faith."

"Obstinacy won't save anything," she said. "Your gods made the Skittersill a slum for slaves. The god-wards keep property values low, and make the place practically uninsurable. Everyone who lives here risks plague, earthquakes, demon infestation. It hasn't happened yet because the old wards hold, but they won't last forever."

"Yet families live, and love, and grow, here. The gods gave this land to the people—as slaves, yes, but it remains theirs in common and in trust, now the gods and owners are dead. You propose to steal their homes. Increase the land's value, allow its fee simple sale, and in five years no one will recognize this place. The god-wards protect it from your . . ."—he did not say "master"—"Boss."

"So you joined the movement."

"I told my faithful to follow their hearts. They wanted more. Their eyes accused me of cowardice. I went to the Square to serve, and as I served my congregation grew. The gods are closer than ever before to accepting our new, bloodless path."

"And the cult of Temoc grows with your church."

"Do you want me to desert them? I trained to serve and fight." He tightened his fists until his knuckles cracked. "It took me years to learn peace, to learn to spare the fat small imitations of men who spit at my feet but cannot meet my eyes. What would be left if I turned my back on service?"

"A man," she said.

"This is a problem of mine with the Kathic tongue," he replied. "In High Quechal, *man* is an honor to be earned. It is not a state that remains when all else is ripped away."

"Fine." Even from this distance she could feel the heat off his skin. "So help them deal with us. That's why we made the Craft—to resolve problems without bloodshed."

"The Craft was made for the same end as any other tool: to bring power to those who wield it."

"Craftwork is more than a big stick to use on people we don't like. We fought to build a better world than that."

"I have no power in the camp."

"Those people look at you like a saint."

"And what will happen when I try to lead them? I am the last Eagle Knight. Priest of the Old Gods. The King in Red has waited decades for an excuse to kill me, and you ask me to offer him one as a solstice present."

"He'll deal with you in good faith, if I have to break his neck to make it happen."

Temoc's default mode was statue, idol, edifice. He did not show weakness or confusion. The old priests had gouged all those from their recruits. But there were cracks in him, and desperation seeped through.

One of Temoc's house windows closed.

"You know I'm right. If you don't pull these people together, they'll listen to someone else. Someone angrier. If that happens, I can't guarantee their safety."

She waited for him to talk. She waited a long time.

"I will do it," he said.

"Thank you." She kept tight rein on her satisfaction. "Send me word when you're ready. Now, if you'll excuse me. Where's the restroom?"

"Inside," he said. "First door on the left."

The screen door opened into a dim tiled dining room. Mina sat at the table in front of a fanned-out horseshoe of yellowed papers. Books gaped at her, propped against stacks of other books. Her pen drifted down the margin of her notepad, and she squinted through reading glasses at a tomb rubbing. She didn't look up as Elayne passed into the deeper dimness of the house. Oil shone from the bellies of glass lamps perched on shelves. Ghostlights were set into the ceiling, unlit. Through the door at the hall's end Elayne saw Caleb pondering cards spread on his bedroom floor for solitaire or prophecy.

She stared at her reflection in the darkened bathroom's mirror for a count of twenty, flushed the toilet, washed her hands, dried them on the towel. Mina didn't seem to notice when she returned, though she did look up when Elayne set a business card on her notepad.

Mina's eyes were large and soft over the rims of her glasses.

"In case you need anything," Elayne said. "In case there's any way I can help."

Mina did not quite smile. "I guess we're not very subtle in this family."

Elayne did not smile, either. Somewhere in the last few years she'd lost the knack of doing so in a reassuring manner. Her teeth seemed to multiply, her grin too broad, as if her bones strained against her flesh: the skeleton in waiting. "I do not need to catch you eavesdropping to see that you're nervous. I would be too, if I was in your position."

"This will get bad," she said.

"I hope not. But if it does, there's my card. Monicola Hotel, room four-oh-four. Or visit our local office. They can find me."

She put the card in the breast pocket of her shirt. "Thank you."

Then she returned to her work, and Elayne to hers.

7

The guards cheered when Chel came to the bonfire for dinner. Forty of them sat in a clearing between the tents, and they set down their bowls to applaud: guys and gals she knew from childhood and from the docks, survivors of the picket lines and the final wicked deal last winter, all muscles, tattoos, dirt and scars and smiles. She raised her hands and sketched an actress's bow, flaring an imaginary cape. Her friends hooted and whistled. When she looked up she saw Tay at the other side of the circle. He wasn't laughing, and hadn't clapped. Well, fuck him, or not, at least for now. "Thank you," she said in the poshest Camlaander accent she could fake, hamming it up. Cozim, by the fire, laughed so hard he almost dropped the ladle into the stewpot. Not everyone here was a dockhand: when they started standing guard others joined them. One of the new women gave Chel a high-five, then winced. Soft hands. Chel dropped back into her normal voice, into Low Quechal. "Not that I mind— but what did I do?"

Cozim passed her a bowl of stew that looked and smelled like it was mostly made from charcoal. "Heard about you and the witch this morning."

"Knocked her right to the ground," the new woman said. Ellen, Chel's memory supplied. Schoolteacher, one of those who came over with Red Bel from the union, which explained her soft hands.

"Choked her half to death." That was Zip, huge and broad. Word around the docks ran that Zip once won a head-butting contest with an ox, and Chel credited the rumor. "Shoulda gone the other half."

"Way I heard it," Cozim said, "you saved Temoc's life."

She stared into the stew, but it offered her no reflections. She tried a bite; something in there might charitably be described as meat. "Cozim, did Food Com send this?"

"Ain't their fault." Cozim pointed over to Zip. "They sent meat raw for us to cook. Something to prove, I guess, after the fight this morning. Thank Zip for the texture."

"Godsdamn, Zip. Your mother never teach you to cook?"

" 'S good all black like that. Cleans the teeth." Zip bared his own teeth, which did not help his point.

"Put those things away," Chel said. "You want to blind us?" She tried the stew again, but a few seconds' cooling had not improved the flavor.

"Why didn't you kill her?" Ellen again—and Chel couldn't tell whether she was scared, or eager. The circle grunted interest.

"You think I could have?" Chel said. "You ever seen a Craftsman die?"

"Saw one crushed by a shipping container once," Zip said. "Walked under the crane. Cable snapped." Someone chuckled, and he glared around the circle, looking for the one who'd laughed. Nobody owned up. "I'd checked it. Hand to gods."

Chel didn't argue. "Did he stay dead? They can come back, mostly."

"Beats me."

"Still, though," Ellen pressed. "Why not?"

"She didn't come to hurt Temoc. She just got the wrong impression when she saw him at the altar. You've been to services." Nods around the circle. "She jumped him because she didn't know what was happening. That was my fault. I should have told her."

"Still," Cozim said. "You got your hands on her throat. Counts for something."

She'd thought so too, at first. But Elayne had healed that girl, and Temoc greeted her as a friend. "It's not like that," she said, and again, louder, for the others to hear over their own laughter: "It's not."

"You taking the witch's side?"

"No." Chel stood. The others stopped talking. Forty pairs of eyes rested on her. She felt suddenly exposed. She'd spoken to rooms before—given orders, addressed crowds in the strike. This felt different. "The King in Red sent her to talk. They want to make a deal."

"We've heard that before. Deals don't end well for us."

"This one might. And we almost stopped her at the border because we were afraid. I jumped her because she didn't understand what she saw. Let's say they really do want to deal—and I mean like people deal with people, not like the bosses dealt with us back at the docks. Any of you want to count how many times we screwed up today? How many times we almost wrecked our chances?"

Cozim stirred the charcoal stew. "What are you saying, Chel?"

"Back on the docks, we knew our job. We've been standing guard here as if that makes us guards, but we don't know what we're doing any more than fresh muscle knows how to load a cargo ship. We almost turned back a Craftswoman who wanted to help us, and we let a poisoner in. If we screw up and a fight breaks out, who you think the papers will blame?" She let the question hang. A few tents over, someone played a slow air on a three-string fiddle.

"What should we do, then?"

"We need rules," she said. "Just like at work. So we're ready for whatever." She sat back down, and picked up her bowl. "What those should be, I don't know."

"We could make a uniform," Cozim suggested. "So they know we're all together, not just some gang. Doesn't need to be anything fussy, just a sign."

"I got a rule I need to know," Zip said. "When do we get to hit 'em?" Some of the boys laughed.

"When they hit us first."

Suggestions came fast after that. Even Ellen joined in after a while. Chel listened more than she spoke, glad to have the focus off her—though once every while folks looked back to her for approval, as if she knew what from what. She added a few questions to the mix, answered others.

Tay turned from the fire and walked away. He hadn't spoken since she sat down. As Zip and Cozim argued over what color armband the guards should wear, Chel left her burnt stew to follow him.

She caught Tay outside the tent circle. He'd lit a cigarette, and offered her one.

"No thanks."

"Suit yourself." He took a long drag, and stuffed the crumpled pack into the pocket of his thick canvas pants. He wasn't a talker, never had been. He smoked a cheap Shining Empire brand he'd started with in Kho Khatang before he got kicked out of the merchant marine, more spun glass and pixie dust than tobacco inside the rolling paper. Got the packs off a sailor he still sort of knew, who'd been jumped by some homophobic son of a bitch during a night of drunken shore leave and was getting the shit kicked out of him when Tay stepped in. Son of a bitch and friends broke Tay's nose; Tay and the sailor did them worse, and Tay got canned for it. He came back to DL to work on the docks with his dad, and these days his sailor friend brought him foul cigarettes by the carton and didn't take payment in return. Chel had called bullshit on the story when Tay told her, two weeks after they first slept together, but she'd met the sailor and he still had the scars.

The faraway fiddle took up a faster tune, and drums joined in. The smell of spiced pork mixed with sweat and weed and tent canvas and rubber from the soles of many shoes. She missed the dock stink. Not enough oil and sea, here. "So you're a hero now," he said.

"As if I know what that's supposed to mean."

"You didn't argue when everyone clapped."

"You're jealous."

"I'm not," he said. She laughed. "I'm not. But if that witch really had come to kill Temoc—"

"She was here to talk, Tay."

"If she wasn't," he pressed. "If she wasn't, you'd still have jumped her."

"Yeah."

"And how do you think that would have ended?"

"They can die," she said, though she'd maintained the opposite to Cozim.

"If she wanted to kill you, she could have."

She'd spent most of the afternoon trying not to think these thoughts. She knew the Craft was dangerous. God Wars vets, those still living, told stories: war machines, crawling undead and demon hordes, sigils that turned your mind inside out when you read them. And every day she saw Craftwork miracles— ships with masts tall enough to scrape the sky, metal sailless hulks larger inside than out. What could the people who made such things do when they went to war? Best not to think, because thinking terrified. "She didn't."

He breathed smoke, tapped ash, examined the ember of his cigarette. "I don't want you to die."

"Me neither."

"Not for Temoc or for anyone."

"You are jealous."

Tay laughed hard, and put the cigarette back in his mouth.

"If the Craftswoman really wanted to deal," she said, "it was worth the risk. And if she didn't, I had to stop her."

"Nine hells of a risk."

"But think of the reward." She turned them both to face the camp beneath the golden sky. As the sun set, signs and slogans came down. Fireside circles bloomed with life. The camp by night became a village, messy and wild and new, in the middle of Dresediel Lex. "If there's a chance at a deal, we have to try. We lost the strike; we can't lose this, too. They want a

Skittersill too rich for Zip to raise his kids. A Skittersill where we don't fit. I can't let that happen."

"Me neither." He touched her on the waist.

She took the cigarette from his mouth and kissed him, and tasted salt and tobacco and pixie dust and glass. "Come on. Let's go back. Maybe Zip's stew is an acquired taste."

"You get my share."

"No fair." She jabbed her knuckles into his side. "You have to eat that shit if I do. We're in this together."

"Yeah," he said, that one word drawn out with a touch of pleasant surprise at the end, as if he'd found a gift inside. Together they returned to the fire.

8

The King in Red's secretary rose from her desk to bar Elayne's way. "If you don't have an appointment, you'll have to wait."

"He'll make time," Elayne said. She'd taken an hour-long carriage ride through traffic and three elevators to reach the King in Red's foyer, on the top floor of the pyramid he'd remodeled into an office building. The trip had not calmed her. The secretary was no fit target for her anger, but Elayne would not let herself be detained in Kopil's lobby, no matter how elegantly appointed it might be.

"He's secluded." The woman pointed to the obsidian doors behind her, carved with serpents and dead gods. Closed, the doors' engravings formed an enormous skull, eye sockets aflame. "No one enters after he's lit the fires. His schedule clears tomorrow at two. I'll pencil you in, or if it's urgent we can squeeze you between his security briefing and the evening market rundowns."

Elayne closed her eyes.

Neon spiderwebs and interlocking ghostlit gears filled the foyer around her. The door was well Crafted, but not well enough to stop Elayne. She found the timekeeping mechanism in an instant, and its bond to the schedule on the secretary's desk. Trivial to twist the schedule's sense of local time; it was always two tomorrow afternoon somewhere.

The door ground open. Grave-blackness gaped beyond.

The secretary gaped, too. "See?" Elayne said. "I told you he'd make time."

She strode past secretary and doors into a shadow that closed about her like a mouth. Stone steps rose through the night. She could have summoned fire, but she needed none.

After a long climb she emerged into a deeper darkness in which the King in Red sat, wreathed by lightning.

He hovered cross-legged in midair, finger bones resting on the sharp protrusions of his knees. Blue-white sparks leapt from his skull to the crystal dome above. Their brief flashes illuminated the outlines of his office: altar-desk, stuffed bookcases, umbrella stand. Somewhere, a Zurish contrabass choir chanted songs of praise and terror.

"What exactly," she said, "were you trying to pull?"

The choir faltered and failed. Crimson stars caught fire in the King in Red's eye sockets. "I see you visited our friends in Chakal Square."

"I did. Especially our mutual friends."

The skeleton sighed, and stood. Robes fell heavy around him. Toe bones tapped the floor. The lightning faded, and normal ghostlight returned to the room: a sparsely furnished crystal dome atop the eighty-story pyramid of 667 Sansilva, from which Red King Consolidated distributed water to the fourteen million people of Dresediel Lex. A long time ago, priest-kings had sacrificed people on the red-tinged altar that now served Kopil for a desk. "I didn't think Temoc's involvement was worth mentioning."

"Wrong. You thought it was worth not mentioning." A carafe of coffee rested on a side table near the desk. Elayne poured herself a cup with the Craft, and floated it through the air to her waiting hand. "You knew about the Alt Selene ruling. You're not that far out of touch. You thought Chakal Square might be a problem. You investigated, and learned Temoc was involved." She drank the coffee. "This is good."

"I add more black to it," he said. "Temoc is the last priest of the old gods. His fathers killed thousands. His hands are not clean."

"You kept news of Chakal Square under wraps, put our work and your city at risk, because you didn't want to deal with him.

And then you tried to start a riot, so your Wardens could arrest him for disturbing the peace."

"Really, Elayne. You can't believe a radical's accusations."

"This morning they caught a man trying to poison the camp. You mean to tell me Tan Batac came up with that idea all on his own?"

"He did," Kopil said at last. "But I didn't stop him."

"He almost poisoned hundreds of people."

"Food poisoning," he said. "Unpleasant, but hardly dangerous."

"If you're in good health, which I can't say for everyone in Chakal Square. That was low."

"Temoc and I have unfinished business."

"I've made deals with actual demons, with a lot less at stake. So have you."

"This feels different," Kopil said. He leaned against the black-red glass of his desk. Bony fingers settled on a silver picture frame. She did not need to look to know what image it contained. Kopil, younger, with his arms around a man she'd never seen alive.

"I know it's hard," she said. "They cut Timas open on that altar. But you've had your revenge. You broke their world and built a better one in its place."

"It's not enough."

She couldn't argue the point. She'd loved, and lost, but her loves and losses had never been so deep, so sudden, or so bloody. "Would he want you to set all you've built at risk for the sake of a grudge?"

Skyspires turned slowly above them. The falling sun lit the smog a million shades of green and yellow and red. "This was easier before," he said.

"In the Wars, you mean."

"Gods try to smite you, and you smite them first. Armies of light against armies of darkness. Craftsmen advancing the cause of knowledge and freedom and humanity against ignorance and oppression."

"Humanity?"

"Or whatever you want to call us," he allowed. "But times have changed. My people turn back to old and bloody gods."

"That's freedom for you."

He bowed his head. Shadows lingered in the folds of his robes and the depressions of his skull. "Everything was clear in the old days. You walked the lines like the queen of Death."

"I was seventeen," she said. "More seems clear at seventeen than is. You were forty, still fleshy, still human, which imparts a likewise palsied perspective."

"What do you want from me, Elayne?"

Once those pits in his skull held eyes, and skin covered his high cheekbones. A long time had passed since then. "An apology. For keeping secrets when you said you wouldn't, for treating me like just another minion. We've known each other too long for that."

"I am sorry," he said, and she thought he meant it.

"Call back your agents. Quit the skullduggery. Work with the Chakal Square crowd. Temoc will gather leaders from the camp. We'll meet, and compromise, and deal. Be wise for once, as well as strong."

She wondered how many people in Kopil's life could bear his gaze without flinching.

"Very well," he said. "But Tan Batac won't understand."

9

Temoc celebrated the sunset sacrifice in Chakal Square. As he chanted he saw Chel near the mats with another man beside her, a broken-nosed dockhand who tensed when Temoc raised his blade.

Hungry gods pleaded, promised: give us blood this time, and joy, and new power. A heart might even wake the old ones, and woken they will dance with you the great gavotte of war.

No, he told them, and himself.

Not all the frustration he felt belonged to the gods.

The knife fell, pommel first, and the echo of sacrifice yielded an echo of bliss. For the gathered faithful on the mats, even an echo was more than they had known. It was enough. New light kindled in the broken-nosed guard's eyes.

After the ceremony, Temoc walked among milling parishioners. Chel seemed ready to lead her companion off, but she stopped when Temoc raised his hand.

"Sir," she said as he approached. And then, an awkward afterthought: "This is my partner, Tay."

Temoc bowed his head to each of them in turn. "Welcome."

"Thanks," Tay said. "I've never been to one of these before. It's one hell of a thing. Excuse me. I don't know what to say."

"The sacrament is strange. It occasions prayer and reflection, and sometimes sacrilege." Temoc wished he felt as sure as he made himself sound. "Are you busy tonight? I would appreciate your company at a meeting."

"Of course," Chel said.

"I—" Tay buried his hand in his pocket, and gripped

something there. Not a weapon, Temoc's old training reported. Cigarettes. "It's my shift. I should go."

Chel touched the man's arm. "I'll catch you back at the tents."

"Sure," Tay said, then stuck out a hand. Temoc clasped with him, and felt his calluses, patterned wrong for a warrior. Tay broke the handshake and walked away. After five steps he lit a cigarette. Smoke trailed him through the camp.

"How can I help, sir?"

"There is no need for 'sir,' " he said. "My name is enough." She waited.

"The King in Red and Tan Batac want to negotiate. I must convince the leaders of our group to speak with them."

"You don't need an escort to talk with the Kemals over at Food Com," she said. "Or with Red Bel or Xotoc. Might even hurt with Bel, if she thinks you're trying to intimidate her."

"All those you mention will listen to reason," he replied. "We will start with the man who won't."

The Major's troops drilled by firelight to the beat of deep drums.

Temoc counted one hundred men and women dressed in street clothes and patchwork armor, fighting mock wars two by two. When the drums beat four-four time, those to the north attacked with fists and knives. When the beat shifted to five-six, the south mounted their assault in turn. Flesh and metal struck metal and flesh. Groans and meat percussion mixed with drummers' blows on taut hide.

The Major's jagged metal edges reflected his army and the flame. He kept time with one hand. No—Temoc saw the beat he kept shift before the drummers' did. He did not keep time. He called it.

"Hello," Temoc said. Chel stood by his arm, playing silent attaché. He was grateful for her presence: the Major came from the docks. Perhaps he would listen more to voices from his homestead.

"Come to join us, Temoc?" The Major's mask warped his

voice into a chorus of wheels and gears and twanging banjo strings. "To teach us ancient arts of war?"

"The King in Red has sued for peace," Temoc said.

The Major's hand faltered. The beat tripped, and the ordered clash dissolved to a chaos more reminiscent of the battles Temoc knew. The Major passed the conductor's role to an aide, and turned to Temoc. "A trap."

"I don't think so."

"You know Craftsmen better than anyone. Their 'due process' is all deadfalls. During the dockworkers' strike they called us to parlay, and those who went emerged from that meeting room speaking competition and market forces like fresh graduates from the Hidden Schools. These people turned the Siege of Alt Selene into a massacre, and torched the jungles of Southern Kath. The only way to break their smug self-sufficiency is to refuse to deal with them."

"Which," Temoc replied, "only makes them angry."

"Good. Then they will show their true faces."

"Most of these people do not want war." He kept his voice low and level.

"War comes whether or not it's wanted," the Major said. "The Craftsmen are too sure of their own righteousness to compromise. There can be no change without revolution."

This was why Temoc rarely visited the Major, though many of the man's soldiers came to service. Rhetoric ran circles in the Major's mind. War was its own end. Temoc, gods help him, understood the appeal. "But are you ready? Are they?"

"History decides the moment for transition."

"I have fought Craftsmen. Your troops are impressive." A sop to the Major's pride: their ferocity had merit, even if their technique fell short. "But they can't beat sorcery. The Craft will scour us from the soil and let our ashes testify that none can beat the Deathless Kings. If you refuse to deal, the others will, and their deal will be more a surrender for your absence. Chakal Square will be the dockworkers' strike repeated. Bide your time. Build your strength. But for now, join us at the table."

The Major's aide broke the rhythm of the measure, and again the drill tangled. Flames danced on steel as the Major pondered the vanguard of his revolution.

"I will come," he said at last.

"Thank you."

Temoc left, and did not let himself sag until he was certain no one but Chel was watching.

Temoc walked the camp in glory. One night was not enough to change the world, but it was enough to start, if one walked fast, and with the gods.

Stars wheeled overhead, and fire in his mind. He mended broken bones. Soothed fears. A woman came to him shaking of withdrawal from a drug he did not know, a drug that, when he looked upon it with eyes of faith, curled as a centipede around her spine. Its jaws he broke, and the legs too, one by one. Screams rose to the clouds. He could not tell the difference between the woman's screams and the drug's.

In the end, the centipede died and the woman lived. She could barely stand on her own, and when she lay down she fell asleep in moments.

He spoke with Red Bel. He wheedled Xotoc. The Kemals at Food Com acquiesced: Bill was eager, Kapania not so much.

Temoc worked until his scars' light faded to the faintest emerald glow.

Chel walked him out. The press of bodies and the furnace cackle of song, debate, and prayer warmed him. The rest of the city, and the Wardens, stood cold and sharp beyond the square. "Do you really think we can deal with the King in Red?" she asked.

"What would you want from such a deal?"

"For him and Tan Batac to stay out of the Skittersill."

"And I want them to let us praise the old gods. The Kemals want housing for God Wars refugees. The Major will settle for nothing less than peace on earth and goodwill toward men, even if he has to kill everyone on the planet to achieve it."

"So, no."

"Compromise is possible. But possibility is a vast empire, and likelihood its smallest province. Still, the province is rich, and so we work to seize it."

He felt her gaze as a weight, this woman he could lift one-handed, in her early twenties perhaps, work-hardened but innocent of war. Temoc had been born and raised in Dresediel Lex. But Chel could say the same and yet she had never seen the Serpents dance before Quechaltan, never known the glory of a true sacrifice or the deep surf-rhythm of a city's voices raised in prayer, never fought the butchery dark sorcerers called Liberation beneath shattered skies and down alleys slick with blood and melted snow. Temoc had not left his city. His city left him, replaced by another. He'd been born scant miles from this spot, yet felt a half a world away from everything he knew.

"My family waits," he said.

"We'll be here in the morning."

"I know." He set his palm on her forehead, felt its warmth and the curve of bone beneath, and sent the remains of his sun-set power into her. Green light danced in the blacks of her eyes, and faded. When he withdrew his hand, she did not stagger, but neither was she still. She seemed to grow in all directions at once. "Watch, in my absence."

He hailed a cab two blocks from Chakal Square and rode home past lit windows in tenement houses, rectangles of yellow light cut with human silhouettes. Old men drank in a bar while a Shining Empire poet played the zither under a spotlight that made his silk gown shine. In an open-air park, a crowd danced to a brass band. Three college kids gathered around a fourth vomiting in a rose bush. Red lights transformed half-naked men and women writhing in massage parlor windows into Old World devils. Foreign music, foreign poems, foreign lust. Never such perversion under the old gods: bodies and their deeds were celebrated in song and story, and sex itself was worship.

The lights of his courtyard gate were lit, but the yard was

dim. Furniture protruded from vines and bushes and cactus swells. By the reflected glow off the belly of the clouds he found his door, unlocked it, and entered the dining room. Mina had stacked her books on the buffet table, bookmarks tonguing at odd angles from pressed pages.

Something shifted beneath his foot and he stumbled. Lifted the offending object: a small rubber bouncing ball, translucent with fools'-gold flecks inside. He shook his head and pocketed the ball.

No lights in the hallway, either, and darker here without windows. Lamp flame flickered in the gap between Caleb's closed door and the jamb. He heard giggles, groans, and shouts in High Quechal: "Mine!" "No!" "Unfair." The language of the priests, the language of his youth, spoken nowhere now but in this house.

He knocked once on the door, and opened without waiting for an answer. "Hello?"

Two lamps lit his son's narrow room and its furnishings: a small bed with a cotton sheet, a table, a bookcase. Mina insisted Caleb learn to own, and care for, books. Sponge-printed multi-colored lizards climbed the walls. They'd done that as a family, when Caleb passed through a brief but intense lizard fixation at age five. The boy printed the ones nearer the baseboards himself, blurred and blotted. Temoc and Mina took turns hoisting Caleb on their shoulders to do the ceiling. Drops of paint dried in their hair, and Mina'd cut hers short to get the clumps out.

Caleb and Mina crouched on the floor beside a lamp, each holding a small stack of cards, with a larger pile between them. They dealt cards into the center by turns, and every few deals one or the other slapped the pile with a triumphant cry, matched by their opponent's wail.

"Be careful," Temoc said. "You'll knock over the lamp."

"Give us some credit," Mina answered without turning.

"Hi, Dad!" Caleb waved, and Mina dealt a card and slapped the pile. "Hey, no fair."

"If you don't mind the game, you lose."

"Can I join?"

Caleb frowned. "We can't deal three equal piles. Someone would have eighteen."

Temoc sat by the foot of his son's bed, legs curled beneath him. Prayer position, they called this in the old days. "I will take your cards from under you."

"No cheating," Mina warned.

Temoc raised his hands, and adopted as innocent an expression as he could manage.

They played Apophitan Rat Screw for a half hour more. Even without the gods' help, Temoc's reflexes were fast enough for him to seize a small stack of cards, though Caleb and Mina both seemed to have access to a side of the game denied him. Caleb sometimes slapped cards he could not possibly have read.

"Counting cards," Temoc said, "will lead to your being thrown from most games."

"If they catch you," Mina pointed out.

"So the idea is don't get caught?"

"The idea is to win through virtuous play."

"Mostly to win, though."

No one lost that night, though Mina's pile was largest in the end. Caleb purified the cards, wrapped them in silk, and returned them to the box. So simple a contest, with no soulstuff at stake, invited only an echo of the Lady of Games, but still they observed her rites. These, at least, the boy understood. Temoc had invited Caleb to his services, and watched him from the altar. Sacrifice scared the boy. The long litanies of heroes' names and deeds that once made young Temoc hunger to prove himself, these bored his son. But Caleb understood games and their goddess, who was for all her limits the last still worshipped openly as in Dresediel Lex of old.

Caleb went to brush his teeth, and Temoc and Mina waited in the bedroom. He sat on his son's bed, and she watched painted lizards climb the wall. "It's late," she said.

"More work today than I planned."

"Good work?" They'd been slow to learn this skill of

marriage: to take time, and let each other bring as much of the office home as needed.

"I hope. A chance for peace."

"Caleb worried." Meaning, I worried, but she had trouble saying that. Neither one liked to admit weakness. Luckily, they knew each other well enough to hear the unsaid words.

"I know. I'm sorry." He smoothed the covers of his son's bed. "I appreciate his wanting to wait up."

"Not just him," she said, before the faucet shut off and Caleb returned.

Temoc let the boy climb into bed himself. Mina kissed their son, and so did he, and hugged Caleb back when Caleb threw his arms around Temoc's neck. There was no word in High Quechal or any other tongue Temoc knew for the way his son smelled.

"Good night. Sleep well. Dream noble dreams."

"You too, Dad. I love you."

"We love you, too," he said, and they left his room, closed the door, and took the lantern with them.

Mina led him down the hall, silent.

"Good day for you?"

"I'm worried about my translation of the Oxulhat ceno-taph."

"It's fine."

"I know. I'm still worried."

Their bedroom lacked lizards. A painting of her family hung from the off-white walls beside a pre-Wars lithograph of his. She closed the door behind him, and set the lantern on the dresser. Lamplight painted her sandstone colors. Shade-swathed, she might have been a bas relief on an ancient temple, or one of the cave-wall paintings she studied. Beautiful, raw, and real.

"You didn't have to wait for me," he said.

"I know." She rushed against him like a wave, and, as always, he was swept away.

He stumbled back, tossed in her embrace, in her kiss, his hand under her shirt, on her spine. Flame flowered in her eyes.

Her smooth lips found his cheek, his mouth, and still stumbling he lifted her and they fell together to the bed. They kissed again, and he held her harder, as if she might slip away and leave the world in shadow. Her fingers caught in the buttons of his shirt; he pulled hers up over her head in one motion, and she laughed.

But as they moved together on the bed, the red glow of her recalled bonfires reflected on the Major's armor, and the War-dens' silver stares. Sunrise flickered on the edge of a knife. He pulled her to him, his line out of the depths, the rope a goddess cast down so poor Temoc could climb out of the maze of his own bad choices.

He clutched her, hard—then let go, and let himself fall.

She felt him change. He watched for disappointment, but saw only a slight, sad smile before she bent close and ran her cheek along his, smooth skin against smooth. He'd never been able to grow a beard. "It doesn't need to be everything," she said. "Just be here, now, with me. Please."

She kissed him, and he kissed her back. Outstretched, they explored each other as if wandering through their house on a moonless midnight. No Wardens, no knives, no sacrifices, no battles to fight. Only her.

After, they lay sky-clad amid strewn pillows. His fingers trailed over her stomach, and she stretched like a cat to his touch. "We don't do that enough," she said.

"What would be enough?"

"Let's experiment."

"A scholar even in the sheets."

"Mankind deserves to know. Womankind, too."

"The boy might notice."

"He needs to learn the facts of life someday."

"I thought that was your job."

"Yours."

"I missed you." He did not know why he said those words. They saw each other every day, unless she was on a research trip, or he on retreat. But still, they sounded right.

"I missed you, too." Her fingers rested against the inside of his thigh, not sensual so much as there. "Sometimes I miss you even when you're around."

"I worry." Hard to say, harder still to hear himself say. But no one in this room could hear them.

Her hand tightened on his leg. She climbed cliffs for fun out in the desert, a regular patron too of the university climbing gym. She was strong enough to hold him. "You don't need to be a part of this, if you don't want to be."

"I told Elayne I would bring the camp together, to compromise. It might work."

The warmth of their sex had faded, and sweat cooled them both. That was all, he told himself: that was why goose bumps rose on her arms and on the skin of her belly beneath his fingertips.

"They need protection," he said.

"The Wars are over, Temoc."

"I was the gods' sword, once," he said. "At least I can be these people's shield."

"I'd rather you be yourself," she said. "My husband. Father to our son." The mattress creaked. She rolled against him, her arm across his chest, her legs clasping his. "No one can ask you to be anything but that."

"No." Their house, their son, her arms, were fortress walls against the desert night. Their bed was a sacred and secret space guarded by dark arts from history.

She pulled the covers over them and slept. He pretended to sleep too, memorizing instead her imprint, the smell of her hair, the weight of her head and leg and arm.

It was enough.

Why shouldn't it be enough?

10

Elayne's predawn world was the color of an Iskari corpse: gray hotel room, gray curtains, gray skyline broken by the Sansilva pyramids. From dragonback the city fit a single grand design, but her fourth-floor window was not high enough to make that order clear.

She stretched, and took inventory of her body. Were her fingers less sensitive to pressure, her joints more stiff, than the day before? The Craft eroded flesh. Forty years ago, at the height of the Wars, her body and soul had been one instrument carrying out the demands of a single will. Even ten years back she hadn't felt so clear a split between mind and form. Some mornings recently she woke and moved her limbs like a puppeteer, triggering muscles one by one to rise mechanical from her sheets. Those days, these days, she waited for the twinge of betrayal in the chest or the small vessels of the brain that would signal the start of her next phase of life. Or if not life, then at least existence.

The betrayal hadn't come yet.

But no matter how carefully she kept herself, someday she would take that final stepwise jump, shed muscle and organ, and survive as—what, exactly? A skeleton, on the most prosaic level, but more. None of her friends who'd gone before her could explain the change to her satisfaction. They offered comparisons, many and myriad and no more consonant than those of blind men feeling up an elephant. How was it to see in cold heartless relief, to abandon the soft colors filtered through—created by?—jelly globe eyes for pure harsh wavelengths, to throw wide and close perception's doors at once? She could imagine such an experience, her imagination was strong, but she had no way of knowing whether her imaginings were correct.

She suspected not.

Still, the face reflected in the hotel window hid her skull well enough. Except for her teeth, which pierced white through the illusion.

The Monicola Hotel had a pool on the top floor, and a gym. Laps sounded pleasant, but Elayne had long since stopped swimming for exercise. Bone density mattered more for a Craftswoman than for other humans, since bones would stay even once she shed her meat. Not that she could afford to neglect her muscles—the chirurgeons were clear on that point. Elayne knew one scholar who still complained of heart trouble and shortness of breath fifteen years after going full skeleton.

"But you don't need to breathe," Elayne had said, "and you have no heart."

"Just because one does not need to breathe," the woman replied, "does not mean one cannot feel short of breath. And the lack of a heart does not save us from heart trouble."

So: bodyweight exercises. A little work on the bench. No cardio. Air filters be damned: in Dresediel Lex, to run was to invite the city into your lungs, and the city was a drunken guest who liked to trash the place. Elayne did medicine ball slams, lifting the heavy sphere overhead and throwing it as hard as she could into the mat, a wood-chopping motion remembered from childhood.

Mirror selves watched her.

The judge. Tan Batac. Kopil, self-styled King in Red, the sorcerer turned revolutionary turned backroom ruler of fourteen million souls. Temoc, who almost died trying to stop that transformation. Who would have died, had she not intervened for reasons she doubted to this day were sound. Sympathy for a boy caught on the wrong side of a war. A faint touch of attraction—to his will to fight for a lost cause, if nothing else—and a naive sense that such passion was worth saving for its own sake.

More mirrors. Elayne was older now, wiser perhaps, colder for certain, and used to power and its ways. She thought of Mina, Temoc's wife. Caleb, his son. Chel. A web spun around them all.

They were not her clients. They were not her problem. She had been hired to mediate between the King in Red and Tan Batac, not to bring protesters to the bargaining table. But she had burned Dresediel Lex once, and she would not do so again.

She threw the medicine ball harder and harder still, until gym mirrors buzzed in their brackets. Her arms sang with the effort, ignorant of the skeletal fate that awaited them. Though in the end, perhaps her body was no worse off than her mind. Bones would endure, at least. No way to tell how much of her self would make the jump.

She returned the medicine ball to its stand, toweled off, and walked downstairs to shower and dress for work.

11

"We need—"

"We need," Tan Batac interrupted, then bit off a piece of doughnut, chewed twice, and swallowed before repeating: "We need those people gone. Dispersed. Out of Chakal Square. That's our goal."

Elayne glared at him across the conference table wreckage of disemboweled pastries and half-full coffee cups. Large meetings were anathema to plain talk and quick decisions, so of course Kopil and Tan Batac had brought three associates each this morning, henchmen and -women who sat and sipped good coffee turned bad by conference room alchemy. At least they remained silent, for the most part.

Batac's entourage were human, all men in various stages of corpulence and decay. One was a Craftsman in his own right, a former Varkath Nebuchadnezzar associate gone in-house. Kopil's group included an Atavasin snakeling, its scaly body coiled around a transport revenant; a golem bearing a vision-gem for some distant associate; and a young woman from his risk management department. A more diverse crowd than Batac's but no more reassuring, the young woman's stare as alien as the snakeling's gold eyes, the golem lenses, the light within the gem. Kopil's crowd, naturally, set the Skittersill team ill at ease, and Batac had spent the last several hours grandstanding for their benefit.

"We need," she repeated, putting more ice into the words this time, "to understand our BATNA."

Batac blinked.

Kopil translated: "Best alternative to negotiated agreement. The best possible result if we walk away from the table."

"We know the worst," Elayne said, leaving Batac no time to cut in. "We force the Skittersill's transformation, the Chakal Square crowd resists, reality ruptures, unbound demons spill through, kill everything, and contort local space-time into an unrecognizable hellscape. What's our best alternative, though? Once we know that, we know our fallback position."

"Best alternative." Batac took another bite of doughnut.

"We can change the Skittersill wards," Kopil said, "to a limited degree without causing a rupture. My people ran the numbers." He nodded to the young woman, who opened a folder and spoke without consulting the papers within.

"We can replace outdated divine insurance and disaster protection schema with privately maintained modern systems. The immediate advantages of disaster protection could be realized with minimal risk: four nines probability of implementation without rupture."

"Still high," Elayne said.

"Much lower than any proposal that includes liberalizing the Skittersill property market."

"Okay," Elayne said. "At least we can privatize the insurance setup."

Batac shook his head. "My people need a liberalized market to develop the Skittersill. Without that, privatizing the insurance market only makes the land more expensive to administer."

"Safety does offer some return on investment."

"We have figures here—" said Kopil's statistician.

"I've seen the figures. If I go to my board with this, they'll laugh me out of the room." He mopped his forehead with a folded handkerchief. "I'd love nothing better than to run a priesthood, dispensing grace for free. But I'm a businessman."

Kopil: "No one here is arguing—"

"It's not enough." Tan Batac stopped, then, and noticed the

silence. The statistician stared at him with ill-disguised horror. The snakeling's forked tongue flitted. The King in Red cocked his head to one side. If he still had eyebrows, one of them would have crept upward. Stars bled out in his eyes.

Elayne wondered how many years had passed since someone last interrupted the King in Red.

Her watch chimed. She pulled it out, glanced at the face, affected surprise. "And that's break." She stood. No one else moved. "I for one could use a stroll. Mr. Batac, come with me."

It was not a question, and before he could say no, she opened the door and waved him out. As the door closed Elayne thought she heard a mountain laugh.

She led Batac to an empty conference room, closed the door behind him with the Craft, and blacked the glass walls.

"Okay," he said. "Fine. I get it."

"I am not certain you do. Kopil, I understand. This case dredges up bad history for him. You don't have that excuse."

"He has nothing to lose but his pride." Batac glanced over his shoulder, though the room was empty. "I know how this looks, and I hate it. I grew up in the Skittersill. My family, we're better off than most who started there, but . . . the place is a wreck. Rents are cheap, there's crime. Stonewood refugees clog the streets. These fixes will help. Took me years to get enough people with use rights on my side to even start these talks. But not everyone on my board is there for charity. We have speculators. Real estate cartels. Construction folks. They want profits, and I don't mean oracles. Some took big loans from ugly banks to buy up use rights to Skittersill land so this deal could happen. If I go back to them—" He pointed to the door. His hand trembled. "If I go back to them and say we got some stuff we wanted but not enough to make this worth their while, they cut and run. My position collapses. All this goes for nothing. You get paid for your time even if these negotiations fall to shit. His Majesty back there, he owns the damn water. What's he have on the line?"

He was breathing heavy by his tirade's end, and looked raw

as a tree in winter. A northern winter, she amended. Trees in
Dresediel Lex never shed their leaves.

"You are afraid."

"Afraid?" His laugh sounded strained. "I have responsibil-
ities."

"Your best alternative to an agreement is quite bad."

"Yes."

"You can blame this on the protesters. Or the King in Red.
You can blame it on the judge, or me, or yourself if you like,
but no amount of blame will change the situation. You need a
liberalized property market. Very well. Then your best move
is to devote yourself to the process. Work with the people of
Chakal Square. Decide what your board can offer, because you
get what you want through this process or not at all."

"What happened to, if they're unreasonable we don't have
to deal with them?"

"They're reasonable," Elayne said. "If they break down at the
table, we have options—but that's no more a plan than entering
a boxing ring with the hope your opponent will tie his own
shoelaces together before you touch gloves. Are we done?"

He nodded. "You set that alarm."

"It was that, or drag you from the room on even less pretext."

"You're a clever woman, Elayne."

"Base tricks hardly qualify as clever," she said. "And I try
not to make a habit of theatrics. But sometimes ends justify unpleasant means."

She released the Craft that blacked out the walls and windows. Sunlight returned, and Dresediel Lex beyond and below
the skyspire.

"Okay," he said, and again: "Okay. Let's get to work."

12

Energy and mass bend time and space—so the Hidden Schools taught. No wonder, then, the meeting seemed to last forever. Tan Batac played fair, but the issues were tangled and the minutiae obstinately minute. Elayne chipped at both parties' resolve until, long past sunset, they teetered on the brink of agreement. Tan Batac was hoarse, and the plate of pastries picked clean. The conference room smelled of aftershave and overactive antiperspirant.

Nevertheless, Elayne was almost surprised when the door opened to admit her assistant, June. She'd forgotten it could do anything but separate her from freedom. June waited through the King in Red's rant about ownership structures; when the skeleton finished, Elayne called fifteen minutes' break, and tried not to betray relief as she left.

She closed the conference room door as if sealing all the world's evil behind it, and stalked down the hall with June in pursuit.

"Good meeting, ma'am?"

"I haven't killed anyone yet. That counts for something."

"The abattoir's there if you need it."

"I wish." She stopped by a window that looked out over the Drakspine ridge. "We'll be fine."

"Of course, ma'am."

"What do you want? Or did you just come to rescue me?"

"You have a visitor downstairs. A Ms. Paxil," with an accent on the first syllable, the clan name, rather than the parental name. June had lived in Dresediel Lex for ten years, but in some ways she remained very much a foreigner.

Lights glimmered from the hillside palaces. Batac probably owned a villa up there. "I don't know anyone by that name."

"Security's on site—Ms. Paxil doesn't have an appointment, and she isn't dressed for business. But she had your name, so I thought I might check."

"She just showed up and asked for me?"

"She claims a 'Temoc' sent her. I can have security point her to the door."

With knives. No, not quite. Demons didn't need knives. "I'll be right down."

Elayne descended the rainbow bridge from the skyspire to the pyramid below, which held the earthbound offices of Kelethres, Albrecht, and Ao. Few Craftsmen worked down here, so far from the starlight that was their sustenance, but since real estate was cheaper on solid ground, they relegated back-office tasks to the pyramid. Compared to the spire this place wasn't much to look at, but the reception hall offered some majesty at least: backless couches and low glass tables and abstract paintings hung from walls not quite the color of cured human skin.

Chel sat on a couch, reading *The Thaumaturgist*. Demons stood around her, faint shapes shimmering in air. Mandible scraped against glassy mandible. Scythe-talons kneaded space as if the emptiness had texture, which perhaps it did, to them. Or else they were simply keeping limber, awaiting an opportunity to deploy their murderous talents.

Not that Kelethres, Albrecht, and Ao was in the habit of killing people who stopped in without an appointment. Suggestions to that effect had been raised at board meetings, but Elayne was relatively sure Belladonna Albrecht meant them in jest.

"Ms. Paxil, I presume."

Chel closed the magazine and stood. She made a good show of ignoring the demons. "Elayne. Ms. Kevarian, I mean. Good to see you."

"You're a long way from Chakal Square."

A demon hissed. Chel steeled her expression. "Looks like it's my turn to meet your guards."

"Payback's fair play. At least no one has tackled you yet."

"Good thing, too. These guys are spinier than I am."

"How's the camp?"

"Growing. Hundreds more have come. They heard the King in Red might deal, and everybody wants to back a winner. By noon we had to push our line out. And the Wardens retreated across the street. Simple."

"Not so simple." She turned to the demons. "Leave us." Light rolled through them as they flowed back into the not-quite-skin-tone walls, leaving only echoes of their footsteps. Claw-steps, maybe. "Did Temoc send you?"

"We're ready to meet your people, if they come to us." She glanced toward the wall into which the demons had vanished. "They don't trust your turf. And he says to hurry. He's not sure how long his support will last."

She thought of the perpetual motion argument in the conference room overhead. "Not a problem." She hoped. "I will visit the camp tomorrow to prepare ground. We'll meet the day after."

"Thanks."

Chel's hand was warm. "You're welcome." Elayne did not let go. "How is it down there?"

"Fine," she said. "Tense."

"Good." With a flick of Craft, she activated a summoning circle. "A cab will be waiting downstairs to take you back. Or anywhere else you might want to go. On me."

"Thank you," she said, and smiled before she left. Something about her gait struck Elayne as odd. As Chel neared the door, Elayne realized she'd subconsciously expected the woman to be carrying a briefcase, or at least a purse. In her rumpled shirt and torn slacks and ragged boots, Chel bore only her pride.

Elayne climbed the rainbow bridge again, somber now, and returned to the conference room. Heads swung round, chairs spun to face her, coffee cups stopped halfway to open mouths. "Gentlemen," she said. "The camp is ready. We are on the clock."

13

The next morning, Warden barricades stopped Elayne's cab two blocks from Chakal Square. She walked the rest of the way, past jowly counterprotesters and buzzard-eyed journalists, past the Wardens' command tent and a table set with pastries and coffee for officers on duty.

Sentries surrounded the Chakal Square camp—all, this time, at an approximation of attention. Each guard wore a red armband, which Elayne did not like. Nor did she like that they remembered her.

She appreciated the escort they offered, though. The camp had grown. Faerie circles of sleeping bags, groves of protest signs and skeleton effigies, marker-scrawled icons of dead Quechal gods—before, all these seemed scattered from a height onto a game board, but as the square filled they'd assumed an organic order. She followed game trails through organizational microclimates toward the fountain. Someone had painted a face on its faceless god.

Temoc met her in a clearing. "You've grown popular," she said.

"Not me. Many have come to support us. Chel"—who waited behind Temoc, with five men in red armbands—"helped organize the guard."

"You didn't stop her?"

"Why would I?"

"She's given these people an identity to set against the Wardens. You know as well as anyone how dangerous that is."

"I can't be everywhere." He illustrated the clearing with a sweep of his hand. "Does this place suffice?"

"We need a tent."

"My people won't like that. They want our talks transparent."

"My clients put themselves at risk to come here. They want to deal, not play for the cheap seats. The negotiations should be private, and insulated."

"We'll bring a tent."

"Good enough. And I'll guard this clearing against undue influence."

"What do you mean, influence?"

She raised one hand, and sparks flickered between her fingers.

"Oh," he said.

"It goes both ways, of course. Kopil is robed in fear as well as crimson, but your people have their own power. Their faith has bent the local noosphere to draw more faith to feed itself. Combined, there's too much interference for a reasoned debate. Not to mention our hidden players."

"What do you mean?"

"We still don't know who publishes the broadsheets, or what that person's goals might be. Better protect ourselves now than wish we had later."

Watchers surrounded the clearing, peering through holes in fabric and around the curved walls of tents. "Your enchantment could twist our wills," Temoc said. "Why should I trust you?"

"A Craftswoman's word is her power. I promise to protect both sides equally."

"Such specificity," he said, and smiled: a flaw in the cliff face. "Do it, then."

She touched the glyph above her heart, and drew her work knife. The starfire blade glistened. Darkness spread from her. Glyphs flared at her temples and wrists, and she saw herself transform in Temoc's eyes from a friend to a being of light and terror. That hurt, though she was used to this particular pain. Their onlookers drew back, as expected. The world of hearts that beat and love that never died fell silent. Only whispers and wind remained.

There were many ways to prepare for a meeting. This was one.

She carved a circle into the flagstones, sixty feet across with a few inches' gap in its circumference. Outline established, she inscribed the ward's terms in unborn script. The space within the broken circle calmed and stabilized. Eyes closed, Elayne watched the green tide of the crowd's faith part around the perimeter she'd drawn.

Dresediel Lex's discontented watched her work. Many of these men and women had never seen real Craft. They knew its artifacts and echoes: crystal-shard skyspires overhead, driverless carriages, airbuses, optera, trapped demons, doctors who dipped their hands through patients' skin, and for every such sign a thousand smaller and subtler. The Craft told merchants how to stock their shelves, and by its power water coursed through the city's sunken pipes. These people lived in a Crafted land, but today, for the first time, they watched a Craftswoman work her will.

Temoc crossed his arms, unimpressed.

"Explain."

She pointed with her knife. "That language defines the space where we'll meet."

"We agreed to meet here. What remains to define?"

"Where 'here' is, for starters."

"These few yards of Chakal Square."

"Ten seconds ago these few yards of Chakal Square were several hundred miles back on our planet's orbit. They've traveled even further relative to galactic center."

"You know what I mean."

"I know what you mean, but the Craft only knows what I tell it. That's why we use circles. Geometry's dependable. Most of the time, a point is either inside a sphere defined by a given great circle, or outside."

"Most of the time?"

"Geometry's tricky. That's why I added the spiraling language: to establish that I'm warding the sphere described by this great circle, as interpreted through standard fifth-postulate spatial geometry."

"This isn't assumed?"

She looked at him sideways. "Standard fifth isn't even true on the surface of a sphere, but we define it to be true for present purposes." The sun beat down, even through the writhing shadows her Craft cast. "Could someone fetch me water?"

He waved to a red-arm, who returned bearing a canteen. She accepted it with thanks, careful not to touch his hand. Frost spread across the metal from her fingertips. She drank until her lips froze the water within, then set down the ice-filled canteen.

She surrounded her first circle with a second, also open, to bind and limit the warded space.

"Why do some symbols fade?"

"They stay where I carve them. But I'm not always carving into rock."

"Into what, then?"

"Notional space, where the ward lives. We don't compose a new ward every time we need one—it's easier to use preexisting forms. Those lines connect this circle to a ward we Crafted decades back, which will remove us"—she winced as she sliced a vicious wound in the fabric of reality—"from the Square. This way I don't have to fight the crowd's faith directly. Instead, I establish that the space inside these circles is not part of Chakal Square, so your people's beliefs about the square will not interfere with us." The last cut was always the hardest, when exhaustion dulled will's edge. There. She stood, and with a wave banished the dust from her trousers and reinstated their crease. "A drop of blood from each of us, and I'm done."

He didn't flinch as she cut between his scars. The skin resisted more than it should have, but at last blood flowed. She caught it with Craft, a red globe in air, drew a drop from her own arm, mixed the two, made her blade long and curved like a calligrapher's brush, and, kneeling, painted the circles closed. Blood smoked and sank into stone. Beneath the daylit world, large gears ground, counterweights fell. Circle, curved runes, spiderweb lines, all shone for a glorious, terrifying instant.

Elayne didn't blink, but someone did, somewhere, and the light died. She crossed the circle, and did not stumble. After decades of slipping from world to world, one found one's sea legs quickly.

The rest of her business was mundane by comparison, concerned with format and food, security and the spacing of bathroom breaks. They ate after, Temoc and Elayne and Chel, a rough hearty lunch of roast pork and rice delivered by red-arms with the Kemals' complements. Temoc did not mention Mina or Caleb. Elayne didn't, either. They were present nonetheless, uninvoked, in the silence.

For all Temoc's scars and strength, she thought, he needed a ward of his own around Chakal Square, or around his heart, or around that courtyard with the cactus flowers and the screen windows and the boy who played solitaire in the dust.

After lunch, Temoc and Chel escorted her to the square's edge. They were near the border when the fight broke out.

First she heard the scream, followed by curses in Low Quechal, and fists striking flesh. Temoc moved, fast. Chel ran after him and Elayne followed, arriving almost too late to see.

A crowd pried two pairs of Quechal men apart. A boy lay between them, clutching his leg. Temoc's arrival shocked everyone but the brawlers, too set on their fight to notice. One took advantage of his captors' shock to fight free. His arm came around to strike—

And stopped.

Temoc had grabbed the man's wrist. The assailant's arm wrenched at an odd angle, and he cried out. Temoc caught him before he fell.

"What happened here?" Temoc said.

One of the men on the right shouted in Low Quechal, and

pointed to the boy on the ground. Temoc replied, earnest, slow, calm.

Neither noticed the Wardens crossing the street, or the red-arms who blocked the Wardens' path, shoulders square, jaws jutting. Chel shouted, "Stand down!" but the red-arms didn't listen. A Warden drew her club.

Elayne moved without moving.

Shadow boiled from the ground. Solid winds thrust red-arms and Wardens apart.

Elayne tossed one of the red-arms six feet into the air and passed beneath him into the road. She blazed, grown large in glyphlight. The Wardens recoiled from her, and raised their weapons with the uncertainty of foxes before a bear.

She let her shadows fade. Frost on stone sublimated to steam. Sunlight slunk back like a kicked dog. "There is no trouble here." She floated them a business card. "I work for the King in Red. A boy was hurt in an accident. Send for a doctor."

Their blank eyes reflected her. A Warden wearing officer's bars recovered his composure first. "We need to see for ourselves."

"Follow me, then," she said. "You alone. The situation is tense."

The officer waved his fellows back, and followed Elayne. A scarred giant with a red armband blocked their way. Elayne was about to make the giant move, before Chel grabbed his arm. "Zip. Don't."

He stepped aside.

A rumble of distant thunder followed the Warden through the crowd. Temoc turned to meet him. "There is no crime here."

"I'll judge that."

"The boy fell," he said. "This man shoved him by accident, and broke his leg. These two are his parents. A fight ensued. That is all."

The Warden stepped past Temoc to address the men. "Is this true?"

Veins stood out on Temoc's neck, but he kept quiet. Elayne marveled to see such control so near to breaking.

But it held.

Wardens wheeled a stretcher through the crowd. Elayne did not like how fast the stretcher came—it implied the Wardens expected trouble. No one wanted to press charges with Temoc watching. The boy and his fathers went with the Wardens, and Temoc turned to the remaining brawlers with a gaze that drained color from their faces.

But Elayne saw the fear under Temoc's rage. This might have been the breaking point. A brawl between red-arms and Wardens would spread, and the whole square catch fire.

She took that fear with her when she left. And she took, too, a broadsheet she found near the fight, which bore an etching of Chakal Square beneath a blocky one-word headline: "Rise."

14

In the heart of Kelethras, Albrecht, and Ao's office pyramid, a
golem sat in a steel chair behind a steel desk in a cork-walled
room and sipped a mug of steaming coffee through a straw.
False stars shone around him: light from the ghostlamp on his
desk glittered off tacks pinning alchemical prints to the walls.
Yarn and wire tied pins to pins, pictures to pictures: a bridge in
Shikaw to a Southern Gleb tribesman bleeding out from a lion
attack, the claw marks in the tribesman's back to a teenage girl
in a floral print dress with white lace at collar and cuffs, her
right eye to a reproduction of a Schwarzwald painting a century
and a half old, some ancient family standing before a castle
in the depths of a wood—three bearded elders, a small round
woman carved from ivory, a young man in a billowing shirt
with a smile bent as an old druid's sickle. And another twenty
lines spread from that man, from the curve of his smile, some
weaving back to Shikaw and the bridge, and others off to still
more distant lands and interlocking wheels of yarn. Thousands
of pictures, and these were only the top layer: more beneath,
long faded, the string in some cases thrice rotted and replaced
by wire.

In that cork-lined room, silent and swift, the golem worked.
Four-armed, with its upper limbs it lifted newspapers in many
languages from the stack beside the desk, and with its thick
manipulators turned the pages. Lower arms, scissor-fingered,
sliced scraps from their context: pictures, lines of text, a three-
word excerpt from a breath mint ad. Lenses realigned to read.
Every few minutes the golem paused for coffee, or for a drag
from the cigarette that smoldered in the ashtray. Thin smoke

rose from its tip to coil against the ceiling, a dragon pondering the paper hoard. Already the evening's work had yielded a four-inch stack of clippings. Shifting gears, pumping pistons, unwinding and winding of clockwork and spring, opening and closing switches, all merged into the babble of a mechanical brook through a metal forest. And underneath it all, always, lay the sound of scissors parting paper.

"Zack," Elayne said from the door, once she'd waited long enough. "I have something for you."

The cutting, and all other visible movement, stopped. The metal brook trickled on.

She walked to his desk. Dead eyes stared up from the top clipping. A woman, her throat slit. Elayne could not read the caption of old-style Shining Empire glyphs. "You can't add this many every night. You'd have filled the entire room with paper by now."

A clock wound as the shield of Zack's head turned right and tilted back to face her. Lenses realigned for focus, and as they shifted she glimpsed the furnace inside him. "I edit." A cello's voice, the music of strings made words by processes she did not understand. She was only a passing student of golemetrics, which required more dealing with demons than she liked. Not that Elayne had anything against demons per se—but her conversations with them often reminded her of a vicious joke in which she herself might well be the punchline. Perhaps the demons felt the same.

Zack hefted the clippings in one manipulator arm. "First cut, most relevant of the day's news. So I believe now. Initial processing complete, I compare. Lotus Gang execution, or Grimwald incursions into Shining Empire territory? Method suggests Khelids, Dhistran death cult from eighteenth century, though current scholarship indicates Khelids were in fact a cover for Camlaander occupationist priests' attempts to reconsecrate Dhistran territory to Undying Queen and Eternal Monarchy."

"Or someone knifed the girl because she had something they wanted. Or was something they wanted."

"Hence: editing. Does new content fit with emergent patterns?"

"Accept facts that fit the theory, throw out those that don't?"

A narrowing of aperture, for him, was a narrowing of the eyes. "A death may be a death, or early warning of existential threat or out-of-context problem. Nothing occurs in isolation. The world's doom ripples back and forth through time." That last word a vibrating chord. "Did you come to mock my methods, Elayne?"

"I came to ask your help."

"You have strange protocols for asking."

"You'll like this." She unfolded the broadsheet and held it before his lenses.

Clicks and realignments, scrape of a needle on a spinning wheel. "Simple propaganda leaflet. This political affair holds no interest for me."

"An army gathering in the Skittersill holds no interest?"

"I have no defined life span," he said. "Nor will you, once you shed that skin shell. We are both difficult to kill. The greatest dangers to us are dangers to our world system. Therefore we may divide all threats into two kinds: global-existential, and trivial. Trivial threats deserve no time or thought. This protest does not threaten the fundamental coherence of reality. It is of no importance."

"What if it causes a demon outbreak?"

"It will not. Too many central decision-makers have nothing to gain from widespread destruction. Even if it did, such events can be contained—we might lose Dresediel Lex, but not the planet."

"Accidents happen."

"Accidents, by their nature, are stubbornly resistant to prevention. The same is not true of conscious threat. This demonstration may inconvenience our clients, but it is not relevant to my extracurricular work."

"What if I told you someone had been printing and distributing these leaflets throughout the Skittersill, for free, since before details of our work on the old wards became public? That no one knows who prints them, or what their angle might be?"

Zack took the paper—a scythe-arc through the air, and it was gone. Her fingertips stung with the speed of its departure. The golem pressed the broadsheet flat and scanned its front page with lenses and knife-tipped fingers. The shield-face opened, revealing a forest of wires, lenses, and hydraulics. Eyepieces telescoped out for greater magnification, and secondary lenses rotated into place. "No further leads?"

"None."

A toneless hum was her only acknowledgment. No nods, of course, while Zack was so close to the paper. Without moving his head—it gimbaled gyroscopically—he took a binder from a low shelf beside the desk, fanned its pages by touch, and found a section that seemed to satisfy. Only then did he retract his eyes and close his face. "Here." He offered her the binder.

"Garabaldi Brothers Printing and Engraving."

"The shop that composed this item. A family outfit in the Vale. Do you have other samples?"

"No."

"Unfortunate. Unlikely the object of your inquiry would use a single printer. Combination of sources preserves supply, anonymity. Though anonymity requires effort. How much effort do you believe this person is likely to spare?"

"I have no idea," she said. "What do I owe you?"

He offered her the broadsheet back. "Tell me what pattern emerges. May bear on my work."

"I will," she said. "Zack."

"Yes."

"What do you do, when you find an out-of-context problem?"

He tilted his head to one side. "Depends."

"On what?"

"On the threat's form," he said. "Threat is another word for change. Status quo ante is not preferable to all change. Consider the Iskari boy stopping the leaking dam with his finger—

romantic image, but futile. If one is to play any other role, one must be open to drastic change. The world some large-scale changes would bring about may be preferable to the one we currently inhabit."

"Have you ever found such a preferable threat?"

He gestured to the walls, to the net of possibilities. "If I had, would I be working here?"

"Thank you," she said, and left, though he hadn't answered her question.

Behind, the golem bent once more to his work. The metal river ran through the metal forest, and a smoke dragon coiled against the ceiling.

15

Temoc worked out in the courtyard before dawn: weighted one-legged squats, handclap pull-ups and pushups, a back bridge held for a slow count of one hundred. When he was done he knelt facing east and drew his knife. He checked the black glass blade as he did every morning and found it sharp. The cutting edge was thin enough for light to shine through.

"You're up early."

Mina wore a white terrycloth robe, and her feet were bare.

"I couldn't sleep," he replied. "How long have you been watching?"

"Long enough to get a good view," she said with a smile he remembered from nights beneath a desert sky. "Meeting's today?"

He nodded. "The King in Red. Tan Batac. Both in our camp, to talk. It might even work."

"You're wearing your deep-thoughts face."

"You always think that."

She walked to him, took his arm in her hand, and squeezed. "Tell me."

"Caleb." He had not known what he would say until he spoke his son's name. "When I was his age."

Mina smelled of sleep, and her robe smelled of laundry. "When you were his age, the world was a different place."

"When I was his age, I earned my scars. They've kept me safe."

"Not against this." She dragged her fingernails across his skin, leaving white tracks that faded fast. He felt exposed with her so close. Vulnerable, bounded. He liked the feeling, though every old warrior's instinct rebelled against it. "You're scared, so you run scenarios. I understand." She slid her hands over his chest. The creases at the corners of her eyes deepened. She read him as if he were a strange text in a familiar script. "It's okay."

He stepped back. "If this meeting goes wrong, I become a target. So do you."

"I can handle myself."

"Caleb has no scars to help him."

"That was the idea. He can be the sweet kid neither of us were."

"But if I fail—"

"You won't." She kissed his cheek.

"You were worried, before."

"I still am," she said. "You mind if I head-shrink you a bit?"

"No."

"You've grown up good enough to want to help people, and strong enough to do it. That has nothing to do with the scars your father gave you, and everything to do with the man who wears them. But you don't know that. You're scared of what happens to us if something happens to you—and since goodness and strength and scars are tangled in your head, you worry you haven't done right by Caleb because you haven't scarred him. But our son will be good and strong without the shit your father did to you, or the shit my parents did to me. My husband is about to make peace with the King in Red. I'm proud of you."

"I love you," he said.

"Damn straight." They kissed again. He lifted her, and she laughed. Her kiss lingered on his lips, her weight in his arm. Later, when he stood in Chakal Square before his congregation, blade raised, sacrifice bound on the altar, she remained. But chant swelled to climax, the blade came down, pommel striking sternum like a hand on a drum, and in that sweep and the exultant rush that followed, he lost her.

16

The morning of the conference, Bloodletter's Street was cordoned off for blocks. Wardens moved yellow wooden barricades to admit the King in Red's carriage; dismounting, Elayne found herself in a field command post that looked much like those she remembered from the Wars. Stretchers against one wall, first-aid station nearby. Wardens marched or ran about. None were armed that she could see, beyond their truncheons. Small relief. If weapons were called for, she doubted they'd be long coming.

Couatl circled sharklike overhead. An adjutant ran off to summon the Wardens' captain, who approached, blank-faced with reflective silver like the rest, unidentifiable save for height and shape and the number stamped on his crimson skull badge. The King in Red drew the captain aside, and they conversed in hushed tones.

Beside her, Tan Batac shrank into himself: hands in pockets, shoulders hunched, head turtled down.

"Nervous?" Elayne said.

"Big day."

"You'll be fine. These people want to talk."

"These people want my head on a pike, and the rest arranged somewhere near as a warning to passersby."

She chuckled.

"Listen to them." Chakal Square was chanting. From this distance, the words melded to a meaningless ocean rhythm. "We brought these people everything. There are fortunes in the Skittersill because of me, because of my family." He struck his chest, hard. A hollow sound. His hand darted back into his pocket as if startled by the noise. "We try to make this place a palace, and what do we get?"

"These people are angry because they think you've ignored them. Their anger will recede as you work together."

"They'll come for me. Just you wait."

Kopil returned with the Warden chief and two deputies in tow. "Is Tan still brooding on his imminent demise?"

"That isn't funny."

The skeleton grinned, of course. "Let's hope this peace conference goes better than the last one, eh?"

The last one: the God Wars. The failed summit before the final assault on Dresediel Lex. Liberation forces approached the meeting scarred by years of war; Elayne herself had been seventeen and suffering nightmare visions of thorn-beings hunting her through deep jungle. They bore their losses with them to meet with gold-draped priest-kings of Dresediel Lex who deigned to grant them audience. The conference failed in the first minute, but days passed before anyone realized. "Let's hope," Elayne said.

Kopil cracked his knuckles. "We'll be fine. The good Captain Chimalli here has ordered us an escort of Wardens." No one was supposed to know Wardens' given names, but of course he did, and of course he used them.

"I hope your people can control themselves," Elayne said. "Yesterday they almost stormed the camp to break up a brawl."

"I'm sending my best with you." Captain Chimalli's voice was higher than his bulk suggested, narrower, with an accent Elayne couldn't place. Elayne always expected the masks to change Wardens' voices somehow, but they did not. "Lieutenant Zoh's in charge, seconded by Sergeant Chihuac." He gestured to each in turn. More names: a privilege extended for convenience. Better than numbers, at least. Zoh was a wall of a man, who in prehistoric days would have claimed kingship of his tribe by throwing the previous monarch off a cliff. He clicked his heels when he saluted, and his shoes were mirror-polished. Chihuac seemed more promising: five-six in combat boots, strong, solid. Elayne didn't trust either one, which said more about her than them. Even in the Wars, she'd seen violent meatheads inside every uniform.

"You understand your role?"

"To preserve respect," Zoh said. "To protect. To pull you all to safety if this breaks down."

"I can protect and pull myself," Kopil said. "But power's a funny thing—people tend to forget you have it if you don't seem to. Do not use force unless we're attacked first. I need perfect beings at my side today, not men."

Zoh saluted again.

"And take care of Tan Batac. He is more accident-prone than Elayne or myself."

Batac glowered at that, but he kept his voice civil. "Thank you."

"Very good," Kopil said. "Now, bring us to my people."

The noise built as they approached. Waves of chanted protest rolled over them, bearing the stench of close-packed thousands, of stale sweat and hope and fresh anger. Even knowing what to expect, Elayne caught her breath when she saw the kaleidoscope crowd—their bright colors and their mass. They raised signs, unfurled banners, sang old songs.

She had told Temoc when to expect the King in Red, and the direction from which he'd come. Now, assembled and indomitable, the Skittersill's people watched their nominal lord approach.

The Wardens formed a circle around Kopil, Batac, and Elayne, with Zoh in front. The King in Red stood taller than their escort, which would have worried Elayne if any weapon this crowd might wield could harm him. His skull held no brain, and the bones were just another anchor binding the long-dead man to the city he ruled. The crown at his brow gleamed crimson gold.

The red-arms who faced them stood aside to reveal a corridor into the camp, lined by more red-arms with elbows linked to resist the crowd's weight. The path was broad enough for their group, and empty save for scraps of trash and one broken, facedown sign. The gathered thousands stared.

They walked into the mouth of the beast. Elayne reprimanded herself, quietly, for seeing the crowd as a single insensate animal, for letting Batac's fear infect her. She'd come here before and emerged unscathed.

But never with the King in Red.

As they walked the noise faded, or a deeper silence blocked it out.

Kopil's bony feet tapped the flagstones three times with each step.

They met Temoc at the path's end, before a green tent. Chel waited by his side. He had not spent the morning's power: scars shone green beneath his clothes. The last time he met the King in Red, they had wrestled in the air above the body of a dying god.

Elayne looked to Kopil, but a skull's face met all changes with the same gallows humor.

Behind Temoc stood the leaders he had promised: the Kemals, Bill sporting an unkempt beard, Kapania's hair bound beneath a patterned bandanna. The Major lurked near them, flanked by a round woman and a lean fellow with graying hair and a black cane. A third man stood by the tent, silver studs at his wrists and scars at his neck and forehead: a debt-zombie, freed.

Six, and Temoc made seven, an appropriate number for a working of Craft, yet so few to stand for such a crowd. Then again, the King in Red represented the fourteen million of Dresediel Lex, and the hundred million souls in the city's banks, into which this camp could disappear like a drop of ink into the Pax. Even Tan Batac stood for the Skittersill, for the community of which these malcontents were technically a piece.

Yet those fourteen million were not here. The crowd was.

Temoc advanced on the King in Red. Chel followed, proud. Her arm sported a crimson band. She caught Elayne's eye, but kept her expression guarded.

Lieutenant Zoh blocked Temoc's way, taller by half a head than the priest though less massive, and, of course, not glowing. Temoc met the Warden's silver gaze. "Did you come so far to hide behind your men, Kopil?"

"No," the skeleton said. "Stand aside, Lieutenant."

Zoh hesitated just long enough for Elayne—and, more to the point, for Temoc—to notice. He withdrew. The ring of Wardens split into two lines flanking Elayne, Tan Batac, and the King in Red, opening Temoc's path to them. The priest strode into their gauntlet, radiating divine power and self-assurance.

He extended his hand to the King in Red, who clasped it in a bony grip.

"You look different," Temoc said.

"The last time you saw me, I had skin. And eyes."

"That must be it."

"You look much the same."

"Clean living," Temoc said. "Thank you for coming."

"Thank you for meeting us. Though your people seem unhappy."

"They are not my people."

"They certainly don't seem to feel they're mine."

"They were never yours."

"I will reassure them." Kopil released Temoc's hand, and the lights of his eyes flickered and went out.

Elayne saw the Craft he invoked too late to stop him without a struggle. So she watched, and hoped the King in Red didn't wreck the conference before it began.

A brutal wind whipped the square, a wind like none these southern people had ever known, a thousand miles' frozen prairie wind contemptuous of all the works of man. Chakal Square onlookers fell into one another's arms. Wails of terror broke against the wind's howl. A shadow closed out the sun, and the sky deepened to the color of a bruise.

The King in Red's face emerged from that sky like a bather's from a dark pool. Red gold burned upon his brow. He cleared his throat, a sound like a bomb blast or a mountain crumbling.

The wind screamed so high and loud Elayne thought her ears might burst. Then Kopil spoke, his voice echoed by the demonic wind.

"People of Dresediel Lex," he said, and what was left of her heart sank, because this was wrong, this was how you inspired an army about to invade some god-benighted state, how you whipped sorcerers and demons and soldiers to a frenzy, not how you addressed scared and angry civilians. "You have called me and I come. From Sansilva's pyramids, I descend to Chakal Square. I have shaped our city for forty years. I pledged to make us strong, and I toiled beyond the borders of this world to that end. My work makes you afraid, and angry. Do not let fear poison you against progress. I come to reassure you." "Reassure" rumbled, thunderous. Someone nearby fainted.

"I will hear your challenges, through your commission. We will find common cause. The future of Dresediel Lex will not be tarnished. We have slain the gods, so we must do Heaven's work ourselves."

At least he'd said "we," not "I." But all the rest was so adroitly wrong, words and delivery alike. To Elayne, the wind-speaking and the cloud-face were cheap tricks barely worth the effort. But as far as the crowd was concerned, the King in Red had seized the very power they wanted to deny him: the ability to awe them.

"Thank you," Kopil said, and the wind ceased. The image in the sky did not so much fade as break. Black hollows of eye sockets became perturbations in the underbelly of a cloud, cheekbones a distortion of wind through smog. Sunlight returned, meager and emaciated by Kopil's Craft. The King in Red clacked his teeth together twice, and said, "That's better."

Elayne almost punched the skeleton in his absent nose. She clenched her jaw instead, and recalled advice Belladonna Albrecht had given her decades ago when she had been the fiercest fledgling at Kelethras, Albrecht, and Ao: We cannot save our clients from themselves. Someday in your career, Elayne, you will represent a man—almost certainly a man—who wants you to help him barter his soul to a demon for three wishes. When that day comes you may refuse his business, you may try to change his mind, but in the end if hell he wants, hell he will achieve.

Chel marched toward the King in Red, furious, ready to run into a hell of her own. Zoh blocked her path. She tried to shove past him, and he grabbed her. Around them, the crowd stood from the flagstones to which they'd fallen. Fearful groans became cries of rage.

How could she stop this? She could take to the skies herself, but the crowd wouldn't listen to her.

Chel tore free of Zoh. Temoc turned.

The cordon almost broke.

An accident might have started it, a stumble cascading through the crowd. Red-arms tripped and almost fell. Wardens raised their truncheons. Tan Batac glanced around, eyes wide as a starting horse's; his face twisted into a weird smile.

Temoc reached for the King in Red, and closed his eyes.

So did Elayne: the remnants of Kopil's speech-Craft hung about them like an untied knot. Temoc grabbed those loops and pulled.

The wind returned—but this was no cold northern gale. Temoc's was a desert wind, the wind of the Badlands before the God Wars, the wind that spoke to vision-questing shamans. The crowd fell silent. Anger stilled to expectation. Eyes turned skyward.

This time there were no shadows, for Temoc was no Craftsman. His scars were divine gifts, and through them he held power gently. His face took shape over Chakal Square, constructed from sunlight and smog and faith.

"Thank you," he said. "I thank the King in Red. We are happy—" Some shouts of protest there, but Temoc ignored them. A tense silence fell. "We are happy you have come. Many Craftsmen would trust magic and Wardens to guard them from dissent. But you come in person to hear our voice. You led a revolution, in your time. You know what it is to be cast out by those in power." The first cries of assent rose. "You will listen to us. You will deal with us." More shouts, these of support. Up Temoc! Preach! "We are not mad, or shortsighted, or desperate. We are not weak. We are the people, and we are wise. We are the people, and we know the future. We are the people, and we are patient. We are the people, and we are strong." Cheers now. And stillness, too, rapture as the river of Temoc's words flowed on. "Let us build a better future. Let us make peace."

Peace echoed across Dresediel Lex. Temoc's face merged with the sky, and the man below opened his eyes. All light had left his scars, spent in seizing Kopil's Craft, but he stood strong and straight opposite his adversary.

The silence of crowds differs from that of an empty room. In Chakal Square after Temoc's speech, thousands breathed. A child cried. Feet shuffled on stone. Banners flapped. Whispers were a breeze through willows. Did you hear?

Yet for all this sound there was still silence between Temoc and the King in Red.

"Good speech," Kopil said.

Zoh released Chel; she brushed off the sleeves of her jacket as if filth, not silver, covered the Warden's hands.

"We needed one." Temoc gestured to the group. "Allow me to introduce the Chakal Square Select Committee. In the coming days you'll grow to know them better."

"Them?" Tan Batac's first word to Temoc.

"I am not a member," Temoc said. "I facilitate. I hope to be a calm counselor to these people, as Ms. Kevarian is to you." Elayne listened for the contempt she'd heard in Temoc's voice when he spoke of Batac before, but she heard none today.

She allowed herself a glimmer of hope. This might work.

"Very well." Kopil hooked his thumb bones through the belt of his robe, and advanced on the Select Committee. "Shall we get to business?"

17

Business was boring. Which, of course, had been the plan and the hope. Scintillating and dramatic negotiations rarely produced good results. Within the green tent and Elayne's ward, the crowd outside might as well have never existed. Here they could sit and talk. And talk.

They sat around a rickety table in camp chairs better suited to the hosts' rumpled practical clothing than to Tan Batac's silks. A water pitcher occupied the table's center, flanked by glasses. No pastries this time. No food at all. Light through the tent's oculus formed an eccentric ellipse on the table as the meeting opened, slowly compressing to a circle. Fitting symbol, she hoped, for their meeting—at least until noon. After that, the circle would distort once more.

The hosts introduced themselves. Kapania and Bill Kemal she had seen in the fight that first day, though she did not realize they were married then; they led Chakal Square's Food Com, and in their private lives ran—had run—a small restaurant with a charity attached. The Major gave his war name, and crossed his arms. Hal Techita, of the cane and the grim countenance, was a community organizer. The large woman was Red Bel. And so on.

After introductions, Elayne poured herself a glass of water, and said, "Let's each present our proposals in clean language. There's no audience to win here; we want to forge a compromise."

"We want to forge a compromise," said Kapania Kemal, "if there is one to forge. From what I've heard of your plan, I don't think there's much chance of that."

"We'll go first," Elayne continued. "Then you can explain your goals. I think we have a good deal of common ground."

Kapania frowned, but leaned back anyway into her chair.

Elayne summoned the Skittersill in ghostlit outline above the table. Not as convenient as pulling them all into a shared dream, but these people were uncomfortable with Craft. Also she hoped that with the Skittersill in miniature, their problems would seem small, too.

"When the first settlers reached Dresediel Lex from Quechal-Under-Sea, they found a natural bay separated from the desert by mountains. Patterns emerged as the settlement grew: social categories and custom divided the land, and gods reinforced those patterns. The Skittersill was reserved for temple slaves. As far as the local wards are concerned, it still is. But Dresediel Lex has no gods anymore. Their death left holes in the protection they offered this community. If we don't patch these holes, disaster isn't just possible—it's certain."

Steel plates clacked against one another and steel wires twanged as the Major shook his head. "You preach disasters that have not occurred."

"Imagine an enormous sand castle. On the first day the tide washes in, and the walls hold—but they're weakened. The next day, they hold, too. And the third day, and the fourth. But over time the battlements grow so weak a breeze tumbles them into the sea."

"Typical Craftsman response," said Bel. "Don't fix a broken system. Don't understand it. Just replace it with something you think works better."

"We understand this system," Elayne replied. "The old wards need gods to work, and the gods are gone. The traditions have failed, too—no one from the Skittersill attends high temple sacrifices these days, for instance, since there are no sacrifices. No one works in the blood vats, because there are no blood vats. Families are no longer dedicated to holy slavery, because the Craft does not permit the purchase or sale of sentient beings."

The Major shifted in his chair, but said nothing.

"The existing wards require such activity of Skittersill residents. The traditions' failure leaves loopholes, ratholes. We need to start anew, and replace wards woven by gods with ones made by and for human beings. In a way, we face the critical question of our post-God Wars century. Can we build a world for ourselves?"

She paused for effect, and to listen. No replies. No questions. They waited for her to continue. The hook was in.

In two states is the mind most vulnerable, she remembered Alexander Denovo saying, in the dark days when they worked together: in sleep, and in rapt attention to a story. She'd used no Craft to bind their will. Her own ward would block such tricks. But rhetoric was a Craft all its own. Elayne's words invited the Chakal Square protesters to share her vision, to join a group of heroes struggling against all odds to save the world.

"So," she continued. "This is what we propose."

And their work began.

"We cannot agree, we will not agree," Bel said two hours later, leaning over the table with her eyes fixed on Tan Batac as if a gaze could skewer him, "to any plan that lets you and your cronies sell our homes wholesale to Shining Empire brokers, or bulldoze them and build casinos."

Batac inflated with outrage and offense. "Is it theft to enrich a poor community? To replace rotting tenements with palaces? Is it theft to improve the lot of my people? I was born here. I played in the same streets you did, Bel. I can talk any slang you talk. The difference between us is that I am trying to give something back."

"Give back?" Bel's voice sharpened. "You can only give back if you've taken first. You take our homes and give back a gutted community. You take our livelihoods and give back vague promises of jobs that never come. You take a place that doesn't belong to you, and give back one that does."

"Volumes of facts. Tables of figures. The opinions of a host of experts from the Hidden Schools and the Floating Collegium and even Seven Islands. Liberal and conservative prophet projections for five decades of development. They all support me. This proposal you rail against, these innovations you call desecrations, will be good for the Skittersill. Our plan brings jobs. Construction. Tourism. Soulstuff will flow to local pockets. The docks won't be the only paying work anymore. What else do you need to see?"

"I can tell you what I'd like to see." She cracked her knuckles against the table.

"Why don't you?" They'd leaned so far toward each other that Elayne half expected them to forego words and simply slam their skulls together. Unlikely, alas. Skull-slamming might have offered more chance of compromise.

"I'm sorry," Elayne said, and Bel and Batac turned to her. She showed them her watch with an expression of regret she hoped was not obviously feigned. "It is time for our break. Sunlight will do us all good."

Batac held Bel's gaze for an elegantly timed heartbeat, then straightened, ardor and anger set aside like children's toys. He smiled an easy, self-effacing smile, the smile of a man caught in an embarrassing situation. "Of course. I'm sorry. I appreciate your candor and your passion, Bel." And he left. Bel stared at his retreating back with a stunned expression Elayne recognized from pankriatists flipped onto the mat.

Elayne started to follow Batac out, hoping to corner the man and talk sense into him, but Kopil's cold hand grabbed her arm. "I'll take care of it."

"We need him in line," she said.

"I said I'll take care of it." A voice of sand-scraped bone. His robes flared as he strode from the tent.

Elayne sorted through her briefcase as, across the table, the Chakal Square Select Committee spoke among themselves. She didn't eavesdrop, exactly, but she was pleased when she saw the Kemals approach Bel and speak in low, conciliatory tones. They glanced over to Elayne, who took the hint and left.

Noon sun burned the sky blue, blinding after the dim tent. Soft dry breezes bore smells of crowd and incense and leather and cloth, and beneath all that the city's brick, adobe, and oiled stone. No sea salt here. A few scant miles from the ocean and they might as well have stood in central Kathic corn country.

Light streamed through her closed eyelids, painted the spiderweb space a rich orange, webs of blood and skin and sun rather than Craft. Elayne's muscles had knotted in their long sit. She reached on tiptoes for the sky, and arched her back. Cracks and pops cascaded down her spine.

"Sounds tense."

Chel's voice. Elayne opened her eyes. The woman stood beside her, hands in her pockets. "It is," she said. "The crowd seems calmer."

"A bit." Chel picked at her red armband. "That thing in the sky pissed people off. Got me thinking."

"What about?"

"You remember that first day? When I tackled you."

"I still have the bruises."

"I thought you wanted to kill Temoc."

Elayne waited.

"If you wanted to kill him, I couldn't have stopped it. At most I would have got myself killed first."

"It was a brave thing you did."

"And that I'm asking my friends to do."

"You mean the red-arms," she said.

"Me and my friends, we're second-, third-generation dockhands. Whatever game Batac's playing in the Skittersill, we aren't winning. Wages are down, and if the rents go up like they will if Batac gets his way I don't know what we'll do. Scatter, most like. Work in the factories, butcher for Rakesblight, sign our bodies to zombie in the almond groves. So we do what we can to keep order here. But, hells, that face in the sky. We must seem like ants to him. And I've put my friends under the magnifying glass."

The others emerged from the tent, two by two. Bel and the Major talked in low voices, Most rushed off for refreshments or the restroom. "If not for your friends," Elayne said, "the crowd would have charged us. Temoc would not have had time to calm them down. You saved the peace. If we make a deal, it will be because of you. Respect that."

Chel raised her head, and closed her eyes, and stood haloed in light. A cloud passed between her and the sun. She opened her eyes again. The shadow passed, but the golden moment was gone. "I do. But I'm still afraid."

"Good," Elayne said. "You're doing something big. Fear helps you manage it."

"Maybe." Chel looked down at her hands, which were small and thick and callused, and back up to the crowd and the redarms and the Wardens and the tangled future.

There was much Elayne should have said then. There were many questions she should have asked. But the King in Red called her name, and raised a bony hand. "I have to go."

"It's okay," Chel replied.

As Elayne left to join the skeleton, she did not feel so sure.

18

The day's end came slowly and too soon at once. Temoc lost count of the shift and retrenchment of battle lines within the tent, as parties on each side surged toward common purpose only to retreat once more to platitudes. He was used to this sort of thing, from parishioners' feuds and the arguments that sprouted like crabgrass wherever two priests met. But at a mediation table he'd hoped for statements of fact, and compromises made on the basis of those facts. He had not realized facts themselves could be ideological.

Tan Batac claimed updating the wards would require allowing the sale of Skittersill property on the open market. Otherwise, the land would remain undervalued, uninsurable. Kapania offered counter-examples: former temple property made public, Iskari palaces converted to colleges and museums. These institutions were obviously insured. But (Kopil interrupting now) they were not insured at a fair price by free men. Their maintenance required constant divine intervention. Iskar, of course, still had its gods. And so it went. Examples from Alt Selene and Shikaw and Oxulhat and the Northern Gleb set against others from Camlaan and Telomere and the Shining Empire. The very definition of ownership under the Craft required that owned property be sellable—but that definition had been first codified a few centuries back, after the founding of Dresediel Lex.

The luminous ellipse their tent's oculus cast crept off the table, glinted against the Major's gauntlets, climbed the wall, and disappeared. Sunset turned the visible sky to a judging bloodshot eyeball.

"If I hear you correctly," said the King in Red, "you are not interested in the benefits this project offers, which by my count include jobs, increased property value, and improved safety as a result of modern construction and modern wards. But I do not understand how this could possibly be the case. Do you prefer the Skittersill poor, unemployed, downtrodden, and decaying?"

Bill Kemal rolled his knuckles under his chin. "We," he began, more to hold his place against the other commissioners than because he knew what he was about to say, "want to help our community. That's all everyone on my side has been saying. I think you're focusing so much on the 'help' that you miss the 'our' in front of community."

"Explain."

"I." Again the placeholder. "Am not sure I can put it clearer. We all live here. We've built lives in the Skittersill. This deal you propose might improve a bunch of numbers, all those values and figures and things. But if it destroys the community, those numbers don't matter. Think of it like this, right?" The sparks of the King in Red's eyes blinked off and on again as the skeleton tried to parse that sentence. Bill did not seem bothered—Temoc believed he would have said "bugged"—by that blank stare. "You have a spider. A normal one, little house spider, not like those big guys down in the Stonewood. It strings its web in a corner of your house and it looks all weird, misshapen and baggy, broken threads, and you think, poor guy, you should help him out. So one day you replace his web with a better one made of wire: sturdy, tight, strong. You think, awesome, little spider guy's really going to like this new web. But you don't see him around anymore. Because the things you thought were important about his web weren't the things he thought were important. Or she. The wire isn't sticky like the web, you didn't get the shape right, the spider can't fix the wire on its own if something bad happens. Maybe he's a sheet web spider, used those loose strands of silk to catch bugs— only you don't have any loose strands in the web you made, because you didn't think they were important. Like that."

"By your logic we should never attempt to improve on nature."

"No, man, that's not the point. Say you went down there to build your new web, and the spider guy looked up at you and said, 'Hey, don't do that, it doesn't work that way.' Do you listen to him, or do you wave him off and go ahead with the wire?"

"I contact the Hidden Schools to report the discovery of a previously unknown diminutive species of talking spider."

"Yeah, well. After that, I mean."

"Perhaps there are things I could do to improve the spider's conditions that the spider himself, or herself, has not considered. Options not open to the spider, as it lacks my power."

"Sure. But you don't know whether any of those will really help unless you get to know the spider."

The King in Red leaned back in his chair, and tapped his forefinger against his jaw. Bone rasped bone. The skeleton did not speak, but the texture and weight of the silence did not let anyone else interrupt. The sky watched. Temoc had read tales of ice-locked Skeldic ships back in the ages of polar expedition: the ice's first crack signalled coming change, freedom or death. And always there came a pause after, as frostbitten sailors waited to learn which.

Better to end at a moment of awkward possibility. Preserve the seed, and hope it flowers overnight.

"On that note," Temoc said, "shall we adjourn? Think on what's been said here today, and how we can move forward?"

Tan Batac did not speak, nor did the King in Red. Ms. Kevarian took up the slack. "Good idea. We've intruded on your hospitality long enough. Let's pick up the arachnid theme tomorrow."

And so they left. Chel ordered the red-arms to make a path for the King in Red, Ms. Kevarian, Tan Batac, and their Wardens. As the crowd parted, Ms. Kevarian turned to Temoc. "Progress." She'd found a new broadsheet somewhere: printed this afternoon, with an engraving of the King in Red's face over Chakal Square. "Committee Meets with Despot." "Provided we can hold the front."

"I hoped the broadsheets would respect our work. Maybe Chel's people can stop them at the distribution level."

"Would that help?"

He let out a breath he did not realize he had been holding. "Not likely."

"Get some rest, Temoc."

"You, too."

"I don't need it as much."

"Because you're a half-undead sorcerer?"

"Because I'm not leading a revolution." The path opened, and the Wardens gathered, the tall Lieutenant at their fore. "See you tomorrow morning."

He watched the King in Red's party leave, and the crowd watched, too—his people, grown so vast. In the beginning, he knew every name. Who were these newcomers? What did they want? If—when—the committee reached some compromise, would they disperse? Or, like magic knives in old tales, would they demand blood before they slept?

The Major caught up with him at the water tent, and waited while Temoc drained a tall tin cup of lukewarm water, cut with lemon to disguise its aftertaste. Temoc poured a second cup, drained that too, and poured a third before acknowledging the Major. "I'm glad you restrained yourself from killing Tan Batac. At least Bel gave him a taste of his own medicine."

"Never anger teachers," the Major said. He took Temoc's arm and guided him away from the onlookers at the water tent. "Will you return home tonight?"

"I need to remember what we are fighting for."

"We are not fighting yet," the Major said. "But we may be soon. And I do not think you should go. Strong forces stand against Chakal Square. Confronting them, full of anger and commitment, and yet not fighting, requires will. The King in Red almost broke that will this morning. He is not stupid. He wanted a riot, an excuse to call his butchers to their business."

"You imagine conspiracy," Temoc said, "where foolishness suffices. The King in Red has spent so long in boardrooms he has forgotten how to speak to people. I dislike him. He destroys homes and lives and civilizations in the name of progress toward some bloodless future in which we are no different from the skazzerai that spin webs between the stars. But he is not such a monster as to do what you claim."

"Either he meant to start a riot this morning, or he did not—either he is foolish, or clever. Either way," the Major said, "we need you. Stay."

Sunset seared the sky. The Major's armor caught and held its light.

"Without my family, none of this has meaning."

"These people are your family."

"I have to go," he said. "I will be late for evening service."

Temoc left the Major beside the water tent, aflame with the dying day.

The crowd pressed so thick around the grass mats Temoc could not reach his altar. An old woman sat on the shoulders of a tall, stooped man. A round-bellied dockworker shaded his eyes with his hands. Three kids jumped, one after the other, to look. All sought Temoc and none saw him, none would even step aside until Chel shoved and shouted, "Let Temoc through!"

They turned then. Drew back. Knelt.

He wanted to run. So many eyes weighed upon him. No man could bear so much hope alone. Master Alaptan, whose crown bowed his long and narrow neck, had warned young Temoc about the eyes, their weight. This was why priests wore raiment, this was the reason for the flowers, the scars, the knife and altar and the beaded skirt: so you could stand beneath such pressure without shattering.

When he was young, he'd thought the old man had meant the weight of divine power, of the people's hunger for corn and thirst for rain. But another thirst remained when all those needs were met.

Temoc was the last Eagle Knight. He had been trained from childhood by his father and his many uncles of the priesthood. He charted a faithful path in a world that rejected faith. Only for this reason could he bear the weight of those eyes and stride toward the altar. Only for this reason could he chant the old songs before this throng. Only for this reason could he bind a sacrifice to the altar and raise his knife and feel faith flood him as he called the gods to sup on unshed blood, feel bliss so sweet he understood at last the addicts who wept before him saying, Father, if you do it once you'll do it again.

And only for this reason could he leave and walk alone through the crowd past the red-arms' cordon and the Wardens'. Walk, rejecting cabs and carriages, deeper into the Skittersill. Turn onto the first side street, the second. Enter the gates of his house. Meet his wife at the door. Hug her close, kiss her deeply.

Only for this reason could he forget.

19

Tay hid the broadsheets beneath his jacket, and only set them down when no one was looking. That was the deal. He paused beside a tent circle and glanced around, saw students and other red-arms and a family gathered by a gas stove, no one he knew. He knelt fast, tugged broadsheets out of his jacket, and left them on the stone, headline facing up. "Committee Meets with Despot."

He straightened faster than he'd knelt. Five hundred sheets they gave him, and five hundred sheets were hard to hide. He looked like he'd gained twenty pounds, and the paper padding made the jacket even hotter than usual.

Two hundred sheets out so far. Another half and he'd be done. Late to dinner, but he'd eat fast and make his shift no problem.

He turned the corner and almost ran into Chel.

She did not look happy.

"Hey," he said, too quickly. "Thought you'd be at dinner."

"I was, but you weren't. What's up?"

"Nothing." Banjo music twanged a few tents over. Always music in this camp at night, and most of it he didn't know. He sweated, though not from nerves. This heat, that's all, the heat and the jacket. "Went for a walk."

"You know people around here?"

"Yeah." He hunched over to hide the bulge in his jacket. If he took his hands out of his pockets the papers would slip, so he pointed with his chin instead. "You know Old Cipher? His kids got a tent over that way. Mending clothes and stuff. I dropped in, said hello."

"Out of the goodness of your heart." She drew close to him, beautiful as always and her eyes clever. One hand circled around his back, another touched his chest—and the papers, under the jacket. "What's this?"

"Nothing." He tried to back up but there wasn't any way to go without taking her with him. She yanked the jacket open. Snaps popped like knuckles, and the sweat-sogged broadsheets fanned out from within. She pulled one free—ripped the sheet in half, but enough remained for her to read. "Meets with Despot."

"Tay," she said. "Qet's cock. The hells are you doing?"

"I can explain."

"You see what's written here? Did you read this thing?" She snapped the flimsy gray paper in his face like a whip: accusations of treachery. Movement in danger.

"I don't like it, just pass it out."

"Which makes it so much better." The air above her rippled like the air above pavement on a hot day. Or else there was something in his eyes.

"We read the sheets before we came here."

"We read the sheets before they turned mean. They don't like Temoc, or the Committee, or you, or me, or the red-arms. They want people riled up. They want fights. Do you?"

"Course not," he said. "But people have a right to know what's going on."

"They do. We tell them."

"You're sounding like a bonehead, Chel. Or a witch."

"Don't." She went tight like an anchor chain in a storm. "Don't even joke about that."

"You want to stop people talking, you come after me just for handing out some papers. What's the difference between His Redness trying to scare us today and what you're doing now?"

"You think I'm a skeleton? You think I'm on their side?"

His mouth was dry. He swallowed. "No."

"We need to stand together, Tay. These sheets aren't printed here. The folks writing them won't get hurt if things go bad. They'll watch us burn."

"You're the one who almost jumped the King in Red this morning." That stopped her. He withdrew a step, two, still hunched around his papers. "You were angry then, and you're angry now, and you're angry at the sheets for making other people angry. Maybe we should be angry. Maybe it's wrong to meet with the King in Red."

"You really think that?"

"I don't know what to think," he said. "But I wonder if you're so mad at me for handing out these papers because you care about what they're doing in that tent, or because you care about the ones who're doing it."

"What's that supposed to mean?"

"You know what it means."

"I don't." But she was lying. She crossed her arms and stared at him. "He has a family."

"You saved his life. He saved yours. I know how that story goes."

"Only it doesn't. I tried to help him because I thought he was in danger. I'd do the same for you or anyone."

"And I'm just anyone, now."

"You're a bit past anyone," she said, "and awfully close to 'asshole.'"

He opened his mouth, not sure what he would say beyond that it would hurt her. But she was not afraid, and in that she was still the woman he'd fallen for the second time they met. Papers jutted from his jacket like a rooster's ruff. He closed his mouth and his eyes and let his thoughts run on while the banjo played. She was still there when he opened them again. "I'm sorry, Chel." She didn't melt, not yet. "Look, they offered me soul, weeks back, before we came here, to hand the sheets around. We sure as hells aren't getting paid while we're here. I give what comes in to the Kemals at Food Com, and they cut us a break with rations. That's why we get the extra meat."

"Just you, or others?"

"A few guys in our crew do the work. I don't know more than that."

"Stop."

"We'll miss the soulstuff."

"We just need a few days of peace. Maybe less."

"Okay," he said. "I'm sorry for the other stuff I said. I was angry."

"Me, too."

"Yeah. But you had reason."

She smiled, at least.

"Come on," Chel said. "Let's find a place to dump that trash."

20

Like a gallowglass floating on open sea, Dresediel Lex spread phosphorescent tendrils across the dark. Its roads robbed the former desert of its night. Eight decades of irrigation and water theft had greened the barrens of Fisherman's Vale—for farms at first, but before long the city's people spilled onto land where orange and lemon trees once grew. Climb snakelike roads up the Drakspine ridge, hug vine-strangled cliffs through hairpin turns, mount the dry summit and behold the Vale's endless grid of streets, an urban planner's nightmare branded on unsettled ground.

The roads ran north and south, east and west, under a flat purple-black sky: a hydroponic lattice for a growing civilization. Houses and shops had filled the lattice just beyond the ridge with fire and ghostlight blooms. Ride a mile or two past the hills, though, and the roads emptied, crossing and recrossing trafficless around concrete fortresses of industry.

The Craftsmen who freed Dresediel Lex in the God Wars wasted no time selling it to the world. Free City, they called it, First City Made for Man, by Man. Come all castaways, all ye scorned by gods and people. Come and build yourself a life. Outcasts and Craftswomen heard, and came, and soon bayside rent and property values grew too high for most industry to handle. Concerns that needed room moved to the Vale for cheap land, and workers followed.

Flickering ghostlight illuminated the block-lettered sign of Garabaldi Brothers Printing and Engraving. If not for the sign, Elayne could never have told the printshop apart from all the other sprawling two-story boxes with parking lots out front.

Elayne paid the carriage to wait around the corner. The bay's tack jangled as it pulled the two-seater off into the dark. A big roan raised its head from the parking lot trough, glanced over, and snorted.

Weeds pressed up through pavement cracks, adding points to pools of shadow. Lights streamed through the big windows of the front office, where a secretary with an updo sat behind a desk cluttered with cartoon calendars.

Elayne ignored the office and walked to the side lot, through an unmarked, unlocked entrance, down a dirty hall, and opened a pair of grease-stained double doors into pandemonium.

Copper, iron, steel, and lead clacked, clattered, and convulsed. Gears realigned and pistons pounded. Torrents of paper surged over drums the size of carriages. Folding machines snapped their jaws. Guillotine blades cut long strips of newsprint into pages. Surgical lights slammed into every surface and edge. She breathed a lungful of hot paper and vaporized ink and melting lead.

With a twist of Craft, Elayne stopped her ears and reduced the noise to almost-bearable levels. When she regained her balance, she saw the workers, forty or so earmuffed humans in tan jumpsuits, staring at her.

The last few days had accustomed her to scrutiny. She waited.

A tall, broad man emerged from behind the giant press, leading a square woman with a smear of engine grease on her cheek. The woman looked Elayne over, and thumbed toward stairs that led to a lofted office. The woman went first, the big guy at her side. Elayne followed, and two more large men broke off from the group to follow her in turn. The others stood, watching, until the boss glanced back and they all thrilled again to work.

Elayne climbed the stairs. Her ears were stopped, but the mechanical percussion still shook her bones. Below, the presses ate fresh paper. Rollers rolled, folding machines folded, stacking arms stacked. Humans moved among the metal. She remembered an early experiment with Craft in which she'd opened an anthill to watch workers tend the queen. They looked like that.

"Talks Drag On," read the headline on the broadsheets they printed. "Wardens Threaten Protesters." Thousands of copies. She didn't expect so many.

The office was austere. Two desks, one unwashed coffee mug each. Three gray metal filing cabinets against the wall. A cheap calendar hung over the cabinets. Scrawled appointments dimpled glossy paper. This month's picture was a view of a waterfall near Seven Leaf Lake eight hundred miles north, white water banked with a vegetative green nobody saw in Dresediel Lex outside of calendar paintings.

The two toughs followed them in, which Elayne didn't like. When the door closed, the maddening grind of the machines stopped. Noiseproof wards around the office. Effective. The others removed their muffs, and Elayne unbound her ears. After the shop floor chaos, the office's dampened air felt dead.

The woman and the tall man sat, and Elayne sat too, in the room's sole remaining chair.

"I didn't say you could sit," the woman said.

The tall man laughed—not a cruel sound: rounded, full-voiced, blunt. Something skewed in his head.

"I prefer to conduct business sitting down," Elayne said.

"Is that why you're here? Business?"

"Of a sort. Are you Ms. Garabaldi?"

"Why don't you start with why you've come?"

"I'd rather know with whom I'm speaking."

"We all have lots of things we'd rather."

The man laughed, again, too loud.

"I'm here to talk with the Garabaldi Brothers."

"You're talking with one of them." The woman nodded toward the laughing man. If she knew about the grease on her cheek, she didn't care. "And the sister."

"What happened to brother number two?"

Garabaldi took a pack of cigarettes and a matchbook from

her desk, tapped out a cigarette, stuck it in her mouth, lit. "Dead."

"I'm sorry to hear it."

"So was I. Who are you?"

"Elayne Kevarian."

The ember at her cigarette's tip flared red. "Don't know that name."

"No reason you should," she said. "I want to learn who hired you to print those broadsheets."

Her lips pursed around the cigarette filter. "Lots of people hire us to print things. They don't hire us to talk."

"You know the job I mean. The sheets you're printing downstairs."

The brother chuckled, a low unhealthy sound. The sister's eyes were amber-green and deep. She nodded, not in response to the question.

Hands seized Elayne from behind, big, heavy mechanics' hands, and squeezed, and lifted, and pulled. The chair toppled. She fell back, dragged toward the door, heels scraping over the rough carpet.

"Take her out," the sister said. "See her off."

Elayne closed her eyes, and noise and terror filled the room. All lights save the cigarette ember died. A million demons' hammers rained down on a million anvils, rhythmless and un-reasoning, a bone-jarring, teeth-rattling clamor that built and built. The brother screamed, a high, whimpering sound. The mechanics who held Elayne stumbled back, clutching their ears, blind in the darkness that rolled from her skin. She recovered her balance, and straightened her lapels.

The office wards dulled sound. Easy to invert them, to am-plify the noise outside. She tossed both mechanics back against the wall and bound them with chains of starlight. Then she killed the noise.

Light returned. What the sister saw—and it was always so important, in Craft as in street magic, to consider what others saw, what they thought they knew, and what conclusions they might draw from that knowledge—what the sister saw was a black tide that ebbed to reveal her two bruisers bound to the wall by sorcery, and Elayne, free, with black fire burning in her eyes. Elayne righted her chair on the carpet, and sat down.

The brother had drawn back from the desk, teeth bared. The cigarette shook in the sister's hand. "That wasn't nice," she said.

"I repay in kind."

"I guess you do. Excuse me." Garabaldi walked to her brother, hugged him, comforted him with words Elayne didn't try to overhear. He put his earmuffs on. The sister hugged him harder, and only when his rictus-grin softened did she return to her seat. "Let my guys go."

"Can we have a conversation?"

"They only would have scared you."

"My line of work doesn't reward assumptions of that sort."

"Let's talk."

"In private."

"Sure."

Elayne raised her hand. The mechanics slumped to the ground, and after a moment found their feet. She took her faintness, her exhaustion, wadded it up in a ball and tossed it to the corner of her mental attic with everything else she didn't have time to feel. The Craft was ideal for manipulating soulstuff on a large scale, for adjusting wards and building binding bargains and cheating death, for moving slowly and with grim certainty. Yes, she could toss a few hundred pounds of mechanic around without preparation, but she didn't enjoy the process.

Sister Garabaldi waved them good-bye. "Get lost, boys. If she's still here in fifteen minutes, come get her with an army."

The door opened, and closed again behind them.

"Private enough?"

"Yes," Elayne said. "What's your name?"

"You can call me Dana."

"Mind if I have a cigarette?"

Dana tossed Elayne the pack. Elayne caught it in midair, with Craft, fished out a cigarette the same way, and lit it with a flick of her fingers. Again, wasteful, but again, appearances. "I am sorry I scared your brother." The cigarette was a pleasant relief, the constriction of her throat and lungs a reminder she was alive, a little boon to a body that worried it would be forgotten each time she called on Craft.

"It's okay. He scares easy." She smiled at him, and he smiled back. "Good kid. Works well, and the others like him. There are doctors, and they say some new drugs coming down the pipe might help. I don't know. Don't feel like I should decide that sort of thing for him, but he can't really decide for himself."

"Let me be clear," Elayne said. "I work for the King in Red, not the Wardens, and I have not come to make trouble. You know about the situation in the Skittersill."

Dana lowered her head—not quite a nod, but Elayne took it for one.

"The Chakal Square crowd formed to protest some high-level work under way in the Court of Craft. How do you unify a district around a knotty question of wards and bargains?" Elayne exhaled smoke. "You educate them. You flood the area with eloquent, forceful, and above all angry broadsheets, calls to action, indictments of those who stand on the sidelines. Fair enough. But now that the protest will likely end in peace, the broadsheets turn to warmongering. Which leads me to wonder, who paid for all this?"

"We only print the stuff," Dana said. "Client asked us to provide a service, we did. It's a free city."

"Nothing in this city's free. Not even the water." Elayne leaned forward, and tapped ash into Dana's ashtray. "Let me tell you a story."

Dana didn't object.

"A young woman is in school—working toward mastery in mechanics, maybe. Or golemetry? Anyway, her older brother dies, something sudden. Heart failure, let's say." And from the sudden tension in Dana's face, she'd guessed right. "Leaving her with a family business and a brother who suffers from a mental condition. Theirs is a business of relationships, and such a fast transition puts those relationships under strain. The sister treads water, but she wasn't groomed for this business. She can keep the machines running, but accounting and client management are foreign to her. The bottom line creeps up, the top down, and if she slips, a hundred fifty employees fall. So when someone shows up talking secrecy, security, and large direct transfers of soulstuff, under the table, she doesn't think too hard before she says yes."

"If you want to piss me off, you've succeeded."

"I want a name. In exchange, I help you and your brother. My firm has contracts with accounting Concerns. We'll send a consultant to get your books in order. Steady hand at the tiller. You'll do fine."

"How, if I feed my clients to the Wardens?"

"I'm not the Wardens," she said. "And your client won't know you've told me. She might not even stop paying you."

"Why do you think she's a she?"

"Why wouldn't she be?"

Dana had smoked her cigarette to the filter. She crushed it out in the ashtray, and leaned back. "You're working for the King in Red, but not the Wardens. You want to find my client, but you don't want to stop her. You don't make sense, Ms. Kevarian."

"I have friends in the Skittersill," she said. "They will burn in the anger your client wants to fan. They need help." She did not look at Dana's brother. "Your client won't know I got her name from you. And I think my fifteen minutes are almost up. If you wish to accept my offer, best do it before the cavalry bursts through that door."

A clock ticked through the ensuing pause.

Dana took a piece of paper from her desk, and a pen, scrawled a name on the paper, and passed it, folded, to Elayne. Elayne snuffed out her cigarette and read the name printed there, in firm capitals: Kal Alaxic. With an address.

"Thank you," Elayne said. "I'll send the accountant."

"Get gone."

She warded her ears before she stepped out into the pounding noise. Mechanics watched her walk to and through the door. The night swallowed her.

Up in the mountains, a dry wind howled.

21

The wind blew dry and hot all night. It rolled down distant slopes and dried across a thousand desert miles, until at last it bore nothing but itself, not even dust. Children in clapboard houses sweltered through sandstorm nightmares. Fights in bars by Monicola Pier boiled onto the street, human beings transformed to tangles of fists and feet and teeth. Even Wardens paused before breaking up brawls that brutal. Better wait for the drunks to bleed it out. Hospital surgeons sharpened scalpels and took drugs to stay awake.

Temoc stared at his ceiling and snatched for the frayed edges of the dream he'd left behind. Fire. Screams. Death. And above it all, a sense of grim inevitable fate.

Mina curled beside him, and uncurled, and yowled catlike in her sleep.

He stood without waking her, and walked their house alone. Caleb's door had drifted open. Temoc considered going in to watch his son asleep. Decided against it, for the same reason he'd not woken Mina. No need to inflict this wakefulness on another.

There were prayers for such nights and such winds. The sky outside the kitchen windows was yellow-orange and higher than usual—the sorcerous clouds Craftsmen used to protect their precious starlight from the city's glare had retreated from the dirt. Still the wind blew on. A bad omen. People waking in Chakal Square tonight would fear for their souls. These winds issued from wounds in the world. Demons rode them.

He drank three glasses of water, which did not help. His heartbeat slowed.

He stepped out of the kitchen and saw Caleb at the dinner

table, watching him. He swore, and drew back a step. An apparition? A message from the gods?

But the boy said, "I couldn't sleep," and was his son after all.

"Hells, Caleb. We should teach you to hunt. You won't even need a weapon. Just do that to the deer, and they'll fall down dead."

The boy didn't laugh. "I'm sorry. I thought you saw me."

"Would you like some water?"

"Yes, please."

Temoc poured him a glass, and refilled his own. They each dipped a finger in the water, and shed a drop on the table. *Water in the desert*, Temoc said, and Caleb replied, *a generous gift*. They sat, shadows inside shadows, encased in dry, charged air.

"Do you get bad dreams, Dad?"

"I do."

"Do they scare you?"

"No."

"Why not?"

"There are two kinds of dreams. Most are false, with no more substance than a lie. Some dreams are true, but truth is barely more substantial. A dream can neither wound nor kill. Why fear it?"

"Mom says dreams connect. Mom says we're all tied together in dreams, and sometimes stuff spreads from one person to another."

"Perhaps."

"So you're not scared?"

"I am not."

"Then why are you awake?"

Because, Temoc thought, fear and dread are not the same. Because to say I'm scared suggests that something has scared me, that I know the shape of the beast that chases me down dream corridors. That my fear has an object, and that object has a name, and this name is known or at least knowable to me. One cannot fear a dry hot wind, one cannot fear to lie in bed awake beside one's sleeping wife, one cannot fear one's child. To say I fear suggests that something makes me fear, and I have never yet encountered a thing I could not break with my bare hands.

And yet this boy watches me with my own eyes under my own brows above his mother's cheeks, and when he questions me I reel. I am Temoc. Once a goddess set her palm upon my brow, once I slew a scorpion the size of a mountain, once I fought demons to a standstill on a bridge over a chasm as deep as death. I preach to those who stand against the King in Red. I am Temoc, father, and husband, priest, and I cannot be all those men at once. What father leaves his wife and child to seek war? What father sets aside his son for an ideal?

Temoc leaned across the table, and ruffled Caleb's hair. The boy squinched up his face and pushed Temoc's hand away. Wiry, lacking Temoc's bulk—but still strong. Strong enough.

"I'm worried about you."

"I can take care of myself."

"I hope so," Temoc said. He lifted the boy from the chair and embraced him. Caleb squirmed, then understood, and hugged his father back.

Outside, that dry, demonic wind blew on.

22

The next morning the sun rose. The tide rolled in. Airbuses drifted overhead. Stoves burned scrambled eggs, and cooks cursed and opened windows to let out smoke. Downtown highway traffic ran nose to bumper, slower even than usual due to rubbernecking near Chakal Square. An unlucky accountant's carriage crashed into a fruit cart. Lemons rolled across pavement, squashed under hooves and wheels. Zest and spray mixed with sweat, horseflesh, hot wood, pavement, shit. The city groaned like a revenant new-woken on the slab, and shambled forth hungry for food it lacked a tongue to name.

In Chakal Square, the parties met. Elayne, nursing a skull-fracturing headache after last night's adventure, strode down the red-arm's cordon at the King in Red's right hand. Tan Batac, to the skeleton's other side, walked briskly—he must have slept well. He seemed to be the only one. Weakened by dawn, the hot wind still dried skin and robbed spit from open mouths. It even chased away the smog, leaving a sky that could not be called blue—pale, only, the color prophets gave death's horse, with vague tones of orange and green and threatening thunder. The crowd did not mutter, did not growl. It watched.

There were no speeches. If Kopil had tried the voice-in-the-sky routine today, Temoc could not have calmed the people. They would have mobbed at once.

Temoc ushered them into the tent, and again they sat, and again the oculus began its slow progression—though today the sunlight ellipse seemed an accusing eye. Each side watched the other, exhausted and uncertain and at bay. They drank water and waited as the day forced itself alight.

No one was more surprised than Elayne when things began to move.

She asked the first question, yes, but she could not be held responsible for what happened next. "We left yesterday with Mr. Kemal's spider," she said. "And the dangers of miscommunication. Perhaps we could expand on that theme: have each side present the other's position, as they see it, with as little emotion as possible."

Temoc objected to the idea that one should set aside emotion when discussing homes and families. The Major refused to describe Tan Batac's goals as anything less than apocalyptic. Elayne resigned herself to another day of shouted slogans and table-pounding, but few commissioners seemed to share the Major's passion. Even Bel frowned as he railed about revolution. After the Major, each speaker took a calmer position, until Kapania Kemal summed up: "You want to tear down our home, and build a place where none of us can live."

The King in Red's laugh held little humor. "Change is inevitable. Even you commissioners are new to the Skittersill. The Kemals have a warrior's clan name, ke, and Techita's family were freeholding artisans before the Wars. Bel's people have lived here since first settlement, but the very fact she calls you neighbors proves how much the Skittersill has changed. Hells, you've enlisted Temoc Almotil to your cause, and I remember when the priests of house Al came this far south only to choose sacrifices. So you'll forgive me if your evocations of community and home sound rich. You want to protect yourselves from change, just like every conservative since the dawn of time. You're on the losing side of history."

Hal Techita struck the table with his stick. "Typical Craftsman's argument, thaumocratic and reliant on false historical progressivism without a shred of—"

"Hal," Bel said, and Techita stopped. "We can't make this about philosophy or we'll fight until the stars fall. You and I disagree on these questions—as do Tan Batac and the King in Red. Our problem is practical, not ideological."

"These gentlemen"—and Techita spared no scorn on that word—"seem to disagree. We explain our position and they can't even repeat it back without reference to the grand shape of history."

"Then let me try," said Tan Batac—the first words he'd spoken this morning, and still with that small smile, still with fingers interlaced over his belly, like one of those cherub-cheeked porcelain sages from the Shining Empire.

Hal eyed him warily.

"Our main difference," Batac said, "is that you care about preserving the Skittersill as it is now, and I care about how the Skittersill must change to survive the next three decades, or five. You think I want to wire your spiderweb. I think you want to freeze it: to lock your current life in place, to keep it from changing."

"We want it to change," Kapania said. "Organically."

"What do you mean by organic? Do you mean slowly? Because living beings move fast. Fifty years ago Dresediel Lex was a theocracy; today we're not. Do you mean, in hermetic isolation? Because I can't think of any living system disconnected from all others. Maybe those blind fish you get in caves, almost—but I don't think you want to be a blind fish in a cave, even if that were an option, which it's not. You're in the middle of one of the biggest cities in the world."

"There's a difference between evolution," Bel said, "and decree. Your plans—" She waved at the maps spread on the table. "You want luxury apartments where we live. Some of these compounds have been inhabited for six hundred years."

"But haven't those houses changed in six hundred years?"

"Sure. After fires and disasters, after victories and marriages and tragedies." She looked about the circle for confirmation.

Even the Major nodded. "Things change. We care for lives lived here, now. Not for some crystal utopia."

"But you don't mind if the Skittersill becomes a utopia over time."

"No."

"So we really disagree," he said, "on the question of how to regulate the transformation."

"Sure."

"Do you have any suggestions?"

And so, two hours into the second day, the talks began.

Elayne took notes. They broke for small group meetings, they broke for water, they broke for lunch, they broke to stand outside under the angry sky and contemplate the possibility of failure.

"I don't believe it," Kopil said. "They're talking."

"They were talking already," Batac said, with a self-satisfied grin. "But we're talking together now."

"They will seek concessions, you realize."

Batac searched the crowd, and nodded at some secret knowledge he gleaned there. "I can handle my investors, within reason."

Elayne tried to shake her sense things were going right for the wrong reasons.

Back in the tent, uncertainty receded. Concessions were offered, compromises raised. If Elayne hadn't warded the tent herself she would have suspected a secret hand of usurping the delegates' wills—but there was no arcane Craft in play. The parties had simply decided to cooperate, like a cloud deciding to rain.

"You want to protect the Skittersill," Tan Batac said. "You don't want it to become a museum."

"The structures should remain," Bel said, "and rent should be guaranteed."

"What about bare spaces, decaying buildings? Do you want abandoned houses to stay abandoned when we could replace them with something new?"

"No," Hal said. "We care about living beings, not dead wood."

"I would be comfortable," Bel said again, "if abandoned or otherwise damaged structures could be rebuilt, repurposed, even sold fee simple."

"So long," Bill Kemal added, "as owners are forced to protect their property. Or I bet we'll face a season of suspicious fires."

"What do you mean," said Batac, "by 'protect'?"

"Full fire suppression, earthquake and flood resistance. Pest control."

"Especially against lava termites."

"Expensive," Batac said. "Few insurance Concerns will offer such a guarantee."

"Someone will," the Major said. "Or what good is your vaunted free market?"

"These terms will chase off anyone who wants to buy Skittersill land."

"If the cost of insurance is high, there will be less demand for Skittersill real estate, which should keep rent and land prices low at first." Bel pointed to the plans. "But the district will change, and after a while you'll be able to realize these dreams of yours."

Batac nodded. "We'll need time to negotiate new insurance deals. Markets develop slowly, and comprehensive property-warding agreements don't just fall out of the sky."

"Not," said the Major, "when you rig their auction to benefit your cronies."

"That is a hurtful accusation," though Batac did not seem hurt. "I don't want to delay this agreement. Neither do you, I imagine."

"What if the new wards require comprehensive coverage as of, let's say, two weeks after they take effect?"

"Two months."

"Within which you can send your arson squads to our homes. Two weeks is generous, to my mind."

"I don't even have an arson squad. Six weeks."

They sparred with words. Sometimes Elayne thought Batac or Bel might flip the table, or the King in Red, grown large in wrath, would shatter them all to pieces. But they recoiled from the brink of each new crisis, and by four o'clock they stared at one another, wordless.

Wordless until Elayne said: "It sounds like we have a deal."

She outlined the terms, read them back, adjusted a few figures, clarified key definitions. Passed copies to each commissioner, which all reviewed in silence. She recognized the shape of their concern. Recapitulation came after every debate, and trembling review: did I compromise my principles because I was tired and desperate to agree to something, anything? Which of us gave more?

"I recommend," she said, "we involve the court at this point. Judge Cafal may have questions."

"We cannot all go to the judge," Bill Kemal said. "People get nervous. The Major has outstanding warrants for his arrest."

"It is true," the Major said.

"Plus, we need to sell this agreement to the square."

The King in Red crossed his arms. "I thought you were empowered to negotiate."

"Negotiate, yes. Not rule."

"If you cannot guarantee their commitment—"

"We can," Temoc said. "The people will listen. But they must know the cause to which they are committing themselves."

"So what do we do now?" Tan Batac asked. "Wait?"

"No," Elayne said. Every delay increased the chance someone would step wrong. Deal or no deal, pressure grew. "The Commission needs to sell the people on the deal while we finalize it with the judge. But we can't go to Cafal alone. We need someone to stand for the crowd, someone they'll trust."

Glances flicked across and around the table. The Major coughed.

"Why," Temoc said, "is everyone looking at me?"

23

"I should talk to them," Temoc said, "before I go."

They stood outside the tent, in full view of the crowd.

Elayne raised one hand. "I'll set it up so you can speak in the sky."

He hesitated, then nodded.

"I never thought you would feel stage fright."

"I do not like speaking for myself," he said. "I speak for something greater, or not at all. And anyway, there is no stage here."

"You did fine last time."

"Last time I had to stop a riot. There was no room for failure."

"If pressure helps—if you can't sell this, I doubt your commissioners will do better, which means that the peace has failed and we're back to square one."

"Much better." He closed his eyes and flexed his shoulders in a way that caused his sternum to pop, a bass noise like an arm breaking. "Let's go."

She called upon her expense account with Kelethres, Albrecht, and Ao. Her blood chilled, and color drained away, leaving only wavelengths of light. The red-arms' armbands lost their bloody hue. A girl with flowers in her hair held a screaming child in her arms, and the child's face lost its flush and the daisies ceased to remind Elayne of a petal's brush against her cheek when she'd been young and almost in love, in that vanishing breath between girlhood and the War. All that faded, but power flooded her instead, which was compensation.

The Craft she wove lacked the King in Red's theatricality,

which was probably for the best, considering the delicate moment.

She extended her hand to Temoc. Green and blue flame danced in her palm, tongues twisting between her fingers.

"You're on," she said, and opened her grip. The fireflower wrapped him round, flashing emerald as Temoc's scars seized control. His eyes rolled back, his body went rigid, and his face emerged from the orange sky above.

"People of the Skittersill," he said. "For the last two days we have discussed terms with the King in Red, and with Tan Batac. We have sought to preserve the city we know. They understand our concerns." Murmurs of disbelief, a shout of "How?" From off to the north, laughter. Temoc laughed himself, his voice rich and full and wet despite the dry wind. "We have a deal. The structures we live in will not be sold or harmed until we wish it. They will consider our needs, our way of life. These talks have bridged a gap that seemed uncrossable. Nor is this is the end. We have shown our strength. We command respect when we stand together. Do not lose faith. I go to the Court of Craft, where I will present our deal to the judges." "Temoc! Temoc!" A few voices raised in chant at first, a few hands lifted to the sky. Then, more. "The commissioners will explain our achievement. You will see that we have made compromises, but have not compromised. The world we want is the world we build, now, together." Strong downbeats in that voice, hammer blows to drive his point home. Short words. A literal speech act: victory was victory because he named it so.

"Listen to the commission. Hear your leaders' words. Do not falter. Wait for my return."

He faded from the clouds. A blue space remained where the Craft had scoured the sky clean.

"Temoc." The chant built and spread, men's voices, women's, children's, bass alto tenor soprano, clear or reedy-rough, angry or rapturous or exultant or simply willing the future bright. "Temoc. Temoc. Temoc."

The man, priest, Eagle Knight, father, old enemy, lowered

his head. He gave no sign he heard them. To him the chant might as well have been the wind that bore it, the wind that whipped clouds and dust to plug the clear blue moment in the sky.

The red-arm cordon strained again, not this time against the protesters' anger but against their need. Wardens surrounded Temoc, and Elayne, and Tan Batac, who seemed no more than a man in a rumpled, though expensive, suit. And the King in Red of course, who stood at Elayne's elbow, and said: "He is dangerous."

"He's on our side."

"Now."

"Did you hear that speech?"

"I heard a dangerous man. And the only thing one knows for certain about a dangerous man, is that he is dangerous."

Temoc smiled and waved as the crowd chanted his name.

24

The judge cleared her schedule—unheard-of in Elayne's experience, but the King in Red was not a normal client and this was not a normal case. Cafal's assistant ushered them to the inner office. The judge sat behind her desk, the same deep lines graven in the same square face, the same broad mouth fixed in the same passionless disapproval. Her sharp blue raptor's gaze flicked over the three of them, lingered on Elayne, and settled at last on Temoc, who returned the stare without expression. Elayne thought about cats and kings, and wondered which was which.

Cafal addressed Elayne first. "Counselor. Have you fixed your problem?"

"Yes, your honor. The Chakal Square Committee have agreed to a compromise. They send Temoc Almotil as their representative."

"Does he have Craft training?"

"I am a theologian," Temoc said.

"Enough to understand the agreement under discussion?"

He nodded.

"It's irregular for someone to claim authority in my court without a document to prove it. Do you really speak for those people?"

"Would we have met with him for the last two days if he did not?"

"You're against a wall, counselor. In your situation, I might be tempted to meet with anyone willing to meet with me."

"With all respect." Temoc did not raise his voice, but they all looked at him. "Evidence is an echo of truth. My people have sent me, and so I am here."

Cafal's laugh inspired neither confidence nor comfort. "Such responsibility. Good thing you have broad shoulders."

"My shoulders have little bearing on the situation."

"I've seen your name in the papers, Temoc Almotil. But it's interesting to learn what sort of man you are in person."

Cafal snapped her fingers, and they stood astride Dresediel Lex. The twin suns of her eyes cast their shadows down its alleys and over its pyramids.

"Very well," said the judge from the vast and arching sky. "Show me your deal."

After two days in the Chakal Square tent, after Bel and the Major and Kapania Kemal, after the staring crowd and the brewing riot and the red-arms and the demon wind and the faces in the sky, Elayne found the afternoon's work straightforward. Not that it was easy—Cafal's gaze was implacable, her mind sharp. But she did not jag sideways in the middle of an argument to question the philosophical foundations of the Craft, nor did she object to basic terms of art.

Temoc answered questions, when questions came. Explained, patiently, about spiders, and about webs, about the Skittersill protesters' need to know their lives would not be sold out from under them. Crossed his arms, and rarely let his hand drift to the hilt of his knife.

Easy. But when the judge said, "So mote it be," and they fell back from the dream in which three long strides could compass the distance from Worldsedge to Stonewood, into their ill-fitting bodies, when they shook hands and congratulated one another on a job almost done, when they left the Court and emerged into the late afternoon, Elayne felt less triumphant than she expected.

The victorious afterglow of the enemies' agreement in Chakal Square faded fast. Standing on the sidewalk in front of the Court of Craft as traffic rolled by, as the King in Red and Tan Batac waited for a valet to bring their carriages and Temoc tried without success to hail a cab, she felt the unease of having walked a quarter mile down the wrong fork in a road. The first year she'd moved to Alt Selene she often got lost without noticing at first: with each passing block the stores seemed stranger, unfamiliar script invaded road signs, caustic spiced vapor drifted from restaurant kitchen vents, until she reached a district that might have been lifted from the sprawling metropolis of Kho Katang. And all the while she'd felt she was on the right road.

Hells. She gave, as always, too much credence to foreboding. Glandular chemistry was subject to pheromones, to context, to the angry orange sky that hung over Dresediel Lex like the sole of the proverbial other shoe.

Two carriages arrived, one crimson-lacquered for the King in Red, and Tan Batac's black and sleek, drawn by a horse that bore the same relation to normal horses that temple paintings bore to normal men: idealized, exaggerated, impossible. Both pulled off and merged into traffic, drivers whipping the horses' flanks.

Temoc waved for another cab. This one slowed a fraction before the driver remembered a pressing engagement somewhere across town and sped past, leaving a trail of dust. In another city, mud might have splattered on Temoc's pants, but late summer in Dresediel Lex was dry.

He's dangerous, Kopil had said, and he was right. But Temoc was also, if not a friend, at least a person she did not want to see stranded downtown at rush hour. "In a hurry?"

Temoc frowned up at the sky. "I hoped to return home and eat before the evening sacrifice."

"Good luck at this hour," she said. "The carriageway's backed up to Monicola, and Chakal Square makes surface streets even worse a gamble than usual."

"Then I will go straight to the Square."

"It's been a long day. How about dinner first? I know a place that's fast."

25

Behind the red counter, a thin man with a wispy mustache ran a knife twice along a honing steel, then carved off the outer layers of a revolving skewer of thin-sliced roast lamb. He set the lamb onto a plate, added chopped tomatoes, hummus, slaw, and pillowy pita bread, then dropped the plate onto the counter, called "Forty-eight!" and turned back to meat and knife and honing steel. Elayne lifted the plate and her own—stoneware so thick they outweighed the food they bore—and led Temoc to a booth near the back, away from the windows.

"I've never been to a place like this," Temoc said. A line curled from register to door. They'd snagged the second-to-last table, the others occupied by a mix of DL metropolitans: workers in denim and cotton, couples on their way to the theater, bankers eating with scavenger speed. A young suited man with a bandage on his chin swallowed wrong, choked, coughed into a napkin. "They should eat more slowly."

"People don't come here to eat slowly."

"I have seen coyotes dine with more grace—and coyotes must eat before something larger comes to take their food."

"Same situation here," Elayne said. "Or, similar. A scavenger eats fast because she's afraid of competition. These people eat fast because they're afraid someone like me will visit their desk while they're at dinner."

"So you are the monster they fear."

"Try the lamb. You make a sandwich with the pita, like this." She demonstrated. He tore the pita in half with grim focus that made her imagine a much younger Temoc at anatomy lessons as a novice. Strike here to break the breastbone.

Carve along this meridian. Puncture here to drain blood fast enough to induce euphoria, but not so fast as to let the sacrifice expire.

Still had a lot to learn about pita bread, though. He ripped one of his halves while filling. "The bread is too fragile."

"Be careful of the browned bits. They break." She finished her own sandwich, built her second. He ate slowly, and licked his lips. "You look pleased with yourself."

"The judge is on board, as is Chakal Square." He stood, took a handful of napkins from the service counter, and returned, wiping hummus off his hand. "We are doing well."

"I'm worried about the broadsheets."

"We have stopped some distributors," he said, "but the papers that remain are passed more swiftly through the camp. With luck they will not interfere with the deal."

"What if you went for the source?"

Temoc curled one fist inside his opposite hand, and watched her over his knuckles. "What have you learned?"

"I don't have time to investigate tonight," she said. "I need to draft this agreement. But I have a name for you, and an address. I'll give you both, if you listen to my advice."

"Go ahead."

A group of office workers stumbled out into the heat. As they left, a gaggle of schoolchildren entered. Hot wind whirled through the open door. "You have a good family. They love you. If this goes south, take care of them."

"Why this sudden concern?"

"You're part of a movement now. You don't know what that's like."

"I fought in the Wars."

"To defend your city, not to change the world. Causes have a gravity that's hard to resist. I never told you what I did in the Semioticist's Rebellion—why they took me off the field and sent me to the King in Red, before I met you."

He shook his head.

"I burned down a forest to kill one man. It didn't work. So

I followed him across a mountain and a desert into another jungle's heart. I killed five gods hunting him. Small gods, but still. I should have died myself. I almost did. He hurt my friends. Someone I loved tried to turn me from the hunt, and I didn't listen." A shawarma joint was the wrong place for this conversation. There was no right place for this conversation. "I want you to take care of your family, not end up bleeding out in a back alley."

"Okay."

She took a notebook and pen from her briefcase, and wrote the name she'd been given, and the address. Tore off the paper, and set it folded between their plates. "Take care, Temoc."

She stood, brought her empty plate to the dish bin, and walked past the children, out the door, into the wind.

26

When Temoc returned to Chakal Square, he felt a change. Beneath the peoples' excitement, beneath the hope, grew weeds of suspicion and fear.

A woman narrowed her eyes as he walked past. Two men in newsboy caps crossed their arms. An old man lit a cigarette and blew smoke. Maybe Temoc was paranoid, disturbed by the name in his breast pocket, by memories he had ignored for years.

Chel caught up with him by the food tents. There was a new furrow in her brow, a pinch around her mouth. She carried a rolled-up broadsheet like a baton.

"Sir," she said, and fell into step with him. Distracted, he did not correct her. "The commissioners presented the agreement. People support you. The Major's troops took it hard. But we're ready."

"And the judge approves of our deal."

"Good." She did not sound happy.

"What's wrong?" Unless he was making it up. Unless Elayne had him jumping at ghosts. He thought of Caleb, and Mina, and tried to think of anything else.

She passed him the broadsheet.

A picture of the commission meeting the King in Red, sketched yesterday morning. Caption: "Deal, or Treachery?" He scanned the article for key phrases. "Allowing Craftsmen to seize our land. Details unclear. What aren't we being told." He handed back the paper. "We've told everything."

"I know," she said. "The article's wrong. But some believe

this stuff and, well, I'm glad you came back for the sacrifice. Lots of angry people tonight."

"I will reassure them."

They came to see the sacrifice, the angry and confused side by side with those of unblemished faith. They listened to his tales of the Wandering Kings, of Old Quechal suffering in the desert, of the peoples' confusion before they found a home. "In the desert," he told them, "we fear, and we lose hope. But we must stand together. We must not be less than what is gold in us." And at the end, drawing from their faith, drawing from the gods, drawing from the woman splayed upon the altar who screamed rapture as he struck her breastbone, he wove them together—guided them through death and rebirth.

They followed, for now

That was enough.

He walked the camp, healed the sick, fed the hungry. He prayed, silently and aloud.

When that was done, he left, and caught a carriage north to the address Elayne had given him.

Temoc hadn't returned to Sansilva in years. The sacred precinct he knew was gone, and the people who prayed and sacrificed there gone as well, dead or retreated to waste away in suburbs. Only artifacts remained, pyramids and broad streets adulterated by modern monstrosities of crystal and steel.

He found the building he sought, a black tower beside the old New Moon Temple, studded with ghostlight logos and Kathic signs rather than High Quechal glyphs: Hyperion Sporting Goods, Osric & Croup Fine Clothiers, Scamander's Deli. Higher floors advertised more arcane Concerns: Alphan Securities, Grimwald Holdings, CBSE, banks and trading firms, scars carved in dead gods' flesh.

Before the cataclysm children and sorcerers called Liberation, incense and sandalwood had lingered on this air. Chant and praise echoed from sandstone walls. Priests prayed to present gods.

We are not gone, the gods whispered. But in forty years they had not overwhelmed him, never surged through his veins with tidal-wave force as they did in the heat of his youth. They did not like his bloodless worship.

So much for memories. There was work to do, tonight.

He reread the slip of paper. The address written there belonged to the penthouse on the tower's twenty-seventh floor.

Temoc opened his scars. He found a current in the air, a stream of coolant Craft. One of his parishioners, an architect, described skyscrapers as furnaces. People, lights, and machines radiated heat. If the cooling Craft failed, these buildings would stew their inhabitants alive. There was poetry in that, a fable he might have told to Caleb when the boy was younger: "Once a man lived in a glass box."

He seized the Craft, and soared.

Gravity bowed. City lights stretched to lines. Fresh wind whipped his face, stung tears from his eyes. Roads shrank to strips. Stars hung hungry overhead, so clear in Sansilva where Craftsmen let them shine. The penthouse balcony approached. Vines trailed over its edge: vines on the twenty-seventh floor, fed by water pumped up twenty-seven stories so a man could live in the sky and still grow grapes.

Temoc landed on the balcony's edge.

He stood on a hardwood floor in front of a glass-walled penthouse. Craftwork dulled the wind he should have felt at this height; the night was calm and cool and smelled of the sea.

The room behind the glass was all cream leathers and plush carpet. False flames flickered in a brick firepit. An old man sat in a leather chair beside the fire, reading, bare feet propped on the brick. His small toes curved inward; his big toes were long and thin and twitched as he read. His skin was dark, his hair long since silver. He still had his teeth, and they were white as his eyes were black.

The old man looked up from his book, saw Temoc, and smiled. He waved to the glass wall, which parted like a curtain brushed aside. Cold, scentless air puffed out. "Temoc!" the old man said. "Good to see you. Come in." He spoke High Quec-hal. His accent had not soured in the last forty years.

"Alaxic." Temoc wished he could smile as cheerfully as the old man. He entered the room, and the glass poured shut behind him. "What are you doing?"

"I'm hurt," the old man said. "Was this how we taught you to behave? Straight to business, even when meeting old friends? Let me fix you a drink." He raised his tumbler, empty but for a sheen of amber at the bottom.

"Tea," Temoc said.

"Of course." The penthouse living room blended seamlessly into its kitchen. The old man filled a kettle and set it on the stove to boil. "No liquor on duty?"

"Life is duty."

Alaxic drank the last of his tequila. "You look well. Active life agrees with you."

"More active than I'd like, the last few weeks."

"Well," he said. "That's to be expected. The family's healthy?"

"Yes."

"A son, you mentioned when we last met."

"A son."

"Only the one?"

"So far."

"The gods have been kind to you in other ways, I suppose. You barely look thirty-five."

"I feel older."

"But you don't feel sixty, either, and you should." Alaxic ex-amined his tile floor through the amber-tinted bottom of his glass, then rinsed the glass and set it on the rack to dry. "Do you ever wonder why you stay young while the rest of us age?"

"Not really," Temoc said. "The gods keep me in good health."

"Meaning they've abandoned the rest of us, or we've aban-doned them."

That was not a question, so he did not answer it.

"I was a priest before you were born," Alaxic said. "I made

a hundred sacrifices with these hands." He held them up, fingers crooked, knuckles swollen. "When war came I fought Craftsmen under the sea, in the sky, on the earth. My Couatl was killed beneath me and I fell and fought on. In an alley five blocks south and west of here I strangled a wizard with his own robe. Do you think I have given up on the gods?"

"Do you praise? Do you pray? Do you lead?"

He laughed, dryly. "Perhaps. Perhaps not. Who's to say, anymore."

"We are."

"Do you praise them, then, in your squat bloodless church, with your followers who pretend to die as you pretend to kill them?"

"That is not pretense," Temoc said. "It is faith."

"Faith," he repeated, and the kettle cried. "What tea would you like?"

"Mint, if you have it. It's late, and I must wake early tomorrow."

Alaxic found a box of tea, scooped some into a tea ball, dropped the tea ball into a mug, poured the water. "Honey?"

"No, thank you."

He slid the mug across the counter. Steam rose from within. Alaxic took a tequila bottle from a cabinet and poured himself a splash. "To the balcony?" He limped over; the glass parted, remained open for Temoc, and closed behind.

"You have learned the heathen Craft."

"We lost the Wars because we underestimated them. Only a fool makes the same mistake twice."

"They taught you?"

"They teach anyone. Their innermost secrets, can you imagine, are published in codices any idiot can check out of a library. Once you learn those, their schools will teach you more, for a fee. It is a different way. Alien to my mind. To see as Craftsmen do, there is much you must unlearn, or learn doubly. Sometimes I think that's why the Wars lasted so long. Not because either side showed mercy. The first necromancers had to learn, as I have, to think in two worlds at once: they were born in a world of reciprocity, of divine fervor, of sacrifice and glory, and they had to learn a new world of tools and of control. The second generation grew up knowing only that new world—and so their every act shored it up. They could best impose their will when they did not realize it was will. To them, conquest felt like sight."

Temoc dipped his finger in the tea, shed a drop on the hardwood floor, and spoke the blessing under his breath. The tea warmed him after the cold of Alaxic's house. "The Craft is no mere point of view. It works."

"It does, but the way it works depends on perspective." He raised his eyes. "I used to fear the stars, you know."

"We all did."

"Demons spin webs out there in the black. True demons, I mean, not the creatures Craftsmen summon—monsters who trap worlds in their nets. They visit us to eat, and the gods and Serpents stand against them. To us the Craftsmen, feeding on starlight, seem servants of those hungry mouths at the end of time. Yet Craftsmen see stars as sources of energy, nothing more. They hope to leave this globe one day and stride through the heavens, free at last. This difference springs, I think, from the fact that their first magus, Gerhardt, was an Easterner, Schwazwald-born, Iskari trained—both maritime mercantile cultures, star-revering. But any Craftsman will tell you his beliefs about stars are experimentally verified truths, not perspectives."

"And that is why you want to start a war."

Alaxic chuckled. "Not the most elegant segue."

"I did not come here to talk philosophy."

"Without clarity of principle, our discussion will have no meaning."

"You always were a priest at heart, Kal—one who thinks and talks. I was trained to be a soldier, too. Why have you spent the last month driving the Skittersill to rebel?"

"I'm trying to explain."

"Then speak plainly, and speak of deeds. Leave ideas for wiser men."

"No," he said. "Our first responsibility—as human beings—is to see the world around us. If I do not look in shadows, if I flinch from pain, I abdicate that responsibility. And to whom?" He swirled his glass toward the obsidian pyramid that towered over the skyline—Quechaltan, high temple to the old gods, forty years usurped. "The King in Red. Tan Batac. Your friend Elayne. The fine doctors of the Craft. Those people in Chakal Square have abdicated all their lives, because they were trained to do so. They've lived with a dull ache where their sense of right and wrong should be, stuck in someone else's bad joke. How many worked every day on the docks, or cut lawns or swept streets or added numbers in a cubicle farm, and drank or screwed that unease into oblivion? When I learned of Kopil's and Batac's scheme, I knew I could use it to open the people's eyes. So I spent my fortunes. I wrote broadsheets and had them printed. The King in Red lit the fire; I showed the Skittersill it was burning."

"Then why fight the compromise we've built?"

"A compromise made in secret. A deal to hum lullabies to men almost awake."

"We built a movement, and you want to destroy it."

"Not destroy. Save."

"The Chakal Square crowd has no weapons, no fortress. You're whipping these people toward a fight they will not win. If we make this deal, the movement builds. The momentum continues. The city changes for the better. If we fail, I see only pain ahead."

"Sometimes we need pain."

"Easy words to speak from the comfort of a penthouse."

"We each aid the cause in our own way. If this sours, do you think it will be hard for the Wardens to find me? You had little difficulty, and the Wardens can be quite persuasive."

Temoc set down his tea. He breathed deep. There was a fire within him, a fire he'd spent so much of the last few days trying to suppress, fed by fear, by frustrated hope, by intimations of mortality. "Alaxic."

The old man turned.

"Stop this. Now. Change the tone of these papers you write. Or stop delivering them. You are endangering my people. And if you continue, I will set myself against you. I will speak, and they will listen. They will know you for a man who wishes to use them for his own gain. You sit behind your desk and concoct revolutions with your pen. These people know me. They look to me. I lead them."

The wind blew from the north, hot and dry and angry as a dragon's breath.

Alaxic nodded. "I suppose you do." He finished his tequila. "Too late to change the morning edition, but I will halt its delivery. Tomorrow afternoon's issue will endorse your compromise."

"Just like that."

"Of course," he said. "You have no idea how long I've waited to hear you accept leadership. I thought your family would keep you away. But it is good to see you walk the true path. Do not waver."

They looked into each other's eyes for a long time, both searching, neither finding.

"I must leave," Temoc said.

"So soon?" Alaxic turned to set down his glass. "Why not stay? We could talk about old times."

But when he turned back, Temoc was already gone.

27

Mina woke to a breeze through the open window, and stretched under cotton sheets. The hand that held her shoulder was warm, and firm. "What?" More groan than a word, elongated, final consonant missing.

"It's me."

Temoc's voice. Well, that was good, at least.

"Hi." She rolled over and sank back toward sleep until he kissed her on the forehead. "Shouldn't you be at work?"

"Come with me today."

That opened her eyes, pulled her upright in bed. "What?" This time with the final "t" in place.

He was dressed, pressed and polished, with that slick wrinkle-resistant way of his, as if he'd sprung fully clothed from some god's forehead. Sharp, and beautiful. "It's a big day," he said. She knuckled sleep out of her eyes, and stifled a yawn with her fist.

"Big day for you to let me sleep."

He laughed, which annoyed her. "I've been pushing you away. I don't want to do that anymore."

"What time is it?"

"Four thirty."

"In the morning."

"Of course."

"How about you push me away until, say, six?"

"I thought you cared."

"I will kill you."

"Someday, maybe. Come on. I made coffee. And breakfast."

He held out his hand. She took it, and he lifted her from bed.

Half-blind, she groped for her robe and cinched it around her waist. "You sign it today."

"Today, we save the Skittersill. Concessions on both sides, but there will be peace. And we can build from here. The Chakal Square Movement will be the first step in something big—the people have a voice now." Such a smile, wide and bright as desert sunrise. She could see it even without her glasses. "What scholar wouldn't want to watch this?"

"When do we need to leave?"

"I have a sunrise service. Forty-five minutes, give or take."

"Coffee first," she said. "Shower. Then I decide whether you get to live."

He handed her a mug, its contents dark and hot and beautiful as any tragedy. She grabbed it from him, spilled some over her fingers, ignored the pain, and drank.

"History in the making."

She staggered out into the hall, into the bathroom, and shut the door in his face when he tried to follow.

"I'll wake Caleb."

"Breakfast better be good," she shouted through the door.

"It is!" he said, and maybe he said something else, but the water cut him off.

The shower improved her mood, or else the coffee. As usual when awake before sunrise she felt like she was moving through an underworld, one of the peripheral hells her mom used to tell stories about. Once she turned the lights on she could at least pretend it was a proper hour of the morning. Temoc didn't need indoor lights, eyes sensitive as a cat's, predawn glow filtered through curtained windows more than enough for him. Breakfast was good, as promised, though heavy: eggs, bacon, fried bread. "We'll need our strength," he said. Caleb sat blank-eyed at the table. Refused offered coffee, shoved food into his mouth. "This," Mina tried to explain, "is a big day for your father. For all of us."

"Why?"

Reasonable question, though answering it would require an entire academic conference. "The King in Red," she started, "has been arguing with people in our neighborhood. Most of the time he wins arguments. This time, we won. And he's coming to sign papers that say we won."

"It's more exciting than it sounds," Temoc said, and Caleb echoed his father's smile, even though Mina could see wheels turn behind the boy's eyes, evaluating, forming questions. Good instinct, though she worried sometimes that he was too quiet.

She wore khakis and a collared shirt, not wanting to seem overdressed for a mob or underdressed for the king. "Will we meet him, do you think?"

"Of course. He's come in person, the last two days."

History embodied—master of Liberation, who deposed the old gods and rebuilt Dresediel Lex from the ashes of the city he'd burned. He'd already entered the folklore of the tribes she studied, leader of a pantheon of devils and trickster-spirits. Perhaps worth the early wakeup call.

Hot wind blew down dry gray streets. Dawn never felt quite like this in the field. Wilderness softened the transition from night to day: flowers opened, birds sang, the desert came alive to drink the dew. None of that here—only stone and sleep. Temoc sat beside her, silent. Contemplating the day to come? Reviewing his forty years of struggle, or the weeks he'd made this journey to Chakal Square alone? She wanted to ask, but couldn't with Caleb between them. Or, she could, but she couldn't trust him to give an answer that wasn't cushioned by the effect it might have on the boy.

"How did we win?" Caleb asked after a few silent minutes of cab ride.

Mina blinked. "What do you mean?"

"The King in Red beat the gods. So how could we win?"

"We fought differently this time," Temoc said.

"It's easier to win some kinds of battles," Mina added, "when you don't fight."

"I don't understand."

"Back in the God Wars, the King in Red and the people of Dresediel Lex were enemies. So he fought as hard as he wanted, without worrying what people thought of him. He's very strong, so he won. This time, he thinks the people in the square are his friends. He can't just kill them, like he did last time."

"That's one reason," Temoc said.

"Is there another?"

She smelled the camp then: woodsmoke, burnt meat, and sweat. Clothes worn and worn again until they became part of skin. Mingled breath. She heard the voices.

Temoc halted the carriage, dismounted, lifted Caleb from the cab. Mina followed, taking Caleb's other hand. The sky was lighter, but the city still felt unreal. Familiar paving stones lay underfoot, and plaster walls stood to either side; they walked past shuttered strip malls and convenience stores. A bail bondsman billboard blared yellow against the sky. The street was empty of traffic, empty and haunted. Then they turned the corner, and before them spread a human sea broken by canvas tent islands and ship mast signs. Chakal Square took her breath.

There was no Craft here, no power like she saw daily at the collegium—only the sheer weight of assembled human souls.

How could so many have dared to come here? Set against the King in Red, their passion was futile. Defiance invited death, torture, prison.

And yet they had won.

She had never been quite so proud of her people as in this moment. Sentries with red armbands called out to Temoc. Cheers greeted him.

As the red-arms received Temoc, as the crowd gave way, she swelled with pride and a little fear. She read the papers, of course, and knew Temoc's role. But to know her husband worked with these people, to know he was their totem against disaster, to know the Skittersill turned to him as nomads turned to shamans and for the same reason—none of this prepared her to walk beside him into the mouth of that crowd. Lead us, the people said. Command us. Be our strength.

She'd slain demons with the man beside her, and argued with the ghosts of desert gods. They'd faced down Scorpionkind and returned alive from deserts where only shadows walked. She had thought she knew what it was to be an Eagle Knight, what life Temoc would have lived if the world had never turned. But this too, was a part of that, a part she did not know. He walked beside her, unashamed, draped in authority.

Her father's people had been cooks in the temples, her mother's people servants. This never mattered to her before. It did not matter now. But it came closer than ever before to mattering.

She wanted to hug him, to slug him, to kiss him, to remind him he was human. But she held Caleb's hand, and walked beside him nobly as she could, chin up, and did not flinch when Temoc said, "This is the other reason."

28

The sacrifice, at least, looked familiar. Mina waited behind the altar, flanked by Caleb and by the woman Chel, who Temoc had introduced as a friend—a strong figure, shorter, broader than Mina herself. Mina stood with hands clasped behind her back as the service progressed toward sacrifice. The people of Chakal Square clustered around the makeshift temple; the few hundred who could fit on the mats knelt there, and the rest, thousands she estimated, pressed near. Children rode on parents' shoulders. Men near the back perched on tiptoes. They muddled through the call and response, sludging the sharp consonants and glottal stops of High Quechal.

She knew this service, but it felt different in the open air under so many eyes. Temoc's muscles rippled as he raised his arms. Scars shone with faith.

Her husband. But he belonged to them as well.

"And nobody's thought to bring more mats in the last few weeks?" Mina asked Chel.

"No."

"It would let more people sit."

"But it would make those who sit less special."

She nodded. "So there's status in kneeling."

"Sure," Chel said, though there was a hitch in her voice, uncertainty.

"How's it decided, who kneels on the mats and who stands?"

"Some wait all night."

"Do the same people always kneel?"

"No."

"Why not? If it's better to kneel than to stand, wouldn't people with enough influence want to kneel all the time?"

"People who haven't knelt before should have a chance," Chel said as Temoc drew the knife.

"Who decided this?"

"Nobody," Chel said. "It's just the way things are. You ask a lot of questions."

"That's what I do," she said. "I study this sort of thing. I don't usually have a chance to see its infancy. This is stuff we speculate about in journals—that makes us scream at one another if we've been drinking."

"What stuff?"

"Construction of ritual. Ossification, or codification really, of performance. The extent to which it's intentional or accidental, or an intentional response to initial accident."

"We're not an experiment."

"That's not what I mean." The blade came down. "Just—it's interesting to think, given what you have here, what it might look like in a hundred years, or a thousand."

Mina turned to Chel, and turned away too, from the gods that were and were not her own, which rose from the altar to lick the sacrifice's blood. She shared Temoc's faith—but in Chakal Square, under the burnt orange sky, she felt alien. "Do you think we'll last that long?" Chel said.

And in that question she heard the fear Temoc buried under false certainty. "Why wouldn't you?"

As the gods feasted before them, she wanted to shake Chel and demand: tell me why you're scared. Tell me why I should leave here now, and take my son and husband home. But she did not.

"A hundred years is a long time. That's all."

"You'll be fine," Mina said, and hoped she was right.

29

Elayne landed behind the Wardens' barricade and released her opteran to buzz off into the morning.

Black-uniformed faceless figures marched around her, fortifying camp, feeding the feathered serpent mounts: a colony of large and surly ants. More Wardens had arrived overnight. A sandbag wall stood between Elayne and the crowd. Bad omen for the morning of a peace.

She sought the King in Red, and found Tan Batac waiting outside the Wardens' command tent, thumbs bowing out his suspenders, head bent, investigating his brown wingtips over the mound of his belly. His cheeks twitched, his mustache trembled. Always in motion, even when still—two thousand years before, Aristocritus used that phrase to describe the universe. He might have been prophecying Tan Batac.

"Is that it?" he said when he saw her, and pointed to the briefcase.

She lifted the case slowly and with effort.

"Looks heavy."

"It is. Only a few slips of paper, but enough Craft's woven through to make them ten times heavier than lead."

"I started insurance negotiations after we left yesterday. Hope I can lock in a good price before this drives us all out of business."

"The deal will bring you more business than it drives out."

"Of course." He nodded, licked his lips, nodded again.

"I wanted to thank you," she said.

"For what?"

"Your sacrifice. If you had not compromised yesterday, I doubt we would have reached an agreement so soon, if ever."

"Sacrifice," he said, and "yes," and: "You're welcome. And thank you, too. Without you. Well. None of this might have happened."

He extended his hand, and she shook it. His grip was strong and soft, his palm cold. His eyes remained unsure.

The King in Red emerged from the command tent, robed in crimson and clinging shadows. "Good morning," he said. "Let's get this done."

Batac hid his fragile edges when Kopil appeared. "Let's."

Zoh led the Wardens, with Chihuac by his side, all clad in dress blacks: high-collared jackets and creased trousers and patent leather shoes. The King in Red cackled when Elayne noted the uniforms. "This is an affair of state," he said. "After a fashion. We must show respect. Besides, a little awe never hurt."

"No," Elayne agreed. "But." Quietly, as they approached the barricade. "Promise me something."

"What?"

"No more sky speeches. And if I ask you to stop doing anything while we're in the square, especially anything Craft-related, listen."

"Elayne. I know how to control my own people."

"These aren't your people at the moment, and this is a dangerous time."

"Whatever happened," he said, "to the woman who razed the Askoshan Necropolis? I miss her."

Elayne let one corner of her mouth creep upward. "She wouldn't have survived as long as I have. She didn't, in fact."

Kopil raised his hand. A length of barricade erupted, sandbags reshaping themselves into an arch. Zoh led the way through, and Elayne, Tan Batac, the King in Red, and their escort entered Chakal Square for the last time. The barricade closed behind them.

Elayne expected the crowd, the red-arms' array. She wasn't ready for the suppressed anger of Chakal Square, for the tension like a long-held breath. She hoped Temoc had stopped the broadsheets. So large a mob, confused and mad, was a solution awaiting a seed to crystallize it into action.

A misplaced word would be enough. A shove, a laugh. A shift in the hot dead wind. Sand blown in the wrong woman's eye. The path they walked to the tent where Temoc waited might seem wide, but was in fact narrow as a blade.

Temoc, she saw as they drew near, had brought his family.

She almost wrecked it all in that moment: almost grew a hundred feet tall and threw him across the square and shouted, What were you thinking?

But she controlled herself. Caleb and Mina seemed like messengers from a cleaner, more composed world, somewhere beyond the stars. Elayne met Mina's gaze, offering as much reassurance as she could without breaking character. For the boy, Caleb, she risked more: she smiled at him, and he smiled back.

The King in Red stepped forth, and Temoc advanced to meet him. "We have drawn up the deal," Kopil said, with the barest touch of Craft woven through his voice so the words would carry. "Are your people ready?"

He offered the amplification Craft to Temoc: a nice gesture, to make his first act surrender. "We are," Temoc said.

Elayne's cue. "This briefcase contains our deal." Likewise amplified. Blood and hells, but she was ready to stop playing for the cheap seats. If she wanted to act out before judge and jury, she'd have gone into another branch of Craft.

Nothing for it. Sometimes even a necromancer had to appear in public. At least there were fewer torches and pitchforks than usual, so far.

"Thank you," Temoc said.

Before Elayne entered the tent for what she hoped would be the last time, she glanced back to Mina—but she did not meet the other woman's eyes again before she passed into shadow.

Entering the meeting tent felt like slipping into a limpid pool after a long hike. They all felt it: even the Major relaxed, free of the Square's anxiety. Bel laughed at something Kapania said, and Hal poured them all water. The King in Red sagged, and for a moment he resembled a kindly, ancient uncle who just happened to be a skeleton crowned with red gold. Tan Batac was the only one who looked nervous, and one for ten wasn't a bad ratio.

Temoc entered the tent last. Elayne caught him before he could take his seat. "What do you think you're doing, bringing them here?"

"This is a historic moment."

"Historic and dangerous."

"I did not expect the crowd to be so tense. We are on the verge of victory."

"To them, victory and defeat look a lot alike."

"Then let us show them the difference," he said.

She released him, and they sat. Silence fell. With her thumb Elayne rolled the briefcase tumblers to her combination, opened the latches, rolled the tumblers random again, and lifted the lid. Bill Kemal tensed as if he expected something to explode, but the case was empty save for a manila folder, a dip pen, and a shallow silver bowl. She removed folder, bowl, and pen, set them on the table, and closed the case. "Here we are."

She opened the folder and slid the document into the center of the table. Five pages, with a signature on the fifth.

"So small," Kapania said. "I thought contracts like this ran for hundreds of pages."

"Hundreds," Elayne confirmed, "or thousands. This is a special case. We've done most of the work. These papers alter the original pursuant to your requirements, most substantially the preconditions of fee simple sale and the insurance and protection mandate. I'd like to walk through the terms of the agreement one by one. Please pay attention. I'll pause for questions after every subsection. I appreciate your holding questions for a pause, since there's a good chance your issues may be addressed in the text." Nods around the table. "Section one."

Fewer questions than she expected, and no outbursts. No

major changes—a few words here or there, easy emendations Tan Batac and the King in Red let slide. Before her watch ticked quarter past ten, she turned the final page and said, "Are we agreed?"

The King in Red nodded.

Tan Batac said, "Yes."

"We are," said Temoc.

"Sounds good," said Bill Kemal, and Kapania, "Sure."

"Yes," said Bel after a long, slow nod.

"Acceptable," said the Major in a steel-string twang.

Xatoc said, "Yeah."

And Hal Techita said, "Sounds good."

And that was that.

Almost.

She drew her knife from the glyph above her heart, savored that old shiver of corruption and universal wrong. They'd been through a lot together, this blade and her. She kept it subtle; only gathered a little light into the edge. The oculus dimmed to pale gold. "Some of you," she said, "may find this next part unpleasant, but it's necessary. You may use your own blade, but unless you do this sort of thing often best let me do the honors." With a stroke of her finger, she honed the moon-light curve.

They all let her make the cuts, even Temoc. She needed only a drop, in most cases so fine a cut the victim felt no pain until Elayne was done. Temoc did not flinch. Tan Batac bit his lip as the blade descended; she did not warn him this was a bad idea if one expected jaw-clenching pain. She added her own blood, to lend the firm's seal to the contract. When the bowl reached the King in Red, the others caught their breath. Kopil held out one hand, palm raised. The sparks of his eyes blazed, and wind howled from a distant, blasted plane. The universe blinked, and when light returned a tiny sphere of ruby liquid hovered over his outstretched hand. He turned his hand sideways, and the blood fell into the silver bowl with a plop. No one asked him for an explanation, and he offered none—only leaned back and sipped coffee.

With water added, and fixative, the blood became tolerable ink. Each party signed in turn. A wheel turned beneath the onionskin surface of reality, giant weights fell into place, and, as Tan Batac signed, the work was done. A long-drawn note on the deepest edge of Elayne's hearing shifted pitch.

This was the part of the job she loved: the world changed, and she changed it. They changed it, together—these people she dragged to the table and guided through darkness.

She clapped. Even Tan Batac joined in her applause.

"Good work, everyone," she said, and returned the contract to her briefcase. They looked around, stunned by victory achieved in spite of themselves.

Then they rose, and as one left the tent.

30

Elayne emerged into the silence of the crowd. The contract pulsed in her briefcase, drawing power from the gathered masses, settling into shape. The sun hovered above the RKC building to the east, a bright orange fire in a bright orange sky whipped by demon wind. People called questions, jawed and joked. Someone even sang. But the voices masked emptiness. Eyes turned toward her, and she read a question in them.

What now?

By the tent flap, clutching Caleb, Mina faked academic detachment, but her concern showed through. Elayne wished she hadn't noticed. She felt as if by noticing she betrayed the other woman.

Temoc's scars blazed, and he climbed into empty air as if ascending an invisible staircase: taller now than the King in Red, his boots above the rolling crowd. Sparrows settled onto the RKC building's rooftop. Wardens marched behind their barricade. Temoc cleared his throat.

"It is done." At first Elayne feared he might stop after those three words. But Temoc knew how to milk a pause. "The deal is signed. People of the Skittersill. My people. We have won."

A dam broke and noise burst forth. Women shouted, men yelled, children screamed. All through Chakal Square the Skittersill's people cheered. Protest signs twirled in whirlpools of dance. The King in Red did not seem to mind the noise. Neither did Tan Batac: he waved into the crowd, his eyes squinted as if searching for something.

Elayne heard joy in the sound, no doubt, but more energy

than joy, a month of harbored rage and fear allowed its first release.

Temoc let the cheer build, but long before it might have reached crescendo he held out his hands, palms down. The noise receded. He lowered his hands further, and the silence returned, deeper even than before. Pressure built.

Tan Batac did not seem to notice the change; he kept smiling and waving, even as the applause died.

Temoc opened his mouth.

Chakal Square was so quiet Elayne could hear her own heartbeat.

Chakal Square was so quiet everyone heard the shot.

A high, sharp crack—Elayne leapt at Temoc, grabbed him by one ankle and pulled, wrapping them both in a diamond-hard shield. Temoc fell to one knee on his platform of air, fought to stand. No bullet struck Elayne's shield, no arrow or Craftwork missile or fléchette. She glanced around, confused: the space swarmed with Wardens, black and silver blurs flocking to the King in Red. Futile. Any weapon meant for him would not be stopped by killing a few Wardens first. They should be guarding—

Oh, gods.

She would remember, later, that when the shot came she'd seen Tan Batac wheel around, hand still raised. Signs she should have noticed: body stiff, face glazed with adrenaline and shock. But she'd dived for Temoc instead.

Tan Batac fell. A red stain spread across his white shirt between his thin suspenders. He flapped at the stain as if to daub the wetness up. His lips framed words she could not hear. Blood gushed from his wound in rhythm, and his hands left red prints on his jacket.

His eyes focused on her.

Noise, everywhere. Rush of her own heartbeat, her own breath. Wardens shouted spells she remembered from decades past, handed down to them by veterans of her Wars, Wars which had never ended and, never ending, never changed.

"Have visual."

"Man down."

"Single shot."

"—Perimeter—"

"—Need cover—"

"Get down get down get down."

"Medic."

"I see him I know I see him."

"Medic!"

"Engaging."

And beneath those spells she heard other cries, the crowd understanding—or not—

"—Who—"

"They can't—"

"Temoc's down!"

Another shot. She raised a second shield.

This time no one fell.

Temoc landed beside her; shadow and green flame swallowed his skin, the gods' aspect summoned to protect him. He glanced from Tan Batac to his family, to Mina covering Caleb with her body, to Chel covering Mina, to the Wardens. Elayne knelt by Batac, pulled a handkerchief from her jacket and wadded it against the wound. The yellow sky reflected in his eyes. She woke glyphs on her hands, wrists, temples—different glyphs than those she used for work, older, cruder, made with makeshift tools in time of war. Darkness swallowed her, an instant's utter vacancy as if some high all-sustaining God had blinked (as, if such a Being existed, she must have done mere seconds before). Elayne pulled poison sunlight down—enough, she hoped, and closed her eyes: Tan Batac's soul was a torn sheet whipped by hurricane winds, but he could bear, for a while, the touch of her Craft. Longer than he'd last without. The cost of magic was ever the calculus of healing.

Tan Batac was an engineering project broken.

Subconscious systems tracked unfolding chaos. Situational

awareness: once drilled in you never forgot, time and therapy be damned. The King in Red drew power to him. "Find the assassin. Bring him to me." Assumptions, always. Might be a her. Might be many enemies. The Wardens aren't police here, now—they're a force in hostile territory. Don't send them in without a clear mission.

"No," she shouted, to convey all this at once, but Batac slipped beneath her, damn hopeless, couldn't even lie still. She turned back to him, cursing. Not that she could have stopped the King in Red, not that Kopil would have heard her over his own anger's roar.

Zoh charged into the crowd. The other Wardens circled around Elayne, Batac, Kopil. The red-arms did not give way fast enough and Zoh struck two men with wrecking-ball force. He swam against a human current. The crowd responded: some fell, but others pressed against Zoh, clawing, biting. Zoh raised his arms to ward off blows: "Out of my way!" With muscles reinforced by Craft he hurled protesters aside, carving a path step by step through thrashing bodies, searching for the shooter he'd seen, might have seen, hoped he'd seen.

"Cop!" "—fucking—" "What the hells are you—" "Temoc!" "—The hells you—" "—broke my godsdamn *arm*—"

Focus. Gut wound. Blood flowing. Find the slug, easy, but was he safe to move? Entry wound below the rib cage but slanted to one side, and back there he had kidneys to worry about, and liver and gall bladder. This would all be easier if he was dead. At least she could stop the bleeding—or contain it, by convincing his blood it ran through unperforated vessels.

Batac spoke. Skin blanched white, lips trembling, he found breath to whisper. "Not at all."

"Not at all what," she asked, faking calm. "Not at all what, Tan?"

His too-pink tongue flicked out, wet his lips, withdrew.

Rocks arced through the air at Zoh. Pebbles first, then larger stones thrown faster. Most bounced off—a fist-sized chunk of masonry hit the Warden's head, but his mask saved him. Made him angry, though—he shoved harder. "Make way" he bellowed with enhanced voice, but there was no room for the people to fall back, no way for them to make.

A chill spread across her skin. The King in Red held fire in his hand, and contemplated the crowd near Zoh. "No!" she cried, and he heard.

"Justice must be served."

"You want to help? Help me. If you throw Craft into this crowd, people will die."

"They will bow to us."

"You'll kill them!"

Temoc shouted: "Be calm. Everyone be calm." But even he could not drown out the roar, or stem the tide of bodies that surged against the red-arms. The King in Red snarled, but at least he let the fire die. "Can we move him?"

"If we're careful. I have the wound contained."

"—At all. Not at all."

They could recover. This was one nail in their coffin, just one, with many pry bars to hand. If they reached safety they could cool this down. Batac was stable, would be stable, had to be. He would survive.

The second nail sounded like a mother, crying.

Fear seized her, but that wasn't Mina's voice: she had drawn back toward the tent, behind Chel. No, the cry came from the crowd, near Zoh.

The King in Red swore in High Quechal, which she hadn't heard him speak since the Wars. His eyes blinked off, then on again.

"What is it?"

The mother screamed.

"Zoh. He—"

She stood, saw for herself the ripple spreading from Zoh, the space where there'd been no space before: a widening circle around the Warden and a kneeling woman. She held a child of maybe six, younger than Caleb. The child's eyes stared unblinking at the sun. Blood poured from his scalp. On the flagstones beside them lay a rock, stained red.

Later Zoh would claim he hadn't thrown the rock on purpose. Caught it by reflex, rather, and tossed it into the air with more strength than he should have used, a Warden's throw, Craftwork-enhanced, and what goes up most of the time comes down. Others said he'd aimed for one of the rock-throwers, to break a collarbone or shatter a rib, but someone jostled him and the stone went wild and by dumb bad luck the kid was in the way.

"Killer," was the word the crowd spoke as the mother wailed. Zoh turned in a slow circle, and maybe he could have saved the peace even then with the superhuman compassion the Diamond Sage of Dhistra showed in tales of his billion incarnations, maybe he could have gone to the mother and knelt and removed his mask and let himself be torn apart. But Zoh was no saint. Masked, he did not even seem a man. He stepped back, arms raised, and if he said "I'm sorry" it was lost in the crowd's roar.

"Temoc!" Elayne shouted, turned, searching—the priest stood transfixed beyond the Wardens' circle, a sculpture of black and jade. "Talk to them."

But the crowd closed in, and the red-arms didn't stop them. The vanguard of the charge was a big man with jowls and a thicket beard: he reached the Wardens and fell, almost too fast for Elayne to see the silver fist that struck him. Others jumped over their fallen comrade's body, only to bounce off a shield of solid air, while a second shield enclosed Zoh. Kopil's Craft cut off the sound of screams. Bodies wadded against the shield, cheeks and hands and stomachs flattened by its curve. Lightning cracked where they touched. Kopil's crown was a dark halo.

The King in Red drew his hands apart and the shield grew, sweeping protesters aside without apparent effort. His teeth ground together. Wardens, braced to resist the riot, stumbled into suddenly empty space. Temoc pressed to the front of the crowd, scars radiant. "Get back," he shouted to his people, and some obeyed, but only some, and others rushed to fill their place.

With her glyphs awake and power chilling her blood, Elayne wanted to fight, to shatter the crowd, to open their road to safety. She was a spring, and did not want to hold herself compressed. The King in Red, too, was ready to fight—weapons formed around him, trembling on hair trigger.

"Give us that man." Temoc pointed to Zoh. "The killer."

Kopil laughed, the same laugh that almost brought the mob down upon them two days ago. Only two days. Then again, only minutes before, they had been about to finish this in pride and peace.

"No," Kopil said. "He will be punished. But I will not give him to your mob. Find the assassin among you first."

"Give him to me and we can stop this," Temoc shouted through the screams.

"Do it," Elayne said. "I'll stay with Zoh."

Kopil shook his head. "Unacceptable. We all leave together."

"I need a concession. Something to calm them down," Temoc said.

"I won't let my people die at the hands of yours."

"Listen to him, dammit," Elayne said.

"I have. For days. And here we are."

"This is a mistake."

"Not mine," Kopil replied.

A drum beat inside Elayne's chest. Shadows crossed the face of the sun. The crowd's screams changed from rage to terror. Elayne looked up. Through the shield's blue arc she saw two feathered serpents dive. With twenty feet to spare, their wings unfurled, braking, and cast scalloped shadows upon the square. Talons gripped the shields' slick surface, and with mighty wing-beats the Couatl rose, bearing the Wardens, Elayne, the King in Red, and Tan Batac north toward the Bloodletter's Street camp. Below, faces merged into a carpet of rage—unbroken save for a small space beside the meeting tent where Elayne saw, in receding miniature, Mina and Caleb, and Temoc fighting toward them.

"Don't let this happen," she shouted, weaving Craft to carry her words to his ears. "Don't."

If he answered, she could not hear.

"Not at all," said Tan Batac, "what I expected."

31

The Couatl landed behind the Wardens' sandbag rampart. The King in Red released the shield, and they settled onto pavement. To the south, the crowd's voices roared.

"We have to go back," Elayne said. "Before this gets worse."

"We must do nothing of the sort," Kopil said. "Bullets. Honestly. Who still uses those?"

"Someone who thinks their target isn't warded."

"So Batac was not chosen at random."

"He was the most vulnerable," she said, and bent again to her patient.

The second Couatl set Zoh down nearby. He staggered when the shield released him, and wheeled with arms raised as if expecting an attack. Even through the silver mask, Elayne could see his fear.

A Warden cried "Medic," and two more wheeled a stretcher toward her; Captain Chimalli followed close behind. "What happened?"

"Someone shot him." The medics lifted Tan Batac onto the stretcher. Elayne helped. She felt very cold. "Zoh tried to find who. It turned ugly. A kid's dead."

"Did he find the weapon?"

"I don't think so. I didn't see."

Chimalli frowned. "That's bad."

"You are a model of perspicacity," Kopil said.

Elayne grabbed a medic's arm. "Get Batac to a hospital. He lost a lot of blood, and I took his soul to keep him from losing more." They nodded, yes ma'ams all around, and ran off, wheeling the stretcher.

Batac's eyes fluttered open as he passed, rolled, fixed on Elayne. He smiled. Smiled. A baby's expression, soft with idiocy. She remembered the dead child in his mother's arms, white flecks of bone against wet blood and black hair. She wanted to strangle Tan Batac for his smile, wanted to tear her Craft from him and let him die.

"Man the wall! Companies Forty-seven and Forty-eight, get up there! Move!" Wardens ran for the barricade. Weapons lockers opened and Wardens passed out stun nets and lightning rods Elayne hoped they knew how to refrain from using. Some of the weapons she did not recognize, which she hoped was a good sign. Crowd control. Nonlethal. In theory.

The medics rolled Tan Batac to a hospital wagon. She noticed a red handprint on one medic's arm, and realized it was hers. Blood covered her hands, and soaked her shirt and jacket cuffs. Sticky, thickening, still warm. She pulled its heat into her. Blood froze into red crystals. She flexed her fingers, and the crystals fell like crimson snow.

"We have a wounded man," Chimalli said. "But no evidence, and with that crowd out there, we won't get any. They'll cover the assassin's tracks. No evidence, no killer. We're in for a bad few days."

A flash from atop the barricade, the colors of the world inverted.

"Or more," he said, and ran to meet the assault. Elayne followed.

The crowd near Temoc convulsed with rage. Ten thousand wills condensed to one around that mother's scream. Couatl bore the King in Red and the murdering Warden north and east to the Bloodletter's Street barricade, and the crowd followed them, united by anger. The protesters near Bloodletter's could not know, yet, about the dead child, about Tan Batac, about the murders. Still they washed against the barricade, first waves of a rising tide.

Temoc flailed among them. Grabbed a passing red-arm. "Find me the one who shot Tan Batac."

The red-arm pulled back at first, not realizing who spoke. Temoc turned the man to face him. The red-arm's eyes reflected the flames of Temoc's face.

"Hear me."

He did not mean to raise his voice, but the words came out as a roar. The red-arm flinched, cowered. Good enough.

"Go into the crowd. Find the one who shot Tan Batac. Now." The man obeyed.

They had to catch the killer, and hope Batac survived. Craftsmen would tend him, which was more than Temoc could say for the child. Gods. The mother. He should have sent that red-arm to shelter her. And—

Mina.

All the world's a mess, and we within it smears of flashing teeth and narrowed eye and clutching hand, cloth and spit and hair. Near the tent, he saw a flash of his wife's face, Caleb in her arms, a blink and then gone. He cried her name.

With power upon him, he moved through the people of Chakal Square. Most gave way. Those that did not, he forced: grabbed a man around the waist, picked him up, and set him down elsewhere, swept confused protesters aside with one arm. Shouts and curses trailed him, cut off as people realized who it was they cursed.

When he reached Mina, he hugged her, crushing Caleb between them. The boy squirmed, grabbed his mother around her waist. Temoc smelled his son's hair, his wife's skin, beneath the rising stink of panic. "You're okay." Perfect, not even bruised. He wanted to pull them closer, pull them inside so they would never be apart again.

He heard a metal twang, a gravelly voice: the Major. "Vultures! They lie and kill and run, afraid to stand for their crimes!"

He ignored everything but her, but him.

"We're fine," Mina said in his ear.

"We're okay, Dad."

"It's falling apart. I'm sorry. I'm so sorry." Cheers ripped through the air. Were they cheering the Major? Themselves? "We have to get you out of here."

"Can you stop this?"

"I don't know," he said. Chel stood nearby, directing a band of red-arms to attend the fallen. "Keep them in the tent. Protect them."

"I will."

"I should stay."

Mina grabbed his arms. He felt her fingernails through his shirt. "We'll be fine." She had to shout for him to hear her, even so close that he could smell her shampoo. A few hours ago, he'd made eggs for breakfast. So few, so long. He'd thought himself clever: the broadsheets out of the picture, the end in sight. You'll see history, he'd said. He hadn't lied. But not all history was pleasant in the making.

The tide grew stronger. People streamed toward the barricade. The Major's voice rolled on, invoking rage spackled over by millennia of civilization. Temoc could not hear the words. Demon wind smelted them to war cry, prayer call. "This isn't what I wanted." Temoc's arms were steel bars, himself a statue, unmoved by the crowd.

Moved, though, by her hand on his chest, pushing him back into the current. He never could resist her. "These people need you."

Mountains fell with less reluctance. Caleb clutched her, and reached for him. So much Temoc wanted his face to show, such pressure building in his chest, in his stomach. But he wore the armor of faith, and he could not show his son weakness. This was what a man did, when it had to be done. Stood against a mob. Led his people. Gave himself to the greater good.

Left his family.

Temoc turned away. He wanted to throw up. He forced himself downstream. Glanced back, once, allowed himself that, saw Mina carry Caleb into the tent, saw Chel and her squad stand guard. A last meeting of eyes. Her lips moved. He wished he could hear what she said.

He waded west through the human flood toward the mother of the fallen boy. Red-arms followed him, confused. He found a clearing: people stood around the woman and her child's body, insulating them from the riot. Kapania and Bill knelt beside her, not speaking. They had a child, too. A daughter. Far away, he hoped.

Bill's eyes widened when he saw Temoc. "What's happening? I ran here right off."

Like he should have. "The Major is leading a charge," Temoc said. "These red-arms will help you."

"What should we do?"

"Take care of her. I'll stop this."

"How?"

"I'll think of something."

Not that there was time to think. Only time to force through the crowd, to call upon reserves of faith to lend him majesty. Robed in shadows he advanced, and this time there was no need to move people out of his way. They bowed to let him pass, shouted his name. Their awe augmented his power: it was blasphemy to offer such a gift to any but the gods, and blasphemy to accept, but he would atone later. He needed the might they offered. He strode through them as in times past he'd strode through the ranks of his army.

Flashes of light from the Bloodletter's Street barricade, and screams. Stun nets—wire webs threaded with lightning which tangled those they caught, rendering them an obstacle to their fellows in a charge. Temoc saw no lethal weapons yet; no Couatl descended to strike. Perhaps they would not. Couatl were vulnerable near the ground. The Wardens would not risk their aerial trumps so early, not when they might serve other uses later: reconnaissance, or bombing.

Old wartime instincts returned so readily. As if he had spent four decades fighting this battle in his head unawares, and now the plans bubbled up like tar pit gas.

He found the Major near the barricade. Armored minions surrounded him, and flocks of angry people watched and listened and obeyed. "Press Bloodletter's Street, but send parties east and west down Crow and Coyote. We're boxed in to the north, but if we flank them they'll retreat. Go!" With an imperious gesture as if parting an ocean.

They went. Gods help them.

Temoc approached. Eyes widened. Men lowered sharpened sticks and lengths of pipe. Some fell to their knees.

"Temoc," said the Major. "Welcome."

"You might not think so when I say what I have come to say."

"Peace has failed."

"It will, if you cut off the Wardens' retreat. They're not trying to hurt our people yet. They will lose restraint if you make them desperate."

"We want justice."

"You want to kill that Warden."

"Don't you?"

"I want to stop this riot before it becomes a war."

"So we let them murder a child and get away with it."

"He will be punished."

"No." So much anger in that last word. "The Wardens will claim it was a mistake. Their man responded on instinct. A fine, perhaps a brief prison sentence. If one of our people did the same to them, they'd be gutted in Sansilva at high noon." Playing to the crowd. This was a performance, not an argument.

"Hold your assault. I will go to the barricade. I will bring us the Warden."

"Talk costs time. They'll cut us off and kill the revolution before it begins."

"Will you throw us into war without even trying for peace?"

The Major raised one gauntleted hand, revealed a wrist-watch strapped between his makeshift steel plates. "Half an hour. Convince them if you can."

A chance. Not much, but still.

"Half an hour," he said, and marched toward the barricade.

32

"It's been too long since my last siege," said the King in Red atop the rampart. Elayne stood beside him, looking out and down.

"This isn't a siege."

The skeleton laughed. "What would you call it, then?"

Protesters climbed the sandbag wall, boosting one another, pressing toward the heights. A bulky bearded man dragged himself up with sheer muscle, two feet from the top, one. As his hand cleared the rampart, a Warden grabbed him and pushed. The man fell, screaming. Elayne cushioned his fall with Craft.

Wardens dropped another stun net over the side, and where silver threads struck climbers the climbers fell. Cries rose from those whose jaws the current did not clench.

"A day at the beach," she said.

"Unfortunate metaphor. The ocean wears beaches down."

"We don't have infinite nets."

"A small oversight, easily corrected. At any rate, we don't need them. I could join the battle. Or you could."

"I won't. And as your counsel, I urge you not to, either."

"You're no fun."

"First, this isn't fun. And second, you don't pay me for fun."

"I suppose I do pay you."

"Trust me," she said. "When this is done, you won't have to wonder."

"They attacked us."

"You don't get a free pass on atrocities just because they hit first."

"We have the deal."

"People are dead, and more are dying. Those nets aren't toys. We have to stop this before it gets worse."

"If they send someone to talk, then I will talk. What's wrong with enjoying a little skirmish in the meantime?"

She pointed to a burst of green light approaching through the sea of limbs and angry faces. "There's your someone. Vacation's over."

He sighed. "Very well."

Temoc crossed Crow toward Bloodletter's Street and the Wardens' wall. A knot of red-arms near the barricade urged the attackers on. Their leader kept shouting even after her fellow red-arms noticed Temoc and fell silent. She did not stop until Temoc tapped her on the shoulder.

"We are changing plans," he said. I must speak, he prayed, and the gods answered, yes. "Fall back," he cried, and his voice echoed. "I will speak with the King in Red."

Stillness rippled out from Temoc. Those among the crowd that could, turned to watch him. Fallen protesters writhed on the pavement, quivering as stun nets sparked.

Kopil spoke. "What do you want?"

"To stop the fighting."

"Your people attacked us. We defended ourselves."

"Murdering a child is an interesting form of self-defense."

Their eyes met across space. They had fought, in the God Wars: wrestled in midair above the obsidian pyramid at 667 Sansilva while gods writhed broken below.

Elayne liked most parts of a Craftswoman's life—liked carving dead things up and waking them, liked manipulating the hidden forces of the world. She did not like waiting beside a client, hoping he would not say something stupid. She knew the King in Red, and knowing him knew he was pondering responses that ranged from sarcastic (But you have so many, surely you can't miss one!) to professionally inhuman (These things happen.). Unfortunately she could not call for a recess in this court.

"I am sorry," he said, and she let out a breath she hadn't realized she held.

"Sorry is not enough. We want justice. We want the murderer."

"He will stand trial."

"Will he stand masked?"

"Masked as a Warden," Kopil said. "He did what he did—if he did anything at all, a claim of which we have no proof—in uniform. His family deserves protection."

"Who will hold him until the trial?"

"We will," the King in Red replied, too fast.

She hoped Temoc would accept that. Hoped he would realize how little ground the King in Red could give. Temoc had to see that, standing atop a barricade manned by Wardens, with Wardens at their back and a mob in front, they could not offer a Warden up as sacrifice. If they had time to convince the captain, then maybe, but there was no time. Temoc was barely holding the battle in check.

"Not enough," Temoc said.

How could it be enough? Temoc could read a crowd. These people wanted blood, and failing that, victory. Blood he could not, would not, give them. As for victory, how might they accept something so intangible as a guarantee the right Warden would be punished?

I need more than that. He glanced from the King in Red, imperious atop the ramparts, to Elayne—could not implore them without losing the crowd, but he wished he could, so much his bones ached.

"How do we know the right Warden will stand trial? He hides behind a mask. Strip the mask and give him to us. We will hold him safely while you prepare the trial."

The skeleton laughed. "You expect me to surrender one of

my people? We have seen the dangers of Chakal Square. Tan Batac would attest to them, if he were conscious."

Unconscious, not dead. One point in their favor, at least.

"One madman's actions do not taint us all. I say your Warden will be safe."

"Let me go with him," Elayne said under her breath. "This will work."

"No." The King in Red could talk without moving his jaw.

"You're trying to protect me."

"I will not give them a bargaining chip."

"You just don't want to lose."

"What happens when you sleep? When Temoc or some gutter witch defeats your wards and you and Zoh wake up to find yourself splayed on an altar?"

"You are being irrational."

"We cannot trust you," Kopil said, loud enough for all to hear.

Godsdamn it to all hells. So close. The refusal with a pause was even worse than one without. The pause showed reflection, consideration, rejection. "Show him to us at least. Give us his face, his name, so we will know him when he stands trial."

"And expose his family."

"You can protect his family. Let the man choose, at least. Let him refuse us."

"That's it," she said. "He can't back down more. Ask Zoh."

"Not without a concession."

"Ask for one."

"He can't concede anything."

"He has control for the moment. Don't waste it."

"I will not show you his face without his permission," Kopil said. "But. Before I ask him—if he agrees, you must allow Wardens to enter the Square. They will search for Tan Batac's assailant. Interview those who saw the crime. Wring the truth from them."

The red-arms shifted, wary. What would the Major say? Where was the Major, for that matter? Temoc should have dragged him along for support. "Show us the man," he said. "Name him. And I will help your Wardens search."

"I'll get Zoh," Elayne said. "Keep talking. If you disappear, Temoc loses his anchor on the crowd."

Kopil nodded. As Elayne climbed down the sandbags he played for time, describing the Wardens' investigation, giving Temoc a target.

Wardens turned to her, and she ignored them. The Wardens relied on masks to present a unified front, to stop corruption and the dangers that followed officers home. Exposure would end Zoh's career. The crowd's cries seemed louder as Elayne left the wall: the narrow street channeling the mob.

She found Zoh in the rear of the camp, near the Couatls' nest. The big man paced, head down. Three steps right, parade-sharp turn, three steps left, and back again.

"Lieutenant," she said, and he stopped, saluted. She did not salute back. "The crowd wants your head."

"And the king will give it to them."

"He's talked them down."

"To what?"

"Your face."

"I don't understand."

"If we unmask you, they'll let us send a team to learn who shot Batac."

"I was trying to find out. They stopped me."

He wanted reassurance. She offered none.

"I guess this is one of those things," he said, and stopped without saying what kind of thing he guessed it was. "You're here to tell me, do it or pack."

"I'm here to ask. You know the costs. This could help a lot of people."

"I guess," he said, and paused, head cocked to one side.

She waited for him to speak again, but he did not. Nor, she realized, did anyone else. The background hum of the Wardens' chatter fell silent. They stood around her, arrested in mid-stride, listening to a sound she could not hear.

Listening, as the riot's noise grew louder. Nearer.

The sound came not from the barricade, but from the east.

She ran past Zoh to the intersection of Bloodletter's and Falcon, and saw Warden pickets brace against charging Chakal Square protesters, two hundred at least already around the corner and more behind. They'd been flanked.

Other Wardens sprinted past her to reinforce the pickets, Zoh and his fellows moving as one. The protesters charged, the Wardens crouched, the charge accelerated, feet pounding the cobblestones, leaping—

To slam against a wall of empty air.

The force of their impact knocked Elayne to her knees. She hadn't time for elegant solutions, just enough to convince a few cubic yards of air it was hard as steel.

Shouts behind her. More red-arms must have circled west down Coyote. She blocked that intersection too, straining to argue with two separate gaps of air at once. In haste, she'd anchored both barriers to her body, which meant she couldn't move without moving them.

Wardens ran past her to the lines. Word spread from mask to mask—Kopil must know by now that Temoc's truce was broken. Which meant—

Red light bloomed behind her, a fiery tower rising to the sky.

Damn and triple damn. She drew her knife, pushed up her shirt cuff, and drew blood from her forearm. Blood splashed against pavement—blood that was arguably a part of her. Kneeling, she strengthened the connection with a a few glyphs of her true name etched in stone around the drying drop. Cheap trick, but it would do.

She passed the barriers' anchor into the drop of blood. They flickered, strained, but held. Good enough for now. It had to be.

The blood boiled.

Shadow and light clothed her, gave her strength. She sprinted toward the barricade.

Atop the sandbags, Wardens took up arms again. Stun nets glittered. They raised other weapons too, long wicked rods and hooks of iron, killing tools. "What are you doing?" Temoc shouted. "We're here to talk."

The King in Red burned atop his makeshift fortress, ten feet tall now and growing, his eyes nova-bright. Lightning gathered between his clawed finger bones. "To distract, you mean. I thought you had more self-respect, Temoc."

"What do you mean?"

"You never wanted to talk." Kopil's voice boomed. "Just to keep us busy while your friends snuck behind our lines."

Friends? Temoc almost said aloud. Then he thought: the Major. "That's not true!" Around him the crowd cursed and cried and surged toward the wall. "This isn't over!"

"I think it is," Kopil said, and raised his hand.

Elayne leapt the sandbag rampart in a single jump. "Kopil!"

The skull, three times the size now of any human head, revolved toward her. Comically large, monstrous. "I am busy smiting."

She almost lost it then, chaos be damned. "They flanked us." Pitched so Temoc could hear. "Smite later. First, save the camp."

He shrugged, and swept one hand through the air in a dismissive gesture. Humans erupted from the barricade, thrown pinwheeling back into the crowd. "Hold the line," he told Chimalli as, now fifteen feet tall, now ten, he floated to the street. She followed, wasting soulstuff on speed to keep pace.

"I should have expected this." His feet touched ground an instant before hers.

"Kettle them with Craft. Stop them from moving north. Contain the riot."

"Expensive. Cheaper to kill a few, terrify the rest."

"Do that and you have a bigger problem."

He stopped. "Who will stop me? You?"

"Do you want to go down in history as the first Deathless King in the New World to use deadly force against civilians?"

"What definition of 'civilian' are you using that includes anarchists in uniform?"

They reached the intersection, and Elayne's glyphs. The drop of blood sparked and sputtered—too much power passing through at once. Her barrier would break any second now.

Wardens screamed orders as the barriers sagged. A narrow gap opened to the east; rioters clawed through.

"So easy to kill them," he said. "If I do it now, fast, the whole movement will shatter like glass on the anvil. Blocking them in gives these madmen credit, and strength. More will die in the long run."

"Kopil."

He stared into her with eyes like needles. Anyone else might have broken. But Elayne knew him of old.

"Don't."

His eyes blinked out. A serpent ate the sun. He snapped his fingers with a sound of thunder.

Her barriers broke like porcelain, and his replaced them. A hundred guillotine blades fell, east and west along Jackal, cutting the Skittersill off from the northern city. Diamond-shimmering walls, pregnant with nightmare: gaze upon them and go mad. Many did in that moment, and fell back writhing with visions of shining teeth and gnawing doom.

The King in Red stood in his own city, his place of power. What force could resist him?

Screams from the east. Rising barriers snapped arms and legs. A woman wept.

"It is done," Kopil said. "We are at war."

33

Temoc watched the peace fail.

He tried to stop it. Shouted until his throat was hoarse. They did not listen.

The King in Red left the barricade. Below, the people of Chakal Square rose, beaten, bruised, and angry, to throw themselves at the wall again. With the King in Red gone, the Wardens seemed less formidable than before. More stun nets cast, and men and women fell, but others helped them, or climbed over their bodies to press on.

"Stop," he cried, but he had lost the people, and they were not easily regained. He had been their heart. Now he was a rock against their flood.

He ordered red-arms to fan out and break the rush. Cut off the supply of attackers, limit the damage. Those scaling the wall were lost already. Triage. He hated the word.

Minutes passed, or seconds, or hours, before he heard the screams. Terror, shock, pain. These were not the cries of men who faced weapons. A weapon you understood. These screams meant Craft.

Diamond blades cut Chakal Square off.

Demonic reflections danced in the translucent barriers, reaching out with arms of refracted sunlight. A woman had been charging the barricade atop a tall man's shoulders. The man stumbled, and she swayed too close to the wall. Spectral claws left white tracks on her skin. She fell, screaming. Temoc heard a loud crack as she struck pavement. Only an arm broken he hoped, or a leg.

"Help them!" he shouted to the red-arms. "Get people back.

Give them room." The red-arms saluted with fist across chest, the old way. Temoc realized seconds later that he'd replied in kind. He was a soldier again.

He heard more wails from farther east down Crow, and west down Jackal. Demon walls rose. Translucent insect nightmares within cast rainbows on the crowd.

They were being bottled off.

He charged through the crowd like a bull through surf, breaking waves and scattering foam. When he saw red-arms, he commanded them: "Go to the barriers. Help the wounded." They obeyed and he ran past, guided by a glint of sunlight off steel, through surging flesh until he met the Major.

"What did you do?"

The Major knelt on his crate, back to Temoc, talking with his soldiers. At Temoc's words, the soldiers withdrew, and the Major stood. "Temoc. How was your meeting?" Black eyes glinted behind his helm.

"You ordered the attack while I was still talking."

"I told my men to get into position. They must have misinterpreted."

"They would have given us the Warden. You ruined it."

"Any deal they made would only be a sop to us. The djinn's out of the bottle."

"They're walling us in. Anyone in the square is an enemy of the city, now. They're declaring war."

"Excellent!"

"Are you insane?"

"The King in Red has named us his enemies. We are soldiers now, together. Everyone who thought there was a peaceful path from Chakal Square will face the truth today."

"There are families here. My family is here."

"Then they will fight." The voice behind the helmet echoed with the tinny noise of marching boots. "They will fight, and we will win."

"Not like this. What will you do against Couatl? Against Craft?"

"What we can," the Major said. "And more, with you at our head. Temoc, last of the Eagle Knights. You could drive them weeping before you."

"The whole corps of Eagle Knights could not stop the Craftsmen in the last war, not with the gods behind us."

"No army opposes you today, no legion of wizards and demons and dragons and undead. Only a few police and an uncertain king."

"The gods are too weak to fight this war."

"Then we will give our lives to their cause," the Major said. "We will sacrifice. We will shed blood. They will feed, and you will lead us to glory."

"Glory." The word sounded good. Sleeping gods stretched in Temoc's heart. They knew these ancient words, and smiled fanged smiles as they dreamed. Rise and fight. Kill, in the old way, as a man. He searched the Major's eyes for some hint of duplicity or madness. He found none. "You really think we can win."

"I know we can, with you at our head."

The Major must have heard Temoc's knuckles pop as he balled his hand into a fist, but he didn't understand in time to duck.

Temoc's punch struck the Major's helm, lifted the man a few inches off the ground and threw him back into the watching red-arms. He fell, a clattering pile of metal, a fist-shaped dent in his mask.

Temoc walked away.

"Where are you going?" the Major called after him.

"To my family."

34

Temoc marched toward the meeting tent. He stopped to heal a young man's broken leg, one hand steadying the knee, the other hand pulling from the ankle. A prayer to Healer Olam, a breath of divinity in his touch, and hunger. The gods smelled blood.

None here, he told them. The world has changed.

He just couldn't offer any proof of that at the moment.

He healed the boy's leg, and a woman's bleeding scalp wound, and fused cracks in a fat man's ribs. They followed. He saw Kapania Kemal gathering followers, with Bill by her side. He walked on. If anyone tried to stop him, he did not notice.

He found Chel guarding the tent. She saluted him. "They're safe."

"Did anyone. . ." He trailed off, couldn't bear to say the words—they were too big to fit out his mouth.

"No."

"We're blocked in. All the roads going north, at least."

"What will you do?"

He frowned. "Take my wife and son home."

"Will you come back?"

"I don't know," he said, meaning "no." And, when she did not answer, only stared at him unmoved: "You should go. Take as many as you can. This will get worse."

"Before it gets better?"

"Before it gets worse."

"My friends are here," she said. "My people." And he heard after that: yours, too.

"I know." And I am sorry. "I need to take care of my family."

"What should we do, Temoc?"

"I told you. Leave."

"I can't." Desperation. Fear. Controlled, before her men. She would have been a good commander in the Wars, if there had been woman commanders then. "Help me, even if you're going to take Mina and Caleb." Your wife and son, again unsaid, who I have kept safe, your wife and son to whom I have done my duty as a soldier. Expecting you to do your duty to me in turn, as commander.

With the shreds of his god-power he pulled her followers' eyes to him. "Chaos will pose a greater threat than Wardens at first. Protect these people." He set his hand on Chel's arm, felt her strength. "They will follow you."

"Thank you," she said. He saw her marshal the will to speak again without shaking. "Get out of here, sir."

He entered the tent.

Mina sat inside, helping Caleb play solitaire. When the tent flap opened she spun toward the sudden light, one hand raised to ward off brilliance or a blow.

"We're going," he said.

"Caleb, it's time." The boy gathered his cards, wrapped them in silk, and slid them into their box.

"What's happened?" Caleb said.

She hugged him. Blood from his cheek marked hers.

"I didn't know this would happen. I swear. I thought—" What? There were words to use, if he could remember them, if the memory of Chel's eyes hadn't torn them all away. Lead us. "No," was a start, but what came after? "We have to leave."

"I'll carry Caleb."

"I will," he said. "I'm stronger."

"Let me do something, dammit."

"Help me get us out of here. That's enough."

She wanted to know more: about Chel, or the Major, about what he would have done if she and Caleb did not exist. Unasked, unanswered questions fluttered about their heads like bats, terrifying and terrified at once.

Temoc lifted Caleb and led Mina from the tent. Chel saluted

as they emerged, and Mina broke stride to salute her back. They pushed through the crowd to Bloodletter's, where a barrier blocked their path—but the barriers didn't run through buildings, only closed off streets. Temoc kicked down a shop's door and they fled through connecting rooms into an alley behind the nightmare wall. They ran down empty streets beneath circling Couatl—an anonymous family homeward bound. Wardens rolled past in black wagons toward the siege.

They reached home. Their courtyard seemed unchanged and alien at once, as if every surface and object had been repainted a subtly different color. The apartment still smelled of breakfast. Temoc set his son down and sat, and Mina sat, too. They breathed in the shadows across from one another, and were afraid.

35

The King in Red laughed avalanche laughs and directed the Wardens with the dramatic excess of a Schwarzwald nightclub impresario, movements swift and sweeping, orders delivered in thundering voice. Wardens ran where he bid.

"You'll be all right?" Elayne asked before she left.

"I haven't felt this good in years," he said. "I should thank them."

"Keep yourself under control."

"I am always, perfectly, under control."

"Listen to me." She stared into the conflagrations of his eyes. "As your counsel, if not your friend. The Wars are over. Let the Wardens do their job."

"The Wars are never over."

"They are," she said, with all the certainty she could muster. A few decades of death had not improved Kopil's emotional intelligence in other respects. She hoped he still had a hard time telling when she was stating a fact, as opposed to willing her statement true.

"Okay," he said.

Apparently so.

The King in Red continued: "Tell me what you find. And keep that briefcase safe."

"I'll file it after I check on Batac at the hospital."

"Let me know what you learn." Without further good-byes, he swept away to harangue more Wardens.

Captain Chimalli caught Elayne before she left. "Lady Kevarian," he said—using the Quechal vocative of address to nobility. "You're going to Grace."

She nodded.

"If you don't mind." The captain took a sealed letter from his pocket. "Bring this to Dr. Venkat. We'll need more first-aid supplies here soon. Nurses, too."

Elayne accepted the letter. "How many?"

Chimalli ground his thoughts between his teeth, oscillating from over- to underbite. "As many as she can spare." He saluted, said, "Ma'am," and turned and left.

How old was he? Early forties, perhaps. She remembered that age. You thought you understood the world, and the limits of your understanding. You thought the worst was over.

She flew north, to Grace and Mercy Hospital.

Dr. Venkat was a round Dhisthran woman about Chimalli's age, who Elayne found in an observation theater that smelled of alcohol, fake mint, and faker lavender. Venkat walked a pen through her fingers. The operating room below was painfully white. For all the times Elayne had wanted to strangle Tan Batac, or flay him slowly, she didn't know how to feel when she saw him butterfly-pinned and bloody on the table. "Will he pull through?"

Pursed lips. A nod.

"Soon?"

"No."

The voice took her by surprise: an alto soft enough to soothe burns. "Can I talk to him?"

Venkat shook her head.

"He might have seen who tried to kill him. We need anything he can give us."

"If we wake him before he's ready, he might never wake again."

"I could walk into his dreams."

"Ms. Kevarian," the doctor said. "The Wardens who brought Batac said you applied first aid."

She nodded.

"You stopped the bleeding, but your Craft drained his soul.

There was hardly any apperception left for me to save by the time he got here."

"I did what I had to."

"And thanks to you, he survived. Barely. We have drugs to keep him under, drugs to help him dream. Exposure to starlight will help his soul regrow. But if you shove around in his mind before he's ready, you might break him so badly that the person who wakes up won't match the one who went to sleep. Which is why we don't usually let necromancers operate on living patients."

"I saved his life." Even to Elayne that sounded plaintive.

"I'm sure his family is grateful."

She resisted the urge to swear. "I have a letter for you, from Captain Chimalli."

The woman's eyes flicked away from the operation. The pen stopped its revolutions, rested on the railing. Neither of them spoke.

Elayne hadn't opened the letter, or read it. She'd guessed. The captain had little time to write and seal a note. There were few messages a man in uniform might keep on his person, just in case—and a few people to whom he might address them. He wasn't related to Venkat. Lovers, then, or close friends.

She didn't like using such leverage, but she needed every lever she could pull.

Venkat slid the pen into her pocket. "Give me your card. I'll tell you when he wakes."

"As soon as. Please."

Venkat nodded. Elayne passed her the card with the letter. "Thank you."

Elayne was still human enough to give the other woman space, to let her stand and watch the blood and read the letter with her hand clenched around the railing. Elayne was still human enough to leave.

A small suited man stumbled into her by the lift. She recovered her footing, and helped him up. He wore pince-nez glasses, which she hadn't seen anyone but skeletons wear since the thirties, and them only because skulls lacked ears. The combination of spectacle-enlarged eyes, narrow shoulders, and forward-sloping face made the man resemble an officious ferret. "Excuse me. Do you know where I might find Tan Batac? I understand he was admitted here."

Assassin, perhaps? Elayne closed her eyes and examined him as a Craftswoman: no glyphwork, little Craft, soul leveraged with a few bad loans, folded contracts in his briefcase. No threat.

"I'm a business associate," he explained. "Jim Purcell, from Aberforth and Duncan. I need to review some specifics for a deal, get a signature."

"You'll be a long time waiting."

"It really is important."

"Talk to Dr. Venkat in the observation theater. Give her a few minutes, first."

The man blinked at her through his pince-nez, but at last he said, "Okay."

"Good luck." Elayne left him, and left Grace, too.

36

At sundown Chel stormed the RKC offices on the Square's eastern edge. She led the charge with Tay by her side, but it was Zip who threw a trash can through the building's front window. Glass showered onto the tile floor and glittered like cutting frost.

They ran through the empty foyer past a reception desk, froth on a human wave. If they stopped running they'd be trampled by those behind, ground into the glass. Not that Chel wanted to stop. Night after night standing guard, pacing through the camp, all that over in an afternoon. She ran, and offices broke behind her.

The charge spent itself down side passages and up stairs. Wood splintered and drywall burst and shattered pipes sprayed precious water onto bathroom floors. The Major's people did most of the damage, hunting trophies, stripping the office accoutrements with which the King in Red's contractors defaced this ancient temple. Holes in drywall bared carved stone beneath.

Chel ran through galleries and past open workspaces, and her red-arms followed.

"I don't see the door," Tay shouted.

"It's here." She was barely breathing hard. "The Kemals said—There." Left through the break room to the office cafeteria, windowless and ghostlit green, past empty tables into an unlit kitchen. Pans and colanders hung from the ceiling, and knives on the wall. She smelled disinfectant and char, dish soap and grease. Behind the kitchen they found the stockroom, piled with boxed onions and potatoes. A steel door took up most of the wall. It closed down, like the door to a garage.

Tay tried the latch first. "Locked."

Chel slipped a sharp-toothed key from her jacket pocket. "The Kemals used to cater here." The key fit, and the lock popped open. The door drifted up. A sliver of sunset shimmered on the stockroom floor like molten gold.

"What now?" Zip asked. "We run for the docks?"

"No. We don't know how long this siege will last, and the Kemals don't have enough food for the camp. They can bring supplies through here."

"The Wardens will catch on."

"Which is why we have to be careful." She addressed the whole room of red-arms. "You hold this storeroom. If anyone goes out that door, we'll tip the Wardens off before we're ready. If we're smart and wait 'til sundown, we can get a few supply runs through before anyone notices. If we're dumb, we get nothing. Got it?" Nods all around. "I'll tell the Kemals."

"I'll come with you," Tay said, and they left together.

He held himself tense until they reached the cube farm. Then he laughed. "I thought for sure everyone would run right out those doors."

"That'll come later."

"Why not now? You saw those witch-walls up on Crow. The Wardens are angry. This won't end well."

"We stay because we can help people. Don't worry. I'll run when time comes."

"When's that?"

From the front hall, she heard screams.

"Now," she said.

Six men and two women knelt on broken tiles—three Quechal, five pale-skinned Old-Worlder types, Camlaander or Iskari blood, Chel couldn't tell the difference. They were desk jobbers: faces and hands soft, smooth. They wore office clothes, creased wools and ironed cotton, ties and jackets, and every one had showered this morning. Most of the men carried a luxury of extra weight in their hips and stomachs and jowls. One was gym-rat buff—his nose was broken and leaked blood, and he pressed a hand to probably broken ribs. Another man was crying.

The Major's troops stood behind them, armed with lengths of pipe. The Major paced in front of the hostages, and pondered each in turn. He'd made it halfway down the line.

"For gods' sake, Stan," said the woman kneeling beside the crying man. Her back was straight, and her cheek bore a fresh bruise.

A circle of red-arms and protesters watched the Major, his men, and the captives. Chel abandoned Tay to shove through. She shouldered aside a larger man, and stormed to the Major. "Let them go."

He turned slowly. His helmet bore the imprint of a fist. Behind the mask, his eyes shone with fervor. Temoc had looked like this during the sacrifice. "Red King Consolidated told employees at this office to stay home. It seems these did not receive the memo."

The man with the broken nose spat blood onto the glass; one of the Major's troops kicked him in the back.

"You want them as a bargaining chip."

"Lives for lives. We return these innocents, and the King in Red sends us the murdering Warden for punishment."

"Don't do this."

"Why not?"

Gods. Temoc asked her to keep the camp together. How could she do that? She dropped her voice, but the room was quiet, and everyone heard. "You hold these folk for ransom and the papers will make us out to be killers. We need sympathy more than leverage. We need food." Which was as close as she could come in front of an audience to saying: you do this and the Kemals won't work with you anymore. And they're the ones with the corn. To put it more bluntly would force the Major's hand. She'd fought enough dockside rats to know you never cornered one. "Our fight's with the King in Red, not his drones."

The crowd was an even mix of her people and his. His troops were armed and armored, but the fight wouldn't be clean, or easy, and he couldn't risk losing.

She hoped.

"We will take them," he said, "to the camp. The Commission will decide what to do."

She knew how that would go: back-and-forth, argument, sideline sniping, balance of power, nobody willing to agree. The captives would be safe, for now.

But she couldn't smile, couldn't make off like she'd won— or let it seem she'd lost, either, which would disappoint her supporters in the crowd.

Gods, was this how Temoc felt all the time?

"Let's go," she said.

37

A city-sized web of light hung between Elayne and the abyss. The web's strands were thicker than mountains, its bonds firm as those at an atom's heart. She scourged the web with Craft. She sliced its strands with fine logical blades, burned them with fury and frustration, lashed them with waves of flame and bound them in paradox.

The web endured. From this side, at least, it was unbreakable.

She drifted through interstices the size of city blocks, into the below. Great and terrible beings moved around her, like the blind fish that swam at the ocean floor. She ignored them, and struck the web from underneath. If she—one woman, alone—could force the slightest flaw in this edifice, could sever its most slender strand, it would never endure a full-on attack. A demonic incursion would bring more might to bear than even Elayne could manage.

She raised both hands. Talons of shadow boiled up from the deeps, hooked the web, and pulled down. Sweat beaded on her forehead. Her arms shook with effort. The web twisted and stretched, but did not break.

"Are you satisfied?"

She did not acknowledge Judge Cafal's presence, or her question, at first. Slowly, methodically, she tested other angles of attack, with no more success.

At last, defeated by her own creation, she rose through the black. A demon caught her around the ankle with a barbed-wire tongue and tried to pull her down into its gaping maw. She killed it, tore the tongue from her leg, and joined the judge in the vasty heavens.

Cafal here looked no different from Cafal in the fleshy world. Seeming and soul in perfect accord: Elayne respected that.

"Your honor. I thought you would be asleep."

"I can't sleep," she said. "A hazard of the profession. Given the Skittersill's troubles, I thought I might check your new wards. I did not expect to find you trying to destroy them."

"Testing," she corrected. "A signed contract binds all parties, whatever their feelings after the fact. The Skittersill riot should not damage the wards. But theory and practice seldom see eye-to-eye."

Cafal laughed. "Don't I know it. You found the wards secure, of course."

"Yes."

"Then why so glum?"

"I'm not," she said.

"You wrought well, counselor. You knew that. You're not here because you're afraid you missed a weakness. You're here because you hope you did."

She considered lying, or playing dumb, and decided both tactics were beneath her. "We can't stop violence in Chakal Square. Conflict is self-sustaining: when attacked, Wardens respond with force. The crowd meets that force with force, and so on. We need to dampen this resonance. We have something they want: the Warden Zoh. But they have nothing we desire, and so the King in Red does not need to listen to them. If the wards were flawed, we would have to resume negotiations."

"You are dangerously close to violating your fiduciary duty."

"My client's current course of action is detrimental to his long-term interests. I am more faithful to my client than he is to himself."

"That kind of faith is beyond your remit. The King in Red is in good standing with the Courts. The Skittersill ward remains strong, as you see. You built the thing, and even you can't break it."

"We have to stop the fighting," she said.

The judge raised one eyebrow. "Do we?"

The answer seemed so obvious that Elayne checked herself before speaking, as if she were back in a Hidden Schools class-room. "I see."

"The King in Red and his people have a civil disagreement. The court has no place in this."

"You wouldn't say that if you had seen what's happening in the Square."

"Perhaps not," Cafal said. "But the Craft can only do so much."

"Is that why we fought, your honor? To let people die need-lessly because the Craft can only do so much?"

"We fought," she said, and stopped. "I fought, that is, be-cause people were trying to kill me, and I would be dead now if I let them succeed. You were young, then. I think the young fight for different reasons, or tell themselves they do."

"Kopil is wrong," Elayne said. "He's hurting himself, and the city."

"No Craft this court can offer will bend him to your will."

"Then I'll find another way."

She thought she kept her voice neutral, but there must have been something naked in it. The judge reached out to her. "Elayne—"

But she was gone.

38

The first night of the riot was the hardest. Temoc lay awake in bed with Mina beside him, also awake, neither speaking. Sun set over the camp, and for the first time in weeks he was not there to celebrate it. Hungry gods murmured in his skull. They slept, though restless. He did not.

He rose, and walked the halls in boxer shorts. No lanterns lit his way, only the soft glow of streetlights through the windows. Eleven years ago they'd moved to these few rooms—small compared to the palatial chambers of his far-gone youth, but after his drunken wandering days the house seemed a paradise. At first he'd resisted moving into slave's quarters, but he grew to love the Skittersill as he grew to know its people: hard honest folk oppressed by crooks.

He sat on an iron chair outside. Metal chilled his back and legs. The clouds boiled and writhed like crowds mashing against barricades. To the northwest, they glowed red—lit by Chakal Square fires?

The door opened. She bent to kiss his temple. "I love you." Meaning: I'm glad you came home.

"I love you, too." Meaning: I'm not sure.

"You did the right thing."

"I know."

"You could go. If you wanted. I can—" She broke off with a sudden ragged breath. "I'm sorry."

"You don't have to say that just because I want to hear it."

"Go back, then. Throw yourself into that—whatever that is."

"I want to be here, with you."

"Don't lie."

He stood and faced her, a single movement faster than he'd meant. His heart beat racehorse fast, as if he'd sprinted a mile. "I'm not lying."

"If you think I'm holding you back, I can deal with that. But I need you to be honest with me."

"I left good people there." He lowered his voice. Don't wake the neighbors, they might think there was something wrong. Hilarious. Absurd. He did not laugh. "But I can't be in the movement and out of it at once, you understand? If I went back, I'd live and die with them."

"Take us with you," she said, but he heard the slight catch before "us."

"You could survive it. Caleb? There are enough children stuck in this thing already. And if I leave you both alone the King in Red will take you hostage, or worse. So on the one hand I have my people, and on the other my wife, my son who I never taught to fight because I thought, in this modern age, he did not need to know. And . . . I love you. I want to be here." He meant to set his hand on the table, but misjudged his own strength and struck it instead. "I wish there were two of me. I wish there were a million. And then the others would go right the wrongs of the world, and I would stay. I promised to stand beside you. I will not break that vow."

The city could be so quiet after dark. Wind blew over tile roofs and brushed vine against vine. A carriage passed outside their house. Her nightdress shifted against her legs. "I couldn't handle a million husbands. One is my limit. So don't go getting any ideas."

He looked down, saw himself, laughed. "I am not wise enough to make these choices. Choosing leaves a wound, and the wound scabs. When I wonder if I've made the right choice, I peel back the scab to look." He mimed ripping open a scar on the inside of his forearm, and she made a twisted face. "When I was Caleb's age, the priests marked me to bear the burdens of the gods. I expected to fight demons from beyond the sky. I should not need so much strength to refrain from fighting."

"This isn't a refrain."

"No," he said. "I suppose not."

"Come to bed."

"I won't sleep."

"Me neither. But at least we won't sleep together."

The next morning he had to walk two miles before he found a stocked grocery store. The market was mobbed but the streets were almost empty. Unnerving. Dresediel Lex was a city of wide avenues. Even the Skittersill, labyrinthine by comparison to other districts, sported streets any other city would call broad. Most days traffic glutted these, but this was not most days. Streetsweeper zombies shuffled along, their occupation gone: no excrement to clean, no dust to remove.

Temoc stopped outside his house to scan the *Times* he'd bought with the groceries. The front page was an etching of Chakal Square. The artist drew architectural features in painstaking detail but rendered humans as a single featureless mass. Temoc grunted when he read the headline: "Skittersill Rising." It suggested a war between the people of the Skittersill and of Dresediel Lex, as if these people were not the same; it implicated everyone in the Skittersill in the Chakal Square violence. Perhaps he should find the journalist, correct him. But he, Temoc, did not speak for the movement anymore. He was not their master, not even their priest. Just a private citizen reading the news.

The *Times* devoted more space to the riots than they ever had to the peaceful movement. Of course. Violence sold. No mention of Tan Batac, just "a man injured in the initial outburst." Nothing about an assassin. The story focused on the mother and her bloody child, and the Warden's thrown rock. Even there, the *Times* shied from the truth. "In the confusion." "Self-defense."

"It's bad to read on the sidewalk," Elayne Kevarian said. "Someone might run into you."

He did not jump. She stood before him, dressed in charcoal

gray, hands in pockets. He had not heard her approach. "I wondered if you would come."

"I wondered if you would leave the Square. Happy surprises for us both."

"Happy," he echoed.

"Go to the King in Red, Temoc. Stop this."

"I am not sure," he said, "that we are talking about the same King in Red. The . . . man . . . I saw yesterday did not want to stop the fighting."

"He'll listen if you sue for peace."

"Beg, you mean. And if I succeed, what then? Return to Chakal Square to announce that though I abandoned them, I have dealt on their behalf?"

"If you make a good deal, they will honor it."

"Any bargain I strike would be a coward's compromise."

"The King in Red wants to win," she said. "Give him a personal victory over you, and you might be surprised how much he'll surrender in return."

"I will not show him that force will make me bend. I will not show my people that we should stand up for ourselves only until a sword is drawn."

"There's no shame in peace," she said.

"There's no shame in general peace. Each specific peace holds its own." He dropped the newspaper in a trash can. "I want to help, Elayne. I wanted to fight, but I left. I denied the King in Red a target. For that, my fathers turn their faces from me. I can bear their disappointment. But I will not kneel to the man who killed my gods."

"You'll let Chel and the Kemals and everyone in that square suffer for your pride."

"They made their decisions. I made mine. I survived. That was what you asked of me."

"Fine," she said.

"I have to go." He lifted his grocery bag. "Before the meat spoils."

"Take care of yourself, Temoc. And of them."

"I will." He turned from her, and walked inside to his family. She left in a shimmer of insect wings.

They did no work that day. They kept windows closed. Mina set her notes and books aside. They played go fish, and gin rummy, and xaltoc, and a variant on Fight-the-Landlord, which Mina won. Temoc asked Caleb about school, and Caleb told stories of his classmates, and some of the stories were true. At two in the afternoon, their windows rattled and water rippled in their glasses. Caleb ran outside, and Temoc and Mina followed him. Couatl flew west overhead in V formation. Talons glinted in the sun. Temoc's grip tightened on Caleb's arm. He did not notice until the boy squirmed and he let him go.

Smoke stained the western sky.

They waited. After a while, they made dinner.

All along, in Temoc's mind, the city burned.

39

The smoke north of Chakal Square was black as the inside of a mouth, and thick. Sharp winds parted it like curtains to reveal buildings burning. Glass in a high window shattered and shards fell into the inferno. Heat surrounded Chel. The curtain closed again and night returned, swirling and absolute.

"Who sets a godsdamn building on fire in the middle of a heat wave?"

Tay, beside her, shook his head. "The Major's people?"

"I'll open him like a tin can."

A large man barreled toward them out of the darkness; Chel jerked Tay to one side and the runner swept past. Screams rose with the smoke. She recognized one voice: "Gather close!"

The Major. "Come on."

She choked on smoke, and so did Tay. The crowd thinned as they ran north. Most of those still standing were the Major's troops, their faces smeared with ash.

The Major stood among his followers, armored despite the heat. His men crouched around him like sprinters, grim and tense, aimed toward the flames that consumed tents and buildings at the Square's northern edge. "Charge!"

"Hells' he doing?"

"I have no idea."

The Major and his people sprinted toward the blaze. Chel tried to follow, but could only guess their paths in the billowing black. Smoke scraped her eyes.

Shapes approached: inhuman silhouettes first, red-lit lurching ghosts, many-armed and triple-backed. No. Not ghosts. Human beings: the Major's people returning. They bore others across their backs, wrapped their arms around limping women and unconscious men, old and young alike, hobbling out of the fire.

The Major came last, slower than the rest. One man over his left shoulder, a woman under his right arm. His armor glowed in places, and not with sorcery.

They helped him: Chel took the fainted woman, and Tay the man, and together they ran for safety, or at least for air.

They found an empty space to set the wounded down. The Major knelt. His armor pinged and hissed as it cooled, and the man inside that armor hissed too, from pain. He could speak, though his voice was tight: "Thank you."

"What happened?"

"A camp near the northern border. One of the tents caught first." The Major pressed his gloved hands against the ground, but could not force himself to his feet. "Or maybe the buildings caught first, I don't know. Bad luck either way."

"You didn't do this?"

"What kind of person do you think I am?"

She didn't answer that question.

"My people are in the fire, helping those who can't escape. Where are yours?"

"Getting folks out of the border zone," she said. "Breaking down camps to keep this from spreading."

He panted. "And the others?"

"Wardens are pressing on the eastern front. The Kemals' people ran to the Skittersill for supplies. Bandages. Medicine."

"The resource war," he said, and she heard his scorn.

"Their medicine will save lives."

The Major heaved himself to his feet, and staggered north.

"Where are you going?"

"Back in." The smoke parted again. Flames shone off his homemade armor. "Come with me if you'd like."

Then he was gone.

"Dammit." She stood. Tay grabbed her hand. She pulled away, but he didn't let go. "If there are people there—"

"We go together."

"Fine."

They ran north into a foreign hell.

The next several hours melted into a slag of memory: heat and sweat and heavy breath through wet cloth, the weight of unconscious human beings, gods!—flesh could drag you down—straining muscle and the sting of hot metal against skin. She coughed ash and spat black. Shouted directions. Cried for aid. Unfamiliar faces took shape from the smoke, a new pantheon of gods and saviors forged in this dark hour.

Someone contained the northern blaze: Wardens, maybe, or the fire department. Tents near the border burned until they scarred the stone beneath.

When the camp was safe, Chel and Tay collapsed side by side. Neither spoke at first. Breathing was enough. Somewhere, the fight continued. Wardens circled, wingbeats heavy.

"We can't do this," Chel said. "Not alone."

"We did it," Tay replied.

"This time. Things will only get worse—the Major saying the Kemals let people die, the Kemals claiming he set the fire. And we still have our hostages."

"Who do you think started it?"

"I don't care. We need to pull together, and we can't do that alone."

Tay's hand fell onto her stomach. She held it in silence. Overhead, smoke and sorcerers' clouds closed out the stars.

40

The next day Temoc took a stroll.

He told Mina he was going to the store, which was true, but he took the long way round, toward Chakal Square.

He didn't enter the Square, so it wasn't even a lie of omission. He just drew close enough to hear the crowd.

The city was dead. Trash lay discarded in gutters. Airbuses and civilian traffic had deserted the sky. Only Couatl swooped above, so high up they seemed small as birds. In darkened shop windows decal monsters advertised new low prices. Chicken breast, six thaums a pound. New cheap combo platter.

Faith and hunger drew him like gravity. Though the sidewalk lay flat beneath his feet, walking toward the Square he felt as if he walked downhill.

Long after he should have turned away, he came upon the fight. Wardens, inch-high black silhouettes at this distance, manned a wall of sandbags at the end of the road. Cries rose beyond the barricade. A red-banded arm crested the wall, and the first rioter lurched over.

The kid was young, clad in browns and blues save for that red band. He slipped the dismount, fell hard to the street, and as he tried to stand a Warden beat him down again. A swarm of red-arms followed the kid, rained on the Wardens from behind. The red-arms fought bravely but not well, and with merely human strength. The Wardens seemed frantic, angry: beat cops, out of their element.

They were strong, though. A woman—Temoc guessed she was a woman from the long hair—ran at a Warden, who kneed her hard in the ribs. A burly man tried to lift a Warden in a bear hug, but the Warden lifted him instead, and threw him down. Some red-arms fell and did not rise again. Dots of white and red stained clothing: blood and compound fractures, broken bones jutting from torn skin.

Temoc's scars itched. Gods growled half-thoughts and broken sentences in the caverns of his mind. For the fallen. Against all enemies. Unceasing and eternal. In defense of the weak. In service of the holy.

He could help. Twenty Wardens might be a stretch, but he could manage. Strike from behind without warning, hit the commander first and move through their ranks as a whirlwind. Chant the blood chants; his enemies' pain would feed the gods. As each Warden fell, Temoc would grow stronger—and with the red-arms at his back he could roll on to Chakal Square, to his destiny. They would cry the gods' names and the heavens would open. The demon wind would break and rain would wash his shriven city.

What then for Mina? What then for Caleb?

He watched the fight.

The Warden commander signaled retreat. The red-arms laughed when the Wardens fled. Foolish. Wardens unhooked slender cylinders from their belts and threw them underhanded. One bounced off the cobblestones, and a second.

Then came the noise.

A god cleared his throat. A goddess screamed. Metal horses galloped through a steel jungle. An enormous insect chewed through a fat man's gut. Temoc clapped his hands to his ears. The Wardens' masks protected them, but when the sound faded the red-arms lay writhing on the street. Blood leaked from noses and ears. A woman retched on a sidewalk. Long white cracks marred a Muerte Coffee window halfway up the block. From this distance Temoc could not hear the people moan.

He left them fallen, and walked to the store, where he bought vegetables, rice, beans, and two pounds of chicken at eight thaums a pound—demand, the butcher said with a shrug, what you gonna do. Eggs, tortillas. Tequila. Newspaper.

Mina was waiting for him when he came home. She sat in the courtyard with a cup of coffee and yesterday's news spread on her lap.

He should have said something about the barricade, about the noise, about the chicken. He didn't.

41

"You mean to tell me," said the King in Red as he paced the war room under the glow of ghostlights and centipede screens, "that with twenty-four hours and practically infinite resources we haven't been able to find a handful of hostages?"

Elayne sat back in her chair and watched. She'd talked her way into the war room without a fight, but getting Kopil's attention was another matter. The Deathless King had not stopped grilling his Wardens since her arrival. How he expected them to get anything done while he asked so many questions, she did not know.

She wondered if it would be ethical to bill for this time.

The room smelled of sparks, sweat, and bone. Captain Chimalli ran his fingers over the map of Chakal Square. In the last hour crayon and colored pencil had crowded out the printed lines. Soon they'd need a new map; they'd gone through three already. In the basement of the squat building that served as Warden headquarters, a print shop churned out charts by the hour, engravers and cartographers on overtime pay. Gallons of acid spilled onto lead plates. Printing presses hammered ink onto paper, fixing scouts' reports into reality. "Since our first attack almost captured the Major, the Chakal Square crowd's grown wary. The hostages are held in the central camp." He waved his hand over a dozen tents, the fountain, and the mat chapel. "None of our people know where. Scrying yields limited results."

"What about the captives we've taken?"

"They refuse to talk."

"Don't you have gentlemen who specialize in that sort of thing?"

"Are you asking me to torture these people?"

Kopil waved vaguely beside the hole where his ear once was, as if a gnat buzzed there.

"My men might object."

"Don't use those men."

"The captives' information may be out-of-date already. And every time we send Wardens in on a snatch-and-grab, there's more risk the crowd will seize one of our guys. At the moment they're scared of us. What happens if that changes?"

"Then it changes."

"Which will encourage aggressive factions in Chakal Square, leading to more loss of life on both sides. Sir, we don't know what they plan to do with the hostages. They've made no ransom demands. Maybe they don't want to be seen as terrorists."

"Bastards hold my city hostage, and we're wasting time. Do you understand how much this siege costs, Captain? I do. And so does the Chamber of Commerce, whose jackals gnaw at my heels even as we speak. What's happened with Temoc?"

"He's remained with his family. Playing the model father. We have him under observation, not so close he'd notice."

"Without him, Chakal Square's defenseless against Craft, or close to it. Maybe we're thinking too small."

"What do you suggest?"

"Stun the Square. Arrest everyone. Sort the hostages out from the guilty."

"We don't have the jail space for so many."

"Send them to prison, then."

"Again, where? Our prisons are twenty percent above max occupancy."

Kopil's hand balled into a fist.

"Your Majesty," Elayne said before Kopil could continue. "A word, please. Outside?"

Kopil wheeled on her, and she bore his wrath without blinking. His skeletal menace might cow theists and underlings, but she was neither. "Captain," he said, at last. "When I return, give me plans. Outside the box, inside the box, burn the box, I don't care. I want Chakal Square back, and this movement broken. Everything else is negotiable."

Chimalli nodded. Elayne wondered if the captain had seen Dr. Venkat since his letter, and what he would have said behind closed doors about Kopil's commands.

The King in Red set his coffee down and swept from the room. Elayne followed. The doors shut behind them.

42

They rode the lift in silence to the roof, which was broad and flat and mounded with feathered serpents. Couatl slept here, coiled. Scaled sides swelled and shrank with their breath. A tail-tip twitched. Wings shivered. Wardens paced among the sleepers, stroked their sides, soothed them.

"Do they dream?" Elayne asked.

"Animal dreams," the King in Red replied. "Flight and food. Hunting."

"Is that all?" A crocodilian head peeked out of a ten-foot-tall coil. Its mouth could have swallowed her whole.

"Of what else should they dream?"

"They belonged to the gods, before the Wars."

"Yes."

"Do they remember them?"

"I don't think so."

They reached the low wall at the roof's edge. The King in Red climbed up and offered her a hand, which she accepted though she didn't need his help.

Behind them, to the north, stood the Sansilva pyramids where the gods had died. Here, downtown, most of the buildings were modern, with slanted walls and bas-relief flourishes to evoke old Quechal architecture. Liberation laid waste to these streets forty years ago—they'd been lined with civilian structures of plaster and wood, less durable than sandstone and obsidian temples. Conquerors built the modern city on the wreckage.

They faced south, toward the Skittersill. If Elayne craned her neck she could see the district's houses: low and streetmazed with adobe walls and brightly painted wood. "You wanted to ask me something," Kopil said.

"End this. Drop the barriers. Let everyone go home."

"If only it were that easy." He stepped out onto emptiness. "Walk with me."

She did, and found firm footing on the expanse. The ground waited twelve stories down. She triggered a few levitation glyphs, minimum power.

"Don't you trust me?" he asked.

"Trust," she replied, "but verify."

They walked south, moving faster than their pace. Downtown streets latticed beneath them, brilliant lines and luminous intersections. The King in Red took a pack of cigarettes from his pocket, tapped it down, removed one, gripped the filter between his teeth, and offered her the pack.

"No thanks. I'm trying to quit."

"Good idea," he said. "These things will kill you." He slid the pack into his pocket, and lit his cigarette with a flick of his fingers. "I should know."

"Was that what did it in the end? Cancer?"

He exhaled a thin line of smoke. "Damn, I should do this more." She didn't ask what he meant. "I went in for a checkup when I was, I barely even remember. Sixty maybe? This would have been before Belladonna transferred you to the DL office."

"That was 'sixty-three."

"A couple years before that. I went in with a cough, bit of a rattle in the chest. Joint pain. There was a growth in the lung. They could have taken it out, even then. Would have hurt, a lot, but they could have done it. I figured, why bother? I'd been working on premortem exercises for a few years at that point. I won't say I expected it—back then we didn't know as much about these things as we know now." He gestured to the cigarette. "But you reach a certain age and you take precautions."

"A certain age," she echoed.

"I hope I don't offend. You were, what, twenty at Liberation?"

"Seventeen."

"So you know what I'm talking about. The long slow night draws near. Looks like you've lived cleaner than I did. I was a mess, after the Wars. Twenty-two-hour days. We rebuilt this city with our bare hands, mortgaged our souls a hundred times over, a thousand, to pull Dresediel Lex out of the shadows. My life was work. No time for love, for the gym, for long walks on the beach or any of the other things people who don't know what it means to give yourself to a cause say we should do with our time. Maybe they aren't wrong. By sixty I carried a lot of extra weight and a vicious temper. I hadn't slept eight unbroken hours in a decade. So when the doctor told me what was growing in my lung I wasted a week on self-pity, then said what the hells, let's get this over with. I wasn't using the body for anything important. Took a couple months' vacation, threw myself into premortem prep, wrestled a dragon for the secret of eternal life, hid my death in a needle in an egg in a chicken in a trunk on an island in an ocean in a safe-deposit box down at First Lexican Bank, then went for the final buff-and-wax. And now I can smoke the occasional cigarette with impunity. I recommend early transfer to anyone who asks. Reduces the trauma."

"Flesh has treated me well so far. I'll keep it as long as it's mine to keep."

"Ever the romantic. That's the bane of your generation, I think, the youngsters. Though I'll grant—your body doesn't seem to have betrayed you as ferociously as mine."

"Thank you," she said. "I think." And, after a few minutes' silent walk: "You do realize you're bringing us toward Chakal Square."

"Really? I thought you were."

"I'm following you."

"Then who's driving this thing?"

She closed her eyes, raised wards, and woke her glyphs before she heard his low stone-grinding chuckle.

"You are an infuriating individual."

"I had you for a second," he said.

"You realize I was about to break your Craft, send us tumbling to our demise."

"Who's we? You're the one still made of meat. And anyway, we'd have thought of something before we hit the ground. Now. You were telling me to give up."

"I didn't mean you should give up, just that you should end this. Drop the barriers. Offer amnesty. Apologize. At the very least punish Zoh for what he did."

"Show weakness, you mean."

"It's not weakness—they know they can't beat you. Why not choose mercy?"

"Because." They stopped. Chakal Square lay a hundred feet below and a quarter-mile distant. Smoke drifted up from bonfire constellations, and the space between the fires surged with people. Any lower and Elayne could have heard their songs and prayers, lamentations and drunken speeches. At this height the voices faded into silence and wind. The people were just currents in the dark.

"Because," she echoed.

"Because we live off dividends of fear," he said at last. "This is a city of millions—Quechal and foreign, rich and poor, strong and weak. We are all races, and none. We are human, and not. We are patchwork, and like any patchwork, our seams are our weakest point."

"Alt Coulumb could say as much. Or Alt Selene."

"Alt Coulumb's god binds its people together; Alt Selene has its death cults and warring spirits, both solutions of a kind. We thought our new order's enemies would be too scared to fight, and for decades they were. The memory of Liberation was enough. We beat the gods, that was the line—and if you don't get on board, we'll beat you, too. But these people." She heard scorn in that word, and a hint of wonder. "They don't remember Liberation. They think the Wardens are my strength, rather than symbols of that strength, and the longer this siege lasts the more they lose their fear. If dockworkers and fanatics can stand against me in Chakal Square, why not the migrants of Stonewood? Why not the settlers of Fisherman's Vale? Why not the Midland farmers, who already resent us for taking their water? Why shouldn't the crime families get in on the deal as well? If Tan Batac and his people saw an opportunity to rebel, they would."

"You worry too much."

"A soft victory here will not keep my city safe and whole. A slow successful siege won't do. I must remind these people what powers hold Dresediel Lex intact. The Skittersill Rising will become a lesson to this city, and to the world."

New depths opened in his voice: the bass expanded, rumbling through Elayne's body, buzzing in her eyeballs. Blue flame licked Kopil's fingers, and sparks darted between his teeth. He grew large again, as his will distorted and shaped reality. When she blinked, she saw him as a nova of blood. Anyone in the crowd below with a lick of Craft could look up and see it, see him, a doomsday sun in the night sky.

"So why," he said, "should I not open the ground beneath them now? Why not rain fire from the heavens? Why not descend into their midst, shadow-winged with a fiery sword, and walk from tent to tent singing slaying songs? I could ash the rock upon which they stand, dry the fountain from which they drink. I could fill the streets with poison gas and rend their dreams to shreds. Fear would stitch Dresediel Lex together again."

"And you would have the blood of thousands on your hands."

"That blood's already there. I'd add a fresh coat to what's left over from the Wars."

"Do you think our colleagues will look kindly on a mass murderer?"

"What is war but mass murder? And they called me a hero for that."

"There are other ways to rule."

"Name one that works."

"You're scared. Tan Batac, shot in the middle of that crowd, it scared you. Nothing wrong with that."

"I don't scare," he said.

Beneath them, the dancers spun faster.

"If you need a victory," Elayne said, "take one. But don't use the Craft. Don't cross that line."

"What do you propose?"

"Let the Wardens do their job."

"You make it sound so easy."

"It is. They're keeping the hostages in the meeting tent, or your oracles would have found them already. You know who the ringleaders are; those are your high-priority targets. Start the press tomorrow, attack with Wardens on all sides. Concentrate the defenders' attention on their perimeter, then hit them from above. Arrest the leaders. Rescue the hostages. Move dispute to the Courts. Prosecute Zoh at the same time. The riot folds. People slink away. You get your victory. They get their lives."

"It's risky, Elayne. Every time we fail, their power grows."

She shrugged. "So don't fail."

"If this doesn't work—"

"It will."

"If it doesn't, I will need to act, to maintain order. Do you understand? My hand will be forced. Fire will fall. I'll have no choice."

"We always have a choice."

"I made mine already," he said. "Long ago."

Below a dancer stumbled, and spun out of control toward a fire. Someone caught her before she burned.

43

Temoc found Mina in the kitchen, swearing over a pan of eggs. The smell of fried sausages lingered on the air. "You didn't wake me," he said.

"It took you long enough to sleep last night. I thought you might need rest. I can manage a few eggs." A coppery burnt odor displaced the sausage smell. Mina cursed, and pulled the pan off the flame.

He left the kitchen without arguing, and walked into the courtyard. Smoke rose over Dresediel Lex, columns and billows from the northwest, and Couatl circled, peering down with raptors' eyes and raptors' hunger. Rumbles from the street: black wagons drawn by blinkered horses passed their gate. Wardens sat on benches in the wagon beds, weapon harnesses buckled across their jumpsuits, truncheons in hand. Row after row they rolled toward Chakal Square.

Gods called to Temoc, and he knew their names. Ili of the White Sails. Ixaqualtil, chanting through his many mouths from the foot of the dead sun's throne. Qet Sea-Lord sang his surf-song, and Isil sang the wind.

Caleb sat at the garden table, shuffling cards.

"What are you playing?"

"Solitaire. I lost."

Temoc looked up at the smoke. "How long has this been going on?"

"Since sunrise."

"Of course. They wanted to surprise people." Temoc sat beside Caleb as his son dealt another game. "Remember that. When you sleep, you're in danger."

"Do you think the Wardens will arrest your friends?"

"If they are lucky. My friends, I mean."

"Lucky?"

"It's not easy to arrest someone without hurting them. Some of my friends will die today."

He set his palm on his son's back: so small, so fragile. Kid had never yet broken a bone. He walked, ran, fell, all carefully. Thought his actions through. Someday he would learn how it felt to break. How it felt to fail. Perhaps he should have learned already. Perhaps this was something Temoc the peacemaker— Temoc who walked away from Chakal Square and left war for would-be warriors to wage—had failed to teach his son. The boy should know by now that not all wounds could be healed by shuffling a deck of cards, that some games were never won or lost, but instead cycled through the deck over and over, seeking an out that never came.

But was that what Temoc's father taught him? Or his father before? To fear the future? No. He learned this on his own, as did every man. He was still learning it. Every year. Every day.

He learned it from the smoke over Chakal Square.

"I am here for you," he said, and tried to look like he believed it. "Whatever happens."

Caleb smiled, and turned over a card.

Elayne was late to the assault. By the time she reached the war room, the King in Red and Captain Chimalli and their aides had already retreated to the vision well. Two Wardens stood guard at the double doors to the well chamber. They stepped aside for her. One saluted, the other didn't.

She opened the doors and closed them behind her without even a finger snap to betray her use of Craft.

"Troop seven to Jackal and Temal," said the King in Red. "Looks like they're about to try a rush."

"Troop seven, rendezvous with barricade at intersection of Jackal and Temal," Chimalli commanded.

"Troop seven," muttered the dreamer strapped to the bed. "Barricade Jackal and Temal."

Under their voices rolled the distant cry of riot.

The room was crowded. In the center stood the well, an older model built of rough stone blocks stolen from a village somewhere, acid-etched with symbols and invocations. Chimalli and the King in Red flanked the well, their faces lit by the images in the water. Around them lay four stone slab beds, one for each cardinal direction. One bed was bare, and one served as a desk, spread with maps and mobbed by Wardens and attachés, reviewing options and strategy with pencil and straight edge. Dreamers occupied the other beds, both bound and blindfolded. Two lines—one, for communications, tied to a dreamer in the Wardens' on-site command tent. The other dreamer ran the well. His whimpers seeped through his gag. The others ignored him.

"Sorry I'm late," Elayne said. "The judge wanted to review our contract."

Kopil looked up. "And you didn't tell me?"

"A pro forma request. Easily handled."

"And?"

"No problem. This is why you hire professionals." She thought she concealed her disappointment.

She approached the vision well. Beneath its smooth surface lay Chakal Square and its environs, writhing with hive-war motion. From this height, the crowd seemed a massive amorphous organism, one beast with a thousand backs. The Wardens, by contrast, assumed strict regimented lines. The King in Red gestured above the living map, and red arrows formed to indicate the direction of assault. He shook his head, and the arrows vanished. The dreamer's cries changed pitch.

"They're fighting you to a standstill?" Interesting. A part of her even found it exciting.

"Not at all. But the battle is more two-sided than I hoped."

He spun the map on its center axis.

"Impressive setup you have here," she said.

"Most people would settle with a vision-gem. We use the dreamers for post-processing and projection. Rides them hard, but what can you do?"

"You know they're making new vision wells now in the Shining Empire that don't use stolen stones."

"Synthetics don't have the same texture. Plus, control's less fine-grained. They'll catch up in a decade or so, but for now no way's better than the old way. Especially for this sort of thing. This setup gets us per-solider resolution, about a quarter-second of time spread. Look." Their viewpoint plunged swift as a hawk toward the battle's eastern flank, where Wardens attacked a red-arm line. Grand movements shattered into human beings. Men with crossbows shot at charging Wardens from second-story windows. Red-arms met the advance with pikes and stones and spears. Closer still the image swept, to focus on a single boy. Sweat stained his pale blue shirt. A bruise blacked his eye, and he held a captured truncheon. He'd seen combat and survived—but he did not know why he'd lived, and each new battle was a chance not to.

Elayne remembered that feeling.

Ghost-forms surrounded the boy: the well's best guess at his next half second's actions, superimposed on the now. Retreating half a step, advancing. Shifting grip on the truncheon. Crouching. Eyes closed, eyes open. Shouting defiance. Clenching lips tight.

The Wardens charged. They seemed monsters from this point of view: black uniforms and black shields, black weapons and blank silver faces, creatures boiling from some hell's depths. The boy and his comrades rushed to meet them. A hundred battle cries joined in a wordless scream.

The boy swung his truncheon, but a Warden hit him in the face with the edge of her shield. The boy fell, flailing with his stick, scrambling to his feet. A truncheon caught him in the ribs and he recoiled, retreating and striking at once, teeth bared. He didn't see the Warden who hit him from behind.

"And he's down!" Kopil's voice swelled to sports-announcer

pitch. "See what I mean? You don't get that resolution with the newer models, though they're cheaper and don't make villagers so angry." He waved his hand in a counterclockwise circle and their view retreated to safe distance: no blood here, only armies strangling in the streets.

"How goes the war?" she asked, to change the subject.

Chimalli answered. "We're pressing them on all fronts. They have limits, and we'll find them. The western camp collapsed soon after dawn, so we pulled back, redistributed. A few battle groups have had a chance to break into the main square, but we don't want to fight there yet. We've been lucky with casualties so far. When we take their people we stuff them into wagons, send them to Central for processing. Slow, but we're not trying to set a land speed record."

"Tell her about the other thing," Kopil said, still staring into the well.

"The other thing?"

Chimalli explained: "They surprised us a little after dawn. Launched a counterattack on the eastern flank."

Elayne blinked. "Counterattack?"

"Around nine-thirty, they hit our eastern bases hard. We've occupied the buildings flanking the Square since we found that the rebels can travel through them to get around the demon wall—" He shot a pointed look at Kopil. "That's where they hit us."

"Look," Kopil said. "I know the people who own these buildings. If your friend cut your house in half to stop a pest problem, you'd be angry with him."

"Are we calling them pests now?" Elayne asked.

"Poor phrasing. You know what I mean."

"With all respect, sir, a little property damage in the short run might avoid more trouble later. They have been burning buildings."

"They burn, and we'll build more. Anyway, you didn't tell her about the thing."

"Yes," Elayne said. "Please. Tell me about the thing."

Chimalli looked from her to his master, and Elayne could see the layers of his frustration: with the rebels, with the riot, with Kopil. "A small corps of red-arms, better disciplined than usual, hit us at dawn. Heavy, room-to-room fighting. We fell back to protect the upper floors and our own men. That's when they ran."

"Back into Chakal Square?"

"Out," Chimalli said. "South and east, into the Skittersill. At first we thought they might loop around, hit our bases from behind, but they kept going and lost us in the alleys." He spoke bluntly, not trying to hide his failure. "It's hard to track locals through the Skittersill. Couatl search could help, but there are covered alleys and markets in that region, and anyway we're saving our air support for the Square."

"An escape."

"That's not the opinion of my commanders on the ground. To hear them tell it, these were good fighters."

"People fight hard to get away from fighting."

"With respect, ma'am, I know that. But they weren't panicked. This was a planned movement, and you don't pull people who can fight like that from the line unless you think they might turn the tide. This looks like a run for supplies, or weapons. We've locked down weapons caches in the Skittersill, and we're keeping tabs—as well as we can with reduced patrols—on local criminal groups and the Stonewood refugee camps, in case they're hunting allies. If they find reinforcements, this action could get bloody. Bloodier," he amended.

"Fortunately," Kopil said, and motioned to Chimalli to continue. The man frowned.

"Fortunately, we have ways to track them."

"Release the hounds!"

She ignored the King in Red. "I thought you were short on manpower. Do you have enough people to run a dog search through the Skittersill?"

"Well," Chimalli said. "Not dogs as such."

"As such?"

"I mean, anymore."

"*Totenhunds* reporting," the dreamer said. "Pursuing ten possibles."

"Oh," said Elayne.

"I know," the King in Red replied. "Cool, right?"

44

Temoc was doing pull-ups in the courtyard when he heard the howls. Two voices chased each other through high terrifying arcs like a human being might make when breaking. "Caleb," he said. "Get inside."

The boy sat at the table, hands on cards. "What is that?"

"I don't know. Go inside until it passes. Please," he remembered to say.

Caleb gathered his cards and left. The screen door swung shut.

Temoc finished his set, concentrating on the pull in his lats rather than the nightmare noises. Sixteen, seventeen, eighteen, nineteen, twenty, a pleasant burn. The howls neared. Desert wolves sounded like that at moonrise—but they sang of hunger and feast, pack and loneliness. You could hear the images in their songs, if you listened. In these cries Temoc heard only the naked hunt.

He dried his face with a towel, and went to see.

The street outside was empty in both directions. A bicycle propped against a palm tree on the sidewalk opposite. Cobblestones swept clean two days ago remained clean still. How much must this lockdown be costing the King in Red? Though perhaps that was the reason for this morning's attack. The price mounted higher than the skeleton would pay, and so Chakal Square suffered.

The howls rose again, and beneath them Temoc heard footsteps. Human footsteps, running.

He turned just in time to see Chel round the corner onto his street.

No one looks composed while running for their life, and Chel was no exception. Her arms pumped like pistons. She did not so much run as fall constantly forward. She listed badly to one side. Her shirt was torn, and gray and red from ash and blood. One sleeve ended at her elbow. Her teeth flashed in the sunlight.

She stumbled, caught herself off the ground, kept running, limping worse now. Gods.

He ran toward her. She saw him, shook her head, shouted "No!" with the last of her breath.

Then the not-wolves came.

He had no other words for them. Their flesh melted seamlessly to metal and back. Dirty diamond eyes burned above wide mouths where metal teeth dripped poison. Long claws tore furrows in the cobblestones. Metal bolts protruded from their necks, and scar-stitching crisscrossed their flanks. The lead not-wolf galloped down the alley, gathered itself, and sprang toward Chel, all steel and flesh and teeth.

Temoc got there first.

His scars opened. He had little power so far from the Square—only what was left inside him, only what sleeping gods could lend. Ixaqualtil, he prayed as he ran. Seven Eagle, guide my hand.

Strength filled him, and righteous anger, and the hells' own thirst for blood.

He thrust Chel out of the way. The not-wolf could not change course in midair. Temoc laced his fingers together, and hammered his fists into the creature's spine. It fell and rolled, clacking sparks off cobblestones.

The second beast leapt toward him. He spun, thrust out his shadowclad arm, and struck the creature across the face. The not-wolf's claws glanced off his scars. He twisted his hips and pushed to throw it off. One claw tore a hot line across his chest. He'd feel the pain later, if there was a later.

"Behind—" Chel shouted just before the first not-wolf landed on Temoc's back. Foreclaws tightened on his shoulders, rear claws scrabbled for his kidneys. Teeth snapped at his neck, bounced off the scars there. Lucky old man.

No. There was no such thing as luck. There was strength. When that ran out, the gods remained.

The second beast twitched to its feet again. His backhand had bent that one's neck sideways; it swiveled on unnatural joints to face him, and growled deeper than any wolf he'd ever heard.

Not-wolves in so many ways: least among them that wolves were alive, and these long past dead.

Very well. He could not kill a dead thing, but he could break one.

He reached back past claws and teeth. The not-wolf's neck was thick as a normal man's thigh. Metal cylinders jutted from skin over the beast's spinal column. Power thrummed within: too shielded by silver for him to seize and steal. No matter. He was strong enough.

He squeezed. The second not-wolf jumped.

Blood and victory, he prayed, and moved.

In one smooth motion he tore the creature from his back and spun, swinging it down and around and up like a golf club. It struck the other not-wolf in midflight, metal on flesh, flesh on metal, claws into belly. Temoc released the creature's neck and the two fell entangled to the ground. Before either could recover, he knelt, raised his hand, and brought it down, twice, three times. Ichor dripped from his knuckles. The not-wolves lay still.

He lifted one, draped it across his shoulder. Sandbag workout, that was all.

Chel was staring at him. The fear in her eyes made him nervous. "Temoc," she said.

He didn't want to hear what she had to say, not yet. "I'll carry these a few blocks over. We want their corpses as far away as possible. And on fire."

She nodded. Had she looked at him that way before, and he just failed to notice?

Turn her away, warned the Temoc who lived in a small house in the Skittersill and tended his flock and did not raise his hand against the kings of this earth. You do not want to hear the message she bears. She's the war, come home.

"Get inside," he said. "I'll be back."

Bearing the not-wolves, he walked away, and felt her watching as he went.

When Temoc returned, Chel lay slumped against the wall, hand clasped over the wound in her side, breathing through gritted teeth. "Can you hear me?" He crouched beside her. Her eyelids fluttered. Her pupils shrank and dilated and shrank again before she focused on his face. "I will lift you."

"I can walk."

"I know." He slid his arm under hers, and pulled her upright. She hissed. His hand stuck to the blood soaked through her shirt. His wounds were already closing, and shallower anyway than hers. She had no protective scars. She did not scream. Most would have.

Chel limped, leaning against him, through the gate into their courtyard. Four walls and ivy and cacti and blank windows mocked them with suggestions of safety.

Caleb stood on the threshold of their house, just inside the open screen door. Obeying, as usual, the letter of command. He stared at Chel and Temoc. "Dad?"

Mina blew through the screen door like a wind. "Gods, what happened?"

"She's hurt."

"I see."

"I'm fine."

Mina grabbed Chel's other arm. "Let's get her to the chair." Chel moaned as they lowered her. "Where does it hurt?"

"Everywhere?"

"Caleb. You remember where we put the first-aid kit?"

"Under the sink."

"Then why are you still here?"

He wasn't, anymore. She turned back to Chel. "You are

sweating blood and bleeding sweat. Did you run all the way here?"

"Tried to walk. Blend in. But the dogs."

"They sent dogs after you?"

"Two," Temoc said. "Not quite dogs, either. Undead beasts in dog form. I stopped them."

"Great, because I'm sure they only sent two."

"Couldn't count the howls," Chel said. "Maybe a dozen, maybe more. Fifteen of us."

"All of them coming here?"

"No," she said. "I gave two others the address. Took the long way. If they're not here already, they didn't make it."

Ten hounds, Temoc thought. Within him Ixaqualtil writhed for joy and bared his teeth. We can kill ten—twenty, even, with ease and pleasure. Temoc doubted this was true, but the god was not awake enough to reason. Distant, dreaming, drunk on spilled blood. "Hold still," Temoc said. "Do not speak." He called upon the god's power. His joy. Make her whole, he prayed. Heal her, so she may fight.

"If the Wardens are chasing her, we all need to leave."

"Not. No." Chel shook her head. Temoc laid a hand on her ribs, and she bit her lip. Her eyes went wide with pain or visions or both.

"Don't bite your lip, sweetie. Come on. I'm not angry with you. Chel." Mina gripped Chel's jaw between her fingers and squeezed the woman's mouth open. With her thumb, she worked Chel's lip out from between her teeth. "It's okay." Caleb ran from the house, carrying the first-aid kit. "I just want to know what's happening, that's all."

"Here," Temoc said. "I have power enough to help. This will hurt."

"There you go, bite down on the gauze. I hate it when he does this."

"Mom? What's going on?"

"Cover your ears, Caleb. And look away."

Temoc laid his hand over Chel's broken ribs. His touch was

light but he felt the bones shift anyway. She groaned through gauze. "Seven Eagle, bind her."

"You're using Seven Eagle?"

Chel's eyes snapped wide, and he saw fear in them.

"He has fed recently. And battle wounds are His domain."

"Caleb. Cover your ears tight now."

"Seven Eagle, bind her. Seven Eagle, heal her. Seven Eagle, make her strong, for the battle that we now fight, for the battle that does not end, for the ending that comes when none are ready." He repeated the prayer in Low Quechal and High. The god heard his thoughts, but ritual still mattered, even so basic a ritual as prayer. He offered blood, hers and his mixed on his hands. Heat built in his bones, and he let it flow into her. Her bones wriggled, danced, snapped back together. Frayed muscles rewove, heart beat stronger. Blood flowed, and Mina sopped it with a towel.

Chel screamed through her clenched jaw: a sound torn from the pit of her belly. Her teeth gnashed the wad of gauze.

When the worst was over the god released her. She collapsed. Mina, too, sagged. The towel she held had been white, before.

Temoc withdrew his hand. The god slept, hungry again. Hungry, always.

The worst of Chel's injuries had closed, her internal damage healed. But Seven Eagle cared little for blood loss, and Chel was still bleeding.

"Caleb," Mina said. "Bring me needle, and thread, and a lighter. Temoc, can you stand?"

His head was not his to move. He nodded by divine leave alone.

"Fetch some water. I'll be here a while."

45

An hour later, Chel sat at the dining room table, wearing one of Mina's old linen shirts. Her bandages showed dark through the fabric. She dipped a finger into her water glass, and watched the drop form at her fingertip and fall to splash against the table. "Water in the desert."

"A glorious gift," Temoc said.

She lifted the cup two-handed as a Camlaander knight might lift his grail, and drank, eyes closed. When she set the cup down, it was empty. Temoc refilled it.

"Thank you," she said after the third glass.

"We do what we are called to do," Temoc said.

"You're welcome," said Mina.

"I've put you all in danger."

"Well." Mina shifted in her chair. "We couldn't leave you out on the street."

"You might have."

She shook her head, though she left it for Temoc to say "No." When Chel didn't reply, he continued: "Why are you here? Has Chakal Square fallen?"

She bowed her head. "No."

He was not sure how to feel about that.

"You escaped, then," Mina said. "That's good. We can hide you."

He poured her another glass. She drank. Caleb watched from the corner of the room. Temoc considered sending him away, and decided against it. The boy deserved to know what shaped his city.

"We'll scrub down the street outside," Mina said. "I can take your old clothes, plant them on a taxi or something, give the dogs a good chase. You can sleep in Caleb's room."

"No."

"Or out here if you like."

"No," she repeated. "I'm sorry, Ms. Almotil. That's not what I meant. I don't plan to stay."

"I won't let you die in the street."

"I'm strong enough to walk."

"Where?"

"Back," she said, and there was no question where she meant.

"Back into a war, to face gods know what. No."

Chel held the glass in her lap, and stared down at the water— at her own reflection, or the ceiling's, or at her own hands. Mina'd washed them clean.

She had run all this way knowing she might die. She faced the Wardens and their beasts with only conviction to bear her forward. And yet she sat here unable to deliver the message she carried from Chakal Square. Because Mina showed her hospitality? Because she saw why he left?

He spared her the pain. "She wants me to go back with her."

"What?"

A bird sang in the garden: four high whistles and the last sank low.

"Why the hells would she ask that? She almost died leaving that place. No way she'd—"

"It's true," Chel said.

Mina fell silent.

"Have you seen the newspapers?"

"Yes," Temoc said.

"What do you think? Be honest."

"You're in trouble." "You're," he said, not "we're." "The Wardens arrest those they can. The fires turned the city against you, even if you didn't set them. And the hostages were a mistake." He caught Mina's warning glance—go easy on the woman. But Chel did not flinch, though she did not look up from her water, either.

"That's what I told them," she said. "I kept us from issuing a ransom demand, at least. Couldn't get them free. The camp's torn. The Kemals scrounge supplies. The Major fights. Bel's calling on citizen groups throughout the Skittersill to join us. Everyone's afraid."

"Bad," Temoc said when she stopped to drink. He could not bear to keep quiet, not with that bird crying in the courtyard. Not with his son watching.

"The Wardens attacked before dawn. We're building our own barricades to keep them out, but we can't stop them from taking our people. The Major thinks this is his moment, his grand struggle."

"Craftsmen do not fight wars of attrition," Temoc said. "They prefer disruptive victories, surgical strikes. If they press you on all sides, they do so only to focus your attention on the periphery so they can strike the center. Beware your skies. Protect vulnerable targets."

"We need a leader," she said.

"You have many."

"The Major will not listen to Kapania Kemal. Bel acknowledges either of them grudgingly at best. I'm one more rip in a torn sheet. We need thread. Like this, we can't fight. We can't even surrender. If you went back, you could save us."

"And doom you. If I go back, the King in Red stops fighting a new rebellion, and starts fighting an old war. People will die."

"They're dying anyway, and worse. They're losing. Your generation got its last stand. This is ours, and we're falling apart. Ten years from now, we'll look around and say, remember when we couldn't fight back?"

"But you will be there to say it."

"Dying by inches is still dying."

"Spoken like a woman who has never died before."

"I thought you would understand." Those words hurt worse than the not-wolves' teeth.

"I would love to put the King in Red to flight," he said. "To wake the gods from slumber and strike against the powers of the Craft. But the world has changed. I thought Chakal Square was a way forward." Her eyes were bright and wet. "This isn't your fault. It isn't the Major's. It is barely the King in Red's. The peace is broken."

"While you wait," she said. "With your family."

"Should I give them up? Should I burn my house to the ground, because others suffer?"

"You preach sacrifice. I liked those sermons. I hoped you might live up to them."

He would not look away.

Chel set the glass on the table, and pushed herself to her feet. Her arms trembled, but she stood.

"You can't go," Mina said. "You're in no shape to fight."

"Then I won't fight. But I'll be where I belong." She nodded. "Thank you for the bandages. The shirt—"

"Keep it," Mina said.

"Thank you."

She limped out into the blinding light where the lone bird cried.

The door took a long time to close.

Mina embraced him. "I know it was hard," she said. "I know. But you did the right thing."

"Yes," he said.

46

Mina could not pull him into conversation. He remained a rock, staring at a blank spot of wall to the left of the screen door. At last she carried her books over from the shelf, spread them on the table, and began to read. Her pen scratched long lines under vital phrases. Mina had a steady hand despite the gallons of coffee she drank each day. When she'd stitched up Chel's side, she stopped her fingers from shaking with a breath. There were no sounds in the dining room other than her pen, and the occasional turn of a page. The five-chirp bird must have flown away.

The conversation they were not having filled the room. Branching vines of unsaid words tangled and knotted and rotted between them. The air smelled dry as library dust.

She was right. Down all the paths and side routes, she was right. He was a father, and a father owed first duty to his family. As a young single man he had walked faith-armored into war, spear raised, eyes bright with sunrise glory. He might have died then, without hesitation or regret, and he would have known, as the Craftsmen's claws tore out his guts, as their beasts ate his skin, that he had done all he was asked. But the gods had spared him from that fate, and they must have done so for a reason.

Or not.

"I will pray," he said, and stood.

She looked up at him, as if a vast distance lay between them. He was that distance, and he hated himself for it. "Do you want me to pray with you?" she asked.

"I think I should be alone."

She pointed her pen at him, but whatever objection she might have made died before it manifested on her tongue. "I'll be right here."

"I know."

"I love you."

"I love you, too," he must have said, because he always did, regular and natural as falling. But after he left the room he could not remember saying it, could not feel the imprint the words should have left—always left—on his soul. He felt only the certainty of habit, which was no certainty at all.

Their house was too small for a full chapel these days. When Caleb was born, they'd used the little chamber by the bathroom for a nursery, and Temoc set up his gods and saints in the bedroom down the hall. When Caleb outgrew his crib they made the switch, their son to a bed in the once-consecrated room, and the gods into the closet.

Closet was too meager a word. Temoc did not know the room's original purpose. Perhaps it had been an office once, or a storage chamber, six feet by six with a slit window. Temoc had slept in smaller nooks in post-Liberation chaos: under bridges, in the lee of Drakspine boulders, in clefts and caves and hidden tunnels beneath the desert. Once he added shelves, tapestries, and a woven grass mat, there was enough room here for his gods.

Most of them, anyway.

He opened the door and stepped into the shadow of divinity, into the oppression of incense. Stone faces stared down from the shelves. Fanged mouths opened. A small beaten iron statue of the Twin Serpents spiraled on the altar, flanked by the Hero Sisters, Aquel and Achal carved from basalt in the sweep of a dance or game. Suspended above the Serpents hung a black pearl, the heart to be consumed, the wisdom to be gained, the names to be transferred from devoured to devourer. And these were but one facet of worship, the central cult among many gods. Qet and Isil, Sea-Lord and Sky-Lady, upon whose praise

Dresediel Lex was founded long before the ancient Quechal homeland sunk beneath the sea, hung in arras form beside the window. Ili of the White Sails watched from the walls, and Ixaqualtil Seven Eagle, and Tomtilat Spider-Lord, and the seven gods of the seventy-seven kinds of corn, and the Hunchback. On each statue's base, beneath the feet of every woven figure, ran double bars of Serpents' scales, the constant reminder: we walk on the skin of a world that at any moment might consume us. This was the mill of ages, and prayer the water that drove it round.

That at least was the idea, though so much was lost—though the gods themselves passed on. Ixchitli, Sun-Lord, torn open on his own altar by the King in Red. Isil gone. Qet Sea-Lord her consort reduced to a hollow husk and that husk imprisoned by foul Craft. The Hunchback burned, Tomtilat's web torn. No sacrifices to the Serpents on Quechaltan in forty years. And the others, bereft of their city, ripped from their people, faded. Slept, not quite dead, nor yet strong enough to speak. Some few still worshipped in their little ways, and the gods' songs and stories would linger in Lexican dreams for generations yet, even if their true names passed away. There would always be a spider who bargained with a fly, there would always be two sisters who played ball with demons, there would always be monsters who tried to eat the sun, even if marrow and majesty seeped out from the myths.

But he kept them alive. He prayed. He fasted. He taught. Others listened, and because they listened they assembled to protest the destruction of their homes, and because they assembled they would die, and he might save them, and even if he could not save them surely he owed them his leadership, or failing that his presence, because what did you call a priest who deserted his flock in their need—what but a liar? And yet, and yet. He was a man, too, no eidolon of justice, no messenger from beyond, no night terror to plague the sleep of evildoers. He was a man, and a man served his family. This was the duty the gods enjoined: for each man to seek his proper hour of sacrifice, and repay the debt of flesh he owed them.

Temoc was an Eagle Knight. He was a servant of the many Lords and Ladies—their champion, their instrument.

And he had sent a woman to her death. Why pretend otherwise? A woman almost broken by her pilgrimage to him, who sacrificed her friends to seek his help. He sent her away. No: he refused her because he was afraid, for his family and for himself. He let her limp into the light, into the courtyard where the sad bird sang its five-note song, because he knew she was right. He could have stopped her. He was strong enough. If she was choosing wrong, why had he not stopped her?

She was right, and strong as well. It was her strength he admired. Purity of intent. Loyalty. She was a fighter. Like Mina.

Isil smiled from her tapestry. Was that it after all? Chel was a beautiful woman. No. Chel was young, and her strength shamed him. Twice her width and six inches taller, he stood nonetheless in her shade.

She was the man he had been forty years ago.

Gods, he prayed. I am lost. Guide me. Please.

They watched.

Is this the path for which you saved me? To throw my life away? To abandon family, duty, hope, and future, to leave my son undefended? You have kept me young. I have a long road left to walk.

But if I walk it alone, I will always walk in the shadow of the pyres that burn in Chakal Square tonight.

He heard a knock on the door. Mina. He could not face her.

The knock repeated. Not Mina: lower on the door, he realized, in the second before he heard his son say, "Dad?"

He considered not answering. "Come in, Caleb."

Caleb hesitated, doorknob half-turned. Temoc had shown him the small chapel, introduced him to the gods, let him feel their warmth and the rhythms of their dance. But he had never invited the boy to join him in his private prayer.

"It's fine," Temoc said. "Come in."

The door opened. Temoc turned on the mat. Caleb looked from him to the staring faces and back. He stood on the threshold, then stepped through with one foot first, as if testing a pool of water.

"Did you have a question?"

"The woman who came. She helped us in the crowd yesterday."

"Yes."

"She was hurt."

"She was hurt. What she is trying to do now—what the crowd is trying to do—it's very difficult. When people try to do difficult things, sometimes they are hurt. Sometimes they are hurt bad."

"I know that," he said, with a tone of mild offense.

"Of course you do." He reached out to tousle Caleb's hair, saw the flinch, and grinned and set his hand on his son's shoulder instead.

"Why didn't you help her? I mean," Caleb said, when Temoc was about to answer, "I know you put her back together. But she wanted you to go with her, and you didn't."

"I did not."

"Even though she's your friend."

"Even though."

"Why?"

"She wanted my help with the difficult thing she's trying to do."

"I heard."

"You're a good listener."

"Mom says that's how you win at cards."

"I don't win at cards."

"That's how she wins, I mean."

"She wanted my help with Chakal Square."

"Are you worried that you might get hurt?"

"Something like that," he admitted.

"But you won't. You're strong. Really, really strong."

"Even strong people get hurt sometimes. And anyway, I'm not the one I'm worried about."

"Me and Mom?"

"You and Mom. It's a big tough world out there."

"You don't need to worry about us."

"That's what fathers do."

"Mom can take care of herself. She's strong, too."

"You're right."

"And so am I."

He laughed.

"I am. We both are."

And there it was. The vow issued, the singing of the choir. His son would be strong. Strong enough to stand without Temoc. Strong enough to make his own way.

We will protect him, the gods sang. We will watch him. If you go forth to suffer in our service, if you cease to be a man and become instead a legend to glorify our name, he will not be alone. We watch always. We care for our people, and their children.

Only pave the way for us.

Only give us what is ours. Promised by your bloodline, father and son throughout history.

Give the boy the strength he needs. When you were his age, you knelt before the altar. When you were his age, you carved us into your skin. When you were his age, you dedicated yourself to the war that has found you now. We do not fault your hesitation. Years have passed, and the greatest battles come upon us unsuspecting. But do you think yourself so vital that your family will fail without you? Do you think time will cease if you die? You lack faith in your own blood. You need them to need you.

The boy wants to help. Let him.

"Dad?"

"I'm sorry," Temoc said. His voice shook. He did not, could not, contemplate this certainty that opened within him now, as if time were skin and the gods the knife that cut and peeled it back to reveal the future. Don't make me do this. Don't pave this road for me. And yet nothing could take away that sense of knife and skin. "I'm sorry. I know you're strong. You can take care of yourself. I just need to help a little."

Caleb hugged him, and he hugged the boy back, and felt ashamed.

47

By nightfall smoke from Chakal Square spread through the sky, darkening clouds. Temoc cooked dinner. Mina offered to help, and he refused at first, then relented, thanked her. She didn't mention Chel or the riots, and neither did he. They cooked together, and when they spoke they spoke of cooking: how many tomatoes, when to add the flour and how long to toast it, could she soak the dried chilis, where'd they leave the can opener, is that enough salt do you think. They filled the small kitchen, the two of them, trading the knife and chopping block. Stove heat made them sweat. This feeling was so easy to forget, so easy to miss even as you felt it: working with someone you loved on something small. Years had accustomed them to each other.

He tried to keep his eyes clear, tried to focus on the hiss of beef in pan, the smell of singed meat, the pop of grease. She slipped in beside him, slid chopped onions off the board with the back of the knife, and slipped away, leaving a memory in his skin and a tang in the air as the onions fried.

They ate in the garden. For once the clouds' reflected light did not trouble him with memories of the stars that should have hung above. He ate with his family. They laughed together. He served them, then returned to the kitchen, mixed the wine, and poured glasses for Mina and for himself, and even for Caleb. "You're acting," Mina said, "as if this were a special night."

"It is," he said. "I didn't go. I might have. In a way, this is the beginning of the rest of our lives."

They drank together. Temoc cleared the table, washed the dishes, and returned to the courtyard where his wife and son rested. Cactuses rose around them, and fern fronds bobbed in a cool breeze. The northern wind had broken, and for the first time in days he felt the breath of the sea.

He wanted to weep. He did not. He could not afford to waste his remaining time.

He told coyote stories beneath the covered sky. No gods in these, not really, no heroes either as such, only clever creatures trying to outwit larger, stronger foes. Tricksters did not lead. No one looked to them for guidance. That would be a good life. That was how human beings learned to live, at the dawn of time: by scavenging and treachery.

When he finished an old eastern fable about the day the dawn froze, he heard deep breathing and looked left to see Caleb slumped in his chair, head lolled to one side. The boy's fingers twitched, but his eyes were still behind closed lids. "Asleep," he said, and Mina said, "That was fast."

"Too much wine." He lifted his son in his arms and carried him to bed. The boy shifted against Temoc's chest. Remember this, he told himself. The living weight. The heat of him, the pressure of his chest rising, falling against yours, and against your arms.

He removed Caleb's shoes and pants and shirt, slid him under the sheets and patted the covers. Caleb hated that, would have groaned if he was awake.

"Look at him," Mina said from the door. Faint light through the window blinds lit the boy, burnished him like bronze, his features perfect as his mother's. Strong, he'd said.

He would need to be.

Temoc and Mina went to their room, and lay together, and loved one another. He wanted so much to drift off to sleep beside her, to wake the next morning knowing the night had passed and the riots of Chakal Square were done.

He rose from bed without a sound, and dressed slowly. Heavy canvas trousers. Boots. A long-sleeved shirt. A belt. And to that belt he added the knife he always carried, the black glass blade that had not drawn blood for decades. The knife was a symbol of his office: its sharkskin hilt, the curved white reflection along its edge as if the blade cut light when drawn. That was all he could take. If he survived, he might not be able to return for a long time. Even if Mina forgave him, the Wardens would not, for the deeds he would do in battle not yet joined.

He had watched the skyline, waited for the fire-fountains that would signal the King in Red's attack. The dread master tapped his finger bones together atop his throne, and reveled in his siege-facade, patient as a spider, waiting for the perfect moment to strike. Temoc hoped he would delay an hour more.

The hall to his son's room was longer in the dark. The boards did not creak beneath his feet.

He lit a candle outside Caleb's door, ran his blade through the flame, and snuffed the candle with his fingers.

Toys loomed in stuffed lumps from shelves and tables. Caleb's cards lay on the table, on their slip of silk. A half-built block city cast strange shadows on the floor—unfinished arches and tumbled towers.

Temoc prayed.

Praise be to the two sisters
To the sisters Aquel and Achal
To Aquel and Achal who descended into darkness
Who descending into darkness found the Serpents
And finding the Serpents bound them with their
    hearts
Binding as we bind, giving as we give
Flesh to the gods, and gods to flesh.

Don't do this. Just leave. Go fight the war you know you need to fight. Mina will take care of him. He will take care of himself.

But the boy needs his father. Without a father, he needs strength to guard him, guide him. And guard and guide both lay in the blade of Temoc's knife.

He turned the covers down. Caleb was still as death. The

drugs mixed in the wine held him fast. No time for vision quests. No time to confront the Gods of the Three Gates—and anyway one of those gods was forty years dead. The ritual would have to do. The ritual, and the scars.

The knife trembled in Temoc's hand.

Hubris, to think he could dedicate his son to gods the boy barely knew. Folly, to think a few cuts would make his son an Eagle Knight.

He prayed, using no traditional form, to any god or goddess who might hear him. Is this right? I must serve You, I must help my son. Do I presume upon Your power, when I pass my path to him? Did my father presume, when he passed his to me? When he gave me the choice, at age nine, atop the obsidian pyramid at our city's heart? Should I not give Caleb the choice I faced?

And what choice was that? Temoc's father had towered above him, a giant, ancient of days, slabs of muscle and a grim countenance: a lord of men, a servant of the gods. When that man asked his son if he would walk the knight's path, how would his son reply? When every day for nine years he'd heard tales of the Eagle Knights as he drifted off to sleep, and hoped one day he would be worthy to join their number? When every eldest son of his line had taken the oath, received the scars, for centuries?

Temoc was an instrument. He was a knife held in the hand of greater men, of forces greater than men. A knight was a servant, and so was a king: a tool of gods who were history, who were the sum of men and transcended men. Their hands held him. Though they slept, they held him still, fingers tight around his hand, around the haft of the knife descending.

The second cut was the hardest—the first almost an accident, a dip of blade into belly-skin, a shallow nick from which blood welled slowly. Caleb did not stir. The drugs held him, and the gods too, even as they held Temoc and the knife. The second cut, though, was a long curve beneath that first puncture. Temoc needed focus and a steady hand. He could not think of the boy beneath him as his son. Caleb belonged to the line. Belonged to the scars his family had worn since before the Quechal homeland sank beneath the sea. Blood flowed faster now. He should have brought a towel.

As Temoc drew the scar, he feared the gods had deserted him. That, sleeping, they might not imbue the scars with power. But the wound his knife left blazed green, and knit itself closed. Still, blood was lost, and more would be. So much more.

He prayed as he worked, spoke the words and fixed his mind in proper posture for the gods. Dead Ixchitli first, the Sun who fixed the sky, fiercest warrior in the battles against the skazzerai between the stars. Envision a man blood-soaked astride a green field under a blue sky. Two spears in one hand, a club in the other. First see his strength, then see his age. See him as a mountain that bleeds. See his feet entangled with the grass, see him as a fire inside all that grows, a fire too in the bowels of the earth. Then his daughters Aquel and Achal, the twins of one heart with the two Serpents who twine beneath the world, guardian and doom of our people. Qet and Isil. The Hunchback. God after god, each presented as a burning curve through his son's skin. Caleb knew the stories. As Temoc cut, they became part of him.

Arms and legs belonged to the Spider whose web was flame, rebel child of the stars. The Serpents coiled around the boy's heart, guarding and troubling it, their stirrings its constant beat, their magma rolling through his veins. The lungs were Isil's and his salt blood Qet's. Steady the hand, ensure the lines meet cleanly. No fine manipulations of the chisel here, no elegant glyphs: he carved gods and their prayers in elemental forms onto his son, into the boy's soul.

Blood stained the bedsheets. Blood stuck to Temoc's fingers when he wiped it away to clear the ground for the next incision. Blood did not stick to the knife's edge. It rolled off, leaving droplet-trails on skin. The boy's breathing did not change. His eyelids fluttered, eyes danced beneath them, but he lay locked in a sleep the gods invaded.

Sweat ran down his brow, and stung his eyes.

Time passed. An angel of blood spread from Caleb on the bed, wings flared beneath his outstretched arms. The wounds closed, most of them, but he was pale, and shivered from the blood he'd lost. Green and silver lines shimmered beneath his scabs.

One final scar remained: the vertical cut atop the heart, below and above the Serpents' gaping mouths. Anyone could draw the other scars, though there was honor in drawing them yourself. Only the recipient could make the last, symbol of the sacrifice he would perform, of the life he would lead, as if he were a man already dead.

No time to explain all this to Caleb. Temoc hoped, this once, that form would be enough. The gods knew his need. The gods guided them both. The gods would forgive one distortion.

He lifted his son's slick, sticky hand and wrapped his small fingers around the knife. Bones ran straight and thin beneath Caleb's inscribed skin: phalanges and metacarpals and small round knuckles. Strong. Temoc's hand held his son's, which held the knife, and the gods' hand held his. The wrist didn't want to turn quite perpendicular to the chest, so Temoc had to lift Caleb's elbow and move it in. He expected the arm to feel heavy. It did not.

One last cut, a finger's breadth. Skin parted slowly, as if the knife had grown dull. This was the signature, the permission, the act that tied the disconnected scars into a whole.

And the gods entered Temoc.

His spine was a live wire. His flesh crisped, his skin peeled back. Fire tore through him, stretched him to impossible size, and passed down his hand to his son's, to the knife, to the blood. Caleb's eyes snapped open. He gasped for breath, and beams of coherent light shone from his eyes. The scars thrummed as if Caleb's soul were a drum with which the gods beat time. A sound escaped his son's mouth, a hollow, animal screech.

It was done.

The scars dimmed, though they pulsed still. Caleb fell back

to the bed. His body struck the sodden sheets with a wet heavy sound. His eyes remained open. They stared up blank, unseeing. Breath ran rapid over his lips, in and out and in and out, too fast. Shadows unfolded from the boy's scars and folded again, spasmodically, no more subject to Caleb's will than were his trembling hands.

Temoc did not remember this. Perhaps he would not have remembered it. Or else this was new, some reaction to the way the deed was done, or to the drug. He would stay, and watch until it passed.

The blade in his hand was clean as ever. The gods kept it so.

He had done what he came to do.

He hated himself. He hated the gods. He hated the war, and Chakal Square, and Chel for finding him, and he hated the King in Red most of all. But what was done was done.

"Temoc." The voice behind him, the waking whisper, wrapped him in ice. Mina's voice. "Temoc, what's wrong? Why are you still up?"

Her footfall on the floor of Caleb's room was soft and clear. A single gentle press on a piano key. The last time he would ever hear that note.

He did not turn. He did not look at her. He was brave enough for everything but this.

She saw, and screamed.

Passed him in a rush, a sweep of hair and nightgown. He tried to stand, and staggered back. She bent over the bed, a curve in the darkness, holding Caleb, her hands stained red. Words were a rush of breath pulsed with consonants: "Oh, gods. Oh, gods." Could she see the light in their son's scars? Or did she only see the blood? "Caleb. Caleb, honey, wake up." Caleb coughed, gasped, shivered, did not wake.

"It's okay," he said. "He's okay."

She wheeled on him. "There's blood, Temoc. There's—"

He held his hands out between them. Voice low. Voice level. "It's okay. Mina. You don't understand. This is good."

He still held the knife. His hands were red.

Her eyes flared black and large in the night.

"What. The *hells*. Have you done."

So many ways to say it. I scarred our son. Gave him strength. Joined him to the ways of his family since the dawn of time. Warded him against the legions that will one day wish to do him harm. The words did not come. None but the simplest. Only an "I."

That was all she needed. "You."

He stepped toward her. She drew back.

"The wounds are closed."

"Go."

"He'll be fine."

"You want to go. So fucking go already." Her voice broke to a ragged edge.

He sheathed his knife. He could not reach for her.

"Get out of here. Get out of here right now or I will—" She cut off. Anger closed her throat. She grabbed a lamp from Caleb's bedside table, lifted it like a mace. "Go."

"Mina."

"Not one fucking step." A scream. Caleb convulsed, moaned.

Temoc wanted to say something. Anything.

He raised his hand.

"No."

That word was a wall, and the wall fell onto him.

Stop her. Grab her, calm her down. Explain.

How? He couldn't even explain to himself.

He stepped back. Turned halfway. By the time he reached the living room, he was running. Fast, and faster still. His eyes burned. His hands burned—from the blood. It stained him, covered him. Waking gods licked his hands and sang sweetly in his ears. He ran faster, as if he could outrun himself.

Faster yet, and every step carried him to war.

Behind, on the rooftops, two figures watched the house, and exchanged a long, silver, hungry look.

Soon, they said. Very soon, now.

They licked their lips, and savored their fangs.

48

Rage flowed cold and waterfall-fast, mixed with and insepara-ble from fear. Mina stood surrounded by Caleb's room. Shelves. Books. Cards. Blocks. Right angles and sharp edges, askew. The door gaped before her, where Temoc had stood a moment ago, and the black beyond.

She had not seen what she had seen. She could not have.

No. That was the reflex of a scared child's mind, to reject reality that did not fit preconception. She saw the knife in Temoc's hand. She heard him try to apologize, in that way he had of not apologizing. She saw him leave. She told him to leave.

And now he was gone, and she remained. Rocking on her feet. Her breath, and Caleb's, both loud in her ears.

Caleb. She turned back to the bed, to him, shaking, asleep, covered in seeping wounds, in blood.

So much blood. Gods. The body contained what, eight pints, a child's less, and how much spilled here? The sheets stained red. All the gods and devils watched.

She touched her son's chest, his face. Caleb groaned. Eyes opened but did not focus. A sweet, dank smell on his breath: some soporific drug, mixed with the wine. He kept that kind of stuff around, for rituals and dream-quests. Out of the boy's reach. Well hidden.

"Caleb. Caleb!" No response. "Caleb, can you hear me?"

No, again.

She wanted to cry. She was crying, big, racking sobs. Her eyes were wet. She wiped them with her hand, unthinking, and the blood stung. Qet and Isil. Damn them. Damn all the gods, and her husband, too.

She recognized the scars. She had written articles on their like, discussed their language and their relevance to modern Craft, had run her fingers over those very ridges on her lover's, her husband's skin. She had never seen them on her son's body before.

Too much, too much, tossed by rage and frozen by fear.

She could not afford to be this person now.

Her body understood before her brain did. Stopped shaking Caleb, stood. Searched the room, found nothing, staggered out into the hall, realized when she reached the bathroom that she was looking for a towel. A cloth robe. Something to cover him. Grabbed both, and returned. Don't drag the towel across the wounds. Whatever he had done—whatever Temoc and his gods had done—to heal the boy, his cuts were too fresh, scabs pink and raw where there were scabs at all. No longer bleeding openly. Not good, there was no good here, in this room, but good enough. Pressing with the towel, she mopped up blood. Some remained, smeared, dried onto his skin. A handprint. Hers, or Temoc's. No. She refused to think that name. It made her freeze, and she could not afford to freeze.

Where to go? Hospitals would be full of riot-wounded. Could drive north, risk meeting rebels or Wardens or those dogs. Don't worry about that, said the small part of her that was no one's wife, no one's mother, no one's daughter even. Don't worry. Get Caleb out of here. First, pull him off that bloody mattress. Scars on his back, too. Fuck. Sop the blood. Drape him in the bathrobe, white cotton with blue stripes and now red ones, too. Fine. Tie the knot at his stomach.

"Mom?" The voice soft, heartbreaking, weak as if through many layers of cotton.

"Caleb? Can you hear me?"

"Mom," again, drifting off. Fine. Good, even. She lifted him, tested his weight. So heavy normally, grown big, but he felt like a feather now. All had gone out of him, everything but life. The life she'd keep, and strangle anyone who tried to take it from her. Drape his arms over her shoulders. Scabs ridged his skin beneath the thin robe. He moaned in sleep, from pain, from nightmares.

Alone. Alone with her boy in a city gone mad. She could walk the streets, try against hope to hail a taxi. Or she could fly. She closed her eyes, took inventory of her soul. She thought she had enough.

The King in Red would have forbidden optera from landing in Chakal Square, but the rioters' need was great—it would poison the air, confuse the bugs hovering above the Skittersill. But her need was greater, and there was no price she would not pay.

She ran with her son clutched to her, out into the courtyard, out into the street. Feet bare against cobblestones. Craft-warped insects that hover in the clouds, chitin angels, hear me. No one has ever needed you as I need now.

The sky spread opalescent overhead, stained orange in the west by fire. Blank walls crowded her in, skyline scalloped black by roof tile. Dew-damp cobblestones slippery underfoot. Hot breath on her neck, Caleb's breath, so rapid, his body rigid too, seizing up as she ran.

Shapes moved on the roof across the street. Humanoid forms, long-limbed. Copper plates glinted where their eyes should have been, like a cat's eyes seen at angle. They leaned forward, watching. Their silhouettes showed claws.

She would not scream. She ran.

I need you.

Bug-legs struck her from behind, and she flew.

49

Temoc ran from himself, and from his wife, and his son, and two decades of peace. He ran toward battle.

Dresediel Lex around him crouched in wait. Behind blank windows families hid, waiting for a signal to pretend once more to live their normal lives. Lit convenience stores stared empty-aisled out on vacant streets, waiting for customers who would not come. A shopping cart lay upended in a parking lot. An optician's ghostlight sign flickered and buzzed. He ran past all-hour groceries, diviners' shops bedecked with crystal balls and tarot cards, a small-time local Craftsman's office, low-roofed bars, a palm-fronted nightclub, a bookstore with barred windows, a row of tailors' shops. Most nights this strip throbbed with people. Now its emptiness throbbed in turn.

The wind shifted north, hot again, and he smelled smoke, dust, and sand. Senses dilated by panic, rage, and gods, he heard the battle in Chakal Square, an ocean of screams and tangled bodies. His world, now. He sank into it, and ran faster. Muscles stretched. Power coursed through him. He became a creature of darkness.

He felt the wingbeats before he heard them. Bass shock waves struck his chest like blows, echoed inside like a second heartbeat. He stumbled, thinking—heart attack? Had he lost everything only to die here? But he looked up, and saw. He might still die, but not from weakness of the heart.

A flying V of Couatl wedged toward Chakal Square. Twenty-meter wings beat in unison. Snaky tails thrashed the air. They flew so high, in such elegant array, that someone raised in another city might have mistaken them for swans.

Temoc did not mistake.

This was no patrol. They came to kill.

The gods were kind, indeed. Cruel and kind. The King in Red had held his attack for night, when after a brutal day's fighting the Chakal Square band would have no choice but to man their makeshift barricades and hope for the best. Then the Wardens' attack would fall in the center, brutal and unexpected.

The gods were kind, unless they had doomed him to see this assault without being able to stop it.

He could not fail now, not after all he'd done. He ran faster, through the scared city's sleeping streets.

"We are winning," the Major told Chel in a voice that brooked no argument.

"Winning?" She swept an arm to compass the mess of Chakal Square. "You call this winning?"

They stood in the Square's heart: the clearing they'd made by the fountain for the wounded, of whom there were too many. Bodies lay on beds of folded cloth, moaning, bloody. Nurses moved among them, lacking any uniform but compassion. Few in the camp had medical training, most limited to half-remembered first-aid lessons from grade school camping trips. Now they tended the wounds of a war. In days, infection would claim most of the fallen, if the camp lasted so long.

Fires roared behind her. Out on the perimeter, the battle raged. Wardens charged again and again at the barricades.

"We have withstood a day's attack. If they thought we would be this hard to break, they would have struck us harder. We have exceeded the King in Red's expectation. We defied him."

Sweat coated Chel. Pain dulled the sharp edges of her mind. Memories of Temoc's healing still sickened, that sensation of her body coming alive, ribs wriggling and blood vessels fusing as a boar rooted beneath her skin. "We're losing people. We can't last another day at this rate. And we won't, because they haven't really hit us yet. Which they will, if we don't give up these hostages."

The Major laughed steel and springs. He'd straightened out the dimple in his helm, but a trace of the knuckles' dent remained. "You'd have us relinquish one of our few bargaining chips, just because you're afraid. Even if we released them, how do we know the Wardens would call off their attack?"

"There's nothing certain here. Best we can do is gamble."

"And you've gambled so well today."

She drew breath, and did not try to kill him. She'd clawed through broken glass to return to Chakal Square. Sprinted the last quarter-mile, or as near to a sprint as her wounded body could manage. Burst Mina's stitches running from those damn dogs. And her men, the ones she led out into the city to bring Temoc home—they weren't back yet. Hiding still in the city, she hoped. They had friends and bolt-holes. They weren't dead. Necessarily. Not all of them, not yet.

Flimsy argument, she knew. Gods.

"I made the right call," she said. "If Temoc were here—"

"If Temoc were here he'd lead us down the same conciliatory road that got us into this mess. If Temoc were here, he wouldn't be able to turn this attack."

"Listen."

"I have listened. You want us to need Temoc, because then your sacrifice won't have been in vain. You want us to lose this battle, due to your misguided fascination with old gods and antique heroes. You refuse to—"

"Not to me, dammit. Listen!"

The Major stopped talking.

The camp around them had gone quiet. Even the convalescent ceased to moan.

A drum beat overhead.

Chel grabbed the Major's arm and pulled him to the ground. He squawked in shock, struggled to rise.

Then the tents exploded.

On any other night Mina would not have realized she was being followed until too late. Ordinarily the sky above Dresediel

Lex swarmed with fliers and airbuses and Couatl and drakes, as reefs of mirror coral in the Fangs swarmed with multi-colored fish. Even at night, the airspace should have been so crowded that a few more fliers would be all but impossible to notice.

Tonight, though, the Skittersill skies were empty. Couatl swarmed near Chakal Square to the west, but she flew north alone.

Alone, she'd thought at first.

The buzz of the opteran's wings rocked and reassured; its claws clasped beneath her arms, around her waist and thighs, strong as architecture. She was less sure of her own strength. Caleb was a light burden, his arms wrapped firmly around her neck, hers around his back, but even a light burden hurt if born long enough.

Caleb breathed. That was good. He breathed, and was not bleeding. Gods. She glanced back through the rainbows of the opteran's two-meter wings and around the tumescence of its body, its glittering eyes, the proboscis through which it tasted and drained her soul. So far gone in the adrenaline rush, she hadn't even noticed the creature's pull yet. Maybe she wouldn't. Maybe anger gave her spirit strength.

The Craft didn't work that way, but she could hope.

She looked back to their house, now vanished amid the maze of similar Skittersill houses, one more wrong turn in the labyrinth of light.

Shadows flitted through that light. Buzzing wings refracted streetlamps' glow.

Optera, two of them. Following her. Faster, too—gaining.

Any other night she would have called herself paranoid. Apophenia, wasn't that the word, seeing patterns where no patterns were? But this was not any other night. She was still Temoc's wife—gods, was she, even in her own mind?—and the boy his son, and he had gone to fight the King in Red in Chakal Square. Of course someone might have watched them. Of course, if Temoc left and they sought refuge elsewhere, they would be followed.

But these were not Wardens. Wardens did not use civilian fliers. They had their own mounts.

Caleb groaned against her chest.

The opteran sucked Mina's soul, she felt it now, a slight slowing of the mind, perceptions grayed and emotions dulled. But she could spare a second's delay to be safe.

She swerved left toward the coast. Needed to look as if she had a destination in mind. What was out this way? Monicola Pier, no fit place for a woman on the run. Offices. A few hotels.

She glanced back, and saw neither of the optera behind her. Lost them. Good.

But where had they gone?

She searched the city lights for the telltale rainbow of opteran wings. There—to the right, following her old trajectory, so fast. And, once she saw the first, she found the second faster: it had swept in a long arc to the left, almost even with her, moving to outflank.

Diving, she bore north once more, keeping the pursuer in sight. Down she fell, down, until she skimmed the tops of skyscrapers. The old monkey-fear of heights clawed at her—she was low enough now that the ground ceased to be preposterous and became real. A long, deadly drop. Faster, north along Jibreel, and there, her western pursuer passed in front of a white and red ghostlit billboard of a grotesque smiling face. She saw long limbs, too long, a pointed head, a glint of metal, and something in its hand, a blunt claw-shaped instrument with crystal tines that shimmered menacingly.

The light swept around and shrank to a point, pointed at her.

She climbed fast. Lightning cracked the sky beneath her, and the answering thunderclap ripped through her body. She veered right, spinning, her arms clutched so tight to her son she feared she might break his bones and rain his blood on the city. His robe flapped around them. Her feet were bare, and cold. She spun through two large circles to make a pattern, then jagged sharp to the left even as a second bolt tore through the sky where they would have been—this bolt from the right, the second attacker. No shot from the first. Their weapons must take time to charge, or else they didn't want to attract attention.

Both flew straight for her now, all pretense of innocence abandoned.

She could not fight them in the air, not while holding her son. Her opteran was hungry, burrowing deeper into her soul. It sucked and drained and writhed. She had to lose them, and find help, fast. Grace and Mercy Hospital was too far east; she'd have to get past the pursuers first.

She remembered Elayne Kevarian's voice. If you need help. A business card for the Monicola Hotel. Not far—closer than the hospital. Chel didn't trust the woman. Didn't trust anyone, now. But Elayne had made the offer, and she seemed, if not kind, at least effective.

How to reach her? Mina couldn't keep dodging much longer. She had to fly fast. She had to be invisible.

Ah. Yes.

She climbed, hoping—not praying, not now—her pursuers' weapons were still building charge. A few more seconds, that was all she needed. Up, into the mother-of-pearl underbelly of Craftwork clouds. Arms of wet cotton held her close.

She could not see, could not even tell which way was north. Vast shapes moved about her in the artificial cloud. But the opteran knew the way. Its multifaceted eyes peered through the dark.

Go, she told it. Take me to the Monicola Hotel.

The tents burst apart into shredded fabric and broken wood. Long furrows opened in flagstones, two sets of three trenches each. Chel hit the stone hard, and the Major clanged down beside her, both toppled by the wind of something massive overhead. A roar on the low edge of human hearing scraped her bones and knotted her stomach. Groaning, weak, she pushed herself off the stone, turned, and saw . . . nothing.

An immense, towering nothing, a writhing space where her eyes would not focus. Again she heard the roar. Wing-wind battered her face. More tents broke. A red-arm ran toward the wreckage, and a distortion in the air, a not-thing with no color, no texture, no features her mind could hold, struck him in his stomach and he flew back to land amid the wreckage of the tents. Thudding impacts from above, more splintered wood, more roars without throats to voice them.

She forced herself to her feet, pulled the Major up after her. He drew the lead pipe at his hip, held it like a storybook sword, but his eyes sought his enemy in vain among the wrecked tents. He bellowed a challenge, and ran toward the nothing with pipe-sword raised. Then a great wind struck him and he flew ten feet to the left, landed, skidded, lurched to one knee. Blood seeped from the torn armor of his chest.

A fallen brazier's coals caught on canvas. Oily smoke parted to wreathe the form Chel could not see: a snakelike body and feathered wings, huge claws and sharp teeth bared. "Couatl!" she shouted, and grabbed a broken tentpole to use as a weapon. "In the smoke!"

The Major heard her, and turned, seeking. What must have been a claw tore an invisible arc through fire, and he swept his pipe around to block. The force of the blow still thrust him onto his back, but the Couatl screamed and reared, and its frustration gave the Major time to stand.

Screams rose around them: the hostage tent, the armory, torn apart. "Couatl!" she screamed again.

No way to tell if the others heard her. The Major swung for what he thought was the creature's body and missed. Damn damn damn. Other red-arms running. They'd never make it in time. Other screams and eruptions of bodies near the medical tent, the kitchens. Each Warden team had come with a purpose in mind, and this one's was to kill the Major. And maybe kill her, too.

Not if she could stop it.

Couldn't see the body, couldn't focus with her eyes. But if it could strike her she could strike back. The body writhed, the claws danced a killing dance. The wings, furled, swept burning cloth and wood away, leaving trails amid dust and splinters. Those were as good a target as any. And if she could climb the wings, she could reach the rider.

She ran, and jumped, and caught one wing as it swept up. Torn through the air, buffeted by wind, she flew and fell and landed on unseen feathers. Muscles surged beneath her, and taut skin over steely bone.

The Craft that clad the Couatl did not warp light, or else the beast's rider could not see. Chel was being ordered blind: enchantment pressed against her, commanded her to look away. But she could still feel, and felt down the Couatl's wing until feathers gave way to taut scales.

The head was that way, following the wings' leading edge. She felt leather straps—a saddle.

She still held the shattered tent spar. She swung it in a blind arc, screaming. Wood struck bone—the rider's skull. The Couatl reared. She clutched its sides with her legs and swung again, connected. The world veered. She drew back her arm for the third strike.

A human hand caught her wrist and twisted. She gasped in pain. The makeshift club tumbled from her fingers, and the Warden—had to be a Warden—threw her. She tumbled off the Couatl's back. Paving stones struck her like a hammer.

Above, outlined by smoke, a serpent's jaws yawned wide.

Mina flew blind in a sorcerous cloud. Buzzing luminous shapes zipped through the haze and away: other optera, riderless, circling above the city as they waited for someone to need them. Once her opteran veered sharply right, and she wondered why until a faceted crystal the size of a building pierced through the cloud: a skyspire rising through artificial haze for a clear view of the night sky. Blurred figures moved behind glass walls, or bent over desks, ignorant of her and of the insectile darkness alike.

Caleb shivered. The wind, she thought, or their speed, or blood loss setting in.

She was losing it. The opteran drained her soul, and she had only so much to give. Her arms tired.

Get me to the Monicola Hotel. I can do the rest. A few miles more. Her students told stories about optera abductions when they thought professors weren't listening: dumb tales in which a person, generally female, someone's sister's cousin's friend, lost herself in flight, never to return, dead husks flying forever in an insects' grip. She did not believe the stories. Too many traditional forms embedded there: the god-ox that stole the Queen of the Old World, the buffalo-bride, even downtown horror plays, everyday tools twisted to implements of liberation. This high up, she felt the stories' seed. Eternal freedom from gravity and ground, from knives and gods. Tempting.

No. She'd lost so much soul already. Even fear faded, incipient mortality giving way to the kind of drawn-out academic detachment that rendered "certain death" as "incipient mortality." But Caleb needed her.

Monicola Hotel, she thought, through the link she shared with the creature, not so much psychic as gustatory, the connection of diner with dinner, no, dammit. Stay concrete. Be here. Your son's arms cold around your neck. The pain where you hold him. The proboscis burns against your skin. The cloud smells of dirt, charcoal, sulfur. The Monicola Hotel. Where?

Here.

She fell.

They fell, the three of them, together.

The ocean of clouds swept past and they broke through. Like a diver surfacing from deep water at night only in reverse, sweeping from darkness down toward jewel-carpet city, Dresediel Lex perfect only seen from overhead—by day the back of a giant basking lizard, a vast cracked scab, a cancer, but paradise by night. It grew. Gods, the fear a coal in her stomach. She'd never moved this fast before, the opteran's wings buzzing to speed their fall, as if gravity needed any help.

And still the city swelled. A postage-stamp scrap of stone with a black pool at its center no larger than the pupil of an eye, ringed by blinding light, larger now, the size of a book and then no longer a mockup of a real place but the place itself, they fell toward a real thing that would break them both, so fast, pull up pull up pull up up *up* the fountain a fist rushing toward her—

The opteran spread its wings and the dive broke, slowing, slowing, still too fast.

Then it let them go.

She tumbled five feet maybe through the air, Caleb clutched in her arms, to land with an enormous splash in the Monicola Hotel fountain.

Ten blind flailing seconds later she found her footing, stood, chest-deep in water, bare feet slipping on slivers of thrown copper. Her arms free. Spinning, searching. There—Caleb, floating face-up spread-eagled. The scars on his legs burned green. His nostrils flared.

"Caleb?"

"Mom?"

She would not cry. Pulled him into a hug. Everything felt so distant, their embrace a mere pressure on her chest, a vague heat. Colors faded. His hair not deep blue-black, his skin not the color of rosewood—only wavelengths of light. Time ticked by in seconds, not heartbeats.

So little soul left.

"Come on. We have to go." Climbing out of the fountain: application of so many units of force against the fountain lip, contraction of near-exhausted arms and back to lift herself up and the boy after. Her son. So hard to form that thought. So much harder than she expected to remember which muscles moved in what order to walk. Left calf first, then right? Apparently not. Left quadricep first, then right calf, but tighten the core for balance, and keep the boy by your side. Toward the glass doors beneath the angular art deco script that read: MONICOLA HOTEL. Forward. People staring, for some reason.

She needed soulstuff. Staggered, with Caleb, still dripping fountain water, through the revolving door into a vault-ceilinged lobby perhaps thirty feet tall at apex. Chandeliers, fake crystal. Gold leaf everywhere. Marble floors. Temperature perhaps fifteen degrees cooler than outside. She shivered.

Had to be a banking circle here. She scanned the room. Suited men wearing metal nametags moved toward her, faces professionally concerned. The one on the left, twenty-five pounds heavier, had cut himself shaving. A bit of white clay under the chin. She turned from them, pulled the boy with her. There: a small booth by the door. One person in line, an old man in a short-sleeve shirt covered with orange flowers, who took a step back and raised his hands, spread, when she approached.

She slid into the booth, pressed her thumb to the center of the silver circle. Static charge built, thin hairs on the back of her arms and neck rising to attention. She shivered again, losing core temperature. The prick of a needle into her thumb, the drop of blood, the answering whir of counterweights behind the wall, and then her skin and flesh and mind jammed open at once by a rush of soul from her savings account.

She gasped, and gulping air stumbled back into the ostentatious lobby, her son by her side, his hair black once more, black as his eyes and set in a face the colors of which she knew. Eyes, rolling back in his head as he slumped into her. "Caleb! Come on, Caleb, stay with me."

The suits had reached her now, the big man with the shaving cut in front. Brass buttons flashed from his coat. "Excuse me, ma'am. Can I help you?"

"I'm a guest of Elayne Kevarian. Room four-oh-four."

"Are you."

"Call her room. Check. She knows me. This is important."

"Ma'am, calm down."

"I'm calm." She growled that word because fuck calm and fuck him. "I need to see her." She sounded desperate. She was desperate. So good to feel again after the fading of her soul, but if she didn't pull herself together they'd throw her out.

The man opened his mouth.

At that moment, her pursuers landed in the courtyard.

She felt their impact: no slow descent for these, no, they fell lock-kneed from the sky to strike beside the valet station, shattering stone underfoot. A horse spooked and danced away. The valet fell. In the instant before a cloud of dust rose to obscure them, she saw her hunters wore black suits. One was pinching his lapels. They had no lips, but many teeth.

She didn't wait for the dust to fade, for the hunters to emerge. The impact, the sudden screams, distracted the guards. She lifted Caleb and ran to the stairs.

Behind, she heard glass break.

50

Temoc took out the Wardens' sentry in silence, the woman's throat cradled in the crook of his elbow. Above, Couatl beat their wings for altitude, circled up and slickened, there was no other word for it. Their shapes smoothed, and they vanished. His scars burned, and pierced the Craft that hid them. As he lowered the unconscious sentry, he saw the Couatl dive.

Then he heard the screams.

The rear of the Warden camp was a mess of stretchers and prison wagons, one full, protesters straining at its iron bars. This too was guarded, by a pair of Wardens, one man and one woman. Risky, and he did not relish fighting women, but he needed to sow confusion, and anyway the enemy was the one who sent women to war.

He struck the man on the collarbone. It snapped, and he went down. The woman did not hesitate at the sight of Temoc, for all his shadow and flame. She swung her truncheon. He dodged. She swung it again, and once more he dodged, but this time his hand followed hers, clung to it, and bent her momentum against her, twisting the wrist toward and past her elbow, slicing down as if her arm were a sword. She fell. Something snapped in her. The male Warden tried to stand despite his broken collarbone. Temoc choked him out. He'd stay down fifteen seconds. Maybe. Ten seconds left on average before the first sentry would wake.

The cage lock was made of iron. He shattered it with his palm and swung the door wide. The protesters within gaped. Bloody, some. Injured. Awed. Still, they could be useful.

"Cause trouble. Distract them so I can reach the Square. "

"Temoc," one said, before he swept away into the night.

The prisoners burst from the cage and roared their freedom. One kicked the male Warden in the face. The female Warden regained her feet, ignoring the escapees, and ran after Temoc. He hit her in the ribs, hard. She flew a little before she struck a stack of sandbags, and did not rise again.

He dove behind a wagon as Wardens rushed past, drawn by the escapees. When the path was clear, Temoc ran toward the barricade, toward Chakal Square where the people—his people, the people for whom he'd given up his life—where his people were dying. Where Couatl fell among them, ravening and invisible, warded from sight to increase the horror they spread.

The barricade swarmed with Wardens, some distracted by the escape, but still too many to fight at once. Past the barricade, the Square boiled with people under siege. He needed to reach the center, fast.

The sandbag barricade spanned two brick buildings, four stories on the left and five on the right, each packed with Wardens and support staff. A fire escape climbed the rightmost building. One Warden crouched on the top level with a Craftwork crossbow, and another guarded her. They were his best shot.

He reached the fire escape in a single sprint. He needed speed now more than stealth. A Warden near the fire escape tried to stop him; Temoc slammed him against the brick wall. The Warden fell.

Temoc leapt to the fire escape and climbed two floors, three, taking entire flights at a jump. Ixaqualtil bared his seven hundred teeth and raked his talons along the iron railings, surged down Temoc's spine into his limbs. So easily invoked, god of murder, hungry gnawer of hidden hearts.

The Warden with the crossbow did not notice Temoc's climb, bent to her sights, but the guard did, and raised his club and cried a warning and crouched beside the stairs ready to strike.

Temoc did not use the last flight of stairs. He sprang, reveling in the use of speed and strength after all those quiet preaching years, after two decades' dull opiate of joy—he sprang onto the guardrail, jumped, caught the thin iron rungs that walled the landing above, and vaulted foot-first over the rail behind the Warden who'd tried to block his path. The toes of his shoes struck the small of the Warden's back, and the man tumbled into the stairwell. The sniper turned, bringing her crossbow to bear. Temoc broke the bow with one hand. Its Craft discharged in a fountain of sparks. Temoc's other hand hit the Warden's jaw, and she fell.

He climbed the last level to the roof, and gazed down on his people. They tossed like an ocean in storm, assailed from all sides and above. At the ocean's heart, near the fountain, Couatl fought, savage and enormous, scattering defenders. He doubted most of the protesters had yet realized the nature of their enemy.

He had to help them.

He called to the gods. To Qet Sea-Lord in chains, to dead Isil. To Ili of the White Sails and Tomtilat and the Hunchback and the seven gods of the corn, to Kozil Who Slept Under Earth, to Thunder Lords and Lightning Ladies, to Temple Guardians and the Keepers of Knives. The square below surged with terror, but also with faith. And he could use that faith.

Help me, sleepers. Help me, you who have gone away. Bear me up. You have given me so much already.

As I have given you.

He jumped off the building.

"Yes!" The King in Red punched the air. "Excellent. Well done team Couatl. Look at them run. We should have done this days ago. Hells, we should have done this instead of all that prattling in the tent. I mean, of course we couldn't have, needed the contract, but damn it feels nice to engage for once, don't you think?"

"Yes, sir," Captain Chimalli said.

The room had long since soured with the smell of sweat and instant noodles. Dreamers mewled upon their tables. These were their third pair today, the first two dragged off on stretchers hours before, babbling about the black beyond the stars. Dinner had been noodles from the commissary, slurped down and bowls dumped in trash cans someone should have emptied hours ago. The King in Red tended to forget others still had biological requirements, and no Warden wanted to be the first to remind him. There would be time enough for hygiene after victory.

"I mean. Yow. I know you weren't here in the old days, Captain, but we just don't get to do this kind of thing anymore. Battles are so clear. Damn, I bet he'll miss that arm. You spend so long debating strategy and ethics, whethers and wherefores. It's like foreplay. And then you actually do something and life becomes so wonderfully transparent, at least until time comes to pick up the pieces. Tell group four to strike in five."

"Yes, sir."

"Four. Three. Two. One. And boom. Brilliant. Tear through those cooking tents. Burn the stores. Hard to replace that stuff. And—oh, good." The image in the pool warped, twisted. "We've got him! The Major's down." His laugh, loud, cackling. "One of the red-arms giving your guys a bit of trouble, Captain— never mind, she's down, too. You know, I'm almost glad Elayne isn't here. I can't talk like this around her."

"Of course, sir."

The image in the well receded, stopped. Zoomed in again. The King in Red blinked. "Captain?"

"Yes, sir?"

"What in all the hells is *that*?"

The Couatl sprang, and Chel rolled to the side. Its snub nose splintered stone behind her. She stood, breathless, a stick figure drawn with lines of pain. She groped for a weapon. Couldn't see the Major anymore—fallen, alive she hoped. The air was thick with screams, human and animal and bird-snake.

She squinted through smoke and stinging sweat. Sweat, and maybe blood, too. Stitches burst. But her fingers found the fallen tent spar. The Couatl reared, a corrupted emptiness where the fire wasn't. It lunged for her and she lurched off her knees, swinging the spar two-handed into its skull.

The spar broke.

The Couatl cocked its head to one side, bemused, if a crocodile could be bemused. Smoke curled between its teeth, and down the soft tracks of its gullet. That, she could see. Bone ribbed and arched the roof of its mouth, like an Old World cathedral. Carrion wind blew through her, and she shuddered at its foul weight.

The Couatl was too near for her to dodge. Even in her prime she would not have escaped its teeth.

Time slowed. A green light enfolded her. She'd heard friends who almost died talk about lights at the ends of tunnels, and distant shining visions, but none had ever mentioned this green, calm and cool, comforting and fierce at once, as if the gods spread their arms to embrace her.

She prepared to die in that light. Good thing she was already kneeling, she thought, and smiled.

The Couatl struck.

And Temoc punched it in the face.

The Couatl's head snapped sideways and hit the ground. The serpent's body followed. One wing drew a broad swath through the smoke. A figure tumbled from its back: the Warden, thrown from his saddle. The Couatl lashed and hissed. The Warden, visible now, rolled through the wrecked camp's coals.

Temoc stood three feet above the ground, shining with hard light.

When he killed the not-wolves in the alley he had been enfolded by shade and scarlight, a man made great by the gods' blessing.

This was that, but more. Shadows darker, scars brighter, tracing geometric patterns and divine icons down his arms and back and legs and over his skull. He seemed larger than he was, and he was large.

Coiled and recoiled in fire the Couatl spread wings and launched itself at Temoc, who stepped to one side as if the empty air was a dance floor. His fist floated out; the Couatl's jaw un-hinged with a snap. The beast swiveled, impossibly fast for its bulk, slithering more than flying, and wrapped Temoc in a twisting coil, from which he freed himself with a surge of legs and arms, and climbed astride the serpent's back, one arm crooked under its jaw and drawing up, up—

But where was the Warden?

Chel found him by the firelight reflected off his mask. The Warden knelt, a slender crossbow raised in one hand, pointing toward Temoc. Craftwork crackled around the bolt's tip.

The Couatl strained against Temoc, losing. In seconds, its neck would break and Temoc could dive free. Too many seconds. The crossbow might not hurt Temoc, but Chel wouldn't take that chance.

She ran. Smoke-tears wet her eyes. The Warden steadied his aim, exhaled.

No time to veer around the fire. She leapt through it, face tucked behind crossed arms. Heat pressed her, and yes there was pain too and shock, and then she tumbled out of the flames into the Warden.

The man fell.

So did the crossbow.

Chel and the Warden rolled together. She clutched him with her legs, grabbed his wrists. He bucked. She was strong, but he was stronger, enhanced by Craft, and better-trained.

She waited for the snap, for the crash of a falling titanic body that would indicate she could give up, that Temoc was safe, but it did not come. Thrashing wings and serpent-tail broke tents and scattered sparks. The Warden pressed his arms up, and though she bore down with all her weight she could not stop his hands' progress, inch by inch, toward her throat. His eyes burned into hers' through the apocalyptic reflections of his mask. Strong fingers, strangler's fingers.

She tucked her chin, let go of his arms, and slammed her forehead into the bridge of his nose. Bone crunched beneath the mask. The Warden swore, and grabbed for her as she pulled clear. Her shirt cuff tore, which slowed her enough for his wild haymaker to hit her side. She scrambled to stand, but he was up already, on top of her. Her clutching hands found something, a grip—the crossbow.

Brought it around, between them, pointed at his chest.

Pulled the trigger.

Lightning without sound, but not lacking thunder. Her heart beat twice. Breath fled her lungs. The bolt disappeared into the center of the Warden's chest. Sparks sped through his body, down his arms, arced between his fingers. Even then he held her, and she thought for a horrified second he might be more than human.

He slumped.

She felt something wet and cold on her cheek, wet and warm on her chest. She pushed the Warden off. He lay sprawled, bleeding. His mask flowed away like quicksilver syrup. Beneath, he was a Quechal man with big black eyes. Older than her, by a few years. Wide jaw, full lips open as if to ask a question.

Her hand rose trembling to her cheek. When she drew her fingertips away, they shone silver. The cold on her cheek had been his mask, weeping. The warmth on her chest, his blood.

Oh.

Not the first man she had killed, she told herself. Enough rocks thrown, enough weapons hurled. She had probably killed others in the escape this morning, when she kicked the broken wall down on her pursuers, when she swung her club. This was not her first, but the first where she'd felt him as she pulled the trigger. The first to die on top of her, his breath in her face and his blood on her shirt.

A scream tore from an inhuman throat, followed by an earth-shaking slam. Ash and burning splinters showered her. A cinder fell into the dead Warden's open eye, and he did not blink it out.

She stood.

The Couatl lay, visible, in the bonfire wreckage of the broken tent: twenty meters of scale and coil and unfurled wings, its huge head limp. A forked tongue twisted between the daggers of its teeth. Temoc stood astride the dead thing, feet wide-planted, wreathed in light. He breathed. She saw no fear in him, no hesitation, no shock at the enormity of what he'd done. No. That was the wrong word. Enormousness, immensity. Enormity was sin—what she had done, and what was being done to them.

He turned to her, and saw her panting above the fallen Warden. Behind him, more explosions, more Couatl fighting. Some screamed in rage as they saw their brothers dead. Temoc raised his hand to her in salute, and she raised hers in response, or tried to. She still held the crossbow. Hadn't let it go.

She had more bolts, one holstered to either side of the crossbow shaft. She thought she could see how to reload.

She lowered her hand.

Temoc did not break the line of their gaze. She blinked, and he was gone—swept away by the fight.

She knelt by the corpse, and with shaking hands set the next bolt into position, cocked the bow, and followed him.

Mina ran up the stairs, ignoring the sounds of battle behind. The breaking glass, that must have been her hunters passing through the hotel doors. Then another crash—a shattered vase. Sounds of flesh and metal.

She climbed the stairs two at a time, Caleb heavy in her arms, so heavy. She was strong after her long desert journeys, but not strong enough to climb stairs with him in her arms anymore, not after all she'd done tonight.

"Mom, what's happening?"

"It's okay." She said, "okay," between pants for breath.

Can't protect him, the voice at the back of her skull jabbered. Can't protect anyone, least of all your son. Your scarred son. The son his father tried to ruin. You failed him by choosing the father. No time for those thoughts. Keep going. Up, up. Fear propelled her.

She burst through the door onto the fourth floor, gray-blue carpet and off-white wallpaper patterned with broad vertical stripes. Sweat burned in her eyes, soaked her shirt. She could have wrung herself out like a towel. Doors in both directions. Room 404. Where am I?

The door opposite bore no number, only a pictogram indicating an ice machine. Surging left, she ran until she came to a numbered door: 433, the next 431, proceeding down on both sides until a sharp right turn out of sight. Behind her, probably, the even numbers. Of course, she'd run for the back stairs, 01 and the like would be next to the lift, but she'd have to cross the elevators again to reach 404, maybe she should turn around but she'd come too far already, almost to the turn. Take it. No time to lose. If she turned around they might beat her there anyway from the lift—if they were using the lift, not following her up the stairs, in which case if she turned around she might—

Screw it. Run. Faster.

After another turn she reached the hallway of the lifts, 411, 409, 407, the lifts dinged, up arrow ghostlit from behind. It's them, no, might be anyone. Still, run. The doors rolled open. 405. 403. A crash from the lift, and a large form blurred out, black and tan and white resolving as the figure hit the wall with a sickening crunch: the guard from downstairs, face a mess of blood and blood on his shirt as well. His eyes rolled back as he slumped to the carpet.

401.

Within the lift as she ran past Mina heard clockwork click, gears spin and grind, flywheels whir. No time to look. "Elayne!" she shouted, a warning, a plea, too late. A metal hand grabbed her arm, but before the grip could close she tore free with a sound between scream and grunt and roar. She struck the wall, and so did Caleb, and he cried out. 402, almost there. "Elayne! Help!"

Ticking gears and winding springs behind her, rush of fabric and curl of leather. Taking their time, playing with her? No, more likely shock, fear, slowing her perception. She set Caleb down. He stared at her. Something swam through the waters behind his eyes. "Run," she said. "Fast as you can. Run." He took one step back. No time.

She spun, hands raised.

Two figures filled the hall behind her.

They were tall, thin, and not human save in general outline. Glassy many-lensed orbs perched in the eye sockets of elongated mock-faces like masks for an Ebon Sea tragedy, smooth as buffed and hardened leather. They wore black suits and black ties. They had long fingers and long hands: three fingers on each hand and a thumb, she noticed in one of those fits of sudden clarity that plague the terrified, and those fingers and hands transparently mechanical, no attempt made to disguise their hinged joints. Metal, and bloody.

Purple light flickered through their white shirts, beneath their thin black ties, where their hearts should have been if they were human. Which they weren't. Mad babbling in the back of her brain.

They did not hesitate.

Nor did she.

A little table bearing a purple fern in a green pot stood beside the elevators; she grabbed that pot and threw it into the first golem's face. At, rather—the golem raised one arm to block the pot, which shattered, but Mina had followed close behind, teeth bared, striking the damn thing in its stupid glowing chest with all her weight, and no matter how strong it was, sixty kilos to the center of mass would make it stagger.

Which it did, and growled a grinding of gears. She bounced off the chest and flailed for balance. The golem stumbled into its comrade, who arrested its fall with one arm and pointed one hand down the hall, oh, gods, at Caleb outside 404, Elayne's room, pounding on the door and shouting "Help!" The hand stretched, fingers merged and split, thumb dislocated as metal bones realigned into a two-pronged claw pointed at the boy, a claw acid-etched with Craftwork sigils and glyphs and circles that spiraled through strange dimensions Mina could not name. Sparks and charge danced in that hollow, and she realized they had not used a weapon against her in flight, that they themselves were the weapon.

She launched herself at the golem's arm as it fired.

Caleb turned, and raised one hand, face blank and distant as if he was still asleep, as if he'd slipped back into the coma from which their fall from the skies of Dresediel Lex had barely roused him. His eyes closed as his hand swept up, fast and slow at once.

Lightning lanced from the weapon to Caleb.

And Caleb caught it.

The lightning struck his palm and stuck there, darting between splayed fingers. Mina hit the golem's arm a second later and slammed it against the wall. Caleb's eyes flew open and they burned from within, bright as an alchemist's fire. The crackling arcs ceased to jump between his fingers, absorbed rather into them, bursting through his many wounds, uncontrollably bright, illuminating the gods and kings his father's knife had left on his arms and chest and back and legs. And then out, again, from his hand, no building charge this time but a single line of coherent white, a rod connecting his hand to the golem's chest.

The light died as suddenly as it had burned, leaving only a bar of purple across Mina's vision, and a hole in the golem's chest slightly to the left of its glowing heart.

It stumbled.

Caleb fell.

Mina ran to her son, but the golem recovered quickly, caught her, pulled her back, punched her once in the face and again in the ribs faster than she could raise her hands to block. She fell to one knee beside Caleb, only to stand again and strike the golem in the chest with both hands.

It retreated a step, and cocked its head to one side. More trickling of gears and wheels. Was it laughing? Was that a thing golems did? She'd never thought to ask.

The second golem, too, recovered. Purple light seeped through the hole in its chest, and it moved slowly, right arm limp, but it did move.

Behind her, she heard a click.

The first golem swung. She ducked under its fist, hit the thing in the side, knuckles bouncing off metal ribs beneath the suit—

And the golem came apart.

No shuddering, no intermediate stage: she struck the thing, and it burst away from itself, ten thousand shards of metal, gears and wheels and wires and springs and cams and pistons disconnected, suit shredded by the force of their explosion. But the shards did not fall, nor did they pierce the walls with shrapnel force. They simply hung in space, the golem deconstructed. The second golem, the one Caleb damaged, looked up, and in the realigning of its gears she heard, and this time there was no doubt as with the laughter—she heard it scream.

Then it burst apart as well.

Shadows floated at the core of whirling metal and shredded fabric: snapping sharp-jawed inchoate forms circled by spinning silver bands which might have been light, or else metal thinned translucent. The shadows strained, sprouted tentacles and pincers and long clawed arms, became steel and stone and mirror bright, but could not burst free.

"Please excuse my delay," a woman said behind her. She recognized Elayne Kevarian's voice before she turned and saw her there, standing outside the open door to her room. The Craftswoman wore a white bathrobe, and her hair was wet. Glyphs glowed on her bare wrists and fingers and brow. She held one hand before her, finger tracing slow circles in the air, in time with the turning silver bands. "I was in the shower."

"It's okay," Mina said, dimly, because she had to say something. "Thank you."

Elayne snapped her fingers twice. The shadows trapped in silver changed once more, to crystal, and shattered. Falling shards sublimated to steam. The metal bits, too, fell, but these did not disappear. They struck carpet with the soft patter of spring rain.

"What is going on here?" Elayne asked, but Mina did not hear her.

Caleb lay at her feet. Blood seeped from his scars, and striped his bathrobe from inside. Mina pressed the robe against him with her hands, but the blood kept coming. Caleb coughed wetly.

"He needs a hospital," Elayne said, and Caleb hovered over the carpet as if he'd been raised on a stretcher. "I'll call us a cab."

"Two more Couatl down."

"Gods' balls." The King in Red pounded the side of the vision well with his fist, and ground his teeth. "What the hells is happening down there?"

Beneath the water, fires still burned, and Chakal Square convulsed in pain. But the tempo of the convulsions had changed, radiating from the battleground by the fountain to the camps beyond. A light shone amid the tents.

"Hostages secure," the dreamer said. "Team Seven lifting off. Carrying a few members of Team Three, whose mount just went down."

"Get out of there," Chimalli said. "Fast, and fly high." The vision well flashed once more, and the image zoomed toward the light: their Couatl outlined in green, and the invader, the newcomer, a moving white dot, humaniform and mountainous when he stood still long enough for them to see. "Sir, we're losing Couatl fast. And people. Five down."

"We can't pull back now."

"Sir, with all due respect. We didn't plan this mission as a battle. We wanted to get in, cause chaos, get out. We've hit their leaders. We have the hostages. The longer we stay—"

"If we don't kill Temoc, all we've done tonight is worthless."

"We planned a surgical strike. We didn't expect to fight the God Wars over again. We pull out now, we tell everyone that we did what we went there to do, we rescued some people and some Wardens got hurt doing it. It's a win. The city will see it that way. Whatever Temoc's doing, we haven't put a scratch on him yet. You're throwing good people away." My people, he didn't say. My people, who did not go into this equipped to fight gods and their anointed. My people, who are dying. "Pull back. Reevaluate."

"We should press our victory."

"This isn't a victory anymore. Now it's a draw we can dress up as a win. You're on tilt, sir. Keep going and you'll have a rout on your hands, and not the good kind."

"Four-six and Four-seven down. Team Four holding altitude."

"Think it through." Please.

Kopil growled. The vision well swept closer to the battle, until the dreamers writhed with agony and a single form filled the water: a light-riven silhouette, a weapon dressed up like a man. A Warden ran against him, a squaddie from Fisherman's Vale Chimalli had met in passing twice, what was the man's name? Temoc struck him so fast the dreamer could not capture the speed of it, and he collapsed.

"Sir," Chimalli said.

Green light glinted off the King in Red's crown. The room was quiet. The others had stopped talking, stopped breathing even.

"Warden down," a dreamer said.

"Fine." Kopil's voice was soft and sharp. "Fine. Call them back. Call them all back. Mission complete."

"All squads," Chimalli said. "Take flight."

Temoc did not understand the cheers at first. He was finishing a fistfight on a Couatl's surging back: a Warden swung a club at his face and he took the club away, dislocated the man's arm, punched his neck twice, broke some ribs with a kick, and knocked him off the Couatl. The Couatl's wings surged, taking flight, beautiful pinions flared—even at night the feathers sparkled, rubies, emeralds, and sapphires extruded to airy thinness. He considered breaking the wings, decided against it. These were still the gods' birds, even if perverted by Craftsmen's hands. These were the gods' birds, and he had killed too many today.

The Couatl was ten feet already in the air and climbing, a corkscrew toward the clouds. He stepped off and fell to land in a clearing where tents once stood. Everywhere around him he heard the roar of human voices, and spun, searching for the new threat.

At last he realized there was no threat. His people were shouting for joy.

He looked skyward. Couatl flew north. They bore captives and casualties, but they were leaving.

He had won. They had won.

At what cost?

A sudden touch on his back, getting old, too far gone to hear someone sneaking up behind him in a crowd. He spun, fast, smooth, catch the hand and twist back, follow the arm's line up to throat, grip the trachea between forefinger and thumb—

When his eyes caught up with the rest of him, he realized he was choking Chel. He released her arm and stood back, hands raised between them. "Chel! Gods, I'm sorry."

"No," she said, hoarse, "that's fine, I didn't need that throat for anything anyway."

She was bloody. A bruise covered her cheek. Her shirt was torn and there were sooty handprints on her face. Blood trickled from burst stitches. Blood on her chest, too, though that wasn't hers. He could tell. The smell was wrong.

In one hand she held a crossbow, Warden make, no quarrels left. Her breath came slow and deep. Again the crowd roared, a wave of sound that buoyed her up. Her thin lips broke into a smile.

"We won," he said.

She nodded. "They're pulling back. The camp's safe for now. Wardens even pulled back from the barricades. Thanks to you."

"Thanks to us."

"No," she said.

"What's wrong?" he said. "How are the rest?"

"I can't," she started, decided against finishing. Took his arm. "You need to see."

She led him through the wreckage of the tents, through embers, flame, and smoke, past bodies smashed like kindling. Moans rose from the dying. The camp smelled of salt and sickeningly of pork.

The Major lay amid the burning tents.

Others stood around him, and their presence was a relief: Bill Kemal was there and Kapania, Bill breaking open a crate of bandages as Kapania applied salve. Temoc recognized the red-arm beside the Major, though he did not know the man's name. Each looked up, over, to Temoc in his or her own time. But they did not greet him like they would have two days ago, as a friend and colleague. There was awe in them. They looked at him as if he was more than a man who had abandoned his family. They looked at him as if he was something good, or failing that, something great.

He knelt beside the Major.

The armor was torn in many places. The first would have been enough: a Couatl's claw pierced the sheet metal over his stomach into the belly below. What damage the claw inflicted, the torn metal made worse, its edges grinding into meat. But the Major had fought on: punctures in his breastplate from crossbow damage, more buckling from the blows of superhuman fists. His sword arm lay at an almost-right angle. Behind his visor, his eyes twinkled red in firelight. The armor did not reflect as it had before. Because of the blood.

But still he breathed.

"Temoc." That not-quite-human voice. "Temoc."

"Hello," he said. He did not know the dying man's name, and could not ask it now. "I came back."

"Thank you."

Temoc wanted to thank him in turn. Many ways the Major could have said "I told you so," many tirades he might have delivered against soldiers who deserted their posts in wartime.

But such words would have served Temoc more than the Major, and Temoc's needs did not matter now. "You're welcome."

"The camp?"

"Safe," he said.

"They'll be back. Stronger. Not just Wardens. The King in Red will come."

"We'll stop him."

"You need—" He coughed, wetly, a drowning man's cough. "You need strength."

"The gods are with us."

"The gods." Another cough. "The gods aren't enough. As they are. Sleeping."

"They helped us fight off the Wardens."

"You need more. You know I'm right."

He was. Kneeling, as the battle-rush receded, Temoc felt more tired than he had in years. He might win another battle like this one, but the King in Red would not repeat himself. Not when he learned Temoc had joined the resistance in Dresediel Lex. The Craftsman would crush Chakal Square with his full weight. "That's why we need you. Let me get this armor off. I can heal you. We'll face them together."

"You don't need me. The people will follow you."

"I'm just one man."

"That's why." He nodded. "You need the gods. Awake. You need them strong. You need them fed."

"No," Temoc said.

"It is the only way."

"We left that path. The people—"

"The people don't care about theology. They are passion and fear and anger and they need gods to fuel that passion, soothe that fear, stoke that anger." The Major grabbed Temoc's arm in one gauntleted fist, and squeezed. The plates of his fingers tugged at Temoc's shirt, and the blood on his hands left a stain among the other stains. "And I'm almost gone anyway."

"I can save you."

"For a day or two, until I die. But you can do better. You can make me mean something."

Blasphemy even to propose it. Well. Not blasphemy. The gods demanded sacrifice. But for twenty years Temoc had taught another way, preached sacrifice in the living body. To feed the gods and live as the modern world could still permit.

But he had come to defend a people the modern world would not allow to live much longer. He set himself against the King in Red as surely as he had decades before, when he fought the Craftsmen in the skies above Dresediel Lex. And tonight he had pledged his son to the gods' service in the old way, with scars and blood and sacred rites.

Had he lied to himself all these years, thinking he could walk any other path? Thinking he could build peace with the King in Red, that all things true and good in Quechal life could survive when the pyramids became office buildings and old calendars gave way to new?

"Not tonight," he said. "There is no eclipse. The gods will not receive a sacrifice out of cycle."

He knew the excuse was feeble before he spoke, before the Major laughed. "The gods have not fed for forty years. They will forgive what they must, to eat."

"This will turn them all against us. The whole city."

"They're against us already."

"I can't."

"Temoc."

"We have come so far." Head bent near the Major's helm, he barely had the voice to speak.

"Give me my death."

Knives in the dark. She'd screamed at him. His son, bleeding, on the bed. And then how many dead in the last few hours? He'd strangled Couatl with his bare hands, in the air. Battle joined already.

They stirred within him, beneath him, around and above. *Is he right?*

No answer came that he could hear. Pride even to ask the question. We know the gods' will through our deeds.

The Major's breath grew heavy. Death pressed down on him. "Soon, now."

Temoc slid his hands under the man's back. The metal was sticky with blood. He lifted, and found the Major lighter than he'd thought. Metal plates clanked as Temoc cradled the living body. A groan escaped the Major, so soft he could barely hear.

"Temoc?" Bill Kemal, kneeling. "What's happening?"

"He has asked for his end," Temoc said. "I will grant it to him."

He understood. Blanched, and stared at Temoc as if seeing him for the first time, or seeing for the first time what he'd been all along.

Temoc turned to Chel. "Summon them."

"Who?"

"Everyone."

51

"All forces withdrawn," the dreamer said. "Groups one, two, three, five, eight confirmed safe. Recovering to secured positions. Awaiting orders."

"That's the last of them," Chimalli said. "We're done here."

"You may go," the King in Red replied. "If you wish. I want to see how this plays out."

"We'll have options for tomorrow's assault on your desk by four in the morning."

The skeleton peered into the vision well. "Temoc's carrying the Major to the prayer mats."

"That doesn't make sense," Chimalli said. "The Major's shown no religious inclination before."

The King in Red did not respond.

"I'm in favor of the stun option myself," Chimalli ventured. "There are health risks, but we can neutralize the crowd with minimal risk to our people. And it's memorable. Everyone in Chakal Square will know that if they work within the system they'll be protected, and if they try to fight, they'll just look foolish. They'll realize protest is a gift we allow them, not a power they hold. And we'll foster a reputation for resolving dangerous situations gently." No response. He kept going, in hope. "We could let most of the people go—jail the leaders, try them. Everyone else wakes up at home in bed."

"Captain," the King in Red replied. "Please shut up. And watch."

"Sir?"

One skeletal finger pointed down into the water. Chimalli

knew he must have been mistaken, too much coffee, too long in that dim foul-smelling room, but he thought he saw the finger shake. "They are making our decision for us."

Temoc lay the Major upon the makeshift altar.

Smoke rose and fire burned. Heat bloomed on his skin. He was not a weapon now. Only a priest, with a job to do.

The thousands gathered to watch. Wounded, seared, broken, blind with exhaustion, they knelt on the grass mats, or nearby.

Not all came. Some manned barricades, some doused fires, rebuilt the shattered camp. But many. Chel stood beside him. The altar strained beneath the Major's weight, of armor and flesh.

The Major had not spoken since Temoc set him down. His breath came faster.

Temoc spoke the gods' words.

"Qet Sea-Lord, Ixchitli Sun-Shaper
The Twins gave of themselves when the sun their
father died
Yes, they gave of themselves—suckled serpents on
their blood
Suckling serpents they became the world
Becoming the world they became a bridge
A bridge—between man and god
A bridge—between our world and the next
Two united, each informing each
Blood for blood, hunger for hunger,
Thirst for thirst repaid."

And on the litany rolled, words first heard in youth and spoken so many times since, words that came easy to his lips yet fell heavily from them to strike the air like an immense bell's clapper.

The people watched. He felt their faith, their fear, saw it even when he closed his eyes, a sea of green he could inhale, make part of himself, and offer as he offered this sacrifice, this willing human being, to the powers that made them all.

The Major's terror grew as he faced death. No matter that he had begged for it. He was still afraid, and Temoc was still the man who held the knife.

He lifted it: not the black glass blade reserved for sacrifice on Quechaltan and for the making of new Eagle Knights. He had found a blade of simple steel. It would serve. This was no great altar, sanctified by generations, but each altar took its first blood sometime.

He'd denied that truth for so long.

Few in the audience could understand the High Quechal prayer. Few ever had, even in the old days, when hundreds of thousands gathered to see the death that made the sun live again.

"The gods ask us all to give according to our strengths," he said in Kathic. "And we fortunate few are called to give our hearts."

He bent over the Major, who lay prone and still. Unconscious, Temoc thought, until he heard the man's voice: "Don't let them see me."

"I will not," he replied.

Temoc gripped the Major's breastplate and tore the steel. The gods gave him strength. The armor opened for him like flower petals, rising to obscure the Major's body.

She wore a thick leather shirt under the makeshift armor, but that could not hide her as the metal had. Temoc said nothing—only hesitated as he cut the leather out of the way. But the Major caught him again by the hand, strong in her, his, last breath. "Do it."

He raised the knife.

He heard Chel breathe beside him, heard nothing else in the silence. His arm trembled above his head. He shifted grip on the knife, pommel down.

He struck fast. The breastbone broke, as needed. There was

no scream. Muscles in the Major's throat corded, strangling his cry.

Gods stirred. Faces pressed through the world's gauze, endless eyes watching him. Mouths, open, hungry. He knew their names, he knew each tooth. They waited for their child to offer them a gift. No matter that he was an unworthy priest, that the gift itself could not match their radiance. Time was a single scream, a single breath. Gods and men trembled on the edge of a knife, a single drop now tumbling toward eternity as the blade swept down, and blood wept, and divine eyes opened, and the whole world sighed at once and was, as ever, saved.

The Major's heart was slick in his hand.

His people cried rapture as he held it high.

And the gods were in and with them all.

Skies opened. Artificial clouds boiled away. Throughout the Skittersill, ghostlights died and fires failed. Night fell upon their faces, and above them all the stars shone.

The Major lay beneath, a husk.

The vision well blazed and died. Water rolled against stolen rock.

"What the hells," Chimalli said.

The King in Red looked up. Before, though Chimalli would never have said this aloud, his boss had seemed angry, petulant—a boy genius thwarted.

No more.

His eyes burned, as always, but hotter now, the darkness around them deep.

The King in Red was ancient, unbowed, no longer human. More, and less. He was a mind of cold blades that threshed the world from its chaff.

He had slept.

Now, he woke.

"Tomorrow," Kopil said. "Tell Elayne."

52

The wounded and dying overran Grace and Mercy Hospital. Couatl swarmed about the roof, depositing wounded Wardens, then winging south to recover more. When Elayne arrived in the cab with Mina and a bleeding Caleb, the orderlies tried to turn her away. She shouted at them, name-dropped Dr. Venkat, and in the end walked straight past the orderlies' desk toward the lifts. Mina followed her, tight-wound, silent. Caleb floated between them, wrapped in towels to stem his bleeding.

She found Venkat in the trauma ward. The doctor looked as if she hadn't slept since Elayne saw her last. Blood stained her white coat. "Do you have any idea how much work you've brought us?"

"One more," she said, and pointed to the boy. "He'll die if without help."

"So will twenty others in this ward."

"His father," Elayne said, "is the leader of the riot." Mina made a strangled sound, which she ignored. No time for niceties. "He is valuable."

"Everyone is valuable."

"He is valuable to the King in Red, I mean."

Venkat's face closed.

"He's my son," Mina said. "Help him." No emotion in her voice, anymore. On the ride over she hadn't been able to tell Elayne the whole story, but the important elements came through. The boy scarred by his father's knife. The old line carried forth into a new generation—the warrior-paladinate handed to a boy unready for the pain or duty the scars promised. Temoc's last attempt to guard his son from a world that

would grip him even tighter now he bore these scars. But
Caleb had saved himself and his mother in the hotel. Maybe
that justified the burden he would bear.

Venkat said, "This way," and led them through a maze of
blood and screams, past operating rooms where bells kept rapid
pace with racing hearts, to a small white chamber with a white
bed where she laid the boy, stripped off his makeshift bandages,
dosed him for the pain, and set to work. Even through the drugs,
her touch made Caleb writhe. Venkat shouted to a nurse, list-
ing chemicals and talismans—some Elayne remembered from
trauma tents in the Wars.

Elayne tried to pull Mina from the room, but Mina would
not leave. "This won't be short," Elayne said, "or pleasant."

"I'll stay," she said.

Elayne walked three circuits around the trauma ward. No
one tried to stop her. Wandering without a child to care for, she
made sense of the building, assembled the hallway maze into
architecture, identified operating theaters and recovery rooms.
She poured a cup of coffee from a pot behind the nurse's station, and drank. The hospital smelled of blood and disinfectant
and burnt fat. She was not Kopil's warrior, or his general. His
Craftswoman, only, his representative in a matter now settled.

The coffee tasted foul. Not the coffee's fault. Ambrosia
would have tasted the same.

She returned to Caleb's room an hour later, found the doctor gone and the boy bandaged, stitched, sedated, and asleep.
The room had a careful, neutral odor of bad smells scrubbed
away by Craft.

Mina sat by the bed, and did not look up when Elayne
walked past.

She poured two more cups of coffee, and returned. Mina accepted the cup without looking, drank, and said nothing.

Elayne sat beside her. A metronome ticked the beats of Caleb's heart. She could have danced to that beat, though it lacked
swing. A tube snaked down his nose, connected to a bag that
inflated and deflated with his breath.

"They had to sedate him heavily," Mina said, unprompted. "They use the tube because otherwise he might forget to breathe."

Elayne drank her coffee and listened.

"They asked me what they should do. I'm his mother, so they asked. I didn't know what to say." She drank. "I carried him across the city. I fought for him. We almost died. And I couldn't speak when they asked."

"They know what to do," Elayne said. "They asked you because you were there, to make you feel better. Don't blame yourself."

"Who else should I blame?"

"Temoc," she said.

"I married him."

"If not for that, this boy wouldn't be here at all."

"I know."

"Caleb's safe. No one will come for him."

"Not more of those things?"

"Assassin golems," she said. "Mechanical forms animated by bound demons. Expensive. We don't like to give demons a mandate to kill—they stretch the limits they're given. Hard to trace, but hard to replace, too. I don't think you'll see more of them. Anyway, this is as safe as you're likely to be in Dresediel Lex, outside of the King in Red's care."

"I won't go to him."

"I did not suggest it."

"He tried to kill us."

"Golemetry isn't his style. He likes a personal touch. And what would he gain by killing you?"

"He could get to my husband."

"Which would just make Temoc angry. Trust me, the King in Red was happy to let him wait out the siege in your house. He wanted you and your boy safe. When he finds out about this, some Wardens will lose their masks."

"Does that make it better?"

She checked herself. "No."

"I'm tired," she said.

Not for the first time Elayne wished there was a way to peer inside another mind without breaking the mind in question. Mina had seen Temoc go back to war, seen his face before he ran. So much depended on Temoc now—where he was, what he had done. She wanted to grill Mina until she wept.

"Would you like more coffee?"

"No," Mina said. "A pillow would be nice. And a blanket. It's cold in here."

Elayne had not noticed. "I'll find one. Sleep well."

No response.

She left, and spent a quarter-hour searching for a nurse who didn't look too busy to interrupt. As the clock ticked toward midnight, she decided that looking too busy to interrupt was likely a survival trait for nurses.

She returned to the station with the coffeepot, in hope someone there could point her to the linen closet. A graying man sat behind the desk, scratching incomprehensible words into the blanks of equally incomprehensible forms. She cleared her throat.

"Excuse me?"

Neither Elayne nor the nurse had spoken. The new voice, from behind, belonged to a sharp woman in a charcoal suit, who stood at rigid attention. The wheels of Elayne's mind turned slowly. "I know you."

The woman nodded. "Yes, ma'am. I work for Red King Consolidated."

"Of course. From the meeting. The woman with the head for numbers."

"Yes, ma'am." She produced a thin piece of folded vellum sealed in red wax with a star-eyed skull.

"You're a courier?"

"The boss wanted this delivered to you in person."

"Thank you." Elayne opened the seal with a narrowing of her eyes, and read the message there.

Read it again, and felt the courier watching.

The assault failed. They turned to human sacrifice. Tomorrow, we burn them out. Come see. Come help.

The signature, a skull in red ink or human blood.

"Thank you," she said. "You can go. I'm sorry he sent you. It's late to run errands."

"What reply should I bring him?"

"Did he ask for one?"

"No."

"Nothing yet," she said, folding the letter. "Nothing, now."

Behind her eyes, the fire fell.

53

Three in the morning. Elayne couldn't sleep, and had given up pretending that she might. She wandered the hospital from room to bloody room. She noticed, eventually, that she still held the King in Red's letter, turning it over, brushing smooth vellum with her fingertips. She returned the letter to her breast pocket.

No more negotiations, no more clever strategies. Dawn would bring the end. This was how Kopil fought the Wars, too. Maneuvers to start, elegant traps, and when those failed, crushing force.

Mina slept in Caleb's room. It had taken her a long time to fall asleep. Dr. Venkat gave her something, in the end. She'd pushed three chairs together and lay across them, beneath the scratchy hospital blanket Elayne had found for her. Her head rested on a synthetic-fill pillow. Her hand lay beside her face, curled into a claw. As Elayne watched, the fingers smoothed, then clutched again, nails raking the seat cushion.

Caleb was not bleeding anymore. His eyes were still beneath closed lids. Too many drugs to dream.

Elayne left them to their rest.

She was not the only one awake. Nurses made rounds, and doctors too, steps quick, clipboards in hand, smelling of bad coffee. A nurse offered to call Elayne a cab, and she declined. Dr. Venkat did not so much walk the halls as blow through them like a storm, her scowl deepening as the night wore thin. Out of the corner of her eye Elayne saw the doctor dry-swallow two pills, which was none of her business. She was a shadow in a building that hated shadows.

She came, eventually, to the room where Tan Batac lay.

From the door she could not see his face, only the body swelling beneath stiff white sheets, fat fingers stripped of rings. A big man for his frame, but a small stone to cause such an avalanche. Even if he woke, healed, nothing would change. The burn would come, the people of Chakal Square would die. One man with a rifle, and everything breaks.

The miracle was not that one man's death could spark such a conflagration—the miracle was that for a while doom seemed escapable, that Chakal Square might have ended in peace if Tan Batac had not stood in the path of a bullet.

They would never know who tried to kill him. The assassin might have died already in the riots, in the Warden raids. If not, he'd be dead by tomorrow afternoon at least.

She stepped into the sickroom.

Batac's face was round as ever and red-cheeked. Machines ticked off his slow, sleeping pulse. His eyelashes were longer than she remembered. No movement behind those eyelids either, and no wonder—more drugs in his system than in Caleb's. This was the shape of his face without a soul to play puppetmaster. And yet his lips curled up in a slight soft smile.

"He looks peaceful, doesn't he?"

At the unexpected voice Elayne jerked around, raised hands wreathed in fire. The thin man in the black suit sat perfectly still, like a rabbit who'd seen the hunter. Wide eyes reflected her flame.

"I'm sorry." A pink tongue darted between the thin man's lips and retreated without wetting them. "I should have spoken up, I thought you'd seen. I mean, I generally sort of blend into a room, and you looked so serious I didn't want to disturb." His fingers twitched and tapped against his leather briefcase. "I'm sorry?" he tried again.

She put the fire away, and ran her thumbs down her lapels, re-ordering her mind. "Don't worry about it. I'm on edge. The last few days have been stressful."

"I know," he said. "That is, I don't mean to say I know what you're going through, wouldn't presume. Just, it's been hard for me, too."

"You came to see Tan Batac that first day. Purcell, from Aberforth and Duncan."

"Yes," he said, and, "Jim," with the inflection of a question. He extended his hand.

"Elayne." He had the grip of a man who'd practiced his handshake with a coach. "Dr. Venkat didn't kick you out?"

"No. I mean, she wasn't happy about my wanting to stay. And they've been busy. But his family gave me a waiver, and I told her she wouldn't need to bother, I could take care of myself and I'm unobtrusive really."

"I would say so."

"I get that a lot. I'm sorry if I interrupted anything."

"Nothing important," she said, and lowered herself into a chair. "Fears and worries, that's all. That's the funny thing about history."

"There's something funny about history?"

She laughed. "When I was a young woman, I thought myself an actor, someone who moved the world. And I was. But the older I grow, the more I feel like everything I thought I willed, I willed because of forces beyond my control. The closer I stand to the center of history's river, the more I'm swept in the current. In my youth, I broke gods, and my power has grown since. But power is time's tool, not mine."

"I don't know much about that," Purcell said. "People have told me what to do more or less my entire life, and people told them what to do in turn, and even the people who told all those what to do didn't seem like they had much choice." He tapped the briefcase again, a double tattoo. "We do what we can."

"Doesn't seem enough, does it?"

"No. But sometimes when the world's falling apart, the best you can do is sit in a sickroom and wait for your client to wake up so he can sign some papers."

"Why are you here, Jim? I don't recognize Aberforth and Duncan."

"We're not a Craft firm as such," Purcell said. "We're an insurance Concern. Anything you want to protect, we'll protect it, for a price. We even have a subsidiary warding idol run out of the Skeld Archipelago, if you want to go a step further. As to why I'm here, well, I shouldn't talk about that. Sensitive times and such, you understand."

"Maybe I could help," she said. "I've done little enough the last few days."

"I don't know what you could do, unless you can wake up Mr. Batac, and Dr. Venkat says nobody can do that except Mr. Batac himself."

"You need his signature."

"Basically," he said. "Emergency modifications to an existing policy."

"And your bosses are okay with you waiting in a sickroom for three days to get a signature? Must be a big policy."

"Oh, yes," he said.

"What is it? Batac's mansion?"

"Not quite," he said.

"I represent him, you know," Elayne said. "And the King in Red. If there's something he needs to know, tell me. Especially if it's urgent."

"Well." Purcell shifted in his chair.

"What are you insuring?"

"The Skittersill," he said at last.

Grace and Mercy employed top-flight Craft to keep its air cool and its temperature even. A team of climatologists could travel from the kitchens to the roof without encountering a fractional fluctuation in temperature. That Craft must have been malfunctioning, because Elayne registered a drop of several degrees. "The Skittersill."

Purcell smiled with an honest man's relief at sharing a secret kept too long. "Of course. One of the many roles of Mr. Batac's Citizens Coalition is to negotiate joint property insurance and protection for the group's Skittersill holdings. About seventy percent of local real estate around the Chakal Square region."

Which she knew. Which she had known. Oh, gods. Five minutes ago she'd been talking about the river of history. Now she hovered overhead, seeing the pattern of its tributaries, their courses and channels dug to direct them. "You're here because of the agreement. The Chakal Square Accords."

"Naturally. He contacted us on Firstday, with stipulations for the new protection and insurance contracts." Five days ago. Before the riot. Before he raised the possibility of insurance requirements in conference. "More restrictive than usual, more expansive. The Chakal Square Accords void many provisions of our old coverage, you understand. Mr. Batac wanted to be sure there was no gap."

No gap, or no appearance of a gap? "Surely someone else at the Citizens Coalition can sign for you."

"It's pretty irregular. The coalition claims Batac has sole signing authority. Under the terms of the accord, it is possible Aberforth and Duncan could be liable for damages to the Skittersill during the lapse in coverage if we did not make our 'full best effort,' I believe are the words, to secure Mr. Batac's signature. So, here I am."

"During the lapse in coverage," she repeated. "Which started when we signed the accords."

"The accords void our existing coverage." He nodded. "My bosses are likely glad he's asleep. My Concern is not eager to commit to such broad coverage under the current conditions. Just between us, I'm sure that if not for the best-effort provision, I would have been ordered home long ago. We're happier collecting Mr. Batac's new, higher premiums than covering so much damage, as I'm sure you understand. Just business. I haven't been down there, but I understand damages run in the thousands of souls already, not even counting the prevention and protection clauses."

Tens of thousands, more like. And tomorrow, when the King

in Red rained vengeance on the Skittersill, that figure would multiply, while Tan Batac lay here, smiling despite the hole in his gut.

The smile had not changed, but it seemed more sinister.

"Purcell." She stood. "Follow me."

"I have to stay here. Mr. Batac—"

"We'll have an orderly contact us if he wakes. I have a friend you need to meet. Maybe he can help with your problem."

"It's late. Will this person even be awake?"

"He doesn't sleep, as such, anymore. Now. Come, or I'll drag you."

Purcell glanced around the room, looking for some excuse to remain, or perhaps a handhold in case she made good on her threat. He found nothing. "My employers—"

"Can wait. We have a city to save."

She walked fast for the elevator, tapped her foot as the numbers climbed, and when the doors rolled back pulled Purcell in after her and pressed the button for the roof. Hold on, Temoc, she thought, as if sheer force of will could send her words tumbling across space. Hold on.

On his bed in his empty room, Tan Batac kept smiling.

54

The people of Chakal Square slept, and gods walked through their dreams.

Temoc knelt before the altar, and listened.

By Bloodletter's Street, a boy armed with a nail-studded stick stood at his post and drank tequila from a brushed steel flask. Fire quickened in his throat, and down. "Don't hog," said the man beside him—massive, tattoos peeking from his ragged shirtsleeve. "Pass it down." The boy drank again, and thought of his sister, who had warned him against joining the Chakal Square protest, who said the family needed him, only death could come of standing against the King in Red. He finished the drink, taking more fire into his stomach. He had died tonight, almost: a shattered spar right through him, blood seeping from the wound. But then the Couatl turned back, and the skies opened, and the earth as well, and he heard a voice like his father's only bigger, older, deeper, words in a language he did not know but to which his body answered, calling him to rise, to stand, to serve. He was one wave in an ocean that had learned to speak. He passed the tequila, and the man beside him drank too, and when the man finished the light in his eyes was the same as the light in the boy's, and they were brothers.

Bill and Kapania Kemal lay in their tent together, stewed in sex. The bandage around her arm smelled of aloe. "You felt it," she said, awed. And he, who never was a religious man, answered, "Yes," because when Temoc's knife went in he'd somehow shared the Major's body, one with him, staring up at the invisible sky. And when the heart rose he'd risen with it, and the clouds ripped away to reveal starlight and the risen gods. "He shouldn't have done it," he said. "Temoc."

"Could you have turned the Major down, if you were in his place?"

"Maybe not. But we're all in this together now. The gods are watching. Before, we could have run."

"Would you run?"

"Yes. No. I don't know. But we can't, now."

She touched him, rolled on top of him, kissed him, and they spoke no more.

"Gods' blessings on you," said a woman who walked the lines of the dead with a statue of Ixchitli in hand. "Gods' blessings on you," to a man whose blank gaze reflected stars. "Gods' blessings on you," to a woman burned to death. "Gods' blessings on you," to an old man who bled out when his broken thigh nicked his femoral artery. "Gods' blessings on you," over and over, though Ixchitli Himself was dead, and the words she spoke only words, not prayers.

Above and beneath them all, the gods moved, and Temoc heard their footsteps. The Hunchback capered among the fallen, raked his fingers through dreams as a man on shore might rake his fingers through wet sand. Ili of the White Sails spread her wings and breathed over sleepers and quick alike, stirring them with raincloud fragrance. Ixaqualtil Seven Eagle panting dagger-toothed chased dreamers through his hells, long tongue lolling, and his breath stank with the devoured. The seven corn gods grew, praise be to them, blessings upon us all who die that we may be ground to powder and that powder used to make new worlds. Gods and goddesses of thunder and of the demon wind, of rivers and mountains long sunk beneath the waves, of war and healing, of death and rebirth, of games and the players of games. From Chakal Square's faith they wove themselves, from the instant's glory of the sacrifice.

You could not see them with the naked eye. If you walked through Chakal Square that night you might not even feel them, without having paid as its people paid, suffered as they suffered. To feel the gods sift the sand of mind for the pearl of you, you must stand with one foot already in their world.

Not the world of the dead. The world of story.

Temoc listened, and prayed the prayers he knew in silence.

He did not look up when Chel joined him beside the altar. What she had to say, she would say. What she could not say was not his responsibility to force from her. Nor his right.

"You came back," she managed at last.

"I could not let you die."

"But we will, now," she said. "The Wardens won't stop."

"Nor can we, now the gods are here."

"They're terrifying."

"They always are," he said, breaking off his prayer. They heard him speak, and drew near to listen. "They are more than us, but they are us too. And we terrify."

"What I did today," she said. "Coming to get you. I had no right."

He did not reply.

"I'm glad you came, though."

He nodded, knew the nod was not enough.

She touched him on the arm. That was the first and only time she touched him, and he did not touch her back. He wished he could have told Mina that, somehow. He had not left her for another. He had left her to die. Which was, he supposed, no better.

An apostate at the last.

Chel let him go, and left him. The gods' breath washed over him like water, and he feared that they were laughing.

A voice in the night cried Chel's name; she thought at first it might have been a god, and realized too late that it was Tay. He forced through the faithful, smiling broken-mouthed. She braced herself, but not enough. He hit her like a train, caught her in his arms, and lifted. "Gods, Chel. When they hit us, I thought . . ."

"I know," she said. "I know."

"They pressed our eastern flank the whole time." He set her down. She reeled on her feet. "The guys would have folded if I left. And then we had the wounded, and then—"

"It's okay," she started to say, but he was kissing her. He tasted sweet, and in that dark hour it was almost enough.

He must have tasted something else in their kiss, because he broke it off and drew away. She followed his gaze over her shoulder. Temoc knelt there, shining. "He's back."

"Yes."

"I heard things out in the camp. Blind men can see. The lame can walk. They say the gods are awake. They say Temoc killed someone."

"He's killed before."

"You know what I mean. On the altar. For real. With a knife."

"The Major was about to die. He wanted to go the old way."

"Gods."

"Well. Yeah."

"They won't let us go," he said. "Not after this. Riots, I mean, whatever, just some poor folks in the Skittersill, right? Dockhands and schoolteachers and shit. But they can't let us do things different from them. Not this different."

"They might." Even she did not believe that. She had said as much to Temoc. But he needed some hope.

He pulled her close. He smelled smoky and unwashed, and so did she. "Let's go. Before it gets worse. Slip out into the night. Bring the dockside guys. There are enough red-arms left without us to hold the camp together."

"I can't," she said. "I brought him back."

"You said this was bigger than people. That we were fighting for ideas. Well, the ideas have changed. This isn't why I came."

"I know," she said. "But I can't leave."

"Then I'll stay, too."

"No, Tay."

"Shit." He broke their embrace. "If you can die for someone, so can I."

"We won't," but she could not finish that sentence. The firelight caught his skin all bronze and ochre and gold, and his eyes chips of jet, the broken and reset nose that made his face the face of an old soldier on a monument, all courage and loyalty and too few brains.

"You want to stand, we'll stand together."

"We might die."

"We're too pretty to die."

"Speak for yourself."

He took a pack of cigarettes from his pocket, pondered them, and put them back. "That's settled, then. We stay."

"Yes." Gods, why did that sound like passing sentence? She grabbed his wrist, thick-roped with muscles. He was sweat-slick and sooty and very real. "Come on," she said. "Let's find an empty tent."

He followed her into the night of the gods.

55

Elayne landed on the summit of the obsidian pyramid at 667 Sansilva, by the King in Red's office dome. Approaching from the air, she'd been overcome by memory: the greatest battle of Liberation was fought here, forty years ago. Here, Kopil broke gods on their altars. Forty years gone and still, to her eyes, rivers of rainbow blood rolled down the pyramid's steps, and ichor slicked its surface.

Purcell clutched his briefcase with both hands, fingers white-knuckled against leather. He did not share the memory. He was just afraid of heights.

No time for appointments or the front door—not that the secretary would be on duty this late. Lights glowed within the translucent crystal dome in the center of the roof. The master was home.

Elayne knocked three times on the dome. "Old man," she said. "Let us in."

"Elayne." Kopil's voice in the air beside her. "A pleasure."

"I've brought a guest. Don't kill him."

"A friend?"

"Not really. But you should hear his story."

"Come along, then."

"Come here, Purcell." She crooked her fingers, and though she used no Craft, he staggered toward her, obedient as a zombie. "Through the crystal."

His face was paler than it had seemed under the hospital's ghostlight. "Do you know where we are?"

"Do you think I'd land on a strange pyramid for fun?"

"But this—"

"He's not as bad as he looks," she said. "So long as he's not kept waiting." And before he could object again, she walked through the dome. He followed her.

The crystal parted, pricking her skin like a waterfall of blunt needles. The King in Red sat at his desk, the sloped block of red-tinged obsidian that used to be an altar. The office looked much the same as on her last visit, maybe a little cleaner than usual.

"You should have seen it, Elayne." Kopil stood, the fires of his eyes stoked and fierce, finger bones scraping over glass. His robe blew about his body in an unfelt wind. Bad form—wasted power, wasted focus. That said, he had power to spare. "I never imagined they'd go this far. They want to fight the God Wars with one priest and few suicidal kids. I will give them such a war as to burn their memory from this or any world." The lights in his eyes went out, and on again. "Who's that?"

"Lord Kopil, Deathless King of Dresediel Lex and Chief Executive of Red King Consolidated, meet Jim Purcell, insurance agent from Aberforth and Duncan."

"Ah," Purcell said.

"Does it speak?"

Purcell tried to reach into his breast pocket and remove a business card. He succeeded on the third attempt. "It's a—a pleasure to meet—"

The card jumped from his hand and floated across the room. The King in Red reviewed its front and back, then vaporized it. Purcell, fortunately, did not faint.

"Elayne, I appreciate the thought, but I'm covered."

"You are," she said. "The Skittersill isn't."

"I fail to see how that's my problem."

"You're about to bring God Wars weapons to bear on the Chakal Square protesters."

"I don't need a lecture about proportional response. They chased off a commando squad. They've started to sacrifice people. Their gods are awake, and gathering strength. If we don't stop this now we'll be fighting full-scale Wars in weeks."

"You haven't stopped fighting them in forty years."

"Nor has Temoc. Nor have you."

"I don't plan to burn a city to the ground tomorrow."

"You've never governed, Elayne. With all due respect. You have never ruled. Sit on this side of the desk for a while, and you'll see things differently. Without the work my people do, there is no water in this city. How long do you think the Skittersill would last in that case? Or Dresediel Lex itself? I must save my people."

"And in the process, you get to kill some faithful. Gods too, if you're lucky."

He grinned. He was always grinning. "I never said I wouldn't enjoy it."

"Why?"

"I dislike the faithful's smug superiority. Their assumption that gods will protect them. They strangled human progress for three millennia, sent millions to their deaths in dumb wars backed by dumb theology. They killed the only man I've ever loved. Or maybe I'm just bent that way. Take your pick."

"I meant, why are you killing them now? The proximate cause, please."

"We're not doing this cross examination thing. I don't have time."

She put the cold into her voice, the chill that had broken better men than him on the witness stand. "You don't have to sleep. And how long does it take to plan a mass murder? If you like being manipulated into a war crime, fair enough, but don't drag me with you." Purcell, beside her, drew back. Poor guy. Should have left him outside until this part was done. "Now. What's the proximate cause?"

"Temoc sacrificed a man in cold blood."

"After all but starving his gods driving off your Wardens, which he wouldn't have done if the Wardens hadn't attacked, which they wouldn't have done if Chakal Square hadn't broken into a riot, which would never have happened if Tan Batac wasn't shot. Isn't that right?"

"Objection. Counsel is leading the witness."

"None of this would have happened but for Tan Batac's attempted murder. Do you disagree?"

"Fine. If not for that, we would have left Chakal Square without incident."

"The question is, who benefits from this state of affairs. Purcell's masters at Aberforth and Duncan insure and protect the Skittersill property Tan Batac and his partners control. The accords void their pre-existing deal—they call for more protection than Aberforth and Duncan provide at the prices Batac and his people pay. Purcell, how high are the new premiums?"

"I don't feel comfortable quoting the precise figures."

"Estimate."

"Ah," he said again. "I believe it's an order of magnitude difference. At least."

"So. Ten times the cost to protect Skittersill properties, as long as they're occupied and used for their current purposes. That was the deal. All along, the accords shackle Batac and his partners. They don't own what they own."

"So Batac made a bad deal. He's only human."

"He made a bad deal, unless he thought most of the Skittersill would be destroyed between the signing of the accords and the new insurance regime's establishment."

"You're saying he might be happy I'm burning the Skittersill. Fine. I'll joyfully oblige."

"I'm saying he wanted you to burn the Skittersill before the accords were signed. I'm saying that was why he agreed to the accords in the first place."

"You think he wanted me to destroy his property, knowing he'd get nothing for it?"

"Nothing but fee simple ownership. The ability to use the burned ground for anything he and his partners want. Those crystal palaces in our plan—the district rebuilt, everything our friends in Chakal Square wanted to stop. Those buildings are undefended now, not even a shade of fire resistance. You attack, and they go up like tinder. People will die—not protesters, people who just happen to live nearby. Batac gets the Skittersill wiped off the map, and he doesn't even look like the bad guy. After all, everything went down while he was comatose."

"You think he took out a hit on himself?"

"I think," she said, taking a slow breath to compose her thoughts. "I think it's possible he had himself shot. There's no evidence. The assassin in Chakal Square may never be found. But Batac will profit immensely from what you do tomorrow."

"You have no evidence."

"Can you think of another reason he'd make that deal?"

"A weak case."

"Are you willing to risk being manipulated into a mass murder? A crime from which someone else reaps the profits?"

"I thought reaping prophets was the whole point of religious war."

"I'm not joking."

The King in Red rested his hips against the desk. He crossed his arms, tapped forefingers against his bare tibia. "What do you want from me, Elayne?"

"Don't let one man profit on the wreckage of a war he caused."

"Look. I understand. You're a genius. I've never known a Craftswoman like you."

"Don't you dare patronize me. You have been playing at war while people die." Visions of the boy bleeding in the hallway of the Monicola Hotel. She forced them from her mind. Growing too emotional. Bad tactic. Skeletons don't like emotion. Makes them nervous.

"You want a clever solution," he said. "You want that moment when whole world ties together in a knot, and you chop the knot in half, because that's the way it works in court, with Craft and pure theory. We don't have that luxury here. History has happened. I need to resume control of Dresediel Lex. I will do that with fire, to show that rebellion and sacrifice will not be tolerated. You can try to stop me." He sounded tired. "If that's how you want to play the game. You might be smart enough. You're cleverer with the Craft than I am. But you don't have the strength. So I'd advise against it."

Which was the other thing about skeletons: he did not know how much his saying that made her want to try. For him, it was a statement of fact, free of adrenaline and glandular rage. Beneath the masks of performed emotion he was just a man still here twenty years after his body died. She stared into the abyss of his eyes, and he stared back.

"You've made your choice," she said. "And you'll live with it."

"To live with something, you have to be alive."

"I would stop you if I could. You'd thank me for it in the end. But I don't think I can. All I can do is ask you. What would you have done, if you wanted to destroy the Skittersill without getting blood on your hands?"

He didn't answer.

"Do you think it's right that anyone profit off what happens in Chakal Square tomorrow? Do you think it's right that bystanders will die while Tan Batac grows richer?"

The sky above Sansilva was the only part of the city not covered by Craftwork clouds. Stars glittered like glass slivers spilled on velvet. Purcell's was the sole breath in the room.

"I won't call off the attack," Kopil said.

"Then help me save the people outside the square. Help me save the Skittersill."

She waited. She did not hold her breath.

He nodded.

"Thank you."

"Even if Tan Batac is innocent, he will be enraged when he learns what you've done."

"I'll survive."

"And in exchange for my aid, I want your word: you will not protect the rebels in Chakal Square. Save their surrounding hovels, and the wretches crouched within them. The people in the Square are mine. Better, in fact, if you stay away from the Square altogether."

She could not meet his gaze, but she did anyway. "I will not protect Chakal Square. I will not protect those inside its borders. Nor will I set foot on its stone." The promise convulsed between them, and settled, harder than steel.

"Very well."

"What," said Purcell, "just happened?"

"We have an agreement," Elayne said. "You're about to give me the contract. I will sign it for Tan Batac."

"You can't do that."

"Allow me to demonstrate."

"No. I mean." He'd retreated from them both already, and he took a few more steps back, hugging his briefcase. He glanced for a door or some other avenue of escape, but found none. "Tan Batac can't sign, and no one else can sign for him."

"I represent Batac and the King in Red in the Skittersill matter. Your insurance contracts are a piece of that matter. I can sign in Batac's place."

"The contract won't bind."

"We'll make it work," she said. "Trust me."

"Batac's Concern will refuse to pay. The courts will not honor the contract."

"I will provide the initial funds," Kopil said. "Batac will settle the rest when he awakes."

"But he hasn't agreed—"

"He will."

Purcell's head jerked left and right. "I'm sorry. I know you think you know the man. But there's a lot of soul at stake. If Batac protests the deal when he wakes up, who's liable for damage to these properties? Or for the expense of protecting them? You can't just—"

"You mistake me," said the King in Red. "I do not say a man will sign a contract because I believe he will sign that contract. I say he will sign, because he will sign. Do you understand?"

Purcell took another step back. His skull made a loud hollow noise as it struck the crystal dome. He looked up at the

Craftsman and Craftswoman approaching him, and held out the briefcase.

"Good man," Elayne said. She opened the briefcase without touching it, and snapped her fingers. Contract pages fanned out to hover in a circle around them. She scanned them, found the page she sought, fished a pen from her pocket, and marked Tan Batac's name on solid line there, with an added glyph tying the name into the contract they'd signed months back to appoint her mediator. Flimsy argument. Any competent court would overturn Elayne's right to sign. But once in a while there was an advantage to being war buddies with the Powers that Were. Invisible gears shifted and meshed as the Craft took hold. "So mote it be."

"So mote it be," the King in Red echoed. The contract stacked once more and floated back into the briefcase, which clicked shut. "He does have a point, though. That signature is too weak to hold by itself."

"I'll enforce it."

"I will not hold back on the assault for your sake," he said.

"I know."

"Fair enough." He turned from her to Purcell. "As for you, Purcell. You will accept my hospitality tonight."

Purcell was sweating. "I'd really prefer to return to the hospital. Or to my family."

"Mr. Purcell. You are privy to a number of plans that cannot be announced until they become accomplished fact. This pyramid is large, and we have many apartments set aside for our guests. Some are more comfortable, and some less. I hope you will agree to stay in one of the more comfortable rooms."

"And if I . . . refuse?" That word only made it past his lips over the extreme protest of his survival instinct. An interesting world we've made, Elayne thought, where bureaucrats risk death for technicalities.

"Well," the skeleton said, turning his head as if he'd never considered the possibility. "I suppose we'd have to house you in a less comfortable room."

There was not much air in Purcell to begin with, but what there was went out. "I'll go."

"Good." Behind Purcell, the floor screeched open to reveal a staircase winding down. Two Wardens climbed from the shadows. "These men will take you to an apartment. Ask if you need anything. It may be granted. And don't worry. All this will be over tomorrow afternoon."

Purcell followed the Wardens down. Elayne felt a pang of pity as the floor swallowed them. "What now?"

"We attack after dawn, as planned. Who knows how long the battle will last?"

"Not long."

"Probably not." Kopil sagged. "I wonder why I am helping you."

"A shred of goodness left in your heart?"

"Not even a shred of heart," he said. "Mostly I'm helping because you asked."

"I should go," she said. "You know how weak that signature is. Aberforth and Duncan will fight tooth and nail for every thaum I pull from them."

"Yes. And I plan to use gripfire."

Stars watched. Worn obsidian carvings danced their frozen dance. Books sat on shelves, dead words on dead wood from dead forests.

"On civilians," she said.

"They've sacrificed to blood gods. That makes them enemy combatants."

"You mean you think they deserve it."

"Well," he said. "More or less."

"More or less," she echoed, and walked away from him.

"Where are you going?"

"To the front." The wall flowed apart, ushering her from the pyramid's chill into the demon wind. She walked without looking back, toward the pyramid's edge and off, and flew south alone toward Chakal Square.

56

Seven things Elayne saw as she flew toward Chakal Square and the next day's burning:

1. Lights flooded a Downtown park. Brass instruments glinted gold from the bandstand, and people danced. Skirts twirled and unfurled around girls' legs. Dancers in slacks orbited as dots around swelling and collapsing suns. Too high up to hear the music, she placed it anyway as swing from the dancers' rhythm.

2. Huge golem-towed trucks snarled in traffic on an elevated highway, bearing goods from Longsands warehouses to train stations and the airport. Spider-golems skittered forward one massive claw limb at a time, and human drovers walked among them, gnats trying to correct the movement of greater forces. The cause of the traffic, farther up the highway: a truck on its side, four golems straining to right it while men ran between them, waving hand torches.

3. A billboard on an old sandstone pyramid, lit by bright blue ghostlights, bore a picture of a geyser and the word ACTU-ALIZE in block letters. If the billboard offered more context or instructions, they were too small to read from the air. She did not remember the old use of the pyramid upon which the billboard stood. Southern temples often belonged to moon gods. Or perhaps it had been a school, or a prison.

4. A half mile from the Skittersill the blackout began, and the sky opened. No lights shone below save the occasional red bloom of a fire. The stars here were sharper and clearer even than in Sansilva, where, despite the Craftsmen's best efforts, some light seeped up to dilute the stars above the city center.

The Quechal gods had reclaimed their city. Black ribbon streets divided black blocks of black buildings below a black sky. Interesting choice, if it had been a choice, for the gods to clear the clouds away: Quechal religion did not trust stars. The night sky, for them, was an iron web enormous spiders wove to steal the sun's light. This new blackness was defiance of a kind, and a reminder to their people: you have enemies, and they work against you.

5. Wardens swarmed in camps lit by the brilliant ghostlights road workers used after dark, which mimicked noon sun but lacked its heat. From this height, their chaos resolved to order: each camp divided naturally into sectors, bunks here and armory there, temporary cells, guard rotations, clinic. Couatl circled. One passed near enough to ruffle Elayne's suit with the wind of its wings. With streetlights lit, Couatl shimmered from below thanks to their jeweled plumage. Without that light, nothing set them off from the sky where the demons lived.

6. Elayne could not read Chakal Square from overhead as she had the Warden camp. It looked like a forest made of people—individual humans visible only around bonfire edges, sleeping or dancing or drinking, making music or love. Beyond the firelight circles they were droplets in an ocean. Tendrils spread down alleys into labyrinthine Skittersill streets. Here and there, half-lit, she saw some structure: the beds of a field hospital, the command tents broken by the Wardens' assault, the makeshift temple. Grass mats, and the altar makeshift no longer—anointed in the old way, with blood.

7. Gods moved through the Skittersill. With closed eyes she saw them. Back in the wars she'd shipped out to the Shining Empire from a port in Xivai where whales gathered by the thousands to mate. Sometimes they exploded from the waves in majestic fountain breaches, but even hidden, they shaped the surface. The sea boiled with whales.

As Chakal Square boiled with gods, tonight. Elayne did not recognize most of them, nor could she see them all at once. Like whales, they presented hints to form: a gnarled face with a fanged mouth, an arm elegant as an Imperial dancer's, a hunched back and a single blinking eye.

They had slept long, and deep, and they had fallen far. So, woken by Temoc's sacrifice, they rooted in their faithful's minds and took strength from the dreams engendered there. Nightmares would rule Chakal Square this evening. No quiet rest before the day, and the fire.

She landed hard on the woven grass mats of Temoc's chapel. The force of impact knelt her, and raised a cloud of dust. Guards and faithful cried out in terror. A bowstring sang and an arrow slipped through the dust cloud to stop inches from her suit. Shaft and feather crumbled. She plucked the arrowhead from the air and held it between thumb and forefinger as the dust settled.

The kneeling faithful recoiled. Red-arms in scrap armor forced through the crowd, brandishing makeshift weapons. Others raised bows with arrows nocked. Torn tents and broken tentpoles rose into the sky. Flames licked the night.

Temoc stood by the altar. His hands seemed clean.

She saw Chel too, and the man with the broken nose, Tay, both running half-clothed from a nearby tent. Hair in disarray. Elayne forced the smile from her face: at least someone was enjoying the night while it lasted.

Temoc walked toward her. The crowd gave way to let him pass. "Elayne."

"Temoc," she said. "We have to stop meeting like this."

"If you have come to fight, know that my gods live. I am your equal now."

"Before you try to kill me," Elayne said, with slight emphasis on try, because it always helped to plant seeds of doubt in a potential adversary, "you should know I've come to help."

"You have come to join us against your master."

"I'm not a fighter, Temoc. Not anymore. I'm here to save people, like I saved you. Like I saved your son."

That broke the paladin's facade. "Caleb," he said. "Is he—"

"Well, no thanks to you. Golems chased him and Mina from the Skittersill after you left. They're fine."

"Where are they now?"

"I don't think I should give you that information."

"So you have come to torment me."

"Hardly." She looked from him, to the crowd, and back. In a blink, she saw the gods gathering too, through lightning-seaweed lines of Craft: not manifest, though awake enough to listen. "I've come to offer you a trade. Tell your people to leave. As many of them as will go."

"And in exchange?"

"In exchange I save the Skittersill. Or try."

"I don't understand."

"The King in Red will strike tomorrow morning. Your sacrifice made him angry. He thinks the God Wars have come again, and he will destroy you. He'll use gripfire. It will catch, and spread. The Skittersill's undefended now—we're inside the insurance renegotiation window. People will die whose only crime is living near the Square. The Skittersill will burn. I can't save the Square, but I can save the surrounding district, and the people there, if you help me. Otherwise, tomorrow, the fire starts, and who knows what Tan Batac will build in place of all that's burned. You'll have lost in every way."

"The gods will help us."

"Can they save the Skittersill and fight the King in Red at once?" And addressing him she addressed the crowd, and the gods.

Temoc did not answer. Neither did they.

"Caleb will recover," she said, after too much silence passed. "He's young. Mina's safe, and angry, and hurt."

"What do you need?" he said.

"The Skittersill. I have to know it. Perfectly. Intimately. I have to know it like someone who has lived here for sixty years. Backstreets. Shortcuts. Rooftops at sunset. Sound of rain in gutters. The color of the alley cats, and their secret names. I need the dream of this place."

"Is that all?"

She had no patience for sarcasm. "I need men and women who know this ground, and these people. The process is dangerous, but I think I can protect them."

"You think."

"We will be a fire brigade in a firefight. There is a limit to how much safety I can offer. But I need volunteers."

His chin sank to his chest. It might have been a nod.

"He'll go." Chel's voice. Elayne glanced up, startled by the interruption, to see Chel shove Tay forward. He glared from Elayne to Chel, shaking his head. "He knows the Skittersill as well as anyone. Born and raised here. The other red-arms too, Zip and them. They'll help you."

"What about you?" Tay said it first, so Elayne didn't have to.

"I'll stay," she said. "I started this. I'll see it through."

Elayne did not interrupt the pause that passed between Chel and Tay, did not speak to draw their eyes from each other. At last, Tay's shoulders slumped. He nodded. He took Chel in his arms, kissed her, broke away, and walked toward Elayne.

"We will send the others," Temoc said. "Good luck."

"Thank you."

He offered her his hand. It was clean, though firelight dyed it red.

They were close enough for him to whisper and be heard. "I had no choice."

"I don't believe you," she replied, with false conviction.

She left him standing on his grass mats before his altar, beneath the stars.

57

Elayne walked on air through Chakal Square to the meeting tent, with Tay beside her. Others followed: red-arms and interested faithful, armored hooligans loyal to the dead Major. She kept her glyphs' starfire damped, but still she glowed.

"You didn't fly when you came to us the first morning," Tay said.

"I prefer to walk on the ground. It's easier."

"Why aren't you doing that now?"

"I promised I would not set foot in Chakal Square. My word binds me."

"We'll leave the Square, then?"

"In a manner of speaking."

They reached the meeting tent. Night dyed the deep green canvas almost black. The tent had served its purpose during those long tense negotiation days, but tonight it would only block out the sky, and she needed all the starfire and moonlight she could catch. With a sweep of one hand she shredded the canvas and toppled the poles. The circle she'd etched into stone glinted silver.

Elayne crossed the circle and settled once more to ground. Gods cursed and threatened, but she ignored them. Those Wars were long done, at least for her.

For some, they would never end.

Tay joined her in the circle, stepping high across the cold flames as if climbing from a boat to shore. He turned, and blinked, like a man who'd walked long in the mist and stood now in the sun. "It feels different."

"This circle is not a part of Chakal Square. Here, I can protect us without breaking my word." She drew her work knife, and lightning sparked along its edge.

"What should I do?"

"Stand still."

The limits of the ward were set, burned into stone and notional space. To change them she would have to wipe away the ward and begin again, for which she had neither strength nor time. So small a space, with so many left outside. But large enough, she hoped.

"First," she said, "I assert my right to claim insurance for the Skittersill." She carved a circle seven meters in diameter within the ward, and inside that a second circle, concentric and three meters across. That circle she tied to the contract she'd forced Purcell to let her sign, and through that contract to her representation pact with Tan Batac. "And then I prove I am who I claim." To the second circle she added a few drops of her blood—always err on the conservative side with human fluids. A little goes a long way.

"Why do you need to prove that?"

"I will draw a lot of soulstuff through these circles tomorrow. The powers I invoke will use every loophole to keep from honoring their agreement—including claiming I am not myself."

"Why do you need us?"

She looked up from her knife's trail. Tay alone stood within the circle. Others had gathered outside: red-arms mostly, some she remembered from that first day when they tried to bar her access to the camp. A withered and scarred man. A giant who made even Tay look scrawny. A woman with short hair dyed shocking red.

"Come in," she said. "Step across the line."

"It's fine," Tay added.

They entered, each by each, the red-haired woman most decisive and the giant the most hesitant.

"You're friends of Chel's."

"I am," the giant rumbled. "Zip."

"That's your name."

"It's what they call me," he said. "My name's Andrew, really."

"Not all of us know her," the red-haired woman said. "She asked for people from all over. I used to work with the Kemals, up by Market and Slaughter."

Elayne let her work-knife fade and her glyphs dull to pale tracks on her skin. Even the shadows of her suit grew shallow. She looked almost human when she was done. Normal enough, she hoped, for them to believe her.

"I need your dreams."

Elayne's deals gave her power to preserve the Skittersill. Now she only needed to explain, in precise and Craftwork terms, what the Skittersill was. The insurance contract stipulated which properties it covered, yes, but tomorrow Aberforth and Duncan would fight those definitions. This building on fire could be any building on fire. Why should we save it?

She had maps, but maps were poor echoes of reality, their accuracy open to attack. She had to feel the Skittersill as if it were her own flesh. She needed a lifetime's walking of its streets.

No way to get there in a night. Fortunately, she could cheat.

They sat cross-legged around her, the first twelve: Tay and Andrew-called-Zip and the red-haired woman named Hannah, and scarred Cozim. With a fine brush and silver ink she drew a glyph-eye on each one's brow. Others joined, and sat, and had their brows inscribed. Tay flinched at the bristles' touch. "It tickles."

It would burn, soon enough.

"Eyes closed," she said, and sat in the center of her inner-most circle.

Zip spoke first. "How long you want us to sit like—"

She closed her eyes, and they fell through sleep into nightmare.

Which nightmare didn't matter: so many to choose from, and knowing each she could find the next most basic terror and

follow it down into the marrow-fears of the race. Love itself
could be a nightmare—a laugh, a touch, a feeling of content-
ment and loyalty to block out life and light and even her own
name, love become one of those old Iskari prisons where they
threw men and women to rot without light or sky or anything
but the crush of the jailer's boot heel on hands thrust through
the slot in the door through which they slid tin plates of bad
food, and she followed that nightmare further down to burial,
her body stiff, dead maybe, as shovelfuls of earth fell into her
mouth, onto her eyes, weight that grew and grew and grew and
she could not breathe or move or see as they packed it down,
dragged heavy rocks over the distant surface and smoothed it
and struck it with their shovels and she felt nothing but heard
the impact and no matter how she strained she could not move
and then the worms came and the bugs that burrowed and the
whole host of crawling hungry things, and still further down
she fell into that single sharp terror, I am being eaten, but so
basic that there was no referent to I, only the chewing, the tearing of flesh, the self swallowed, to—

There.

She hung in the central fear, tangent to all human minds at
once. There was no geography in this place that was not a place,
but topology, yes, a web of minds each of which contained its
own webs of minds, a billion-dimensional space all but impossible to navigate untrained and unwarded.

But Elayne was trained, and warded, and knew the secret
ways of fear.

The drawn glyphs called to her, the eyes she'd scribed herself, and she reached out with a hundred hands, each one a
mercy, like a sage from the mountains west of the Shining
Empire, generous and omnipresent.

She found Zip screaming, chained to an anchor that fell to
crushing depths, and took his hand and broke his chains. She
found Cozim sobbing in bed beside a woman's skeleton that still
wore scraps of rotting flesh, and lifted him from his failure. She
found Eleanor tearing at worm-flowers that sprouted wriggling

from her belly, pulling each up by its roots only to draw forth gobs of her own meat and corded nerves—until Elayne tore her free of herself.

As she wandered the nightmares, to her surprise she found another, without her eye-glyph but of immense gravity: Temoc, who stood over an altar where his son lay bleeding.

She did not hold out her hand to him. He did not ask for it. But he reached into his chest, drew forth the Skittersill in miniature, and passed it to her.

"Thank you," he said, and turned from her back to his own private fear.

They hung together between dreams, Elayne and Tay and Cozim and Zip and Hannah and the rest. "Show me your city," she said.

And their city took shape.

There was no single Skittersill, as there was no single sun, no single moon, no single god. But a city grew around them nonetheless.

Their dreams were grand and old and private and new, their roots deep and facets many, held together by memory, analogy, and metaphor rather than logic. For Tay the Skittersill began with the smell of dust and fried plantain, with streetcorner sweetness and cheap drink, with street dances each lunar new year, brawling and turning cartwheels to the rapid beat of a brass band. For Hannah it began with fear and a breath of air from the distant sea, the feeling of sudden freedom. The images slid through Elayne's mind, fast and fluid. And she added her own memories, her own dreams, and Temoc's: the city seen by a preacher to deserted rooms, through ten years of depression and alcohol, two decades more of search and prayer and hunger, followed by twelve years of love. Ten thousand sunrises give or take: some found him streetside with feet in gutter, head hanging sickly between his knees, some streamed through glass windows as he donned priestly regalia and raised false knife before a sparse but curious crowd, some called him from feathered sleep to wake in Mina's arms. Sunsets too, and music: horse hooves and rain and three-string fiddle, the song of soapbox politicians, drums on stage and in dancer's veins, drums in his wife's flesh and his own chest.

These dreams would take years to infiltrate her waking mind, years she did not have. But there was another way.

Her eyes drifted open, and her hand rose to her chest, drew her work knife from the glyph above her heart. Dreams weighed down her arms. The stars above thronged with all the monsters Quechal myths had planted there. Spiders the size of trash bins skittered around her, spinning webs. Chakal Square was a charnel house, an orgy, an inferno. The city crumbled into ash, built itself again, was knocked to pieces by flaming serpents taller than the tallest building, perished in a single blinding light, towered black and invincible above. A Craftswoman's mind was an edge for cutting her will into the world, but an edge could scrape as well as cut, and this she did now, scraping away years of judgment to dream and wake at once.

She touched her knife to stone and drew the first line. Then she drew another, crossing it, and a third.

A map unfolded from her blade. Set beside surveyors' charts this map was warped and imprecise, streets crossing at the wrong points—if the lines she drew were streets at all. She cut a long curve sharp as a sickle, and lines like rays from it, that might have been the Forty-first Skyway. This was no navigational aid, nor was it art exactly. But it was useful, it was real. Working, she saw the city, each crossing and square painted with memory: this corner good for afternoon preaching, that alley where migrant workers slept if they'd stayed in town too late to risk the crossing back to Stonewood, this the square Mina painted three times in watercolor, that the rooftop with the hammock where Tay and Chel slept in good weather and happier times.

She worked for hours or minutes, probably the former. Dreamtime could not be laid upon a line, as dream maps did not yield to an alphanumeric grid.

Around her the people of Chakal Square prepared themselves for death, and hungry gods danced.

She finished before the moon set. The map drank and digested starlight. It breathed.

She returned her knife to her heart, laid her hands in her lap, and let her eyes drift shut.

She had done what she could. What she was allowed to do. Now she could only wait and gather strength.

Elayne did not sleep, surrounded by her circles and her mad map and her fellow dreamers. But she rested in a way that was not altogether unlike sleep.

The night passed.

Morning came.

58

Temoc woke before dawn, and found the skies above Chakal Square clear.

Dreams contorted in his mind: dreams of Mina, of her hate for him. Of Caleb, who did not understand.

Of Elayne.

That memory shocked him to his feet, on the dry grass mats spread before his altar. A red flaking stain lingered on the table where he had lain the Major. Gone now. He'd burnt the man himself. The husk did not matter, once the feast was done.

Men and women slept upon the mats. Some few early risers drifted among the rest like priests or robbers through the wounded after a battle. Chel stood close by, and watched him stand, stretch, exorcise the night by movement. The sky brightened from amethyst to sapphire. Temoc wished he could stop the sun from rising, stop time from turning, leave them all sleeping here on the morning after their finest hour. No need for a final battle, no need for him to honor his promise. No need to tell them they were doomed, or face the choices he had made. The knife. The flight.

Chel approached him. "Bad dreams," she said.

"Of course."

"We're ready, because of you."

"That is a sentence," he said, "not a commendation. What did you dream?"

She licked her lips. "You don't want to know."

"Leave it there and I'll imagine worse. What did you dream?"

Her eyes were deeper than he remembered. They must have deepened in the night, or he had. "My father was a mechanic at Longsands, and I've worked the docks since I was a kid. I dreamed I sailed a ship on fire. Not one of the container hulks, but a real old ship, a tea clipper, burning. Its hull caught, and the decks, and the sheets. Still we sailed. We suffocated, our skin melted, and still. The captain sent me to the crow's nest. I climbed through the heat. By the time I reached the top, my left hand was blistered and my right was bone. I couldn't see. Wind came, and at the last second I thought I saw a flash of green. Then I fell and woke." Her voice stayed level. "It's not a good dream, is it?"

"Not the best," he said. "Do you remember who the captain was?"

She hesitated. "No."

Others woke. They rose in the heat, fathers and mothers, the men and the women and the children. They uncurled from one another, they rolled their sleeping bags, they stepped out of their tents, they blinked in the light. Lines of smoke lay like blades against sky's throat.

Red-arms took up their posts, staring over barricades at empty streets. The wounded tried to stand, and many found they could. By night the gods had walked among them with healing hands. Chakal Square would be ready for the day.

They gathered to hear him. He wondered how many came from faith, how many from fear, how many because they heard the stories and wondered what new miracles today would bring. He did not care. They came, and filled his mats; they came, and stood, and listened.

He bent his head and prayed. Let them hear me. Let all of them hear me.

He was heard.

Hungry eyes watched him watching them.

"This is the last day," he said, softly, and he saw the ripple of shock as each person in the camp heard his voice at once, clear and direct as if he spoke to them alone. "This is the last day. I have seen the King in Red come. I have seen his weapons, and they are grand."

"We'll fight!" someone cried from the back, a man, a boy really. He knew nothing.

"We will fight," Temoc said, not agreeing. "And we must know what fighting means. The battle we face today will be the fiercest we have known. The gods stand at our side, but our enemy grew strong by killing gods. We cannot expect to win. Life is a debt, of which death is our repayment."

No shouts after that.

"We have flowered here, and now we must seed: we must not perish in this battle, but spread. Ideas, and blood, and determination, all must fly from Chakal Square and take root in rich earth to spring up again, and again, and again, until we cover the world.

"I ask you now, if you are strong enough, to walk away. If you have children here, take them and go. The hero's path today is to leave. Be the seed that flies from the fist of the King in Red, and floats away to bloom where he does not expect. Tell the truth of Chakal Square: of human beings defending their beliefs, their homes, their ways of life, from an enemy who gave no quarter. If you accept this burden, you will prove yourself stronger than those who stay. It is easy, fast, to fight and die beside your brothers in the sun. It is harder to build, to teach, to live, and to remember."

He waited, savoring the pause in his speech—a beat as near as he could come to timelessness.

"I will fight," he said, "because I was born to fight. That is my path, but it need not be yours. If you leave now, know your brothers and sisters love you. Know they respect you. Know they trust you to build the world we seek in the years that come.

"It is time for sacrifice. It is time for the gods to know us by our gifts. I will not perform the bloodless rite, in respect for one who gave himself last night to help today. But I will give my own blood. I encourage you all to do the same. Feed the gods on yourselves. Join them in body as you do in faith. Join together so no man can tear us apart."

He held his arm high where all could see, and his knife, and drew a cut between two scars on his forearm. Blood wept, gathering at his elbow. A drop formed, and fell, and splashed against the altar stain.

A tongue lapped the blood from his arm, a talon held him, and he felt himself lifted. His eyes opened, and they stood in the sky surrounding him, miles tall and minuscule at once, grounds of being, and he was with and within them, was the Spider spinning and Ixaqualtil gnawing the bones of the dead, was winged Ili who spread her sails through the sky, was the Hunchback burdened with the weight that is the future. He was the corn and the mortar stone and he was the mouth that consumed; he was the giver and receiver of the great gift.

And then he was himself again, weeping.

He lowered his arm.

The sun rose.

The congregation came, one by one. Their blood wet the altar, and the gods drank, and they left. He did not count how many came. Hundreds perhaps. Time seemed slow that morning.

But before long it was done, and he stepped back from the altar and felt himself complete, and spent, and filled with power.

"Do you believe what you said, about seeds?" That was Chel, beside him. Always.

"I think so."

"Hells," she said. "I never was that strong."

He clapped her on the back. Above, the sky glittered with new-risen sun. "Neither was I."

Some left Chakal Square. Not all. Not as many as Elayne hoped. Not as many as Temoc hoped, either. But some.

Many were parents, families. A couple who brought their two children to a demonstration that started peacefully and became something else. The woman whose boy Temoc had healed when he fell—she left, holding her son's hand. They were not cowards. Their lives were not their own to give. It was a sacrifice, of a kind, to reach this point and step out of the river of history. To be the seeds.

Kapania Kemal stayed, and her husband Bill. They had a daughter. She was twelve, she was living with an aunt in Fisherman's Vale. She was cared for. And they asked themselves how they could look in her eyes, later, and say they left the people they fed and guided and protected because danger neared. They did not know whether this was the right decision. They hoped to survive. They hoped Temoc was cautious, as a leader should be, but that in his heart he believed they might triumph.

Some left to accept Temoc's challenge: because they were strong, and they could bear their scars in secret, and teach the many meanings of Chakal Square. To a bent wiry man with the first strands of gray in his beard, Chakal Square was the resurgence of the Quechal nation, decades crushed beneath a foreign heel. To a young woman with flames couched behind her eyes and a rippled burn scar on her face, Chakal Square meant the gods, meant the rebirth of faith in the face of danger. To a journeyman poet come with his notebook to write the movement's history, the Square was a dream made real. To a Longsands union worker it was one fight in the war between men and the undead powers that sought to rule them. Chakal Square was a beacon. Chakal Square was the moment everything went wrong. Chakal Square was the future. Chakal Square was the past, Chakal Square was the path between. Chakal Square was birth, and death, and all these meanings followed those who walked away.

Some left because they were afraid. They glanced nervously at the sky. They recoiled from the rapture of those who saw the gods. They quailed from the divine call. A red-arm who just the day before had crushed a Warden's skull with a brick, who roared atop a barricade, looked into her future and saw only a simple, short struggle, and then death. So she went.

Those who remained did not ask one another why. They had

passed beyond words, would be one way to write it—a poet's lie, almost true. They stayed, that was all. Whether from fear or hope, for fellowship or isolation, in joy or sorrow, did not matter. They stayed. Reasons were for those who left.

Across the city, Wardens yoked new weapons to their mounts. Chains glittered with silver glyphs. Upon the serpents' skulls they rested crowns, and each crown glowed with the light of a fallen, captured star. To Couatl bellies they bound big metal drums that sloshed when shaken, because even black magic relies sometimes on chemistry. One Warden's grip slipped as he levered a drum into position. The drum tumbled from his partner's hands, and struck stone. Wardens dove for cover. The drum did not explode. It was a good and patient soldier. Its time would come.

59

Captain Chimalli had not slept well. He'd sought Dr. Venkat in the hospital, and found her with blood-soaked hands, too busy to do more than shoot him an angry, delaying look. He lay alone on his hard, simple bed in his hard, simple room, and thought about the morning. Sleep must have come eventually, but he remembered only the first blue threat of sunrise.

He stood on the summit of the 667 Sansilva pyramid, the hub around which his world revolved, waiting as the King in Red drank coffee. His boss, sort of. There were many councils in Dresediel Lex, many overlapping guilds of Craftsmen and Concerns, and laws emerged from their grinding gears. But there was only one King in Red. "We're ready, sir. Airborne on your command."

"Thank you, Captain," the skeleton said, and finished his coffee, and set down his newspaper. "How do you think the papers will report what we do today?"

"Sir. I think they will report whatever's in their interest to report."

"You mean I should tighten my grip, I should control them."

"No, sir. I mean that we all do what's in our interest, most of the time."

"Even the people in Chakal Square?"

"I suppose so, sir. On some level."

"I have many interests. What if they compete?"

He thought about that for a moment. "One wins. That is the one which was more in your interest. Or else it wouldn't have won. Sir."

"You live in a deterministic universe, Captain."

"With respect, you don't pay me for philosophy."

"Is it in my interest to attack Chakal Square this morning?"

"You seem to think so."

"And yet I could stop it all now. I could order the men to stand down. I could extend an amnesty to any who left the square by nightfall, and order Lieutenant Zoh to reveal his face, and stand trial for the girl's murder, as an act of good faith. I could end this peacefully."

Talking with a Deathless King played strange tricks on the mind. Without all the subtle facial cues fleshy humans gave—cues even a Warden's mask offered if one knew how to look—one could not tell when a person was sincere. Every word might be a trap laid by a man with a perfect poker face. Fortunately, with Deathless Kings, every word tended to be a trap, so there was little risk of guessing wrong. "Will you?"

The King in Red examined the stain at the bottom of his mug. "I suppose not," he said. "Let's go. I've ordered Lieutenant Zoh to lead the raid. Seems appropriate, don't you think?"

Chimalli said nothing.

"Come, Captain. We have a long day ahead. No sense starting all morose."

The King in Red dug in the pocket of his robe for a second, finding at last a toothpick that, when he shook it three times, became a brass-shod staff taller than he was. Walking jauntily with staff in hand, he passed through the crystal dome, raised his hands to the newly risen sun, and called for his ride.

Elayne woke and sat, and watched the people of Chakal Square ready themselves. Around her the circle members opened their eyes. "Is that it?" Tay asked.

"No. When the fire comes, I'll need you: living dreams, in living minds. If you want to go, you can."

He looked back toward the fountain, toward Temoc's camp, toward Chel. "I'll stay. If it will help."

"It will," she said.

The crowd thinned. Those that remained fanned out to fill the space.

She had warned them. And the King in Red had warned her. No aid and comfort to the enemy. Save the Skittersill if you must, but leave the people to me. And she said yes.

To break her vow was to break her power. Technically, she had done neither.

One hell of a risk to run on a technicality. Many hells, even.

Temoc walked among his people, wreathed with gods, offering blessings. Where he touched, the light of his scars lingered. Chel followed him.

Elayne said yes, because she did not want to fight the King in Red. Because the Craft was the way of peace, truth, freedom. So she believed. If the system is broken, do what you can from within to fix it. What else was there?

The argument tasted like sand in her mouth. She said yes for those reasons, and also because she could not defeat the King in Red in his own city.

She tested once more the reins of obligation with which she held the Aberforth and Duncan contract. She never could have made that signature stick without Kopil's support. If she hadn't agreed to work with him.

Yet the deal tied her hands. Once, young and fresh with illusions of independence and power after heady victory in the Wars, she'd let another bind her to his will. She fought free, beat him at his own game, cast him into the outer darkness of academia, but years had come and gone and here she sat, bound again by her own tongue.

We gain strength from ties, she thought. That's the Craftswoman's way. Web yourself to others with bonds and debts, mortgage your life for power, and use that power to make nations dance.

Until one day you are called to dance yourself.

Reviewing the dream map of Skittersill she'd carved in stone, she frowned, and drew breath, and centered herself.

A drum beat in the distance. She looked north, and saw the war approach.

60

Gods guided Temoc through Chakal Square. They stroked his skin, and left glyph-trails in his wake. Their voices thundered beneath the world: turn here, stop, left, place your hand on this stone.

He blessed his remaining people as he passed. The gods are here for you. You are ready for this struggle. He knew a hundred ways to ready warriors for their end, and he deployed them all.

Then it was done. He returned to the altar, knelt, and bowed his head.

Gods' eyes watched him from inside his mind.

"Make this worth it," he prayed, in the silence of his heart.

The gods should have some gentle touch, now at the last, for their servant before their altar—but the dark gaped, hungry and certain. The gods were tired, and the gods were old, and the gods did not need to keep up appearances with him. A sacrifice had woken them, but they were no more ready for this moment than was any soldier of Chakal Square. They were scared.

He smiled.

Well, he thought, that makes all of us.

His heart beat strong in his ears, a pounding drum like Shining Empire priests used to call their mountain men to wrestle.

No. That was neither heart nor drum.

He opened his eyes, and stood.

Chel stood beside him. She held the Warden's crossbow from the night before. In their wander through the camp she'd collected more discarded bolts—replenished the crossbow's supply and strapped the rest to a bandolier. She stared into the sky.

Black birds approached, high up. They neared, wingbeats slow and heavy, their snaky tails snapped javelin-straight behind them, for speed.

Chel cocked her crossbow, though they were far out of range. He did not stop her. She had to do something. Around the camp, others readied bows and spears and sticks and rocks. Temoc laid one hand on his blade, and opened his scars. Shadow flowed cold from them, and light. He gave himself to the gods and became less and more than human. Time ran slow.

Above, as one, Couatl folded their wings and fell like arrows toward Chakal Square. Sunlight coruscated from their wings. Stars glared from their foreheads, and silver chains draped their bodies.

But then the first wave pulled out of their dive, wings flared to brake and swoop above the square. Rainbows poured from them—no, not rainbows at all but a translucent fluid, a shimmering wet curtain that covered the sky and, as it fell, caught fire.

The Square began to burn.

The Couatl flew with clockwork precision, and the Wardens released their payload well. But gripfire was never an exact weapon.

Elayne had first seen it in a delaying action in the Schwarzwald, near Grangruft University—local small gods animated the forest to destroy the school before it could take flight. Roots lifted from the earth, twigs sharpened to thorns, vines braided into serpents. The grass itself sharpened to cut tendons and snare defenders' feet. The faculty released gripfire in a circle around the university, pointed outward. At first, it worked, burning a dead expanding ring around the campus grounds. But the stuff was treacherous. A breath of wind, or a god's dying curse, pushed it back onto the grounds, and they had to abandon half the campus before the end.

So when fire fell on Chakal Square, it hit the surrounding

buildings too, and where it touched stone or wood or brick it caught and burned and spread.

Elayne knew what to expect, had tensed herself for it, holding the warding contract close, but the fire's sheer weight staggered her. Sunlight crisped to ash. Noxious fumes seared her lungs. The fire ran through her veins, melted her skin. She'd woven herself through the Skittersill, and felt its pain.

The members of her circle writhed. Zip's eyes popped open, rolled back in his head; white froth flicked from his lips.

A rainbow curtain covered the square.

She raised a shield within the meeting-tent ward: a shield technically outside Chakal Square, and so proof against her bargain with the King in Red. It buckled and flared spark-green, but held. Ozone and caustic alchemical stench tangled.

Outside, human screams rose amid the crackle of flame.

Temoc raised his hands as the curtain fell, and willed the gods' power to roll forth from him, to block the fire.

It did not.

Shadow flowed, yes, and spread, but directly over him, in a small bubble surrounding the altar, a few feet from center to edge. Enough to enclose Chel and a frightened few beside him, but no more. The glyph-lines he'd walked woke too, but offered no shelter. He strained, pulled, called to his patrons. Help us.

He received no reply but the shuffling of divine feet. Silence, tension, delay.

He strained with all his soul, his eyes bulged like the eyes of a racing horse, but he was one man and they were more, and the fire fell.

His people burned.

The fire coated his shield, pressed against it, heavy with the distance it had fallen. Through the haze of heat he saw the others die.

Everywhere caught fire at once. Tents flared incandescent. People fell beneath the fire's weight, and screamed where they lay. But Elayne and her circle were safe. Sweat beaded on her brow.

"We have to help them!" Tay leapt to his feet.

"Stay still," Elayne shouted. "Temoc's gods—"

"They're doing nothing!"

"Stay in the circle. I can't—"

"Fuck your circle." Tay dove out into the fire before Elayne could stop him.

She needed Tay. Old reflexes took over, combat reflexes, extemporizing logic: she sat within the ward, and she was threaded through her dream-circle: she was inside Tay's mind. So by protecting Tay she was protecting the part of herself in him—and she was, by definition, outside the Square.

She clad Tay's limbs in a shield of hard air. The dream map around her swam, and her mind ached with the effort of maintaining the interlocking arguments that guarded them from the inferno.

Her shield buckled. At the edges of the Square, geysers of flame rose from a tar rooftop, and spread to nearby structures.

But Tay lived.

He ran through the heat, a rippling ghost, dipped his arms into the fiery lake, lifted a slumped body, and ran back to the circle. Elayne's Craft wiped fire from his limbs, and from the woman he held. Her skin was blackened, her blouse burnt. Elayne saw a trace of bone, and smelled singed meat. The woman screamed, her throat raw. She was not the only one.

In the Square, they all were screaming.

But she was still alive.

Elayne drew the heat from the woman's burns, and the pain. Pain was a form of art, after all: a concentration of the soul, an extension of time. Pain gave power, and with power, Elayne could—almost—hold the dome upright, and keep the Skittersill from burning. Maybe the woman would die. Elayne had seen worse burns—

—not since the Wars—

—but she'd not die yet.

Tay and the others stared at the woman, horrified, in the half-light Elayne's Craft left as it drained the world to the dregs.

This was what came of staying within the lines.

No more.

She could not stand against the King in Red, but she could do more than she planned. She could save some of them. Not enough.

"Go," she said. "All of you. Bring those you can. As many as fit inside the circle. Now!"

They ran, and she went with them in pieces.

Men fell, and women, aflame. Fire erupted from the viscous liquid the Couatl let fall, and flowed and stuck and dripped and rolled, splashed and clung and covered. Many screams became one scream from many throats, wet and hoarse at once as fire trickled into open mouths.

The grass mats burned. The water in the god-fountain burned, and the faceless god wept burning tears into a fiery pool. A woman struggled to stand, pressing against the fire that clung to her body. Her skin melted. She struck burning hair with burning hands and tried to breathe, but fire filled her lungs.

Temoc felt the first death at once. The second, a breath later. After that they came fast, each flowing into the next until only a single death remained, ugly and enormous as a scream. The air stank of oil and meat and singed hair. Chakal Square died around him, and yet he lived.

Beside the altar, Chel threw up.

The lake of fire rolled with waves where bodies tossed, whitecaps that were hands half flesh, half bone, clawing out of underflame.

Overhead, the Couatl wheeled around for another pass.

Is this it? he cried to the gods, through the torrent of death. Is this what you wanted?

Wait, the gods said.
For what?
For now.
And then there was light.

61

Elayne almost lost the city.

Her volunteers ran through the fire, senses webbed to hers: sulfur and acid vapor and char, burnt leather and metal and melted rubber from the soles of shoes. Around her, atop that perfect-imperfect map, the bodies piled, packed close: in a few minutes they'd rescued dozens, and Elayne took what she could from them, the heat in their flesh and the pain in their souls, to keep them safe. Her shields trembled and almost failed. If she had not been familiar with this feeling—if she had not learned from a twisted master in her youth how to span the gaps between minds, to split and recombine herself—if she had not learned those black arts, she would have broken in the first minute.

She nearly broke anyway.

The Skittersill blazed. A slick layer of flame covered the wooden shops that lined Bloodletter's Street and the brick-and-timber fronts at Crow, fire eating stone, crisping and cracking earthworks—fire that laughed at the rules of fire, fire that burned what could not burn.

With all the focus she could spare, she opened the line to Aberforth and Duncan, called on the insurance contract, invoked true names and serial numbers. The dream map she'd drawn seared her thoughts. The city burned, and she, with stolen power, told it to stop.

Beside her, a man curled into a ball and wept.

The insurance contract responded grudgingly to her call. She felt buildings burn, heard them scream in her mind, and demanded Aberforth and Duncan to perform. This would work. Had to work. She hoped.

There had been no time to negotiate Purcell's agreement; a poorly written contract might let his employers slide out of their obligations to protect and to defend. But though she did not trust Tan Batac in any other particular, she trusted his greed and cunning to have negotiated a good deal.

But still the firm moved slowly, so slowly, to honor her call. Fiery plumes erupted from rooftops. Screams bubbled and choked off. With her eyes closed, she saw the green web of the crowd's faith pulse with their deaths. Hundreds in a few minutes, tight spiraling souls burst like fireworks.

All for nothing, all for a scorched stretch of earth where some developer would build a shopping mall, and everyone left alive would profit, and none would remember, unless this contract moved. Now.

The power came.

It flowed smooth and slow and gold and heavy as a flood of honey down from Aberforth and Duncan, into her, and from her into the dream map. Eyes still closed, feeling rather than seeing the contours of the map, she directed the power to dormant wards in the Skittersill's nails and mortar.

The argument was easy enough: the gripfire tugged matter from matter. Windowsill, rafters, casement, insulation, and drywall all burned on their own. But each piece was part of a building, and the building as a whole did not burn merely because one piece burned. And yet how could a part be burning if the whole was not on fire?

Sophistry, but you didn't need to work hard to outfox flame. Even Craftborn demon-fire was pretty dumb.

The Skittersill burned around her but was not consumed. This trick would not work forever: even the most massive building had a flashpoint. For the moment, wood and insulation glowed, but they did not erupt—excess heat seeped into surrounding stone and metal. The Skittersill's buildings would not burn until they all burned together.

It hurt, intensely.

Not as much as the men and women around her hurt. Even

those she shielded were singed by metal buttons and buckles, parboiled in their own sweat.

The bodies—the people not yet dead—mounted around her as Tay and Cozim dragged the fallen to safety. She saw no one she knew. They must be on fire already.

Chel. Bill and Kapania Kemal. Bel. Temoc.

They should have been safe. No sentimentality here, simple fact: they should not have died so easily. Temoc's sacrifice woke the gods. Even weakened, they might have saved their worshippers for a few seconds, given Chakal Square an instant's defiance to trumpet through history. Why not?

She searched the Square for the vast and immanent presences she had seen.

And found them.

The Quechal gods stood overhead, arms open to receive burnt offerings.

Elayne's stomach turned. She wanted to be sick. She could not afford to be sick. Good thing she was no longer precisely human, or she would not have had a choice.

There was a logic to it, she had to admit.

The gods had slept for decades, eking out a life off Temoc's little sacrifices. Last night's exercise woke them and left them hungry. After the Wars, even gods knew their limits. The choice, from their perspective, was simple: waste what little power they possessed in a defensive tactic that posed no threat to their adversary, or gather the dead and use their sacrifice to power an assault.

The gods sent their power forth. A wind moved among the dying of Chakal Square.

Elayne opened her eyes to watch the first of the doomed things rise.

"Temoc," she said, though he could not hear her. "I am so sorry."

Scorched hair and baked flesh, bubbling skin and crisping muscle, ash and bone and the cries of the dying, and everywhere the stench of alchemy. People dove for cover under the remains of tents that were themselves aflame. Temoc stood in the end of the world.

Through the smoke, through the haze, he saw columns of pure white light ascend.

At first he did not understand. Stared blankly into the sky, into the Couatl wheeling overhead—some new weapon, some mercy to kill his people faster? But these lights rose heavenward, and as they neared, Couatl spun in disarray.

Then Chel cried out in fear, in pain—an animal noise pressed from her by contortions deep within. She knelt, clawing at her skin. Her back muscles wriggled like snakes, and where her nails touched, her clothes and flesh parted and through the cracks flowed the purest, brightest light Temoc had ever seen.

Her screams became a roar.

That light seeped from the wounds she'd torn, a viscous shining fluid that scalded as it coated her shoulders, arms, neck, spine and back and legs. Beneath the light she remained herself: charred clothes and skin, heaving, screaming, standing. She stood, wracked with pain. Her face was a radiant mask.

The light flowed and bulged at Chel's back and folded itself into feathered wings.

Yes, the gods said, and he understood.

He understood, and wanted to fall to his knees and weep hot tears into the consuming fire, that took everything from him, and left him with—

Power.

Once he'd seen a dam break, no small backriver dam but one of the great waterworks of RKC's youth, a structure of concrete and stone fifty stories high. Hundreds of thousands of gallons battered forth, a white wall tearing through the plain, scouring soil to bedrock, shredding houses and farms, shattering the fleeing horses it overtook. Water became solid in two states: frozen, and in motion.

Each cell in his body was wired to a lightning generator. If not for the scars, if not for sixty years of prayer and twenty of war, he would have broken like those horses on the flood. He stood, instead, as light ripped through him, as the shadows of his skin sunk deeper than black, a hunger more than a color. And he was strong.

He grew strong with the deaths of hundreds. One sacrifice, last night, had woken the gods. They found the people of Chakal Square in their dreams, and sang songs of faith to them as they slept. This morning, they tasted the blood of those who remained. As planned.

We few, he said when he raised the knife, we fortunate few, are called to give our hearts.

Rise, Seven Eagle sang in his blood. Fly, and fight.

He wanted to tear his scars from his skin. Wanted to curse the gods and run from Chakal Square, to crisp himself to ash in the fires the King in Red made fall.

But some choices could not be unmade.

Not when Chel spread her glorious wings. Not when she looked at him sadly, and flew.

The shock wave of her rising bent him to his knees. And he knew, as he had known once but forgotten, that his gods were wise, and also clever. They knew Temoc of old. They knew Eagle Knights. They knew he would not leave his people.

Not when there was vengeance left to take.

The Couatl turned for another pass.

He rose to meet them in the air.

The square's heat bore him up as he flew, arms at his sides, chin up, no need for wings. Swept past Chel in a blur, and past the others, too. Senses dilated open by this rush of power, he saw them, the risen of Chakal Square: twelve altogether. Not all whole, or wholly alive. One woman had all the flesh melted from the right side of her body, skin replaced with divine light. A man flew still aflame, his burned-off hands replaced by shining talons. A child, gods, they'd chosen a child, he'd thought all those gone—a child was brightest of them all. Twelve, against the Couatl.

The Wardens' mounts broke in confusion. Scales and serpents, silver chains, star crowns atop their heads, and Wardens rode them, faceless masks reflecting fire.

Temoc aimed for the lead Warden, and, accelerating, recognized him. The tall one, the broad one, who threw the rock that killed the child that started it all. Sent here, by some twisted logic, to see the end.

Temoc held out one hand, tightened his fingers into a ball, and struck Zoh in the face at a large fraction of the speed of sound. The Warden's neck snapped, the Couatl roared, and the other angels joined the battle.

Temoc fought so he would not weep.

"Sir," Captain Chimalli said. "There seems to be a problem."

They stood atop the King in Red's steed, a mile from Chakal Square and the battle. Chimalli flicked through various Wardens' fields of view. The King in Red, behind him, watched.

The first run went smoothly: gripfire deployed, on target within operational parameters. Casualties high. The second wave turned strange.

Lights danced among a cloud of Couatl. Occasional bits of dirt fell from the mass: Wardens tumbled from their mounts. Many were caught; Couatl swept to snag them with their claws. Others died.

Voices chorused in his ears.

"Move like nothing I've—"

"—Out of nowhere—"

"—Dive, dive, dive—"

"It's on my tail, it's coming, it's—"

"—Got one with a net, but she's *burning through*—"

He could only glimpse the forms that moved among his Wardens, killing. A flash of wing, an image of an impossible face, a melted hand, a claw. He recognized, at least, the shadow whose sweeping fists ended too many transmissions. "Sir," he repeated.

The King in Red's star eyes shrunk to crimson dots. He stood motionless, hands on his brass-shod staff, wind billowing his robe.

"All teams," Chimalli said back over the link to his Wardens. "Burst out. Surround them. Javelin units on my mark."

"Acknowledged." Couatl took flight from surrounding rooftops. Chimalli counted twelve lights, and Temoc. His men could handle so few, surely.

Far away, he heard gravel grind against gravel. He realized, with sudden deepening horror, that the King in Red was laughing.

"Sir?"

"Clever. Not Temoc's idea, unless I'm very much mistaken. And here I thought all we'd have to do today was hammer a shield until it broke. Captain. Bring us in."

Rainbow wings and black scales flashed. The world was a cloud of ash and blood, prisms and nets, claws and teeth and glass and death.

Chel danced within her light, a splinter tossed on a torrent of divine will. Jaws snapped where she had been moments past, and she turned and struck back faster than she had ever moved before. She tore open the Couatl's head, and blood steamed in the air. A claw battered her from behind and she fell, spinning, wings flared to catch herself on emptiness in time to block a talon meant for her throat—and then she broke the talon, grabbed its wrist, and spun the Couatl around into another, sending both wheeling toward the fire, wings beating desperately against the empty sky.

Couatl seethed around her, and divine lights darted through them, killing. Two lights landed on one Couatl's wings, and pulled up until bones broke. The lights zipped away, and one flew into another serpent's jaw. That light pulled free, but the beast's jaw slowed him enough that a thrown net caught him and he tumbled toward the ground, faster, faster, until his wings cut through the strands and he soared up to fight.

The sky was a mess of blood. She felt the other lights, their joy and pain. They were together, wound through one another to carry out a grand task.

And that was all that remained of the others. They were singular as blades: when one broke, pinned through the chest by a Couatl's lucky strike, she felt his passing: the joy of purpose served, and gone. The others were dead, or hovered on the verge of death, their pain and final rage giving their new forms strength. They were part of this miracle machine, built by gods to do their will. Chel lived. Beneath the rush of power, she smelled the melted human bodies from the square below, and wanted to die. It would be easier.

Temoc leapt from Warden to Warden. He was a gift of violence to the world. A javelin darted toward him, and he shattered it with a backhand. Nets caught him and he ripped them open. He strode on air. Couatl struck him from all sides, and he laughed. Blood stained his hands, and his eyes burned.

The surge and pulse of battle eased, the whirlwind slowed. Through the confusion of serpents and wings, Chel saw the sky, and the city below. For the first time in ten frantic minutes of battle, she had no immediate target, no one to strike, no one to kill.

They were winning. Gods. All the dead, and all the dying, and still they were about to win.

Did that make it worthwhile?

Couatl corpses splashed into the lake of fire that was Chakal Square.

Someone cried victory.

She glanced around, talons raised, new instincts awake to the chance of threat. More Couatl took off from surrounding rooftops, moving into position for a barrage. The Couatl they'd fought winged to shelter. Chase after them, catch them. Easy. The gods sang war song in her blood.

Then the northern sky rippled and turned black, and the gods began to scream.

Elayne burned in the city's stead. Fire crowned the Skittersill and would have eaten it but for the Aberforth and Duncan deal; Purcell's firm, meanwhile, tried to pull free of its obligations, and would have succeeded but for Elayne. She bridged the fire and the firm, and the two met in battle, on her and through her.

She was too far gone to scream. Fire could not consume wood and brick and stone, so it torched instead through her mind. The iron-wrought cages where she locked her memories melted. Images long discarded, moments of weakness and pain chained in dim corners, broke free, and she:

was a twelve-year-old girl hiding facedown in cave mud, breathing moss and muck as a mob poured past the cavern mouth, torches in their hands and whiskey on their breath. She tasted fear and bile and ice-cold anger. Run, she had to run, but could not—and wouldn't it be better to crawl into the dark and remain, and grow a twisted thing twisted more by shadows?

was fourteen and killing for the first time, with a simple steel knife in those days of sorcery, entering a man's ribs again and again and again, the shock of his body's weight through the steel as he bore her down.

was the snow that fell on Dresediel Lex for the first and last time, and left smoking holes in stone. Gods died in the sky, pierced by thorns of light, as Craftsmen clad in war engines marched through the city's wreckage. Stench of motor oil and blood, saltpeter and ozone, brick dust and sand. Life's million colors faded black and white from soul-loss as she staggered from her war machine down an alley, fatigues bloodsoaked, her eyes shining and her body wet, toward where Temoc lay impaled.

was a body in a dim-lit room in Alt Coulumb, given away from herself, robbed even of the right of rage. City lights outside the window, sharp as instruments of torture, while in her soul's depths delicate mad hands gripped the roots of love and pulled, and pulled, and pulled, and willed them to come loose.

was a hundred moments of pain and defeat, anger and sorrow, innocence lost, and none mattered, because from each she had emerged stronger than before, welding out of horrors new truth, new determination. To be what? Professional? Successful? She was both, she'd been both, and here she stood, saving a city's bones even as its people died. She had grown strong. But what world had she built with her strength? A world where she saved what could be saved and left the rest to rot?

Around her the circle closed, her emissaries soot-smeared and broken. The wounded lay crying.

She saw out every window in the Skittersill. Her senses filled the air. She held the city in her hand as the Quechal gods transformed their dying faithful into weapons, and as those weapons killed the Wardens and their steeds. The dogfight twisted above, a roil of scales and wings, of razors and rainbows. Bodies fell broken into the fire.

She saw Chel in their midst, shining like a star, and winged. Elayne heard Tay say the woman's name, but he could not join her, only watch. She lived, as far as Elayne could see: a human woman winning against all odds, with her patrons' help. Perhaps Temoc's people would have their vengeance after all.

For a few minutes, torn between fire and Craft, she almost believed that. The Couatl broke, fleeing north. More took flight from rooftops around the Skittersill, smaller breeds, built for ranged combat, but Temoc and the angels were fast, hard to imagine a marksman hitting one even with a clear shot.

The angels gave their fleeing enemies chase.

Temoc held back at first, and Elayne saw why. The Couatl fled north in a single narrow stream. If this was a true rout they would flee in all directions at once. The gods, flush with sacrificial souls, were being tempted by a target. They took the bait, humanoid weapons darting forth blood-hungry, rejoicing in the strength with which they put their foe to flight.

Then the Wardens folded their wings at once and dived, and the sky before the Quechal angels rippled, twisted, inverted, and went black with spreading scaly wings, a battleship-broad back, tail long as a highway and thick as a magisterium tree, cavernous jaws with teeth three times the height of a man. Even the eyes were enormous. A ruby glared from the creature's forehead, supernova bright, and in state at the root of its neck stood the King in Red.

In her shock, Elayne almost let the Skittersill ignite.

It was not a dragon.

Well. It was not a dragon anymore.

Dragons, in their age, and wisdom, and might, rarely meddled in human affairs. They took sides in the God Wars, when after long decades the struggle finally threatened to crack the egg of the world—lent aid to Craftsmen, then retired once again to their quiet slow empires and millennial games. Some, young and curious, hired themselves out as carriers for air freight, but the elders kept apart.

But dragons were not sentimental for their dead. The dead were landscape, the dead were for devouring. Humans had some atavistic reluctance to transform their corpses into weapons; dragons had no such qualms, and did not flinch at Craftsmen's first careful question as to whether they would mind, so much, if humans ran a few experiments with their bodies. And so in death they were reborn—the dead ones lacked the living's supernatural cleverness, but their immense frame and unique biology, their polymer scales no artificial process could duplicate, their muscles stronger and more durable than any hydraulic system, the bones from which an enterprising engineer could hang a fortune's worth of weaponry, their colossal lift, and of course the atomic forge within that could power much more than mere fiery breath, Craftsmen could find use for these.

Expensive to operate. A thousand souls or so to fund a minute's combat. But then, war always had been a chance for great powers to play with their most exquisite toys.

Elayne closed her eyes, and within, between, beneath the

scales of the King in Red's dragon, she saw Craftwork weapons spin to absurd heights of power. And, as the Skittersill angels broke for cover, the guns spoke.

Chel did not wait to understand the shape that emerged from nothing in the sky. Immense, claws, teeth, fangs, nightmare eyes, swallowing up the sun: that was enough. She dove, twisting, forward and down. The godsong split into cacophony as divine minds realigned. She ignored them, and let herself fall.

A cloud of cold iron fléchettes erupted from the dragon's wings and filled the air where she'd just been: hundreds of thousands of metal slivers flying at the speed of sound. The others had no time to guard themselves; the gods did that for them by instinct, forging magnetic shields in the air around their servants. But the fléchettes did not ricochet. Glancing off the shields, they darted out, turned, and sped back for a second pass, a third, a fourth. A cloud of tiny knives surrounded her comrades, and some pierced their shields to draw shining blood.

Chel cut her dive, and began to climb.

Temoc saw the dragon, heard the gods scramble to respond, a dozen different concepts rippling through divine minds that understood the contours of the physical world but barely. Their voices pulsed through his scars, their minds through his:

—*attack—turn—parry—preserve*—

Time, for gods always a confusing and imprecise parameter, dilated out, and they swatted each fléchette away: easy to do when they all came from one direction, but on the second pass—

—*many—hunger—resolve—turn—charge—adjust— iron*—

He ran toward the dragon, trailing footsteps of shadow through ozone-charged air. Gods did not deal well with small things moving quickly, and especially not with cold iron. Swatting each sliver aside would strain their powers and attention. Instead, they charged the angels themselves. The iron shards burst away from the winged lights, straight out in all directions. The risen of Chakal Square flew toward the King in Red atop his war beast, laughing.

Laughing, as was the King in Red himself.

The storm of iron lost its animating life, and fell.

Temoc ran faster.

And then the lightning spoke.

Elayne watched. Elegant. The fléchettes first, too fast for the gods to turn aside one by one, and enchanted to seek their target. The easiest response to which, if you were a god, was to apply a single, powerful charge to the entire field of combat, fléchettes and divine wings and armor alike, so the King in Red's iron splinters could never come close enough to hurt the angels. Which, of course, left the angels charged.

So now you have a fléchette storm, positively charged, and a number of angels whose wings are as well. Drop the fléchettes, and you're left with a field of charged targets. Which means, no matter where they run, no matter how fast they move, you can find them, and hit them.

And so as the angels flew toward the King in Red, dragon-wing antennae sparked and popped. Lightning lanced across empty air.

The angels burned.

Chel was behind and beneath the dragon when the lightning hit.

She was aware only of a discontinuity, of flying toward the dragon and then of falling a hundred feet or so beneath, below, every muscle clenched at once, blood in her mouth and ozone in her nose. Ground approaching, fast, faster—she tried to spread wings but the wings did not spread, she spun and fell and flailed as the gods' voices clashed in disarray, but there, her fingers twitched, and the tips of her wings, and out they flared, arresting her in mid-fall, slowing so fast the world went gray but at least she rose.

Above, the others hung in brilliant webs, arrayed in a ring around the dragon's vast head. She must have dodged the worst of it.

Her fellows were not so lucky. They writhed, a twitching agony of seconds that stretched for years. Hooks and beams and instruments of torture manifested in the sky, pierced their wings and pulled, and tore.

The gods' song faltered and grew faint.

She flew faster, a rising spark, a streak to embrace the sun, toward the dragon.

—adjust—scramble—pain—pain—escape—fly—

Temoc, running, heard the gods recoil as the King in Red tore their emissaries. The dragon threw its defenses against him: shields manifested in his path and he broke them. His distance to the dragon doubled and doubled again with every micrometer of space he crossed, and yet still he crossed the space. Demonic claws glanced off his shining scars.

Divine voices clashed discordant in his mind.

Lose the wings, he prayed, fervently. They're too much—gives him something to grab and tear. He knows you want them, so he tries to take them from you. It's only a matter of time before your power runs out.

—perhaps—

With a roar of tearing paper, the risen of Chakal Square burst from their plasma wings and leapt forth, fingers grown claw-long, teeth sharpened to points. The dragon's wards sparked and flashed; two dropped insensate to the city far below, but eight more landed, three on the dragon's skull, three on the left wing, two on the right.

Temoc himself touched down above the creature's ruby forehead. The head twisted; the dragon screamed an iron scream. Around, beneath, to all sides Dresediel Lex wheeled, one with its sky. The shadows that clad Temoc's feet gripped the dragon's scales, held him in place. One more of the risen fell, contorted with insensate rage; the rest dropped to all fours and scampered down the long neck toward the King in Red and his Warden captain.

On the wings, more Wardens ran to intercept the risen, weapons shining in their hands. Fast, so fast, but not fast enough; claws tore silver masks and teeth ripped silver throats. The three from the skull leapt down the neck, from scale to massive scale toward the King in Red. Grinning still, grinning always, the Craftsman stretched out his hand. Invisible knives flensed the fire from the risen, but it rekindled and they advanced—slower, though, a bare but perceptible change, and still the knives spun and skinned. The second of the risen fell: her own body sprouted thorns that grew inward, piercing flesh and bone. Still she advanced, spurred by divine fervor. On the wings, Wardens recovered their footing, ringed the risen and stabbed them with spears as if baiting bears.

He's playing an attrition game, Temoc prayed. Forcing you to spend power you don't have, power you can't recover. Spreading you between obligations until you break.

—our city—our power—

Not now. Not after forty years. You can retreat, but that doesn't mean you can win.

—no retreat—too long asleep—

He thought, at the last, of Caleb, and of Mina, and of the family he'd given up for it to end here, on dragonback.

And then, because he saw no other way, he opened himself to the gods. He pulled their power into him. Light surged through his scars. He sprinted up the dragon's neck. Demons barred his path; he shattered one with a punch and threw himself into the second's chest, breaking crystal with his weight. Close now, so close. More shields, easily sidestepped. Disregard the captain. Focus on the King in Red.

Kill him and this ends. You don't win, nobody wins this kind of war, but at least it ends.

The dragon swooped toward Chakal Square. Another risen tumbled off. The Wardens pressed the attack.

And the King in Red stood before him, undefended, his eyes

twin red stars in the black of his skull. Temoc swept his arm around, fast—

And the King in Red raised his staff in a blur and blocked.

Chel was airborne when her wings failed and the fire of her flesh changed shape. New animal instincts rushed in, mixed a cocktail with the fear in her blood. Even without the wings, momentum carried her up, up, don't think about the drop, the hundreds of feet give or take a death or two she'd fall to solid rock. Focus on the dragon, reach with your claws, never mind how you got claws exactly, just *reach*—

She caught the edge of a knife-sharp scale. As the dragon dove and lurched she pulled herself up, one hand at a time, forcing her feet between the beast-machine's immense scales, and she climbed and climbed until she stood atop the back.

Gods called her to battle, but she splayed flat. The gods had not made good decisions so far. A Warden approached over the swell of the dragon's body: mistook her for a corpse. She did not disabuse him of the notion, not until he was close enough, gods, until *she* was close enough for Chel to grab her ankle and throw her off into the void.

Screaming, she fell.

Distractions: who was that Warden? How old? What family? Was she young? Married? Children? Happy? What path brought her here?

Below, the Square was dead. And that woman, too.

She crawled across the dragon's back.

Captain Chimalli felt the wind as Temoc sprinted past him. He turned in time to see the King in Red defend himself, warglyphs shining from his bones. No time for Chimalli to help: the monsters of Chakal Square had almost reached him, climbing up the neck.

The first, still pressing through a squall of knives, its flesh stripped to bare bone, would be the easiest. It pounced and he sidestepped, struck with both hands on the back of its neck, heard the spine snap. Fallen, it spasmed, started to slide off the dragon's neck. Bones wriggled and realigned. He'd have to kill it again in a minute. Fine.

The second, the one that had been female, with the thorns growing through it, was slower, and more difficult. Pain made it canny. A feint forward with a claw, from which he retreated a step. He drew his truncheon. Another feint, another step back. It knelt and growled, as behind it the third approached.

Two against one were not odds Chimalli liked.

He lurched back. Hungry, the monster struck with a claw. Chimalli did not need to recover his footing, had never lost it, faking only—he grabbed the clawed hand, twisted and pulled and hoped these things' joints still worked like those of men.

Yes. The wrist popped, and the elbow and shoulder when he twisted his waist. A blow with the truncheon to the side of the skull sent that one sliding down the slope of the dragon's neck, clawing with one arm to halt its fall. Which left the third—

The third hit him in the back. Claws dug through his uniform jacket, through his armor plates, through slick silver into skin. He grunted, no screams yet. Teeth on his neck, not through the mask. He fell forward, pushed up with his legs and arms. Bad idea, this, but no better ones with claws in your back. He jumped, and for a sickening moment was airborne over the dragon's neck—then the monster hit scale, and he hit the monster, hard enough to break its grip and roll to one side, his arms weaving around its arm and tightening to dislocate the joint. He stood, hands empty, truncheon fallen. The King in Red and Temoc were a tempest of red and black and silver and brass, but he had no time to help, with the first monster recovered almost already and standing.

Chimalli hit it in the face, and it dropped again. He turned to the second, and hoped.

The fires of the Skittersill were not dead, but they banked low. The gripfire was two parts, fuel and spark, the plan being that the fuel would last the spark long enough for it to catch. Elayne had broken the cycle, and the fuel was almost gone.

Minutes more, and it would all be over.

Elayne's senses filled the Skittersill, and she watched the dragon swoop toward Chakal Square, wings beating. She watched the battle on its back. The sparks, the angels, faded. With each death they slowed, reduced. Captain Chimalli fought three at once, while behind him his master and Temoc traded stroke for stroke. And Chel, where was Chel, lost already, fallen? No. Elayne saw the woman crawl along the dragon's back, light dimmed, keeping low. She remained herself, despite the gods.

And Elayne watched from the sidelines.

"She's still alive," Tay said. "Save her."

"I can't," she said. "That was the deal."

Around her, the King in Red's victims wept.

"Break the deal."

"I can't."

You're not a warrior anymore, Temoc had said.

A peacemaker. A restorer of life. That was what she wanted to be. A counselor.

And so far she had failed.

Soon, at least, the fires would go out.

Temoc and the King in Red danced an old dance. Faster, faster they spun. Temoc lashed out with a kick, blocked by the staff, as was his second. Invited his adversary to attack, sidestepped the staff strike when it came, grabbed at the weapon which was gone already—it swept in a blurred circle to clip a temple that was not there because Temoc had already ducked back.

Fiercer they fought, power flowing into both from greater fonts. From their perspective the exchange contained long pauses, slow shifting moments in which each examined the other, considered options and rejected them, feinted and countered. Still they moved too fast for an outside observer to see anything but a blur.

Temoc had never fought like this, not even in the God Wars.

Accelerating mass and perception to such heights cost Craftsmen dearly—more efficient to slay from a distance, to destroy targets that could not defend themselves. One might lose a fistfight.

As the King in Red would lose. Temoc's hands were so close to his neck. He would break those bones, piece by piece. Craftsmen were hard to kill, but he could manage. He was faster, stronger than he had ever been. A bringer of vengeance. The last true knight in the world.

The monsters slowed. When the next came for Chimalli, he caught it, lifted it, threw it off the dragon. The second, when killed, did not rise again. There was pain somewhere in his body, from cuts and scrapes, and blood everywhere. He would deal with that later. The third monster jumped him, and he flipped it to the ground, knelt on top of it, and hit it in the face, again and again. Bones cracked. He hit it a few more times, and stood, trembling.

The King in Red fought Temoc, so fast. He tried to track their bodies, to tell his boss from his enemy. Maybe. Somewhere. Suggestions of shape within the blur.

He reached for the holster at his thigh.

Chel felt the gods fade and herself reduced. No. *She* remained. The divine grip that held her, the wrath that pulsed through her veins like a second blood, that eased. She became herself again, on this dragon's back, a human being crawling toward the crimson-black cloud that was the King in Red, fighting Temoc.

Not good. Not bad, either, she decided.

At least she still had weapons.

She rose into a crouch, crossbow at the ready.

The last of the fuel consumed, the fires of Chakal Square began to die.

Elayne watched the dragon, and saw what was about to happen.

"Help her!"

Yes. To all the hells with the Craft and its rules, with word and bond. Just *help*.

She called her power to her, reached out—

But at the last her own promise bound her, held her. I will not save them.

Her Craft broke. The shield that warded them cracked, and oven-breath seeped through the gaps to sear their lungs.

She fell to the stone.

Temoc fought the King in Red. The gods' power was his. Immense strength, battering the Craftsman to a standstill. He drew his knife and it splintered the staff, chipped it, sheared it in half.

He kicked out the back of the skeleton's knee, caught its spine in the crook of his elbow, tightened. Bone creaked. Craftwork sparked and spasmed against him. Seconds more.

Temoc laughed, in the fullness of his power. "Why haven't we done this before?"

"Because," Kopil said, "I never needed to get you into position."

Blur and whirlwind, dust and smoke, shadow and light, all coalesced into two arrested forms, the King in Red in Temoc's grip.

And Chimalli had the shot.

His finger tightened on the trigger.

Elayne was too far away, but still she thought she heard the crossbow's string, a single note plucked on the bass of the world.

Chimalli fell. The crossbow slipped from his fingers.

Chel stared down at the weapon in her hand, still singing its one note. She looked up again. The King in Red roared, threw Temoc back, and turned toward her. His eyes burned bright as he raised his hand.

She did not tremble, though she was afraid.

Elayne saw the captain fall, crossbow bolt through his neck. She saw the Craft the King in Red invoked, which she could have stopped, so easily, the slightest flick of her will even at this distance. But she was bound.

And so she saw, too, the round hole appear in Chel's forehead, before she fell.

Tay screamed. She barely heard him.

Temoc tackled the King in Red, an instant too late.

He struck Kopil in the chest with a blow that would have shattered marble, and the skeleton staggered. Temoc hit him again, and again. The King in Red swept his arm around—the hand with which he'd killed Chel—and Temoc seized it and moved faster than even Elayne could see. Kopil's wrist bent at a sharp angle, and there was a sound like a shot, of wards giving way.

Then the King in Red swelled, and his teeth grew long and the sparks in his eyes sharp and fierce as any hell. He thrust out his staff, and Temoc flew back through the air. His scars burned to seize the edges of the Craft that held him, but this Craft had no edge, just an endless torrent of will. The King in Red could not last long with such power in him—his mind would shatter in ten seconds, but he needed less than ten.

Temoc was about to die.

As the people of Chakal Square had died. As their risen remnants died. As Chel died.

And now Temoc. Old soldier. Broken shell. Father. Fool.

While Elayne stood in her circle, immune, because she played the game. Because she kept her word. And because she played the game she would be allowed these few she'd saved, scorched and shattered, to live as testament to the futility of change. Scraps at the table. The King in Red might pay their hospital bills, if it amused him.

She closed her eyes. They stung from smoke and other things. Through the forest of contracts and bargains and powers the King in Red called down, she saw the Quechal gods, shrunken to angry shades and fading, power spent in their rush toward victory. Betrayers and last casualties of Chakal Square.

No, not last. They would die first, and then Temoc.

She could not do this. Not her place. Not her fight. Not now, after sixty years of a chosen side.

For the first and last time in her life, Elayne Kevarian prayed.

Not to the gods above, traitors and accursed. Not to the gods of her childhood, whose people had hunted her through wood and field. Not to the Lord of Alt Coulumb or the squid kings of Iskar or the Shining Empire Thearchs. She prayed up, and in, and out, in broken desperation, in case something might hear.

Save him.

Please.

The answer came at once, so sudden and swift she mistook it for wishful thinking: a cold rush that covered her skin. But there was a mind beneath and behind the answer: cold, vast and alien and personal at once, a voice she'd known since she first caught a falling star, a voice to which time was something other people did.

How? it asked.

So little power left. The King in Red blocked Temoc's avenues of retreat. The Quechal gods' might was all but spent keeping him alive.

As, in Chakal Square and the Skittersill around, the last of the gripfire's fuel gave up. Flame danced on rooftops, on corpses—no longer the King in Red's fire, but anyone's for the claiming.

She felt the fire through the dream map she'd drawn. Gathered it into her hands: not much power but, she hoped, enough.

Here, she said. *Use this.* Might have said more, set terms and conditions, proposed a bargain or a contract. She did not.

Was she mad? She heard no rage in that voice, no vengeance, no hunger. Had she merely committed the oldest error, called for aid in extremity and imagined a voice to answer her?

But with eyes closed she could stare into the horrorland the

King in Red created, its grinding wheels and chains, its talons and its teeth, the million knives and its space warped in answer to malevolent will, and see Temoc. Then, impossibly, the darkness broke, and he was gone.

She opened her eyes. She knelt in and beyond Chakal Square, in a circle of Craft and of the living burned. Around her, the Skittersill stood beneath a blue sky—the same in every particular but for the dead.

Wardens and Couatl lay tangled with protesters. Charred meat clung to bones. Blood crusted on rock. The god melted atop his dry fountain in the center of the square.

Had they saved a hundred? Perhaps not even so many.

The dragon hung above them all. On the undead beast's back, Wardens moved. The King in Red stood, staring. Chel and the captain lay still.

The square and the whole city fell silent.

Elayne felt that silence press her down. She wiped sweat from her face and her eyes. Only sweat.

Thank you.

No answer came.

Around her, the twelve wept, and Tay.

The people they'd saved moaned in their sleep.

The sun shone overhead, and she cast no shadow.

EPILOGUE

The King in Red descended from the sky to the still-warm stone. Far away, ambulance sirens wailed. The smell of death and fire lay heavy on the air. Elayne strode forward to meet him. She did not permit herself to waver. The King in Red leaned on his broken staff. His ribs rose and fell, as if in some long-buried corner of his mind he remembered that he should be breathing heavy.

Behind her, moans rose from the circle she had saved. Around them, the Skittersill remained. People lived in those buildings, worked there. They were safe. This was not a total defeat.

She almost believed that.

Fires danced in the pits of Kopil's eyes. "You defied me."

"I did not," she said, "to my shame. I should have, long ago. We were supposed to be better than this. Our rule was supposed to make people free, and safe. You led a revolution against bloody gods. But what god ever did for his people like you've done for yours?"

"You protected those within the square. They were mine."

"I gave you my word and kept it, or else I would have broken. The men and women in that circle are not yours. They never were."

"Stand aside." Lightning slithered along his crooked bronze-shod staff. He'd bound it whole with Craft.

"No."

"Elayne."

"Look around." The square was fire pit and charnel house in one. Bones jutted from scorched skin. Slagged tentpoles were skeletal arches above blackened stone. "You wanted the God Wars back. Is this the clarity you missed? Because I don't see it. Maybe you could show me."

"Let me pass."

She met his gaze. "Try it, and I will break you."

Dry wind whipped the hem of her charred jacket. His crimson robes snapped like a sail. He was tall, and mighty. "You cannot fight me."

"Let's see."

He might have won. She had powers he had not guessed, and he was weary from battle with gods and their champion. But he saw her, and saw too the young woman he had known, who flew in the vanguard of his army and smote their enemies to rubble. And he saw her fury and scorn and smelled too, the cooked meat.

His own face stared up at him from the cobblestones.

Kopil's eyes guttered like a candle flame drowning in wax. He stepped back, and grew smaller. "The ambulances will be here soon," he said, and left.

Later, Elayne found Temoc bleeding beside a trash can in an alley. His eyes were closed, his legs straight out. His hands lay limp by his sides.

She approached, one step at a time. No gods nearby, but sometimes gods were hard to see. She stopped a few feet away and waited for him to breathe.

He did, after a while.

"Just like old times," she said.

"Just like." His eyelids fluttered open. Behind them his eyes were black as ever. "How do I look?"

"Like hell."

"You, too."

He was right. Her suit was scorched and torn, her face caked with soot and the salt remains of dried sweat.

"Have you come to take me in?"

She shook her head.

"To kill me, then?"

"No."

"Why not?"

"Why would you deserve it?"

His chin touched his chest. "For Caleb and for Mina, at least. That was my fault. The rest—the rest I should have seen coming. Should have stopped it."

"You're no more to blame than any of us."

"No less, either."

"No," she said. "No less." Neither of them spoke for a while. At last, she did. "What will you do next?"

"Someone has to make him pay."

"The King in Red, you mean."

"Yes."

"That's not what I hoped to hear," she said. "Wars beget wars."

"Then kill me now. I will come for him one day. If it takes decades, if it takes centuries. Not all the armies of this earth will stop me."

"Your son," she said, "needs a father."

"He needs a world less broken than this. All the sons need that. And the daughters, too."

"Is there such a world?"

"There must be."

"I don't know," she said. "Perhaps." And: "I kept, and broke, a lot of promises today. To save you. I don't know if I saved the right person."

"Neither do I."

"I should go."

"Elayne," he said to her retreating back. "Thank you."

"You're welcome," she replied, and left the alley for the sunlit streets. Gods gathered in her wake.

Mina stayed by Caleb's bed for days. The papers announced the Skittersill Rising's end, published detailed comments from key players on the council and a brief interview with the King in

Red—so class was back on schedule. She went to the campus for department meetings, for journal review; sat on a lush, watered lawn beneath a blue sky as she adjusted her syllabus for the next semester. The campus was the same as ever, but her papers and sources had changed when she wasn't looking. Etchings of High Quechal glyphs bled with her son's blood.

Most of her colleagues had never met her husband. Those who had, did not ask after him. Their house was far enough from the riot that she did not have to lie much.

At sunset she returned to the hospital, sat in the chair, and watched her son sleep with needles in his arms and a tube down his nose. They had a bed for her at the hospital—she did not know whether the university insurance paid for it, or Elayne Kevarian, and she did not ask—but she could not sleep there through the night. Around two or three, without fail, she woke and went to his room, sat in the old familiar chair, and drowsed off to the ticks that timed his heart.

One night she woke in his room, cold, with a crick in her neck. The machines ticked, and Caleb breathed. Must have been the breeze through the half-open window that woke her.

The window had not been open when she went to sleep.

A shadow moved on the other side of her son's bed, a thing of darkness without contour or dimension. She recognized the silhouette.

"Get away from him," she said.

The shadow drew back. It walked toward her, stiff and silent. The black opened, acquired the contour of familiar muscles, familiar scars.

"Mina." Her husband held out his arms to embrace or supplicate.

"No."

He stopped.

"Get out of here."

"I had no choice," he said. "He saved your life."

"You thought you had no choice. You didn't talk to me. You didn't trust me. Or him. You left us."

"He will be well. Three more days. That's all he needs."

"We'll see."

"I. Gods. I wish I could take it back. I wish I could make this up to you. How?"

"Leave," she said. She turned from him, and crossed her arms.

In a breath of wind, he was gone.

She sat, and remained in the chair for a long time without crying. Then she did, and then she slept.

On the third day Caleb woke, asking for his mother.

When Elayne next saw the King in Red, in the hospital, he looked smaller: still tall and thin, but reduced in a dimension she could not name. He toasted her with his coffee mug as she emerged from the elevators. She nodded in reply. He grinned, but his heart wasn't in it.

"Are we okay?"

"No," she said. "But we can be professional, at least."

Dr. Venkat ushered them into the room, which looked like all the hospital chambers Elayne had ever seen, only more expensive. Slick cushions on the plush seats, every surface polished chrome, the bedsheets silk. Perhaps the occupant's family had refurnished to their taste; perhaps the hospital reserved such rooms for a particular clientele.

Others had arrived already. Professional nods from a Craftsman and a Craftswoman she vaguely remembered meeting at a seminar a few years back. Batac's wife, who Elayne had never bothered to imagine, was everything she would have pictured if she had: round-faced Quechal beauty, heavy lashes and a slight curl to the hair. The daughter stood beside her, uncomfortable in a purple dress with lace, ten years old maybe or eleven, face framed by thorny black curls.

Tan Batac lay in the bed, white-robed, beatific, and, as Dr. Venkat adjusted the mix of his intravenous drip, awake. His eyelids fluttered, pupils dilated, shrank, focused.

"I'm alive," he said, and smiled.

His wife and child went to him first. He hugged them both, and kissed the girl; then the various Craftsmen and colleagues closed in, offering reports and memos, summaries of missed business. They, too, left: no one wanted to linger near the King in Red.

And then they were three, as they'd been on that carriage ride from the judge's office.

Someone had to talk, and that was Tan Batac. "No one's told me the details."

"It was bad," Kopil said. "It started bad, and got worse."

"But the agreement stands."

"The agreement stands," Elayne said. "As does the Skittersill. You'll be glad to know that almost all your property, and that of your colleagues, escaped unharmed."

She'd practiced the words in the mirror, so she could say them with nonchalance, and as she spoke she watched him, lying in the bed, curious what a man looked like who had damned himself and received nothing in exchange.

She knew how it would have looked were he an actor on stage: the extended pause, the exaggerated jerk of the eyes to the upper left. In reality the signs were smaller. Batac smiled, but there was a hitch before his smile, a dart of tongue against upper lip. Did his hands tighten on the sheets? Did he lie unnaturally still? Did he flinch from visions of the deaths he caused?

"Ah," he said. "Good."

They discussed the deal, caught up on the suits the city faced, on the expense of the operation, on the need for repairs and the newspaper editorial remonstrations calling for justice of one kind or another. Shoptalk. Batac lasted for a quarter of an hour before he paled and sank back to the pillow and said, "I'm sorry, friends, but I need rest."

"We'll get the doctor." Kopil patted Batac's shoulder, and turned to leave the room. "Feel better." It sounded like an order.

"Well?" Kopil asked when they reached the street.

"I think so," Elayne said.

He bowed his head. They stood by the road for minutes, silent. Then the skeleton raised his hand, and called for a cab.

In the heart of Kelethras, Albrecht, and Ao's office pyramid, a golem worked in a cork-lined room. A steel brook trickled as newsprint pages turned. A dragon of smoke curled against the ceiling. Lenses telescoped out and back, filters clicked closed and irised open.

Zack did not look up when Elayne sat down. His torso twisted around and spidery arms flickered out to pin a picture to the wall: the faceless god of Chakal Square wept above his cracked, burned fountain. Zack's neck gimbaled to keep his head bent over the desk.

"If you want to ask a question," Elayne said, "do so."

Voicebox gears ground. "I have insufficient data to frame my query. You came to me; you have your own opinions as to what I should ask."

"I heard a voice in the Square," she said.

His torso snapped back into place. He raised his head. Light flickered behind the lenses of his eyes.

"Explain."

She did. He listened, and took notes, and asked some clarifying questions. The steel brook stilled, and the lens light shrank to a point.

"I do not understand," he said.

"Neither do I. But someday I will."

When Alaxic returned to his balcony that night, he found Temoc waiting. The big man had tripped no wards, set off no alarms. He was an edifice against the city lights.

Alaxic swore, and dropped his tea. The mug broke, and a black stain spread over his balcony tile.

"Something wrong?" Temoc asked.

"You startled me." Alaxic pressed one hand against his chest, counted heartbeats, counted breaths, tried without much success to slow them both. "You owe me a teacup."

"I'll pay it back." And, after an interval in which neither of them moved or spoke: "You've had a busy few weeks."

"My connection with the Skittersill broadsheets came out. The King in Red has pressed me from all sides, with some success. Fortunately his own principles forbid him from doing much—speech is free in Dresediel Lex. Our dread lord and his supporters claim their suppression of the rising was a response to open armed conflict; the jury of public opinion has rendered no verdict, but I think they will agree. Since I never openly encouraged armed rebellion, they'll have a hard time making charges stick." Heart rate down. Breath not yet normalized, but deeper. He smiled, weakly.

"I wonder how they discovered your connection."

"Doesn't matter, much." He set the papers he carried down on a side table, and approached Temoc. "Your friend the Craftswoman, perhaps. No matter. How do you like being public enemy number one?"

"Life is simpler now," Temoc said. "Especially with the gods awake. Much becomes clear that once was clouded."

"For example?"

"My purpose. My role in this war."

Alaxic sighed. "I'm glad to hear that. So much needs to be done. If we are to change the world, we need all the help we can get."

"I'm not finished," Temoc said.

"Fair enough, fair enough." Alaxic raised one hand. "I did not mean to interrupt."

"Much becomes clear," Temoc said, "but not all."

"For example?"

"For example. After I . . . left my family. They were attacked by demon creatures. Chased across Dresediel Lex, through the skies, on the earth. I wonder what purpose that served."

Alaxic shrugged. "The King in Red takes revenge in strange ways."

"Did he think my family's death would break me, rather than fan my anger?"

"If so, he didn't know you very well. Not as well as I do."

"Why not arrest us all in that case? Or take them hostage?"

"Maybe he didn't think so far ahead."

"And why not use Wardens for the purpose?"

"Wardens are a funny breed," Alaxic said. "They think themselves peacekeepers. They establish order. It's a hard job, fighting criminals and monsters. But an innocent woman and a child—I wouldn't want to convince anyone they were enemies of the state. Golems are expensive, but they don't talk back, and he has the resources. One of the few who does."

"So you think he knew I would leave?"

"Perhaps they had orders to attack whether you left or not. Might have been timed—you're a holy terror when you're on your guard, Temoc, but even you sleep sometimes."

"Interesting," he said.

"The man's bloody-minded. He wanted a war, and you're an old enemy. It's vicious, but it makes sense."

"That's not what I find interesting," Temoc said. "I find it interesting that you mentioned golems, when I did not."

"Did I?"

The big man nodded.

"Must have been in the papers."

"I have an alternate theory," Temoc said. "Let us suppose someone wanted me in the fight. Someone who saw me on the sidelines as Chakal Square bloomed into a riot, and did not want to leave me there. Say this person thought my family held me back. And so they thought, remove the family and Temoc will charge to battle—especially if he thinks a Craftsman is responsible. If he thinks the King in Red challenged him. So he sends agents of his choosing, faceless creatures, no threat to me, but fatal to those I love. Caleb and Mina die while I am out. Or, even better, while I'm there to fail in their defense."

"That's a hell of a theory," Alaxic said, or tried to say.

Temoc moved.

The old man tried to guard himself, but Temoc caught him around the neck one-handed, and lifted. Alaxic twisted in Temoc's grip but the hand might as well have been iron forged around his throat. Scars shone on Temoc's arm, across his bare chest, on his scalp and brow. He swung Alaxic over the balcony's edge, over twenty-seven stories' drop. Wind slapped Alaxic's clothes and roared in his ears, but the wind was not so loud as Temoc's voice.

"You tried to kill my son. You tried to kill my wife. Because you thought to guide me back to the gods' way." Temoc's grip tightened. Black and brown spots swam through Alaxic's vision, haloed by the light of Temoc's scars. Breath came in trickles when it came at all. "You are proud, oh so proud. So sure in your faith. But if I opened my hand, do you think the gods would catch you?"

Alaxic could not move to shake his head. His skin was paper and about to tear.

"Do you?"

His voice was thunder, his voice the tide.

"No," Alaxic said, which took all the air his lungs still held. He pulled for more, chest aching, but no breath came.

"The gods have let you age, priest. They will let you die." Temoc's grip tightened. So close, so close to death. He knew, as Alaxic knew, the precise pressure needed to snap a man's spine. One twist, and that was all. "They have kept me strong."

Then it was over.

Alaxic crumpled, panting, on his balcony. Air all around him, and he could breathe none of it. He vomited, and again.

When he recovered, Temoc stood above him, lit still by shadow and stars and divine wrath. "But I have need of you."

Hot, wet needles jabbed into the corners of Alaxic's eyes. He tried to speak, but could not.

"I will stop the King in Red. I will fight his people, who crush ours. I will be our sword in the dark. But I need resources.

A base of operations. Soulstuff to acquire tools and contacts, and to build. Do you understand?"

Alaxic nodded.

"You will give these things to me. You will help me do the gods' work, at first. When I am satisfied, you will be free to pursue your own goals. But if you betray me, I will kill you. If any harm comes to my family, no matter the cause, I will kill you. You have been drafted into the gods' service. Do you understand?"

Again, he nodded. He could do nothing else.

"Good," Temoc said. "Your tasks will be made clear to you."

Alaxic did not know how much time passed before he looked up, but when he did, Temoc was gone.

He lay on the balcony for a long while, beside his vomit and spilled tea and the fragments of his mug. Slowly, shivering, he stood.

"Good," he said in a grinding voice. "Good to have you on the team again, Temoc."

The sound the old man made on the balcony could not have been called a laugh.

Elayne helped Caleb into the cab, and sat across from him and Mina as they drove south and west from the hospital into the Skittersill.

The streets seemed larger than before, or emptier. Pedestrians still wandered along the sidewalks, blind men still played three-string fiddles outside bars, carts and cabs wrangled over cobblestones and along paved roads. A child in a dirty gingham dress ran down the center of the street, holding her hand up to passing drivers, hoping for an inkling of soul. Yet the Skittersill had changed—it no longer fit her dream.

Not her dream, of course. Temoc's. Tay's. The dreams she'd borrowed for a while, that lived still inside her.

The house was clean, floors swept and linens laundered, wood and glass and silver polished, scoured free by Craft of all physical and spiritual trace of blood. Mina entered, turned a

slow circle, and did not quite smile. Elayne did not need thanks.
Maid service in D.L. was cheap.

She had planned to leave, thought mother and son might
like some time alone, but they did not let her go. Ordered take-
out instead, and while they waited, they played gin rummy.
They did not talk much at first, but the game built its own space
between them, and the room assumed a green tint as the goddess of the cards bound all three together. Caleb won by plac-
ing a huge hand down at once, with a smile so wide it seemed
his cheeks might burst from holding it.

"If you don't mind," Elayne said, "I'll drop by once in a
while. I'm not in Dresediel Lex often, but there is an office here,
and my firm expects a lot of business from the Shining Empire
in the next decade. I'll be around."

"Thanks," Mina said. "I mean, I don't need help. But it would
be nice to see you more. There aren't many games you can play
with just two."

"Speed," Caleb said. "But you don't like speed."

"Speed's fine. I just lose. War's the one I don't like."

"More games with three, though," he admitted.

"That's right. More with three."

"Some forms of poker work with three players," Elayne
said.

"If you don't mind me stealing your soul."

She laughed.

A bell rang from the street. "I'll get it," Elayne said, and
stood, and walked through the tunnel gate to the sidewalk. The
delivery man passed down a paper sack, and she passed up a
coin with twenty thaums and a tip. He doffed his hat, and the
wagon rolled on.

A shadow flickered atop the house across the way. Might
have been drifting leaves, but no trees nearby were tall enough.

"Go," she said, knowing he would hear. "Maybe you need
them. But now they need you gone."

She searched the rooftops with her eyes open and closed,
and saw nothing.

She returned to the courtyard walled with cactus and ivy, where Caleb and Mina waited. Caleb had put away the cards.

They ate together, and played until the light was gone, and then they drank wine and slept—Mina in her bedroom, Caleb in his, and Elayne on a cot in the courtyard. She placed a ward upon the house, and another around her cot, and slept without dreams.

ACKNOWLEDGMENTS

Each book is a child, and one of those takes a village, so here we are.

Kind villagers this time around included: Alana Abbott, Chris Ashley, Vladimir Barash, John Chu, Anne Cross, Gillian Daniels, Amy Eastment, Tom Gladstone, Kristen Janz, Siana LaForest, Lauren Marino, and Maggie Ronald. Steve Sunu and Sarah Gillig Sunu demonstrated surprising generosity and forbearance when a long-absent friend spent much of his visit to their home pacing its halls muttering to himself about people who don't quite exist.

Stef Fisher and Anna Pinkert also contributed in a critical way, by stepping in to help my wife and me win a charity auction for which the prize was a sixty-day unlimited supply of coffee from Three Little Figs in Somerville, Massachusetts. The management of 3LF no doubt expected the coffee to go to an attorney. Its possession by a full-time novelist may have impacted their profit margins slightly during *Last First Snow*'s completion, for which my apologies.

Thanks also to my editors, David Hartwell and Marco Palmieri, for guidance, hand-holding, and the occasional, ah, let's say "gentle nudge." Irene Gallo and Chris McGrath continue to offer up the best covers anyone could ask for. Ardi Alspach, publicist, rocks—as does Patty Garcia, but she knows that already. My agent, Bob Diforio, presides over enormous conceptual battlements I'm relieved I don't have to defend.

Tom and Burki Gladstone, and Bob and Sally Neely,

blood- and law-parents, remain surprisingly supportive of my strange career choices.

And Stephanie is the best. A list of her qualities I value would be the length of this book again, so I'll save Tor some ink, and sum up with: best.

Turn the page for a sneak peek at
the next novel in Max Gladstone's Craft Sequence

Available July 2016

1

Tara Abernathy's first job as in-house counsel for the Church of Kos was to hide a body.

A Blacksuit led her down a winding stair to a windowless stone room, empty save for a sturdy table, a counter, a sink, and Alexander Denovo's corpse.

Her old teacher and tormentor looked much as she'd last seen him—at least, physically. Even in death his lips kept their self-satisfied smirk. The eyes had lost their triumphant gleam, though, the conqueror peering from behind the country scholar's mask. He wore off-the-rack approximations of his usual wardrobe: tweed jacket with elbow pads, red suspenders, brown shoes. Of course they hadn't let him keep his own clothes in jail. A Craftsman's jacket might hide anything.

He was dead.

"Did you kill him?" she asked the Blacksuit. "Did Justice?"

The burnished silver statue answered: *No.* Familiarity bred neither contempt for nor comfort with Blacksuit voices, which did not carry through the air so much as manifest in the mind, built from screams, skewed cello notes, and breaking glass. *He died in his cell, of a heart attack.*

Blacksuits did not lie, at least not in their official capacity as representatives of Justice. Nor did they murder. They preferred to execute.

Tara walked a slow circle around the body. The signs were right. They would be, no matter Denovo's true cause of death. No one who went through the trouble of breaking into the cell where the Blacksuits held the man, killing him, and escaping without detection would leave sign he'd perished of anything but natural causes.

"He's a Craftsman," Tara said, to remind herself as much as the 'suit. "He's murdered gods. He bound the wills of hundreds to his service. He almost destroyed this city. Hells, he almost became a god himself. He wouldn't die like this."

Nonetheless.

"I won't bring him back for you," she said.

We did not expect you to. Quite the opposite, in fact.

"You want me to make sure he stays dead."

The Blacksuit nodded.

Tara cracked her neck, then her knuckles. "All right. Let's get started."

The problem was simple, insofar as the necromantic logic of the Craft was concerned. A hundred fifty years before, as the first Deathless Kings formed a society free of divine meddling—and, incidentally, of mortality—they'd faced a practical concern: how does one discourage antisocial behavior among formerly human beings for whom life imprisonment is a brief inconvenience, if not an undefined term, and the death penalty a slap on the wrist? How do you keep a necromancer bound to the world by thousands of debts from climbing back out of her grave?

The many answers ranged from grotesque to merely inhumane, but shared a theoretical foundation: you don't let the dead go free.

Tara set her purse on the counter and produced from within a retort, a piece of silver chalk, three gas burners, several large pieces of glassware, and two silver bracelets. She shucked her jacket, rolled up her sleeves, donned the bracelets, and struck them against one another. They sparked, and slick black oil rolled from them to cover her hands. The glyphs machine-tooled into her forearms glowed silver against her dark skin. She drew her work knife from the glyph above her heart, and its moon-lightning blade cast queer light into the corners of the stone room.

Denovo lay before her.

She took a deeper breath than she cared to admit she needed, and touched the cold dry skin of his temple.

"Hi there," the corpse said.

Ms. Abernathy?

"It's all right," Tara told the Blacksuit. She forced her heart back to a slow and proper rhythm. "He's dead, but there's still power inside his body. That power can . . ." she groped for terms the Blacksuit would understand, "push on my memories of him, like organ keys. The gloves keep most of it out, but he was strong. I'll be fine." She made her knife sharp, took hold of his collar, and carved off his clothes.

"Fine," the corpse said, in a wry voice. "Will you be fine, Tara, really? Fine, in this benighted city, slaving for a mad Goddess and an equivocating God not fit to kiss a Craftsman's boot?"

Answering a phantom's taunt was bad form, but she was not being graded here. "Kos Everburning is a good God. He stayed out of the Wars. He's needed an in-house Craftswoman for a long time. And Seril isn't mad any more."

Ms. Abernathy?

"You can wait outside," she told the Blacksuit, "if you'd rather. This will take a while, and you'll make me nervous if you just stand there."

The statue flowed out the door, and shut it after, leaving her alone with the body.

She removed his shoes one at a time, and cut his trousers off. He lay nude on the slab, paunchy and pale.

"Such service," the corpse said. "I should come here more often."

"You're an asshole," she told him, without rancor. What rancor could there be in a statement of fact? She donned a surgical mask and returned to the table with a glass jar, a rubber tube, and a silver needle. The needle she slid into his arm, and the glass jar began to draw his blood. Eight pints; fortunately the jar, like her purse, was larger than it looked from outside. "You always were."

"I helped you, Tara, as I helped all my students. I made you part of something bigger: a community dedicated to the pursuit of knowledge, the advancement of Craft, the salvation and elevation of the race."

"You stole minds. You tried to break me, and when I fought free you tried to destroy my career." The exsanguination vessel worked fast; his skin tightened as his veins collapsed. "When that didn't work, you followed me to Alt Coulumb, and now you're dead and I'm not." She pressed the skin taut below his collarbone's V with her knife, sliced a straight line down to his groin, and peeled back his chest. Slabs of muscle and fat glistened, and she cut into these until she bared the bone. "I guess that settles the question of whose methods work better."

Spectral, familiar laughter answered her. "Please. You had two gods, Elayne Kevarian, and a host of gargoyles and Blacksuits on your side. You didn't beat me so much as outnumber me. But you can't outnumber what's coming."

She pressed her lips together, and flensed his legs. Silver glyph-lines sparked around tibia and femur; his patella sported a star with six, no, seven, no, six points. As she filleted him, she carved through Craftwork sigils, hidden mechanisms and machines. In his left thigh she found a bullet wrapped with scar tissue.

"I wanted to kill Alt Coulumb's god and take his place," he said. "It was a long shot, but if I'd won, imagine the rewards."

"I'd rather not." Corpse-meat squelched beneath her gloved hands. Blood did not stick to her shadowy gloves.

"But now—do you have any idea of the weakness of your position? Your moon-goddess Seril has returned, in secret of course, since half the city still hates her. They've hated her for decades, since she abandoned them to fight in the Wars and died. That she's back, concealed, changes nothing. Kos will defend her to the death—so she's a weak spot, pure leverage for your enemies to exploit. Hundreds of Craftsmen find the very existence of a godly city in the New World an affront. You've given them an opening. When they learn Seril's back, girl, they will come for you. They're not as smart as me, nor half so ambitious. They won't pussyfoot like I did. They will kill your gods, and your friends. They'll carve them to pieces. They will occupy this city, and remake it into a gleaming citadel of Craft and commerce. No more Criers—newspapers on every corner, and zombies in the market. You'll weep if you live to see it. You'll wish you'd never clawed your way out of that fleaspeck town where Elayne found you."

She scooped out his organs, one at a time, weighed them piece by piece, and burned them to ash.

"You have my job for the moment, sure. Enjoy it while it lasts."

"This wasn't your job," she said. Meathooks of Craft raised and turned the body. She tore off his back in a single sheet.

"I was the Cardinal's advisor for forty years."

"And you used him to kill his own God."

"If you don't use people, they use you. The whole world's chains, Tara—Gerhardt said it, and the God Wars proved him right. When I worked with the Church, I made sure I wrapped a chain firmly round its neck. You've fused one around yours, and handed them the dangling end. You can't command these people from within—and command's the only way you'll beat what's coming."

The slab lay empty save for the bones. To a laywoman all skeletons looked more or less alike. Experts could read differences: healed fractures, specific ratios of limb length to torso. Tara had never seen Alexander Denovo's bones before. She would not have recognized him, had she not carved him apart with her own hands.

"This city will stand," she said.

"What city? It's a mess of gargoyles and priests, Craftsmen and common folk, gods hidden and revealed. When trouble comes they'll tear out one another's throats. You can't stop them. Either you'll be chained to them—one piece of a breaking machine—or you'll be alone, a girl naked against a flood. They won't trust you. They won't follow you. They won't work with you unless you kneel to them, and if you kneel, they lose anyway."

"You're lying." She made her knife thick and sharp and heavy, a cleaver built of light.

"I'm in your head. I'm your worst memories of me, your greatest fears. And the greatest fear of all, the one that still makes you sweat at two in the morning when the world's quiet—is the fear I was right all along. That I was right, and you are—"

Her blade parted skull from spine.

The voice stopped.

"Come back," she told the Blacksuit. "I'm ready."

She nestled the skull in a lead-lined box filled with packing immaterial, and followed the Blacksuit to the lowest levels of the Temple of Justice's evidence locker, past impounded drugs and weapons and grails and tools and artifacts too strange to describe with a single word. She placed the skull-box beside his personal effects, and warded them thrice with shadow and silver to prevent Craft from leaking in or out. When she closed the door, the light above clicked from red to green.

She woke that night, on her bed in her coffin-sized bedroom, to moonlight through the window. A goddess sang.

Tara's heart beat fast. She lay in her own sweat, and waited for dawn.

The day after Tara moved into her new office, once she unpacked her books, installed the nightmare telegraph, set up the astrolabe, and routed out the spy in the lobby, she laid a piece of cream-white paper on her desk and wrote, in large ruby letters at the top: "In Case the Survival of the Moon Goddess Seril or the Presence of Her Gargoyles in Alt Coulumb Should Become Public Knowledge Before She Regains Sufficient Power to Defend Herself."

This did not leave much room on the piece of paper in question. Fortunately, or rather *unfortunately*, she did not know what to write next.

She stared at the paper. She clutched the pen barrel between her teeth. She threw a tennis ball against the wall and caught it until her neighboring tenant asked her to stop. That consumed roughly two hours, during which no further words appeared on the paper. She walked Alt Coulumb's streets. She immersed herself in its libraries. She consulted the stars, and the scholars of Craft, though in the latter case she kept the details of her query general. She spoke with gibbering horrors from beyond the edges of time, and erected elaborate palaces of possibility, networked and interlaced contingencies, none of which satisfied.

After all this, she returned the piece of paper to her desk and wrote, in small letters beneath the overlong heading, *We are probably screwed.*

Then she burned the paper, because it was a stupid document to leave lying around, even in an office secured by the finest geases and traps she, a graduate of the Hidden Schools, could Craft.

Tara scattered the ashes in Alt Coulumb's harbor on three separate days. Then she devoted herself to Establishing a Sufficient Worshipper Base for Seril, and to the other, more public duties of the in-house counsel for Alt Coulumb's other, more public God—and in this manner she passed a nervous year, until Gabby Jones spoiled everything.

ABOUT THE AUTHOR

MAX GLADSTONE is a fencer, a fiddler, and a two-time finalist for the John W. Campbell Award. He is fluent in Mandarin and has taught English in China. Max lives and writes in Somerset, Massachussetts. Find him online at www.maxgladstone.com.

CPSIA information can be obtained
at www.ICGtesting.com
Printed in the USA
LVHW041122141121
703288LV00005B/636